ASHES OF
DESPAIR

ASHES OF DESPAIR

MARY SCHALLER

To order additional copies of this book, contact:
Xlibris
1-888-795-4274
www.Xlibris.com
Orders@Xlibris.com
735318

Chapter 1

The News

The middle-aged white man in a black pin-striped suit ran franticly down Market Street, searching for the BART station stairway to the trains. Four younger brown men with weird hairdos, tattooed faces dressed in black leather, draped in chains trotted behind him, sneering and jeering at him. He shuddered from a cold chill at the sound of their chains as they trailed after him for blocks. If he could only reach the stairs to the sanctuary of the station, there he would be safe. As he crossed yet another street against the light, he saw the BART station sign ahead. "Thank God!"

When he got to the staircase, he swung his briefcase in an arch to give him the momentum to make the 300-degree turn and stumbled down the stairs. Out of breath but at the bottom, he spun around and looked back up the stairs. There were the four young men taunting him with ugly names and laughing at him. Arnold tried to ignore them and looked around to see if there was anyone he could talk to on the platform so he would have a witness if they came down the stairs and attacked him. He saw no one but a ragtag homeless man going through the garbage, and at the far end, there was a family speaking Spanish while juggling a screaming, tired child. Pacing back and forth gave him some respite. "If only the train would come," he mumbled to himself. To his relief, he heard the train in the distance, and when it arrived, he scrambled aboard it with terror-driven quickness.

On the BART train, he sat morosely in his seat, grasping his briefcase close to his chest and thinking of how he got himself into this terrible situation. His love of young boys was going to do him in. They have such smooth hands and innocent faces. The way they are so easily aroused made him tingle. He wanted to touch them, kiss and caress them, but even if they were gay, they may not find him their type. This time the boy he flirted with was a decoy, and he had friends nearby who had surrounded him with their fists clenched, wicked, cruel grins and that look of greed in their eyes. They all wanted to get into a violent, sex scene—for money, of course like blackmail. Arnold had barely slithered out of the grasp of this gang of violent teenagers by running with the dogs of hell close at his heels. The boys were there with their jeers and steel knuckles. They were rough, tough kids with large linked chains looped around their middles, circling their necks, and across their chests with all the equipment hanging off the links. They had black tattoos to emphasize their eyes, and their hair was spiked in dyed weird styles that gave them a terrifying look. He thought they were into sadistic stuff, and although young, they were not his kind of fun—that is, unless he was in control. He shuddered to think he could have been violently gang-raped. Even to him that is too scary. The sweat was running down his face just thinking about his close call.

In Oakland, he got off the train. The night air was cool and soothed his hot face. Mechanically, he ran his hand through his thick, black-dyed hair. It was a way he relaxed himself. Briskly, he walked to the parking lot to find his black BMW and got into his car. As usual, he inspected the backseat for unwelcome guests, but there were none. The loyal car roared to life, and he drove cautiously out of the parking area. The streets were almost empty. It was a relief to be out of danger, and he gradually relaxed. Driving through Oakland and then into Berkeley, he thought about how he didn't always park in Oakland, but he moved around from one parking lot to another just to keep any followers off guard. After winding through the streets, he drove up the steep grade to his home in the Berkeley Hills. The driveway led to the garage, and he punched the open button to activate the door. Carefully, he drove in and closed the door behind him. In the dark garage, he could relax. He gave a great sigh of relief. At last he was safe.

***

The Next Morning

Time was flying as she combed her stubborn, soft, dark curls until they succumbed to looking civilized. Elly, already dressed in her nurse's uniform, was late going to work. It had been a frantic morning. Todd, her significant other, had been teasing her and trying to coax her back into bed. He didn't have to be at work at the San Francisco Police Department until nine o'clock, and he wanted to make love to her one more time before she went off to work.

"I can't have a profession if you want me on my back all the time," she told him as she dashed out of his grasp. "I can't be late again, Todd!"

There was a lot of traffic that morning, and the buses were gorged with passengers. Gracefully jumping off the bus, Elly ran past the parking garage door and was almost hit by an equally desperate employee driving recklessly into the garage. She ran across the street instead of waiting at the crosswalk in an effort to get to the hospital on time, and the cars had to come to screeching halts to avoid hitting her. Once in the hospital, she considered the stairs, but the elevator was open, beckoning to her. But just her luck, her boss was in it. Elly tip-toed in and tried to make herself look as insignificant as possible. The head nurse was talking to one of the doctors from anesthesiology about the scheduled case that had been canceled that day. Elly concentrated on the elevator floor tiles as if they would save her. She tried to be as small and insignificant as she could possibly be.

The voice of the supervisor startled her out of her reverie. "Elinor, I want you to go and work in ER this morning. One of the regulars is sick," Ms. Howard said and then resumed her conversation with the doctor.

At the news Elly rolled her eyes as she faced the door, nodded in agreement to the new assignment, and waited until everyone was gone before she descended to the emergency room. The ER was amazingly quiet that morning, and Elly found that helpful as she needed to get oriented to the work area because it wasn't her usual place to work. Jean, one of the regular nurses, was helping Elly feel comfortable.

Taking Elly aside, she said, "We're short one of our best ER docs this morning. Dr. Jamison is sick. By the way, did you know that Dr. Martin died last night from the complications of AIDS.

"Oh, that's so awful. I liked working with him. Did he get AIDS from one of the patients?"

"We are assuming that, but you never know these days whether a person is gay or not. And on that subject, we need to be super careful to wear gloves whenever we go near a patient. Every other patient seems to have contracted HIV either from unprotected sex or blood transfusions. It's a scary time to be working in medicine. I have heard that some of the surgeons are refusing patients because of the epidemic," Jean announced as if she told this to every newcomer.

"That sounds like you had better orient me fast in case one of these patients arrives," Elly said as she gently pulled Jean over to an empty examination bay.

Later in the afternoon, Ms. Howard paged Elly and said, "I need you in my office. I have a very insistent man here who says that it is urgent that he speaks to you. You can use your lunchtime to come to my office. Is it busy there?"

Elly wondered if one of her sons was injured or something. "No, Ms. Howard, it's slow here. I can do as you asked."

After finishing a patient's admission, she took her lunch and went up to Ms. Howard's office with fear in her heart. The nurse in charge welcomed Elly and introduced her to an imposing man in a black pin-striped suit with a briefcase in his lap.

"Hello, this must be Elinor Longacre DeMartini," said Arnold Smith as he rose to his full height of six feet and extended his hand for Elly to shake. He was a man of about fifty or older who apparently colored his hair black, and he had a ruddy face with caterpillar eyebrows and bags under his eyes.

"Do you want to talk in private with Ms. DeMartini? If so, you can use my office," Ms. Howard announced and left.

Arnold graciously thanked Ms. Howard for the generous offer, and taking Elly by the arm, he directed her to the office.

When the door closed and it was just the two of them, Elinor asked, "Who are you that you know the Longacre name?" Elly sat nervously down on the closest chair, trembling. She wished she was with her patients and clutched her lunch sack tightly to her chest. "I'm sorry, but I need to eat my lunch, so if you don't mind, I'm going to be munching on a sandwich, but I'm listening."

"I need your attention. I am here on official business, Elinor. I am Arnold Smith, and I am the lead attorney for the Longacre Estate. When I was younger, I worked with your grandfather and father. It is my pleasure to tell you that you are the heir to a large estate, and it is my job to inform you of that. I will also be your guide in taking control of your new inheritance. Do you have any questions?" Arnold asked.

"Yes, why me? I am just the bastard daughter of James Longacre," Elly said in a small voice and nervously took another bite of her sandwich. Her sweaty hands resisted messing up her white uniform, so she clung to her bag of food in her lap with one hand while she worked on the sandwich with the other.

"Evidently, your grandfather was very fond of you, and he made provisions for you if Annette, your half-sister, died before you. As you know, she sadly died in an auto accident a few years ago. She died without a will or immediate heirs, and that means that the estate follows the will of your father and grandfather. I don't mean to rush through this, but I know you have an important job, so let's make an appointment to meet at my office on Montgomery Street. Here is my card," he said as he extended his hand with the blue and white card.

Elly took the card and held it like a precious jewel and said, "I will call you tomorrow when I am off. Will that be soon enough?

"Yes, unless you have some questions that you want to clear up now," Arnold gently asked.

"I'm sort of in shock. I wasn't expecting anything from the estate. So I don't even know what to ask. I loved my grandfather. He was a very kind man. Do I have any other relatives I don't know about?" she asked in a small voice.

Arnold braced himself. He did not want to discuss the family members. He had enough problems with them without these relatives joining forces against him. So he offered, "There are some distant relatives of no importance. I don't know if you want to meet them, but it is up to you. I must say I don't advise it at this time because they are rather bitter that they didn't inherit anything."

"Okay, then I want to thank you for coming here to give me this wonderful news. Do you know how to get out? This hospital is like a maze. I don't want you to get lost."

Arnold rose to shake hands with Elly, who was juggling her lunch and trying to find a clean hand to extend to him.

He said, "I am looking forward to working with you, Elinor, and I can find my way out. Thank you."

"Yes, me too. That is, I am interested in hearing more as well. There is so much I don't know!" Elly said as she swallowed her doubts and hurried out the door.

***

Later That Day

Her arms were full of groceries as she trudged up the stairs to her apartment and fumbled with her keys to open the door. The door flew open, and a tall, athletic man with tasseled blond hair and warm brown eyes greeted her. "Hi, Babe, what have you got there?" Todd asked while he took some packages from Elly.

"Have I got some good news for you!" Elly blurted out.

"What happened? Did you win the lottery?" he asked playfully as he took her in his arms.

She kissed him lightly on the lips and danced away to the kitchen to start dinner.

"So what is the news? Did they make you the head honcho at the hospital?"

"No, better than that, I think I might own the hospital!"

As Elly prepared dinner, she carefully explained about the attorney that came to visit her and what that implied. "Now let's get some things straight. I do not want to turn into a snob like my sister. I really don't want to change anything; however, we'll never have to worry about the bills. We might buy a house and a really nice car. We can travel and see the world. But to tell you the truth, it all is very scary. The attorney that I talked to seems like a nice man."

Todd stood there, looking at Elinor with worries running on wild horses in his head. "I know you are happy, and I don't want to be a dead head, but all that money is going to change your life in a way you may not like. I hope you don't decide to marry someone of your new class so that you and your partner are equals," he said with sadness.

"Oh, Todd, I know you want to marry me, and I know I have put you off over and over again. I will feel more positive about marrying, when I get through this transition. I don't want to lose you," she said softly while gazing into his eyes. Tenderly, she wrapped her arms around his neck and drew him close for a kiss.

"I love you too much to let you go now, but I love you enough to let you have what is best for you," he said simply.

"Todd, please be happy. This is good news for both of us. I'm going to make a special dinner for you tonight, all of your favorites, and we're not going to argue about how we're going to change our lives. We'll just be able to travel and live wherever we want," she said, reaching over to him and drawing him closer.

"I need to talk about this. Annette, my half-sister, lived a life of wealth and privilege. She was taught from an early age about this estate and all the finances. However, I know she wasn't happy. If she'd been happy, she never would have done all those ugly things," Elly began.

"She tried to kill you ... and almost succeeded. If— I'm sorry, I don't want to dredge up those old memories that need to stay buried with her. But if she hadn't died in that accident, then we would not be having this conversation, and we are lucky that she drove so recklessly that she ended her own life," Todd added.

"Yes, she had a lot of power. Now, after three years of waiting, I may have some of that power, but because I was the bastard daughter, I didn't have the chance to grow up with it. So I desperately need to learn how to manage it, now. I do not have a clue how to cope with this estate," Elly said sadly with her head in her hands. "There is a board for this estate, and it is full of men and women with educations and experience that takes a lifetime to learn. And then there is me with no experience and no time to learn. I'll get dumped into the middle of these sharks, and they'll have me for lunch."

"Speaking of eating, isn't dinner ready? It smells delicious. Let's eat, and we'll work on these problems after dinner," Todd said as he started to set the table for two.

***

"Margot? This is Arnold. I talked to Elinor, and I don't think she will make any trouble for us. She's naïve and uneducated in the world of high finance," he said into the phone with haughty confidence.

"I hope you are right. If we keep it on an informal level and spare her all the accounting, we can intimidate and scare her off like we couldn't do with Annette," Margot added.

"Don't worry. We'll manage her. Have you scheduled your surgery?"

"Yes, finally, it will happen next month, and I'll be so happy to have it over with. They are going to rearrange my male organs, so I will pee like a girl soon. I am thrilled. The doctor is a real artist. He will take the tissues from my discarded organs and fashion for me real female sexual parts."

Her description made Arnold squirm. "You sound like you have really researched this. I know you have been working on this for several years. How did Annette handle your change, or did she know about it?"

"No, I have been dressing as a woman since I was a kid. It's been twenty years or more, but I didn't have the funds for the surgery until ... You have been a dear to help me. I really like being a woman. It has been my lifelong dream. They are even going to move my fat around to give me luscious curves. I am so ecstatic about this that I want to shout it to the world, but that will come later. So tell me about your plan to keep Elinor miles from us."

"I was thinking of suggesting that she call me Uncle Arney and make it sound like a family affair that she can trust. She wants to meet with me tomorrow at my office. She needs to bring her birth certificate and other identification to finalize the paperwork. I think we are lucky to have to deal with Elinor rather than some of the cousins who are very knowledgeable, pompous, and greedy. Many of them have mentioned contesting the wills of David and James Longacre, but they don't stand a chance. Those cousins are only blood relations of James Longacre's wife. There isn't a drop of Longacre blood in them. They have been reviewed so many times in the past, and always Elinor has held up. We must have Elinor attend a board meeting so she can meet everyone. I was thinking in a week or so," Arnold advised.

"I like the family line. She will be less suspicious if she is comfortable. What about Jacob? Is he going to give us trouble?" Margot said with a worried tone in her voice. "And isn't she a divorcée? Maybe her ex-husband will want to cause problems by demanding a share."

"I talked to Jacob last week. I think he is getting senile because he didn't remember Annette was dead and who Elinor was. I don't think we have to threaten him or anything heavy. I reason that he'll be his quiet, unassuming self, and if he says anything inappropriate, we'll all laugh it off. I have a friend in his office, and he records conversations that he feels are important for me. He is my favorite lover, which is an asset," Arnold said. "I have also looked into the ex-husband, Gerald DeMartini, and they were divorced so long ago that he shouldn't be a problem. We'll only worry if she remarries."

"It worries me that you have so many lovers. You and your boys are careful avoiding all those venereal diseases and HIV, I hope. It is not even safe to use a public toilet seat these days."

"Oh, don't worry about me. My boys are clean, and I avoid the riffraff."

You're so crafty. I'm glad you are my friend and on my side, Arnold. Now, I need to go. Call me if there are any new developments," Margot said as she hung up the phone.

★

Elly and Todd were just finishing their dinner. They talked a little more about the past and what the future might bring, but Elly was aware that Todd was troubled. There was a heavy curtain of uneasiness that hung between them, and their conversation was scarce and only about safe subjects. Then Elly decided to bring up a difficult subject.

"Todd, I think we should plan a wedding for this summer or sometime. I have been thinking of different places to have it. Would you consider one of the party boats that go out in the Bay? Or the Golden Gate Park?" Elinor proposed.

"All of a sudden, you want to get married! I don't understand you sometimes. You have put me off with excuses for years. You use excuses like your former marriage and all that rot. Now you are acting like there has never been a barrier and you want to abruptly jump in. Tell me what is going on in that beautiful head that you, without any warning, want a wedding?" Todd asked with suspicion.

"I need your strength to lean on and your presence as my husband in order to have someone on my side. You are the rock that I need to give me grit. Without your protection, I'm a leaf blowing in the wind. These are ruthless people, who learned their craft from the professional men like my father and grandfather. I, on the other hand, have had only one economics course, which is nothing. They will look at me as a poor, unmarried, stupid relative who has no knowledge of business, and they will take advantage of me at every turn. Please. I need you at my side," she pleaded.

"Do you think these people will have any more respect for me as a detective? I'm sorry, but they'll see me as a little person too. I am just a detective or a cop with little more going for me, but I am no match for those high-flying, slick lawyers. You need your own legal counsel and a reputable accounting firm behind you," he said quietly.

"See, already you are a big help. Now how do I find these people?" she said with excitement.

"I'll ask the district attorney for his advice. He goes to professional seminars, and he has encountered important attorneys and CPAs. He'll give you good advice. If you want, you can look in the phone book for CPAs. I'm sure you will do fine without me," he said sadly.

"No, I won't. I want you at my side, sweetheart. If I held a wedding, would you come?" she teased and then kissed him sweetly on his mouth.

Chapter 2

The Next Day

"Hey, Todd, hop over to my office. I have something to show you," Jim called out from his office. Jim was Todd's partner and his best friend.

"What's up?" Todd said with little enthusiasm.

"What's got you in such a funk, buddy?" Jim joyfully asked.

"Elly suddenly wants to get married, but I think it's for the wrong reasons. I feel out on a limb. If we marry and she gets bored with me, she will find some one of her own kind and leave me," he said listlessly.

Jim closed the door to his office and took a long, hard look at his partner and friend. "Why have you made such an abrupt decision that you think you can't trust her when she has been so steady up to now? This is so out of character for you."

"She is inheriting that huge estate that Annette Pace left when she died. I don't think Elinor will turn into Annette, but she will be rubbing shoulders with all those high mucky-mucks, and I will feel like a fish out of water, if I accompany her. They dress differently. They eat and live on a higher plane where I'm not comfortable. Elly tells me she needs me, but I feel grossly out of my league," he mumbled with his face in his hands.

They sat in silence for a few minutes as Jim waited for Todd to recover. Then he said, "I have never known you to not take up a challenge. It's admirable that Elinor wants to share her legacy with you, and you need to put your worries aside. You're as good as any of them, and best of all, she can trust you. I can see you in a tux with patent leather shoes and all that jazz. There you'll be, walking up to meet the mayor. Oh, I know you can't see that you are equal to them, but if you take their clothes off, we're all alike. And don't you forget it. We all take a shit! It is just a costume and nothing more," he said with sincere empathy. Then with a dreamy look, he continued, "I sure wish my wife inherited a fortune. I would be dancing in the halls like mad. You just don't know how lucky you are, kid."

***

Elly dressed carefully in her best blouse that morning. Then she chose a nice conservative blue suit she had bought at the local department store. Her appetite was diminished by stress, and she picked at her cereal. The clock's hand seemed to stand still. To make the time go faster, she ran around, straightening the pillows and empting the garbage. Finally, it was time to take a taxi to the Montgomery Street address.

The hallway of the building was marble all the way to the ceiling twenty feet up, and her heels clicked, loudly echoing off the marble floor and walls as she walked to the elevator. In the elevator she rode with three men in black suits who towered over her. They reminded her of penguins flapping their wings as they squawked quietly together. On the third floor, she got out and went down another marble hall to a huge office complex with "Smith, Cornner, and Blum" on the door. Little did she know that Cornner and Blum had died years ago but their names had never been removed because they looked good. She opened the door and went in. Standing as tall and straight as she could muster, she announced, "I am Elinor Longacre, and I have an appointment with Arnold Smith."

The receptionist responded, "He will be with you shortly. Just have a seat, and I will ring him."

A few minutes later, the tall, imposing, middle-aged man neatly dressed with a slicked-back mop of black hair strolled in with an air of authority. His charming smile lit up his face like a road map as he said, "How nice to see you again, Ms. Longacre. Follow me to my office."

Once again, she walked down another marble hallway to his office. He had a cup of coffee for her and offered her a comfortable leather chair opposite him. "Have you been celebrating your new inheritance? It will change your life in so many wonderful ways, and I have the pleasure of leading you through the confusing twists and turns. We are going to become very close friends, and I want you to think of me as your Uncle Arney. With your dad deceased and all, I will take his place. Now I understand you are single. Well, that won't last long. You will have suitors hanging all over when the news gets out."

Elly sat and listened to Mr. Smith and found he was not telling her anything of much value, but she was afraid of offending him on the first day by asking for more details, so she kept silent.

At the end of the speech, he gave her a letter from the board and explained that they were meeting tomorrow. At the end they discussed the time and place. He then stood up and ushered her out the door. "Now remember, if you have questions, just ask Uncle Arney," he sang in a musical voice that made Elly feel like a child.

Walking down the street after the interview, Elinor felt she had been patronized, and she resented it. He never gave her a chance to ask him questions. With abruptness, he just rushed through the information and treated her like an inconvenient teenager. It worried her that he was treating her this way because he wanted to control her. She decided to visit an old friend. It was a nice bright day in February, and the flower sellers on the street corners brightened the day. The daffodils lightened her mood, so she bought a bouquet. With some searching, she found the family bank on Samson Street and walked in. It had been twenty years or more since she'd entered through these doors.

With an air of purpose, she ambled up to the receptionist and asked for Mr. Jacob Mendelsen. The woman's eyes got big, and she asked, "Do you have an appointment?"

"My name is Elinor Longacre, and I am here on bank matters."

Several minutes passed, and then a tall, skinny young man with a mop of bleached blond hair with black roots and a sweet, round face crowned with black eye brows came and took Elly up the elevator to the second floor. A hunched-over elderly gentleman with white hair met them at the elevator door. "How good it is to see you. It has been so long, Elinor. My, look at you, such a fine young lady you are now. Come into my office where we can have some privacy," Jacob offered.

"Do you want me to take notes for you, Mr. Mendelsen?" the mop of blond hair offered.

"No, no, Mike that is not needed. This is a friend I haven't seen in years," Jacob said in a shaky voice.

Reluctantly, Mike sauntered to the door and slowly opened it as if he was trying to find a way to remain and hear the conversation. When the door was shut, Jacob took Elly's hand and led her to a comfortable chair.

All afternoon, they reminisced about the former years and her grandfather. Elly felt so secure talking to Jacob until they got on the subject of the board.

"You will have to use all your powers of restraint in dealing with the board the first several times. I must play senile, so they don't bother me. At the meeting you should not talk to me. Is that clear? We can only talk here in my office as I had it scanned for *bugs*, and I don't trust anywhere else in the bank. Every Tuesday we can talk here but not at any other time and never by phone," he said, and his eyes spoke of fear.

"Why? What is the problem with the board? Are you saying I can't depend on them?" she asked.

"They were difficult when Annette was alive, but she held them fast with her personality and bribes. She would play one against the other, and they have become bitter. They have resolved to not let you have the same power over them. I am worried that they have become corrupted during the years between Annette's death three years ago and you becoming the head of the board," he explained.

"What? You're saying that I am the head of this board!" she said with surprise.

"Yes, my dear, you are head of the board. You need to look at this as if it is a poker game. You need to keep your cards very close to your chest," he advised.

"Shut my mouth? But if they are corrupt, what cards have I been dealt? Will I need my own attorney and accountant at my side?" she asked. She was trembling with anxiety and confusion.

"No, not this week, but later that might be interesting. First, you must gain their respect. Once you have been introduced to them, and you know something about them, then visit each on their own turf. You need to know them, and you must be willing to ask for their records. Even if you don't feel qualified to read them, act as if you do. This business is often run by mystic moves and deception, and you need to look through the resistance they put up. Do it gently with sleight of hand and you will do well."

"Oh, Jacob, you're talking in a baffling way, and I need concrete methods," she said and sobbed.

"There are none. You must feel your way through the maze ... alone. They want to convince you that they don't need you. Think about how you are going to deal with that. We have a situation where the tail wants to wag the dog. You, my dear, are the dog! You must be strong and act like a very sly fox or ... even a wolf. And now I need my nap. So come back again sometime when you need to review my records. I'm your servant. So are they. And don't you think otherwise."

Elly felt stunned when she walked out the door. Then outside on the street, she took a deep breath and thought a moment. *I need to learn more about my investments. Maybe I will visit one of my businesses I am familiar with, the cardiology clinic.*

***

The taxi took very little time to get to the destination. To Elly the cardiology clinic seemed strange. It had been several years since she had last walked into this place, and it brought back memories of rape and losing her first job in medicine. *They are painful memories, but I must remember that now I am now a registered nurse. And more importantly, I own this clinic.*

Clair Minix, the stylishly dressed wife of the head cardiologist, Dr. Minix, met Elly and greeted her warmly. "How nice to see you, Elinor, it has been a long time. Is this an official visit, or are you just dropping in to see if we are behaving ourselves?"

"I am here to get to know you all again. It is my wish to help you in any way I can. I feel more comfortable with this business than the others, so I want you to catch me up on all the changes you have made, Clair."

With a joy-filled toss of her straight black bob, she started, "We have a new doctor now and a nurse practitioner. I would like to introduce them to our new boss, Ms. Longacre, who is our very special guest and new leader. Let me get you a cup of coffee, and I will round them up," Clair said with a reassuring smile.

When Elly was settled with some coffee, Clair brought in Dr. Roger Garcia and James Yang, the nurse practitioner. Both men were eager to meet Elly, and they made her feel so comfortable and important, something she so badly needed.

"Dr. Garcia is valued among our growing immigrant population from Central and South America. Mr. Yang is also important because he knows how to approach the Chinese community in this city. With these two men, we have doubled our patient load, and we are financially moving ahead in the black. I hope that is all good news for you," Clair said with enthusiasm.

James Yang had a large long-haired golden cat in his arms. "This is Jack. He helps me bring down the blood pressures in some of our patients."

"He is beautiful. I am sure your patients are fond of him. I have read that animals are very valuable therapy for many ailments. It seems the stroking of their fur and their delight in having a warm lap partner helps the patient relax, and then their blood pressure will follow. Do you encourage the patients to get a pet like Jack?" Elly asked with sincere interest as she stroked the soft fur. The cat responded positively with a deep rolling purr. James answered her by nodding with a smile.

Dr. Garcia told her how valuable the clinic was to the community and how he felt privileged to work there. He didn't let on that she had worked with him in the hospital. They were very kind to treat her as a valuable and powerful person in a new job.

Later Dr. Carpenter came in and said, "Elinor, it is so nice to see you here under better circumstances. It is interesting that we are all working to support you now. I knew you had what it took to rise above your difficulties, but I had no idea that you would become the heiress to this fortune. What a change and I hope it will work out well." His voice was full of unnatural tension. It was obvious that his experience of firing Elly, many years ago, was still making him feel uncomfortable. In addition, he could not stop the noise in his head that made him feel Elly was responsible for Doctor Allen Pace's murder and soulfully he grieved for his dead partner.

With grace, Clair stepped between Dr. Carpenter and Elly and changed the subject. "Yes, well, I think we all appreciate having a new leader, don't we, Dr. Carpenter? It is high time for us to move on with this business."

Dr. Carpenter turned and went back to his patients with a shuffling gait and quiet resolve.

Alone again, Clair smiled at Elinor. "It will take him time to adjust. He was very saddened by Allen and Annette's passing, but he will get over it. He also lost his invalid wife a year ago, and that has made him rather stone-faced. On another note, I should take you shopping some afternoon and visit our board's fashion queen, Margot Carter, in her beautiful showroom. You should get to know her, Elly. She has what it takes for you to step stylishly into your new role. She is also a powerful member of the board."

"Oh, I would like that. I need some fashion advice, and she's the perfect one to set me on my new path. Do you know a hairstylist too?" Elly was excited by the idea of looking chic.

***

It felt so good to open the door to the apartment and leave all her worries outside. She changed into her most comfortable jeans with a worn sweater and decided that she needed a night out. When Todd arrived, she convinced him that they needed to celebrate her fortune. They chose their favorite Chinese restaurant on Grant St. As Elly told Todd about her day and her encounters with Arnold, Jacob, and the cardiology clinic, she began to relax. During the dinner she told him, "I can't express it better than saying that I am so appreciative that we can talk together. I want to be your wife. I need a partner in my effort to understand this business. Please let's plan a wedding. I need to do something positive."

Todd smiled and reached for her hand. "I will do whatever you want. I would like to have a little house to share with you. It could have a picket fence, and our children would play all around our feet. However, I know reality is not going to give me my dream, but I will help you in any way you need. I love you very much," he said, gazing into her expressive eyes.

"Wonderful! And maybe our fortunes will create that picket fence and the children. We can always adopt, and there are Victorian homes near Castro Street that have picket fences. I have dreams too. I want the man in my life to love me unconditionally whether I am a nurse or the chairman of the board. I like the funky little restaurants and wearing jeans. I love the parties at the police department and taking hikes in the woods. Please don't think that I will change into a selfish witch like my half-sister because it ain't gonna happen."

"I'm sorry I was so worried last night. Jim talked to me and told me I was being a wimp! I love you very much, and that is what is most important here. We will have a happy life together," he said apologetically.

They talked all evening about their plans, dreams, and wishes. Between the wonton soup and the fortune cookies, they chose a date in May. For the honeymoon they couldn't decide whether they should go to Paris or Venice. They couldn't decide which one was the most romantic, but that was their only disagreement. Under the table their legs intertwined, and he often took her hand to stress the ardor of his love.

***

In another part of the city, a young man was calling his lover. "She visited Jacob and spent four hours with him. I taped the conversation, and I'll give it to you if you pay me," Mike said in a whisper into the phone.

"Come and see me tonight. I would love to punch your ticket. We can listen to the tape together and decide what to do," Arnold said.

"Can you get it up for me? I can tie you up and make you squirm like a drag queen should," the younger man proposed.

"Oh, God, you make me want you so. I'll get all dressed up for you, and you can take those naughty red panties off me. Hurry up and get here before I come all over the phone," said Arnold in hush tones. After hanging up the phone, Arnold was deep in thought. *If she is talking to Jacob, that could be dangerous. I must knock her down a peg. Who does she think she is, going behind my back? No more Uncle Arney for her anymore. The gloves are off.*

Chapter 3

The Board Meeting

Elly dressed in her best tweed brown suit with a mossy green silk blouse. Her freshly styled hair was customized so that her dark curls nicely framed her face. Carefully, she applied her new eye shadow, which brought out the lavender in her blue eyes. When she was ready, she was stunning. She looked as if she was ready for the most important date of her life.

The taxi took her to the Montgomery building, and she hesitated before she walked in. She needed time to go over in her head everything she wanted to accomplish and the information that she wanted to gather. The elevator seemed to stop at every floor, and many of the men getting on looked her over like she was the new woman in the building. She smiled and nodded to them, but no one said anything. At her floor she swiftly walked in the direction of Arnold's law firm. When she opened the door, the receptionist recognized her and stood as Elly walked in.

"We have been expecting you, Ms. Longacre. I'll take you to the board room ... unless you have some other plan," the receptionist announced.

"That would be fine, Sara. Is there coffee and something to eat in there?" Elly asked.

"Yes, madam. I made it fresh and ordered sandwiches like your sister always preferred."

"Oh, thank you," Elinor responded.

The board room was a large wood-paneled room with a long walnut table in the center. The chairs matched the table, and there were twelve of them with one at the head of the table. Elly took stock of this arrangement, and since she was the first one there, she had a choice of chairs. In her heart she knew she should sit at the head of the table, but her worried brain protested. She decided to wait for others to arrive before sitting down. On the walls were several portraits of her ancestors, and she delighted in exanimating them, especially her father and grandfather. She tried to imagine that they would send her their strength and the wisdom that she now needed. All wrapped up in her thoughts, she didn't hear several people come in. When she turned around, they were all sitting in their chairs, staring at her.

The door opened at the far end of the room, and Arnold walked in, "What? You haven't started the meeting yet, Elinor? I thought I would find you at the head of the table, asserting your place. Oh, well, I can run the meeting ... if you aren't up to it," he said and walked over to the head of the table and took up the gavel.

Feeling two feet tall, Elly took the only chair left at the far end of the table, the one facing her ancestors' portraits. *God, how I am failing you, Grandpa,* she thought as she trembled and her heart raced. Elly had difficulty looking at the members of the board. Even Jacob was staring into space. She felt like a shabbily dressed little girl again, the family bastard among all those well-dressed society people. The horror of the shame was written all over her face and body.

Through the fog of her emotions, she heard her name called, and then there was a great silence. "Elinor, are you going to stand and introduce yourself?" Arnold said gruffly.

Elinor tentatively stood and stammered, "I am Elinor ... Longacre. Di Martini. I am ... er ... here because my grandfather was a kind and ... a generous man." Then she collapsed in her chair. The rest of the meeting went by as if she wasn't there.

It seemed to go on forever, but when she thought she could not stand a minute more, it came to an end. Elly wanted to just bolt out of the room, but something tied her to her chair. She didn't want to mingle with them. They were all chatting together and laughing like old friends. There is nothing like feeling totally left out. Small talk was not her thing anyway, she gallantly rationalized.

"Elly, are you all right?" Clair startled Elly, when she sat down next to her and reached out for her hand. "This is just your first experience with the board. Mine was not a wonderful experience either, but you will learn, and someday you will feel comfortable. Would you like to go and have a drink with me and talk about your strategy for working with the board?"

It was music to Elly's ears. "Okay, I have much to learn and nothing to lose. I had such ambitions. However, I now see that I have to know more about my role, and I feel such shame that I made such a poor showing today."

"Well, you aren't a race horse that failed to come out of the gate. Let's not have that drink tonight, and instead we can get together tomorrow and go on that shopping adventure we talked about. How about having some lunch, and then we'll go to some of the most fashionable stores and shops in San Francisco," Clair softly promised.

***

"It was awful, far worse than my first day of being a real nurse. I'm totally out of my league, and I don't know what to do," she said. "I had the feeling that they were talking down to me or treating me as if I had no importance. Not all of them. Arnold, the corporation attorney, and Margot, the fashion leader, they were the worst with their noses in the air. Clair Minix was there, and she at least smiled at me. They were all dressed in black, and I stood out like a huge, ugly brown pimple. They looked me up and down as if they couldn't believe what I was wearing or who I was," Elly said as she collapsed on the couch.

Todd soothed her hair and lifted her tear-stained face and kissed her tenderly and whispered in her ear, "We'll need to plan better for your next board meeting. First, you buy yourself the most fashionable black suit you can find, and then you plant your sweet bottom on the chair at the head of the table, grab that gavel, and bring it down hard. Another tactic is to visit each member separately and establish some connections to them. If you think they are hiding something from you, then ask them probing questions. Then tell them that they had better clean up their act and that you are going to conduct an audit," Todd advised.

Elly's eyes got big. "I think you are right. I have to stop thinking like a mouse. It will get me nowhere I want to be. When I went to the cardiology clinic, they gave me a nice reception. Clair is a straight shooter, and I am certain I can count on her. We talked a little after the meeting. She is supportive and wants to take me shopping for some appropriate clothes. I trust her judgement because she always looks like she stepped out of a fashion magazine. I tried to talk to her today, but I was too upset. And she had an appointment after the meeting anyway. I am going to have lunch with her tomorrow, and then we will go shopping. She is good with choosing clothes that are in vogue, and she can tell me the best store to buy that essential black suit," Elly mused.

***

Across the bay in a large 1920s house in Berkeley, Arnold sat by the phone, anxiously waiting for a call. Suddenly, the phone sprang to life. Arnold grasped the receiver and said, "This is ASS. To whom am I speaking?"

"You're stinking formal. This is the doer. My exchange said you needed job done. They said you had a parasite that you needed to have eradicated."

"I do need such a service. They tell me you are really good at what you do, and that is what I need. You will be discreet, won't you?"

"Certainly, sir. We need to meet somewhere safe to talk about the particulars. May I suggest a beer joint in Alameda? And by the way, dress like a longshoreman with a red bandana around your neck. If you look too clean and neat, I'll not give you the time of day, let alone a deal," The doer grunted.

"I'll follow your instructions explicitly," Arnold said, his voice trembling.

Chapter 4

The Next Day

Clair had chosen a tiny restaurant near Union Square. After the orders were taken, Elly said, "This is a charming restaurant. I have never been here. You are so kind, Clair, for meeting with me today and giving me a chance to get acquainted with Margot. I have a lot of worries connected with this. But you are being generous with your time, and I have everything to gain." When the food arrived, Elly sat stiffly in the chair and picked at her salad.

"You don't have to worry about Margot. She likes to sell her best to the top women, and she will warm up to you. Money opens doors, you know. I will handle her, and you can just sit there and look in the mirror and marvel at your transformation."

Elly looked at Clair with awe. "I've never had someone make me look different since I was a little girl, so I'm looking forward to this with curiosity."

They ate quickly and left for the shopping district. As they walked down the crowded street, Elly asked, "Are we going to the department store?"

"Oh no, we are going to the Margot's store on Maiden Lane. It is where she serves her most distinctive patrons. She hangs out more there than she does in the department store. Besides, we want something really exceptional for you because it will help your ego, and we want something that will turn heads," Clair explained.

"You're so wise, Clair. What would I do without you?"

"I made the appointment for 1:30, and we have to hurry, so let's cross the street here and walk through Union Square to save time."

The store was called Madam Carter's Designer Apparel, and it had a heavy brass door that led to a lobby and a staircase to the second floor. The display room was large with two French Provençal couches with brocade pillows facing the open area of oak floor. A woman in a lovely blue suit approached them.

Clair said primly, "Margot Carter is expecting us."

"Yes, Ms. Carter will be right with you. May I bring you some refreshments?" the attendant asked.

"No, that won't be necessary. We just had lunch," Clair said as she held her head high.

Several minutes passed. Elinor began to relax. Her neck ached with stress, but she tried to take deep breaths to calm herself. Then without an introduction, Margot entered the room, sweeping in like a queen. She was a tall, elegant woman with an elaborate hairstyle to highlight her auburn tresses. Her stunning, chic silk maroon suit glittered as she entered the room and approached Clair and Elly. Margot's eyes were directed to Clair only, and when she spoke, she stood right in front of Clair.

"Good afternoon, Clair. It is nice to see you. I understand you want to look at some of our designer suits for Elinor. Is that correct?" Margot said in her stuck-up way.

Elly felt like a doll that they were going to put new clothes on to bring her out of the gutter. She felt numb, but a voice inside her said that this was an opportunity and she shouldn't pout.

There was a parade of models with lovely suits. They came in a rainbow of colors, but Elly wanted something that would not stand out at the board meetings. She wanted to blend in with the pin-striped suits of the men. She leaned over to Clair and whispered, "I want something more conservative. What do you think?"

"Yes, I agree. Margot, could we look at something more for business. You know, something elegant but conservative," Clair suggested.

The parade of models changed. Now they came with black, gray, and navy blue suits that were the opposite extreme compared to the first group.

Clair spoke up, "Elinor has very lovely eyes. Have you noticed, Margot? They are almost lavender blue. Do you have something in black with lavender trim or a black dress with a lavender jacket?"

"Ah, I understand. I have a lovely dark gray and lavender outfit that may look very nice on her." With a snap of Margot's fingers, a model entered in a lovely but simple silk suit that shimmered in the lights with its lavender highlights.

Elly's eyes grew wide with interest. She had never seen anything so beautiful. Turning to Clair, she said, "I would like to try that one on. Is that the procedure?"

"Margot, let's see what Elinor looks like in that number. You might have your people measure her please," Clair suggested.

Margot ushered Elly into a private room, and her attendants went to work with their tape measurements and helped Elly take off her clothes and put on the silk masterpiece. Elly used her black pumps on her feet, but she could see that they clashed in style and quality. Self-conscious, she walked back to where Clair was sitting.

Clair smiled and winked at Elly. "It looks like that one will work. Did you see yourself in the mirrors?"

"Oh, yes, but I need new shoes to match, and my hair needs some styling," Elly said with some embarrassment.

"Margot can help you with all of that." And turning to face Margot, Clair said, "Let's wrap up that number and send the bill to Elinor.. She needs accessories. Let's take her to the shoe department to see what you have to match this lovely suit. And include a handbag too. . Is Felix available? It would be nice to have him see what he could do with Elly's curly hair"

Arnold will be so upset with me embellishing Elinor, Margot thought. *I cringe about what he may say if he gets wind of how accommodating I am being. However, he did say that we should get her confidence, and besides, I am making a lot of money off of her, so let's not mess that up.*

Later in the afternoon they entered Felix's solon. The elegant shop was all done up in pink and purple, and Felix stood in the middle with a big smile on his face. He was charming and said in a singsong falsetto. "Look at this gorgeous creature you have brought me, Clair. What can I do for you, honey bun?"

Elly smiled back and said, "My name is Elly. I would like something special done to my hair. I would like a hairdo that is easy to care for, but uniquely stylish too."

Under the lights, Felix assessed Elly's hair, and he purred, "Your curls are so enchanting, and I think an asymmetrical cut will show off the beauty of the bone structure of your face. Does that appeal to you?" As he talked, he drew back one side of her hair back to show the effect it would have. "Also, you can sleep on it, and it will still look ravishingly sexy in the morning."

Elly's eyes grew bright. "Yes, that would be interesting."

"We also have a makeup consultant you might like to talk to. You have such lovely eyes. Those should be enhanced more."

"I will take your advice. You are nice to work with, Felix," she said with conviction.

***

As they drove up to let Elly off at her apartment, Clair advised, "Someday you need to rethink where you want to live. You don't have to live in Sea Cliff if you don't want a house, but there are other nice neighborhoods around that would work for you. I don't mean to run your life, but the security here is not the best, so think about it."

"Thank you, Clair. You have been so kind to me today. I couldn't have done that shopping spree without you, and I will consider moving. I just have too much on my plate right now. I just need to do one thing at a time. Everything is happening so fast," Elly said as she got out of the car, but the conversation continued through the open door.

Clair hung on to Elly's hand and counseled, "You don't have to work as a nurse anymore. I know you love healing people, and my husband raves about how well you take care of his patients. But you are now in a different league, and moving is important. Just make that a priority."

"I will think about it. The changes in my life are overwhelming me."

With all her bags in her arms, Elly trudged up to her door. It was so nice and comforting to be in her old apartment with her ancient worn-out chairs. She missed her former innocence and longed to not have the responsibility for this estate; however, all that money was not to be denied, and it could be useful. She looked at herself in the mirror. *You promised Todd you would not be like Annette. But today I was putting on the trappings of an heiress, and there was something about it I did like. A nice home with a fireplace and a wonderful kitchen would be wonderful. But will Todd find that uncomfortable? I need to talk to him about this, and I don't want him agreeing with me just to please me.*

Without warning, the phone rang, and Elly picked it up. "This is Greg Curtain. I am an attorney that works with estates. Arnold Smith said you might need a personal attorney and suggested I call you. Would you like to meet and talk over how I can help you?"

"Well, I would sort of want to pick my attorney from another office so there would not be a conflict of interest."

"I assure you that I would keep all our correspondence confidential. In addition, you need an attorney from one of the best offices in the city."

"What do you suggest?" Elly asked with trepidation.

"May I suggest an informal meeting at your home or with lunch downtown?"

"Let me think about it. Is there a phone number where I can reach you?" Elly asked in order to get rid of him. He gave her his number.

***

Arnold was in his office on the phone with one of his clients when his secretary knocked on the door. She slipped in and placed a note on his desk and scurried out. Arnold finished his conversation and looked at the note. The note said that Margot would like to meet him at their favorite bar for a drink. She only did this when she wanted a secret way to bring him information.

Several hours later Arnold walked into the dimly lit bar and sat at a table in the back. It was his favorite meeting place, and they knew him well.

"Will it be the usual, Mr. Smith?" the bartender asked.

"Yes, Bob and I am expecting a lady, and she likes martinis. So bring a double of that one too," Arnold said with a flirtatious smile because he knew the bar man was gay.

Margot came in shortly after Arnold had settled himself. She took the empty chair and carefully sat down so that she didn't crush her skirt. "Thank you for coming here to talk to me. I had an encounter with our mutual ... er ... friend. Clair brought her to my shop, and I couldn't resist making as much as I could off of her. She looked better when I finally made the sale. You are right. She is not at all sophisticated. I don't know why you are so worried about her."

"I thought we agreed that we were not going to help her in any way. We want her to stay ignorant. I am nervous because she has talked to Jacob and Clair and now you. We need to box her up and throw away the key. She could be treacherous to us," he hoarsely whispered to her.

"All we talked about was fashion. There was not a word about the finances or my books. She is a country bumpkin and not a person to fear. In addition, I love making money, and she has plenty. Besides, she came with Clair, and she is one of my best customers. She has brought me many of her friends, and they have become part of my loyal clientele. This is the way I make my living in case you have forgotten."

"Okay, but I think we need to distract her so she doesn't learn about how to control us. That is what bothers me. I have a plan, and I think it needs to be put into action."

"Just scare her. I don't want to read in the papers that she is dead. You can do what you think is best, but I do *not* want the cops at my door. Do you understand me?"

"Don't get your feathers ruffled. I just want her to stay out of our way. You don't have to worry about her dying. I don't want the cousins ganging up on us as our enemies, either. They have the knowledge to come after us. So if they get involved, we have to get rough."

***

Eagerly, Elly stood by the window, waiting for Todd to come home. She was brimming with excitement about her new look and purchases, and the time seemed to drag. He had called about being late, and now he was later than he had estimated. The sun had set, and the streetlights twinkled in the night air. This evening the streets were really quiet, and there were only a few pedestrians walking purposely along the street.

Elly turned away from the window and decided to read a magazine to pass the time. She sprawled out on the couch. She was wearing a new purple sweater. She loved the texture and design and she wanted to wow Todd with it ... if he ever came home. It was fuzzy and warm, and the color was sensuous. She chose a nursing magazine to occupy her and read the first article about trauma patients. *Goodness, gunshot wounds are the worst, and stabbings can be deadly if the blade is withdrawn.* She was suddenly aware that someone was at the door. Throwing down the magazine, she ran to the door.

"Oh, Todd, I am so happy to see you. I have missed you all day," she cooed as she wrapped her arms around him.

"My sweet Elly, I am so sorry I'm late. Are you still interested in dinner out?" he said and then realized she looked different. "Wow, you look ravishing. Let me get a good look at you."

As she pirouetted gracefully for him, she softly said, "I was worked over by Margot Carter at her place on Maiden Lane. It is a very special and expensive store full of delights. Clair took me there. I just loved the clothes, but they treated me like an old teddy bear they had dragged out of the garbage bin and were fixing up."

"If my opinion is of any value, you look very classy and beautiful. Don't be so hard on yourself. A teddy bear, indeed. I want to wine and dine my lovely darling and then treat you to a sensuous night at home. Are you ready, my love?"

They chose a small intimate bistro a few blocks from Elinor's apartment. Elly's eyes glittered in the candlelight, and Todd realized how much she meant to him. He reached out for her hand. "I am so glad you want to plan a wedding, and May is not that far off."

Elly smiled at him and nodded. "I have lots of ideas, and this weekend we can look at all the selections. Like reception venues and the church."

"I thought you wanted something different like the Bay cruise boats or a wedding in the park."

"I guess I am feeling rather conventional tonight, but I do want something romantic."

Elly looked into his warm brown eyes. They were full of sincerity, and they filled her with a fiery longing that made her want to wrap herself around him. "I just want to eat a satisfying meal and go home and make love to you."

"Well, I am not against that. So let's order and get out of here."

Chapter 5

The Next Morning

Elly had overslept, and now she was rushing to get to the hospital. She gulped down some juice and a croissant as she wiggled into her white nursing shoes. *I'll get some coffee at the hospital when I get there*, she thought as she dashed out the door. Todd was waiting at the base of the stairs to give her a lift.

"How is my beautiful angel of mercy this morning?" he asked as he held the car door open for her.

"I need to go to bed at an earlier hour so I'm not late or killing myself in my effort to get to work," she announced as she slid in.

"If you were not such a honey-wrapped morsel, we would both get to work earlier." Then he added, "I almost envy your patients when you are giving them tender care."

"Oh, come on, Todd. The guys I am caring for are all on monitors and other gear supporting their weak hearts. If I excite them, they might die. Dr. Minix thinks that their pulses go up when I hold their hands, so he doesn't let me do that when I assist him."

"See, I told you that it would be great to be your patient. When you get off today, let's go and talk to the wedding planners. Does that sound like a plan, babe?" Todd asked.

***

In a small café in Menlo Park just thirty miles south of San Francisco, two men sat discussing their problems over breakfast. The fair-haired brother sat on one side of the table, and the other with a darker complexion sat on the other. Their heads were close, and they spoke in hushed tones.

Leland, the darker cousin, said, "I still do not understand why a bastard takes precedence over those of us who are legitimate. That jerk Arnold is not looking out for our interests, even though he supposedly represents the family."

Hank, the fairer cousin, agreed. "We either have to get rid of Arnold or Elinor, and of the two I would say that Elinor is the easier target. However, the real problem is that we still have to deal with Arnold. He is a corrupt and ruthless character. We would need professional help to get rid of him, and that is the beast."

"You mean a contract?" Leland responded with interest. "Do you have those connections?" he asked.

"It's one of those 'friend of a friend' sort of deals. Nevertheless, it would not be cheap. Maybe we should work on Arnold first because that would send a message to the board that the business is out of control, and then we can step in and take over, pushing Elinor out," Leland added.

"You know, I had another idea. Elinor is single, and maybe you or I could date her and win her over. She is a nurse and does not have the legal training that you and I have. Maybe we can blindside her with romance and legal protection," Hank offered.

"Hmmm ... you mean I should romance her? How old is she? I understand she is in her thirties. We were all spoiled brats together. Do you remember? I was about ten. You were seven. Annette was four, and the odd one, Elinor, was about five. She was the ragged one. Now the question is this. Is she worn-out thirties or youthful, inexperienced thirties? She is supposed to look like a Longacre. I hope that isn't the old man they are talking about. Maybe I will go up to the city and check out this lady. If she looks anything like Annette, I won't come out badly in this deal," Leland said as he tried to imagine this unknown woman.

"Okay, you check out Elinor, and I will find a man for the other job. Then we will meet again and compare notes. I like meeting in these neutral places rather than discussing this on the phone. We should pick a different café each time," Hank advised.

***

"Elinor, there is a call for you on the outside line," Ms. Howard announced and then added, "This is getting too frequent, Elly. Be careful."

"This is Elinor DeMartini. Who is calling?"

The voice on the other end was weakly scratchy, and Elinor could hardly hear, "Someone ... is trying ... to *kill* me!"

"Who is this? Tell me quickly before you pass out," Elinor urged.

"This ... is Jacob. I am at the bank. Someone ... switched my ... heart meds. I need ... my nitro ... for heart ... pain."

"Oh, my god! You're having a heart attack. Call 911! Quick!" Elinor advised and then said, "I will call them for you right now, Jacob. You just stay on the line."

Elinor punched another outside line and kept Jacob on the first line. She called 911 on the second line and gave the information, including how they needed to bring the nitroglycerin tablets. Switching to the first line, she advised, "Stay calm, Jacob. They are coming to help you. Just keep talking to me."

Jacob was quiet, which made Elinor more anxious. "Please stay with me, Jacob!"

All of a sudden, she heard loud sounds on Jacob's line. "What is happening?" she yelled into the phone, and then the dial tone came on. Someone had hung up the line. Elinor was stunned. The paramedics would not do that. She tried dialing the number, but no one answered. In a panic she called Todd and said, "I am sorry to bother you, but Jacob Mendelsen at Longacre Bank on Samson St. called to tell me someone was trying to kill him. I called 911. Then someone hung up Jacob's phone, and now no one answers. Could you go over there and check it out?"

"Elly, this is quite irregular, but I will look into it," Todd assured her and hung up.

***

The office of the president of the bank was crowded with EMTs, police officers, and equipment. Todd arrived and brought the coroner with him after he talked to the 911 operator.

When they entered the office, Todd ordered the officer nearest him, "I want the drawers of this desk scanned for fingerprints as well as the phone. What is in that pillbox on the desk? Take that as evidence too."

Jacob lay crumpled on the floor next to the desk. The EMTs had attempted CPR but had failed to get any positive response from the victim. Tim the coroner did a preliminary examination of the body and the pills and said, "I need to do some lab tests on the pills and what the man has consumed. The victim is an elderly man, possibly in his eighties. Todd, did I understand you right? This man is a possible murder victim? Then that is what I want to determine with these tests."

"Yes, Elinor was on the phone with this man, and he indicated that someone had replaced his heart meds with something else and that he was possibly having a heart attack without his regular meds. Do you recognize the medication in that box?"

"Sure. It's nitroglycerin, which is commonly prescribed for angina or chest pain. Did Elinor say anything else about the incident on the phone?"

"Elinor said that there was a loud noise and that someone hung up the phone. I am going to question all the bank staff to help answer these questions. Right now I want to understand if this investigation is valid for the costs. This man may have been senile and confused, or someone may have really wanted him dead. My boss has been harping on me to justify the expense before I run down a rabbit hole without a good reason."

Tim, the coroner, advised, "This is difficult. The man is a fragile old man who could have mistaken his medication for something else. However, someone hung up that phone? You need to find out who that person was, and I will do the toxicology tests to see if he took something beside the nitro. You also need to talk to the victim's doctor. It's here on the box I am taking. It won't cost an arm and leg to conduct a few tests and make some phone calls. But it will clear up the cause of death, and everyone will sleep better."

"Thanks, Tim. I was worried that I was just being Elinor's private detective. She can be demanding sometimes."

***

Going to the bank after work was Elly's priority, but unfortunately, it was closed. *There are so many unanswered questions,* she thought. *Why didn't Todd call me and alert me as to what happened to Jacob? Maybe I should see if he has been admitted to one of the hospitals— that is, if he is still alive and if I knew the hospital. But Todd didn't call me. Has he let me down, and is that what's frustrating me?* She walked home with a troubled mind. However, the long trek through the neighborhoods was soothing and gave her time to think. *Poor Jacob,* she thought. She wondered if he had survived and really was in the hospital. *I hope Todd got there in time to save him? So much is unknown.* Then she finally forgave him for not calling and looked forward to talking to him when he got home.

As she approached her apartment, she was still deep in thought and not aware of her surroundings. At the door while she was fumbling with her keys, a man in a ski mask slipped out of the shadows and grabbed her arm and wrapped it around her back surprising her since she was concentrating on using her key. With speed, one hand covered her mouth and the other grabbed both of her hands and tightly held them behind her back. He said very softly but sternly in her ear, "I won't hurt you if you just cooperate and come peacefully."

Her mind was in turmoil of desperate thoughts. Waiting for a chance to bite him, she looked desperately for an opportunity to struggle free as well. He felt her body stiffen as he dragged her to a gray van and into the interior through the back doors. When the doors were shut, the van lurched forward. The man used masking tape to close Elly's mouth, and she shivered with fear. It was difficult to breathe, and as she struggled for each breath, she was stung by the vision of losing her life. Those dilated blue eye stared up at him, beseeching him. That pleading look had to be covered. The attacker fumbled for a sack and pulled it over her face.

God help me. This sack's nasty odors are suffocating and debilitating. She felt herself sinking into a swirling pit of anguish. Then he tied one hand to her ankles, putting her in an awkward position to prevent her from fighting back. Struggling to gain control, she tried to squirm to loosen the bindings, but they were too tight. The man held Elly's other arm out straight, and put a tourniquet tightly around her upper arm. Then he braced her arm against his leg, and injected a drug into her vein as he loosened the tourniquet. Dizziness enveloped her, and she sank into the blackness as every muscle lost tension.

He watched her body relax, and when her breathing was slow and steady, the man took the sack over her head off and looked at her. She was an attractive bitch; he mused, and then hurriedly replaced the cloth bag over her head. It was just a job, he reminded himself as he bound her other wrist to her ankles. There was something he liked about this moment. When the victim was in his power, he had all the control over this innocent and attractive woman. It was an exhilarating sexual high. If he let his imagination go wild, he could be in another situation with her. He would run his hands over the warm curves of her body, and he would jump her bones and give her a good fuck. A smile crept across his face, and then the dream was gone. Refocusing his mind back to the job, he changed his attention to the admiration of his knots. They were professional. When she awoke, she wouldn't be able to straighten out, and the ties would make her suffer. It was just a job.

Over a bridge and through the city streets, they drove for more than an hour. Elly lay still in an induced unconsciousness. Then they came to a stop at warehouse on a deserted street somewhere in the Bay Area. Two men dressed in black covered her with a gray blanket, and one tossed her over his shoulder and carried her into the building like a sack of beans. The building was large and gave a feeling of creepy emptiness. They headed down the staircase to the basement. At the bottom of the stairs in a spooky, unlit hallway were doors leading to rooms. They laid her on the cold cement in the middle of a secluded room. The concrete walls reared up without windows, creating an atmosphere of total blackness. The chilling hard floor and ceiling completed the isolation. They closed and locked the door as they left. "We will leave her here overnight and come back tomorrow to see if she is cooperative," said the man with his ski mask now pushed up above his face.

***

Todd was at his office, finishing up some reports when the phone rang. The man's voice was muffled, but he said, "Your lady friend is not available. Don't look for her, or she will die." Then he hung up. Todd was stunned by the news, but he was alert enough to immediately dial the exchange in the police department and asked if they could trace the call. The operator informed him that the call was too short to trace.

A sudden panic crept over him. Why hadn't he gone home sooner? He rose with an abruptness that toppled his chair, and he rushed to the parking lot. He drove with a frantic fury to Elly's apartment, and at the door he found her purse open and her keys scattered. But there was no sign of her. Turning, he lashed out at one of the other apartment doors, pounding on the door with all his strength. When he got no answer, he went to the next and the next. An old lady answered one door, but could not give him any information. She was so frightened by him that she was struck mute and whined incoherently.

Frustrated, he excused himself and went back to his car to call his partner, Jim. "This is Todd. Elinor has vanished. I got a call that said if I looked for her, she would die. I need some assistance."

"Do you have an idea of the spot where the abduction took place?" Jim asked.

"I found her purse and her keys in front of her apartment door. I am speculating that is where they grabbed her," Todd said in a tight voice.

"I'll get some officers out there and yellow-tape it. Did you go into the apartment?" Jim asked, knowing his friend was in shock. "I'll take care of everything, including calling the newspapers and giving them the abduction address. Someone must have observed something. What time did you have your last contact with her?"

"I saw her this morning, and then she called me about ten to tell me about this man at the bank who was having a heart attack that she thought was murder. I wonder if there is any connection between the two," Todd said, and the idea sent his mind tumbling down many alleys.

"Was this man a confidant of hers, and is there some connection to the estate she inherited?" Jim probed.

"Yes, the bank is in the estate. I think we need to talk to those people on the board that were so hard on her," Todd added.

"Let me get the officers out there now, and you go and get some rest. I will talk to you tomorrow, okay?" Jim advised.

***

In the wee hours of the morning, Elly slowly woke up. She could see nothing but blackness. Was the room dark? Or am I blinded by something. It was a cold, quiet, and forbidding place. The smell of motor oil and old rags suffocated her and made her nauseous. She felt the ice-cold hostile cement under her body. Her world had shrunk to utter blackness with aching bones and numb hands. When she tried to move, she found she couldn't straighten out, and this caused her angst and pain. The creepy chill crawled over her, causing her to shiver. The chemical stench of the tape that covered her mouth and the scratchy cloth that brushed her face smelled foul. Nausea clutched her throat, and heaving brought no relief. It only made her mouth taste of acid. A desperate moaning rose up in her gullet, echoing off the bare walls. The lonely void of no sound and no sight stunned her. She shrieked at the void. It was somehow comforting to hear her own voice, even though in was muffled by the tape, so she bellowed with all her strength until she was hoarse. The only sensations left were cold pains and a feeling of creepy wetness with the unwholesome odors of vomit, urine, and excrement. In her emptiness she saw visions of men with black with eyes that bored into her psyche. She had visions or guns and needles that came from her distressed subconscious. Her numb hands groped the air as she again lost her grasp on her sanity and passed out.

The Next Morning

It was a few minutes to eight at the Longacre Cardiology Clinic, which Elinor now owned. Kat, the assistant for Dr. Carpenter, picked up the paper. "Doctor, here is an article that will interest you. It seems our Elinor has been kidnapped, and they are asking for anyone who witnessed or knows about it to come forward. You would think that detective friend of hers would be protecting her from these nasty people."

"Let me see the article. I hope they didn't mention us. We don't want to get involved with anymore bad press than we have to. That woman is always getting herself in the papers. It's disgusting. Don't say a word to our patients about this."

Kat was silenced by his reaction and went to the waiting area to clear out any newspapers that might be there. Clair Minix saw her. "What are you doing, Kat?"

"Dr. Carpenter does not want the patients to see this article about Elinor in the paper, so I was gathering them up."

"What article?" Clair asked with genuine curiosity.

Kat thrust the paper in her face. "It is Elinor. She has got herself kidnapped! That woman has a habit of bad press!"

"Oh, that is terrible, the poor thing. I think I will call the police department and offer any help I can give them," Clair retorted with distain.

"Suit yourself, but do not leave the papers out for the patients, okay? Dr. Carpenter insisted on that because it will upset them," Kat said emphatically.

***

In Menlo Park, another newspaper was being read over breakfast. Leland put down the paper and called his brother Hank. "Did you read the article about Elinor? You know who I think is at the bottom of this. Do you think we should call the police?"

"You are ahead of me on this one. You just woke me up. What does the article say?" Hank said, trying to arouse himself.

"She has been kidnapped! Isn't that something Arnold would dream up?"

"Be careful. He is playing with fire, and we don't want to get burned," Hank cautioned.

"Come on. In this case, where there is fire there is also opportunity. Maybe we can help the police take him down. Then we will have a chastened, grateful Elinor, and we can get Arnold disbarred," Leland said.

"Let's think this out carefully. For instance, what could we tell the police? However, being a fag doesn't get Arnold disbarred. His corruption might be a real problem or not, and we might use that as a weapon if he is at its base. We need proof, and we need—let's tell him we are taking over the board in Elinor's absence. That may do two things. It might save Elinor and get Arnold to show his true self, and then we would have the opportunity to ask for an independent audit."

"Now you are cooking! Let's go up to the city and see Arnold," Leland offered.

***

"Hi, Jim, are there any results from the apartment inspection? Or witnesses?" Todd asked.

"Nah, just the usual type of witness statements with made-up stories, and the only fact that they all agree on was that it was a gray van. I put a call in to the FBI, and they should call back soon. The only unusual item in the apartment was a call on the machine from a male cousin on the peninsula who wanted to have lunch with Elly. I have the phone number, and I was just getting ready to call it. I'm curious to see if he knows someone who would do this sort of thing. Do you have any ideas?" Jim asked.

"Yeah, I know. I've never heard Elly talk about a cousin who lives on the peninsula. Maybe we need to call this guy and find out where he was last night," Todd added with enthusiasm. He went to the phone and dialed the number for the cousin. After several rings the answering machine came on. Todd left a short message and a phone number to call.

***

The drive into San Francisco was a simple dash up the freeway in Leland's late-model blue Mercedes. He loved the leather seats and the surround sound speakers. They were on Montgomery St. in less than a half hour. Leland was just concluding his critique of Arnold. "I can't wait to hear what Arnold has to say when we tell him our plan."

"Knowing him, he isn't going to roll over and beg forgiveness without a knockdown fight. I hope you brought your boxing gloves. You might need them," Hank said with a smile.

They parked in a garage and walked to the office building where Arnold worked. In the elevator, they scanned the occupants and stayed silent. The receptionist recognized them and asked them to wait while she conferred their appointment. Then she led them to Arnold's office.

As they entered, Arnold stood up and offered to shake their hands, but they refused. "Why are you being so unfriendly? You didn't get kidnaped," he said with sarcasm.

"It is funny that you are bringing up that subject up so fast because my brother and I have come with a proposal. You see, with the unfortunate absence of our dear cousin, we think we need to take her place until she can return. We will take charge of the estate and protect it in her absence. . . . We do not want you and your friends walking off with anymore loot than you already have," Leland growled at Arnold.

"I beg your pardon. Who the hell are you to accuse me?" Arnold yelled and pounded on the desk for emphasis.

"We also think you hired someone to kidnap Elinor. Wouldn't the police like to hear that?"

"They would laugh at you. I am not involved in this dirty work. It is more your game, not mine. Didn't you want her inheritance? You have the motive, not me."

"Look, if you aren't involved, that is great, but if she does not show up by tomorrow morning, then Hank and I will destroy you. We don't want you thinking that you can run over this family like a mad ox," Leland said with barely disguised antagonism.

"Arnold, we know you are corrupt. You have been siphoning off all the money you desire every month from this estate, ever since Annette died. And you are desperately trying to hang onto that option. This is your motive. Our purpose is to shield the family estate, and we will do that with or without you. But first, Elinor needs our protection. It is obvious that you know something. We can turn you into the police, or you can cooperate with us. Which is it going to be?" asked Hank.

"Be careful, my fine young friends. You are getting into deep bullshit. Don't get too close, or you will drown in it. And then you will really smell bad," Arnold responded.

They sat glaring at one another for several minutes. Then Leland stood up and said, "Come on, Hank. We are not getting anywhere with this rat. He's caught it his own trap. We will find other ways. I'm sure the police with be interested in talking to us."

***

"We got the report from Tim about the medication that Jacob Mendelsen took before his death. Evidently, he had some digoxin in his blood, which would speed up his heart, and that is what gave him the fatal heart attack. His doctor says this was not prescribed as it was contraindicated. I think we have a murder on our hands. I wish Elly was available to see me eat crow," Todd said and looked sadly out the window.

Jim was well aware of the grief that Todd was experiencing. "She never has held a grudge, and she won't this time either. I think you are as frustrated as me with the lack of any leads to Elinor's whereabouts. I have contacted all the stoolies out there, and none of them have heard a word. The FBI is speculating that it is a professional job. The way she was abducted is a pattern that this one assassin uses. We interviewed Arnold, and he professes that he knows nothing. In addition, he thinks these cousins on the peninsula are to blame. Of course, I cannot reach them."

"I think whoever attacked Jacob wanted us tied up and distracted so they could snatch Elly," Todd said.

At that moment the phone rang. Todd picked it up. "This is the downstairs desk, and we have Hank and Leland Dreassler here. They want to talk to you. Should I send them up?"

"Yes, June, we want to talk to them."

Within moments there was a knock on the door. When Jim answered the door, there stood two tall men in their late thirties or early forties who were both dressed in slacks with suede leather sport coats and no ties. The introductions went smoothly, and the officers provided chairs for their guests.

Todd asked Hank and Leland to tell them why they asked to speak with them. Leland explained their relationship to Elly and said they were worried about their safety.

"We are certain that Arnold is corrupt and is protecting his interests by threatening the family. Hopefully, Elinor will be returned to us. We admonished Arnold to return her to her loved ones, or we would make certain his life would be difficult with legal suits. Hank and I are both attorneys and have experience with corporate law. Arnold is a very experienced attorney, but I think we can win our case for the family against him in court," Leland explained.

"Our responsibility is to first clear you of any part in the murder of Jacob Mendelsen and the kidnap of Elinor Longacre. We need to know where and who you were with on these dates and times," Todd said as he passed a document to each of the brothers.

"Murder? I wasn't aware of a murder," Hank and Leland almost said together.

"Yes, one of the board members was murdered yesterday. He was the president of Elinor's bank, and his name was Jacob Mendelsen. We think there is a connection between this murder and Elinor's disappearance."

"Well, Hank and I were both tied up with court cases yesterday, all day. We will happily get you all the documentation and witnesses for that. We are shocked and dismayed by the chaos connected with this board and the estate it represents. The last time we saw Elinor we were just children having fun together. We lost touch with her, and I am sorry that I know so little about her. The board's problems are not due to anything Elinor did but rather due to neglect that was caused by the legal process of identifying the proper heir. Her background may be lacking in experience to control these characters. Whatever service we can be in finding Elinor or managing the board, we are happy to help," Leland said in a sincere manner.

Todd sat back and tried to understand these men and their motives. "Tell me how you are related to Elinor."

"We are related by marriage. Our mother is the sister of Elinor's father's wife. She was a Davis, and that is how we are related. There are very few of us of this generation. We are not really in line to be heirs to the Longacre estate because Elinor has two sons. Isn't that correct? The court would only grant us heirs if something happened to Elinor and those boys," Leland said in a know-it-all attitude that annoyed Todd.

"Well, thank you, gentlemen. Please return the documents for your alibis as soon as possible," Jim instructed.

"I will show you the way out," Todd said as he stood up and walked to the door to open it. He realized that he was sounding like he was dismissing them, but he didn't care.

***

Later

After they left and it was quiet, Todd said to Jim, "What did you make of them?"

"I think it was smart of them to come to us. They have a motive, but so do other members of this wealthy group. Being attorneys, they know it is wise to lay their cards on the table first. I can't imagine that they have much loyalty to Elinor when they don't even know her. They likely want to control her, maybe even marry her," Jim summed it up.

"Oh, give me a break. I can't imagine Elly going along with them or even liking them," Todd said, but his confidence was at a low point.

"My friend, let's find her, and then we will take the next step."

***

In north Berkeley on a quiet street, a beautiful arts and crafts house built in the 1920s stood on the corner, guarded by large redwood trees. A boy of about fifteen with a head of light brown hair trudged up the walkway and up the stairs. He used a key to let himself in and slammed the door behind him. A man's voice called out from the living room. "Davie, is that you?"

"Yeah, Dad," he mumbled as he took off his jacket and defiantly threw it on the floor.

"Just one minute. I want to talk to you," called out Jerry DeMartini, a tall heavyset man with a ruddy, clean-shaven face and graying brown hair. Jerry DeMartini had been divorced for ten years. His former wife, Elinor DeMartini, and he rarely had a conversation, and when they did, it was usually concerning their two boys, David or Davie and Ted. He had custody because he considered his former wife an unfit mother. That was easy to understand when she was a student. This had worked out well for the older son, who was now a student at UC Berkeley and no longer lived at home; however, the younger son had problems with school and his life in general. Elinor had wanted him to get some psychological assistance, but Jerry didn't want to admit that the child needed help. Now he was working himself up to attack another problem his son was having. He did this by drinking a half bottle of scotch whiskey. Slowly, he approached his son. Davie just stood there full of worry with his drooping shoulders and bowed head.

"Have you heard anything new about Mom? "Davie asked, choking back tears he was ashamed of.

Jerry stood in front of his son and shoved a letter at his face and said, "I don't give a damn what the news is about your mother. I want to know why you haven't been in school this week."

Recoiling from the alcohol on his father's breath, David screamed like a wounded bear, "You don't give a flying fuck about her. You are too drunk to care, aren't you! In fact, you want her dead. You probably had her kidnapped!"

Jerry didn't know this news, and it made him stop his tirade. "I'm sorry. I didn't know she was in ... in danger," he said more softly, slurring his words. He reached out to his son to put his arm around him. "Let's go and sit on the couch and discuss this."

David shook off his father's arm and yelled, "It is on the news and in the newspapers. Why don't you know?" Davie tearfully gasped and covered his face to hide his despair.

"I've been so worried about you I haven't read the papers or seen TV or listened to the radio. Tell me what is going on in your life that you aren't in school," the father pleaded.

"Don't give me that act that you really are concerned. You don't really care about me or Mom. You only like Ted because he is a bad ass student at UC. And all your friends know about his brainpower."

"Oh, it isn't that awful. You are a smart kid too, but you don't apply yourself or use your head. I have never doubted your abilities. It's just that Ted is such a winner, and I can brag about him to my fellow professors. He is more like me, and I can understand him. You mystify me. You must take after your mother. And your mom, as you remember, left me for a woman in her life. I find it hard to have feelings for her."

"Yeah, I have heard it over and over. You are never wrong, but I am bored with all that. I don't go to school because there is nothing there for me. The teachers are stupid and don't answer my questions. I don't like dealing with the bullies either."

Jerry was not impressed with Davie's defense, so he said, "Let's talk about it over dinner."

After eating and watching his dad pass out, Davie slipped upstairs to his room to pretend to study. He knew from experience that study was an excuse that his father would believe. *Ever since I was five, I knew I was different. Sometimes I just didn't like being a boy. Other times I liked other boys too much. I have heard that there is a place in SF where boys like me hang out and are accepted. I hear that many are homeless. They have left their families because they are different. I want to do that too. I want to try drugs that make me brave like other guys. I want to be with boys who think like me. Maybe I should visit that area and see if it works for me. If I go tonight, maybe I will hear something about mom.* Later he pretended to go to bed. Lying there in the dark, he plotted his escape. *If I wait until Dad has gone to bed and then tiptoe down the stairs to the kitchen, I can get out the back door without a problem.* He dozed off, but when the clock downstairs struck three, he woke up.

With quiet secrecy, he dressed all in black with a cap on his head. The jacket had a hood and he pulled it over his head to hide his face. In his backpack, he placed a small blanket, some nuts, and some fruit that he had in his room. Carefully, he counted out the meager amount of money he had saved and stuffed it all in his pocket. Silently, he slipped down the stairs to the back door because he knew he could open it quietly.

Once he was outside, he ran silently the three blocks to the BART station. It was deserted and closed. He hadn't thought of that. Discouraged, he sat on a cold steel bench to rethink his plan. Finally, he decided to walk south to the next BART station, which was in a busier part of Berkeley. Maybe he could hitch a ride to San Francisco there. But he found that he was thwarted again. The world was not friendly like he had imagined. Downtrodden, he walked back to his house and returned to his bed to sleep, feeling defeated.

Chapter 6

Discovery

As the early morning chill slipped in with the fog, it caressed the buildings in an ominous shroud. In downtown San Francisco, every street was basically deserted. Cable cars had stopped their runs hours ago, and it was the same for the buses and streetcars. Only a lonely street urchin prowled the streets with his great hulking sacks, picking through garbage looking for food, but then even he curled up in some doorway around two in the morning. In the distance was the wail of the fog horns. Then when it was as quiet as the bat in flight, a gray van drove up the street. They were driving very conservatively so that they didn't attract any attention. When they reached a certain driveway, they entered into the parking area, backed up to the rear door, and stopped. Two men dressed in black with ski masks got out and opened the rear doors of the van. Hurriedly, they dragged out the blanket wrapped bundle and dumped it near the door of the building. Quickly, they returned to the van and sped off. Once again, the shade of silent, foggy pall descended as if the scene had never been disturbed.

***

Several hours later a phone call was placed, and the answering machine recorded a message. "Package delivered!" the disguised voice said.

***

Kat McKinney arrived at work at eight as usual. She was the first to encounter the bundle on the door step. "Ugh, what disgusting odor these homeless people have! Don't they ever bathe?" she said as she stepped around the motionless form to open the door. "I am going to leave this problem for Clair. She always has *all* the answers."

A few hours later, Clair Minix arrived at the cardiology clinic, and she was greeted by Kat. "Have you noticed what we have at our back door?"

"No, is it something I need to address? I really have a mountain of papers on my desk to organize and attack, so I am not interested in games this morning, Kat."

"Games indeed! We have a very smelly homeless person sleeping there, and I vote for calling the police. But maybe you have other ideas," Kat said with jealous defiance as she stood there, her hands on her hips, her elbows sharply pointed.

"Well, let's have a look. I'm not sure the police are necessary," Clair said as she walked to the door Kat had mentioned.

Clair looked through the window and then opened the door. Kat had described one thing right. The odor was intense. "The person may be injured or sick," she said as she walked outside for a closer look. Kneeling down, she pulled back the blanket and discovered a battered head, matted hair, and an abused face. "Let's call 911. I don't like the looks of this."

Kat went to the phone and dialed 911. When the operator came on, she passed the receiver to Clair. "This is Clair Minix at the Longacre Cardiology Clinic. We have a maltreated person wrapped in a filthy blanket outside our back door, and I think he or she needs medical attention. In addition, maybe the police should be involved."

"Thank you. We will send out a team," the operator responded.

"Please come to the back of the building because that is where the person is, and we have sensitive patients who will be arriving soon."

Within a few minutes, Clair could hear the sirens in the distance shattering the peace of the morning. The ambulance was the first vehicle to arrive. Then the fire department came, and then the police showed up. The tiny parking lot was filled with vehicles and people. Efficiently, they scooped up the bundle, blanket and all. Put the person on the gurney and were off to the hospital. The fire department went back to their base, but the police followed the ambulance.

At the hospital they discovered that the woman was wearing a nursing uniform. She was under the influence of some drug, confused, dehydrated, and feverish, and she had multiple abrasions. The doctor in charge of the emergency room asked the nurse to tell the policeman in the waiting room to come inside. "I don't want to be too hasty with this assessment, but this might be the missing person you have been looking for, the woman who was kidnapped."

When the officer came in, the doctor told him about his suspicions.

"If you think she is the kidnapped person, I'll call my boss and tell him," offered the officer. Then he got out his portable phone.

"Yes, she has a name tag on her uniform, but we need someone to identify her as soon as possible," the doctor said as he turned to go back to his patient.

Todd and Jim arrived within the hour. The front desk directed them to the emergency room and told them which doctor to talk to.

Elly's face was bruised, scraped, and sunken. Her lips were cracked and bleeding. Her beautiful hair was matted with vomit, and the nurses were trying to clean her up as quickly as possible. In her delirium, she was confused, and she tried to crawl off the gurney, so they had to restrain her. Todd tried to talk to her, but she didn't seem to recognize or respond to him. He noticed her wrists were deeply injured with groves where the ropes had been. "Did she come with the ropes that made these marks?" he asked.

"Over there is a pile of stuff she came with. I don't remember any ropes," one of the nurses offered and then added, "She has those marks on her ankles as well."

They gave her drugs to reverse the sedatives she had been given, but they didn't help the agitation. In the end, they sedated her more so that they could keep the intravenous fluids flowing and put her in a quiet room. The head nurse told him that it may take twenty-four hours before Elinor could talk to him.

Todd put a policeman at the door to regulate visitors. Then he directed another officer, "Pick up all those garments and the blanket to secure them as they are evidence. See to it that they are logged in at the station."

Down in the lobby, he gave the story to the press. When that was over, he decided that he needed to visit the cardiology clinic where she was found.

Clair welcomed him and told him about how they found Elly. "I'm so sorry I didn't recognize her. Otherwise, I would have called you right away."

"Did anyone see the vehicle that brought her?"

"No, she was resting there when Kat arrived this morning," Clair responded.

Going out the door, Todd looked at the pavement for tracks or something. It was very clean except for some fibers of string. As he was crouching to pick up the fibers, he saw something glittering in the sunlight. It was a beer cap. He picked it up, thinking it wasn't valuable, but you had to try everything.

Then he left the clinic and went back to the forensic lab to look over the blanket and take few other items to the forensics lab for analysis.

Much later Todd arrived at the hospital and went to Elly's room. The officer at the door told him who had tried to visit her and who he had turned away. "One of the males who came to see her was Leland Dreassler. He said he was her cousin, but since he wasn't on the list you gave me, I didn't let him in. Is that okay, boss?"

"You did the right thing. I think I will talk to her nurse before I visit her," Todd told him.

The nurse explained to Todd how Elly was still ill, disoriented, and walking made her dizzy. She informed him that the FBI had been there looking over the records and that they said they would talk to you tomorrow about their report. Ms. Longacre's doctor gave them permission to let them read Elly's chart.

"Was that Joe Sanchez you talked to?" Todd asked.

"Let me check. Here it is. Yes, it was a Mr. Sanchez," the nurse responded.

"That is a relief. He is the only FBI person assigned to this case, so don't listen to anyone else who wants to see her records. I have given a short list of persons allowed to visit her. I am worried that her life may be in danger, so be careful who goes into that room."

"I understand, sir. We will keep a close eye on her."

***

In the hills above Palo Alto in a very modern house with a sweeping view, the great rock fireplace blazed and crackled, warming the winter night in the great room. Leland was sprawled out in one of the leather couches, the phone receiver in his ear. "Yeah, I agree.

The ol' boy caved in. I guess he took our threat seriously. I tried to visit Elly, but they said I wasn't on the privileged list. My guess is that they are being super careful because someone may try to do her in."

"Before you go to see her again, call first so that you aren't wasting your time. I speculate that Arnold might have hired a professional torturer, and I don't like it. If he did, it must have cost him a million at least to do that, don't you think?" Hank replied.

"I agree. I wonder if this man or gang would be interested in taking out Arnold," Leland said.

"Don't worry. He will take out himself. Arnold is playing with damnation just being gay, sexually free while this AIDS crisis running amuck in the homosexual world. He is always seducing stray young boys, and who knows what he picks up with them? In the paper this morning, there was a story about a gay middle-aged man who died in his home in Oakland recently. They think it was someone he brought home. The guy rolled him and then beat him to death. That very thing could happen to Arnold without our help, and it couldn't happen to a more deserving person. I've got to go I have a critical court case in the morning, and I need to bone up on some details before I go to bed," Hank said as he signed off.

When he hung up the phone, Leland rolled Hank's words around in his mind. Hank was gay. He worried that his brother was in denial and was vulnerable to HIV as well as Arnold.

***

The house stood on a winding street in the Berkeley hills off Marina Blvd. Downstairs, the phone was ringing. Upstairs, Arnold slept with a boy he had picked up in Albany. He rolled over and dragged himself from his bed. *Why didn't I put the answering machine on?* he asked himself as he tumbled down the stairs. He got the receiver on the last ring. "Hello?" mumbled as he picked up the receiver.

"This is Mike, you rat. I just got free. They had me locked up for a whole day in the slammer, and I never want to go back."

"Calm down, sweetie. I posted your bail, and you'll get compensated. If you had been smarter, you wouldn't have been in jail at all," Arnold said sleepily.

"Look, I had to be there to replace the meds. I can't help it that someone called the EMTs," he whined.

"Let's talk about it in the morning. Maybe you can take a vacation in Brazil or something. I'll call you first thing. Now get your rest."

***

The Following Night

At another house in Berkeley, David DeMartini dressed in black once again, slipped out of the house, and ran to the BART station. This time he boarded a train to San Francisco. He got off at the first stop in the city and walked to 6th Street. The air smelled salty like the ocean, and it calmed him.

As he walked along the street, the black buildings rose up like monsters around him. He would ask the boys his age if they knew where he could find drugs and a sugar dude. The people on the street were of all sizes and ages. He couldn't tell many of their genders. They would look him over and shake their heads. He didn't understand that they saw him as competition or just a boring new kid. There were so many of them. Some were standing. Others were leaning on the buildings or flopped in the corners of doorways, and so few of them were marks. As he turned a corner, he was aware of an older man in a black suit who was picking up boys. Davie boldly walked up to him and asked him if he was interested in having his cock sucked. The man reeled around and looked Davie over. Then he told him he only wanted experienced boys. Then the man thought a moment.

"There is a man who takes the newbies. Go look for him. He is called ASS, and he would make you a good sugar daddy. ASS has an appetite for new blood. He could train you to do his will."

As the night went on, Davie got tired and sat down in a doorway and watched the traffic go by. So far he hadn't had any offers. He dosed off and dreamed of being in a hard bed in the slums of the city.

At about one in the morning, Arnold, who was dressed in his dark gray suit, had just walked from Montgomery to the Tenderloin to see if there was any new action. The man in the black suit found him and told him about the new boy that he had talked to and told him where he last saw him.

"Do you think he is my type?" Arnold asked, hoping to learn more.

"He's as green as grass. If you like to teach them, then he is your type. If not, then he isn't. He is one of those boys who think he is different and comes here to start a new life."

Arnold walked the street, looking for the stranger. He found him slumped in a dark corner of a doorway with some other homeless boys.

Through the fog of sleep, Davie felt a man's foot nudging him, and he woke up, aware that a man was standing over him.

He looked up to see a tall middle-aged man who then asked, "Are you gay, kid?"

Davie stood up tentatively and took a deep breath and said, "Oh, yeah, I like cocks and rim jobs if you will give me drugs or money." It was a speech he had rehearsed. Standing at his full height, he was almost as tall as Arnold.

Looking him over like he was a new puppy, Arnold was taken aback by the young man's boldness. But he liked the look of the kid because he didn't look overused, and the kid avoided eye contact, which could mean he was shy or hiding something. He didn't have chains on, and that could be good or bad. So he said, "Do you have any experience?"

Davie looked at his feet and mumbled, "I have some magazines that show gay sexual acts, and they really ... turned me on. I even came all over the page."

"Hmmm. Will you come to my pad and service me?"

"Where do you live?" Davie asked timidly.

"I live in the Berkeley hills, and I take BART. If you are interested, we have to go before BART shuts down."

"Okay, er ... what is your name?" Davie stammered.

"Just call me ASS. Those are my initials. And what do I call you?"

"I am Davie. Will you be good to me?" he asked plaintively.

"Sure, I will take exceptional care of you ... if you do the same to me."

***

The Following Morning

Arnold rolled over to see if he had just dreamed about the boy in his bed, but there he was. He had been a joy, willing to give him anything he wanted. The remembrances gave him an erection. Gently, he pushed the tangled curls away from the sweet face. Now that it was light, the face looked familiar. Arnold lay back and tried to think of somewhere he had seen such a face. Then he thought of

Elinor, and his erection disappeared. He turned back to the boy and nudged him to wake up. "David, what is your last name?"

Davie turned toward Arnold and yawned, "My last name is DeMartini."

That name sent a chill over Arnold. He racked his brain for some way to take advantage of this sweet kid and make it a win for him against Elinor. "Davie, I know you are underage, and I am worried that your parents will come after you. You aren't going to be a fink, are you?"

"Gosh, no. I like you, and I want to have more sex with you. What you did for me last night was so super. I can't tell you what a great fuck that was."

He rested on his left arm, and with his right hand, he drew Arnold's face to his. Very tenderly, he kissed Arnold's upturned lips. Aroused, Davie moved his kissing down and licked his lover's neck. Then lick by lick, he moved through the forest on his chest. The dancing tongue skipped through the forest and down to the abdomen. Now he was Ranger Rob crossing the wasteland, licking and kissing as he went. At the groin he met another forest with a tower nervously twitching in anticipation. To Davie this was an ice cream cone that he grabbed with his right hand firmly like he did when he was three and didn't want to drop his cone. He sucked, and his tongue danced on the top with glee. Arnold writhed in erotic ecstasy with the sensuous treatment to his erect soldier. *Oh, God, it may be the end of me to love this boy, but I will enjoy every moment of it,* he thought as he ejaculated.

Davie asked with a husky voice, "Did I do it right? That was my first time."

"God love you. It couldn't have been better," Arnold whispered in his ear.

Arnold couldn't help himself. He drew Davie's head close to him and erotically kissed him while he felt for Davie's erect penis that was prodding him. At his touch, Davie reacted by breathing hard and running his hands all over Arnold. As he expertly stroked Davie's member, he kissed him. The boy ejaculated easily.

***

Over breakfast Arnold asked about Davie's family and school.

"I used to live with my father, but he tells me I am stupid and will never amount to anything, so I ran away. He likes my older brother better than me."

"How about your mom?"

"She has her own problems. My ambition is to be a successful fag. I would like to go to a school full of boys like me."

"Where do you go to school now?"

"I go to a Catholic school in Oakland, and I hate it."

"If I found you a private boy's school where you won't be harassed, would you be interested?"

"That would be cool. I really like learning. I just don't like being teased and bullied."

"Good. We will visit it, and you can make a choice. We will have to tell your dad because the records from your other school must go to the new school. By the way, have you seen the newspaper this morning?" Arnold asked as he shoved the newspaper across the table.

"Wow, far out! They found my mother!" Davie said in awe. "I need to go see her."

"We can't do everything in one day, so you have to make your own choices. Tell me what you want to do," Arnold said in a hard, cold voice.

David stared at Arnold as if he was seeing a different man. The silence went on as David tried to understand his situation. Finally, he said, "Today I want to see my mom, and I can look into schools later."

"Okay, if that is what you desire, I will take you to the BART station, and you can go to San Francisco on your own."

Chapter 7

Rehabilitation

Sunshine poured in through the window, and the view of the Golden Gate was stunning. Elly sat on her hospital bed, daydreaming about running in the streets of the city. It was all a fantasy. She felt listless, weak, and depressed. When she stood, it was like she was on a carousel spinning around. She couldn't steady herself.

"I looked in the mirror this morning and didn't recognize myself," Elly recollected to herself just as stout woman in a police uniform came in the door.

The officer carefully shut the door for privacy and walked over to Elly's bed. "I've been finishing up the arrangements for your discharge and our transportation to the safe place, a cabin in Marin County," Sergeant Maria Fuentes announced.

"This is all news to me. When did this happen?" Elly blurted out.

Maria had been advised that Elly had some memory problems and that she should redirect her as much as possible. "Todd was here and explained it all last night. Do you remember him coming?"

"I vaguely remember him," Elly said haltingly.

"The cabin is in the hills of Marin, and you will get as much rest and exercise as you need. Your doctor agrees that this is the best plan," Maria explained.

"Why isn't Todd here to explain this? I know that isn't your problem, but I feel like I am being shuttled away like a difficult child," Elly complained.

"You still have some healing to do, and Todd and Jim hold your safety as very important and want you in as secure a place as possible. This is in Marin County, where you can have peace and fresh air, and it is close enough to San Francisco so that your family can visit. I am going to be with you during that time to keep you safe," Maria said.

"No one will know where I am, and I will be so lonely," Elly complained again.

"Your family can visit. Your son Ted said they were looking forward to spending time with you there. Todd will spend his days off there, and you can have picnics in the forest and all sorts of fun. There are some cousins who say they will come and visit too. We have a cook and a housekeeper. You don't have to worry about a thing," Maria said with a smile.

"Cousins? Who are they?" Elinor asked

"It is my understanding that they saved your life!" Maria said and wondered if that was appropriate to say.

"Really? Then I would like to meet my heroes," Elly said with a broad smile.

"Okay, then let's get you dressed and out of here," Maria said with enthusiasm.

***

"The FBI man says that the wounds on Elly and the general way they treated her boils down to one suspect, a professional by the name of Jason Roberts. Or several other names he makes up as he goes along. They are on the lookout for him and will get back to us," Jim announced as Todd walked in. "They also said he is probably several states away by now."

Todd took a chair and slumped in seat. "Elly is still fragile. I know she is not going to like a safe house, but as you know, she is better off. The sooner we get this jerk and the guy who hired him, the better. I have been tracing phone calls, but no luck. Let's put a tail on Arnold. We need one on Mike Nikcols too, who is still a suspect in Jacob's death and is out on bail," Todd added.

"I'm ahead of you. We tailed Mike after he left the jail, and he went almost directly to his apartment. But a day later he was at Arnold's house, and we have not seen him move."

"How patient should we be before we get a search warrant for Arnold's house," Todd asked.

"I will try that again. The problem with the first time is that we have no evidence he was remotely involved, but with Nikcols there, we have a better argument for the judge," Jim offered.

"Let's try that and make sure there is no other way out of that house that Nikcols might use. Alert all the airports about him. I don't trust Arnold, he is liable to jettison this inconvenient person," Todd warned.

"I'll get on it today; we have Nikcols' passport number. The airports and airlines will be alerted and they can track him by the passport number. Ya know, the FBI fellow is probably on that right now." Jim assured Todd. Just then the phone rang, and Todd answered it.

"This is Todd Markam. Hi, Joe!" He listened and then said. "That's great news. When is the flight? Okay, we will get some plainclothes guys out there and nab him. Thanks and same to you."

Todd hung up the phone. "You were right, that was the FBI fella, Joe Sanchez. He tracked Arnold Smith's credit cards, and the passport number. Arnold has made reservations for Nikcols for a flight to Brazil tonight at 8:45 p.m. from SFO. We can get some men down there and arrest him for jumping bail unless we can catch him at Arnold's house. We can bring in Arnold too for aiding and abetting a criminal. It is nice to see some movement to this case.

"Yeah, but these aren't the big charges. We still have to find the relationship of Elinor's kidnaping to Jacob's death with a link to Arnold plus Nikcols. We need to get a confession out of Nikcols. Then hopefully, Joe will come up with the professional assassin and make him talk."

***

David arrived in San Francisco about ten o'clock and walked the mile and a half to the hospital because he had no money. In the hospital lobby, they asked questions, and David rebelled against the investigation. "I just want to visit my mom! Why aren't you telling me where she is?"

"I will call the officer and ask her if you are allowed in. We only have one son on record, and he has a different name," the clerk explained.

"That must be my older brother, Ted," David said with anger mixed with jealousy. "Can you call the cops? Like Todd Markam? He knows me," David said with hope.

"Let me call up to the floor and see what I can do," the clerk said with a smile.

"This is the fourth-floor nursing station. How can I help you?"

"This is Amy at the front desk, and I have a young man by the name of David DeMartini here. He wants to visit Elinor Longacre DeMartini. I know he is not on the list, but he says he is her younger son. The problem is that he has no identification."

"Ms. DeMartini is getting ready for discharge, but we are not to let anyone know about that. All I can do is ask the officer here. So tell him to wait and I will call you back."

"Okay, I will tell the lad. He is very anxious."

Amy laid down the receiver and said, "The nurse is going to ask the officer, and she will call back with the answer."

David looked broken and uneasy. "I must see her," he said, close to tears.

Five minutes turned into ten, and there was still no call. Then the phone rang. "Front desk, this is Amy," she said eagerly.

"This is Officer Maria Fuentes. May I speak to David DeMartini?"

"Yes, he is right here."

Running to the desk, David called out into the phone, "Mom?"

"This is Officer Fuentes. Your mother wants to see you. The lady at the desk will escort you up here. Is that okay?"

"Yes, whatever!" David said with concern and handed the receiver to Amy. "You have to take *me* up there," he said with a voice full of resentment that he was being treated like a baby.

They rode in the elevator in silence. David's head was hung low, and he was staring at the floor of the elevator. His heart beat hard in his chest. At the fourth floor, they got out, and Amy turned David over to Maria Fuentes. "Hello, David. We didn't know where you were, or we would have called you. Come. Your mom has been asking about you."

David brightened up. "Yes, I have been worried about her, too."

They walked down the hall to a room with another police officer. "This is David DeMartini. He has come to visit his mom," Maria explained to the other officer.

Elly was dressed in jeans and a lavender sweater, sitting in a comfortable chair. She was thrilled to see her son. "I was worried about you. Your dad didn't know where you were."

They hugged and kissed. David was crying, "I was so worried about you I was going crazy. I am sorry that I worried you."

Elly put her arm around David and softly said, "We need to talk about your problems, David. They are going to put me in a safe house to protect me. You can come and visit when Ted comes. Will that work?" she asked her son.

"Are you going right now? I don't want to go back to Dad's house. Can't I come with you?" he asked plaintively.

Elly looked at Maria beseechingly. "I will consult Todd," Maria responded and left the room.

Maria called Todd Markam. "This is Maria at the hospital, and we are ready to go. However, David DeMartini showed up this morning and wants to go with us to the safe house. He is a runaway, and his father has to be notified. I am in a difficult position here. What do you advise?"

"Don't leave yet. I will call Jerry DeMartini and tell him his son is safe. Does David have a problem going home?"

Maria responded, "Yes, that is what he said."

"I really don't want to report this to child protection services. This kid is too dear to me. I will call the father. Just don't leave until you hear from me. I will try to get away to come there and support you and Elinor. Does that sound like a plan?"

"Yes, thank you, Todd." Maria hung up the phone and returned to Elly's room.

Elly was glad to have Maria back. "What did Todd say?"

"He is coming to talk to David. He should be here within a half hour. The hospital staff has agreed to delay your discharge until this matter is resolved," Maria said with a smile. She felt more secure with the boy's problem with Todd getting involved.

Elinor was delighted to see her son. She didn't say much, but she had him sit on her bed. Then Davie told her why he had run away. "I don't want to go home, and I won't go to that horrid school again."

"What is the problem with the school?" Elly weakly murmured.

"The bullies tease me and steal things from me so I will fight. These guys are bigger than me and I'm a lousy fighter,."

"Did you tell your dad about this?"

"You know, Dad. He doesn't listen. He goes on the offensive. He tackles me when I am weak and makes my head spin every way he can. He asks why I don't go to school, but he never calls them and tells them they have a bully problem. I am told to fight back, but I am not that kind of a kid. I am supposed to take care of myself, so this is my solution. I want to go with you."

The door opened, and to Elly's delight, Todd was there.

"Todd, you are here at the perfect moment. Are you going to Marin with me? And can Davie go with us?"

Maria looked at Todd, beseeching him to solve the problem. Todd cleared his throat and said, "I'm here to talk to Davie, and then we will talk about Marin and us."

As Davie and Todd walked down the hall, Todd told him he had to work on the issues with his dad.

"My dad likes his whiskey more than me or Mom. He is impossible to deal with, and if you force me to go home, I will just run away again."

They reached a waiting room with some privacy and entered. Todd quietly closed the door behind them. "It's time to tell me the whole story, Davie."

"My dad doesn't listen to me. I hate that school, and I am not going back to it."

"Tell me what you find so painful at that school."

"The kids are cruel and horrid to me. I like basketball, but they trip me when the coach isn't looking. So he thinks I am a klutz. I get kicked around like an old shoe. They say I run like a girl and throw a ball like a monkey. If they didn't trip me up, I could score just like them," Davie said and sulked by sitting on the chair with his elbows on his knees and hung his head.

"It sounds like they are teasing you to keep you off the team. Why would they do that? The whole idea of sports is teamwork and cooperation. Why do they say you run like a girl? Davie, look at me. Do you think you are gay?"

Davie raised his head to look directly at Todd. "Do I look gay?"

Todd chuckled. "I'm not sure I know what *gay* looks like. Are you gay?"

"Yes!" Davie announced proudly, and then he said, "I have a lover. I want to live with him."

"What is his name?"

"I don't really know his full name. He calls himself ASS. I love him. No one has so completly loved me since Mom left."

"Your mom needs to rest. She has gone through a terrible experience. The place she is going is north of here. Don't tell anyone, including your dad, where she is hiding. This is for her safety. Will you promise you won't tell anyone?"

"You can trust me on that. Why can't I go with her?"

"I know this doesn't sound logical to you, but we have to follow the law. As long as your dad has custody of you, we have to follow that order, or we are in deep trouble. I am expecting a social worker to show up in a few minutes. She will be a liaison between you and your dad. When your mom is well enough, she can go to court and get custody of you. If the social worker thinks your dad is not capable of being your guardian, then she has the power to change things. I worry about this because if your mom is not well fast enough, you could go into foster care. So please don't protest too much about your dad. I think that maybe another school would be better for you, too."

At this moment the door opened and a lovely Asian American woman stood there. Todd acknowledged her, "Dorothy Chan, I was just telling Davie about you."

"It is nice to see you too, Todd. Is this Davie DeMartini?"

"Yes, I'm David. Are you going to help me talk to my dad?"

Todd eased himself out of the door and hurried to visit Elly before she left. Back in Elly's room, Maria was packing Elly's suitcase with a limited wardrobe. "I think we are ready to go."

"What is happening to Davie?" Elly said in distress.

"It is okay. The social worker will talk to Jerry about Davie and work out a solution. I will keep you informed as much as possible."

Just then the wheelchair arrived, and Elly along with her baggage moved out the door and down to the lobby.

Chapter 8

The Place in the Woods

A white van was waiting at the hospital's dock. It was a standard van with darkened windows so no one could see in. Maria took charge and assisted Elly into the backseat where she could spread out. She gently propped up her head with a pillow and covered Elly with a blanket. When the luggage was loaded, they drove away.

Elly stared at the scenery that rolled by through the window. She felt totally disconnected from it. *Like it's a boring movie I am watching. Oh, God, this van reminds me of the kidnap. I am so uneasy.* Horrid visions of that afternoon were swimming in her head. It felt like yesterday. That creepy, cruel man who grabbed her—his eyes were not punishing, but his actions were different. It was such a strange encounter that I never want to experience again. There was guilt mixed in there too. There was something about the way he looked at her. Did she not fight hard enough, or could she have encouraged him. It was like a rape without sexual *contact.*

Maria chatted away as she drove. Elly had trouble connecting to her words. But the words were gentle and soothing. Elly was lulled into sleep.

The hours dragged by as the road got smaller. They made their way through the mountain area of Marin. The curvy road turned into a dirt road, and it was afternoon by the time they pulled into another private road ending at a meadow. Several rustic log cabins with rock chimneys circled one side of the meadow. Smoke was curling up from some of the chimneys. It was a warm and inviting. Neil, the officer in charge, was at the gate, waiting for the guests. With him was Dusty, a large police dog that resembled a wolf with brown and black fur.

As Maria drove up, she rolled down the window. "Is everything ready for us?"

"Yes, Georgie has the lunch ready, and your cabin has a fire going that you should enjoy. Georgie will serve lunch in your cabin."

"Which cabin is ours?"

"Sorry. I am getting ahead of myself. Yours is the first one. Just follow me, and I will show you where to park."

Neil was dressed like a mountain man; however, he had a holster with a police-issued handgun, and on his chest he wore a bulletproof vest. His head was shaved down to a fine fuzz that he covered with a black and orange baseball cap.

Maria drove slowly behind Neil and Dusty. He directed her to park next to a cabin underneath a bay tree. Neil opened Elly's door. She was still fast asleep.

He gently touched Elly and said, "Hello there, sleepyhead, I am Neil, and this is my partner dog. His name is Dusty. Welcome to your safe house, or maybe we should call it a community."

Elly opened her eyes wide and smiled. "Oh, I like dogs, and it smells so nice here. I must have slept the whole trip. I don't remember anything."

"Here, let me help you into the cabin. Are you hungry? Georgie has been cooking all morning for you, and I made a fire in the fireplace to warm you. It is a very cozy place."

"Thank you. It is very nice. I couldn't have chosen a nicer resort to stay at."

The cabins all had porches with chairs. Each cabin's interior had rustic walls of knotty pine and rock fireplaces that made the rooms welcoming, warm, and friendly. Most of the cabins had two bedrooms and a kitchen. Elly sat down at the table and waited for lunch. As Elly looked around her, she loved the friendliness of the overstuffed chairs and couch. *The handmade table and chairs are charming. It is a fairy-tale place, and I can revel in the fantasy. Somehow this is a dramatic change from my life in San Francisco, so it will be healing.*

Maria also sat at the table in anticipation of lunch. She noticed that Elly was more alert and happier. The retreat to the woods was working already. This was a relief for her because she worried about Elly coming out of her terrible experience. It made her insecure to be a nursemaid. It wasn't what she had been trained to do.

"After lunch, let's take a walk around the meadow to get to know this place. Would you like that?" Maria offered.

"Oh, yes, that would be delightful. I'm so glad we are here. I think my mind is working better already. I miss Todd, and I worry about my youngest son. But I know I need to work on getting strong again, and that is most important. You know, as a nurse, I have to be strong for the patients, and it is the same for family. I have to heal myself before I can help them."

"I agree wholeheartedly with that statement. I think our lunch has arrived," she said as she opened the door for Georgie.

"Greetings to you beautiful ladies! Do I have a feast for you!" George Collinger said with a flare of presentation of his masterpiece. Before them he placed beautiful salads and a tray of fresh meats, freshly made breads, and vegetables for sandwiches.

"It looks grand. You are quite a chef. Where did you learn your craft?"

"Oh, here and there. I just like food, and I like it to look really inviting. Now what would you like to drink? There are all sorts of drinks in your refrigerator in the kitchen area. But if you want wine or beer, I have that at my cabin, and I am happy to bring that to you."

"No alcohol yet, Elly. The doctor said to wait for that, and we will do fine with the soft drinks for now," Maria cut in before Elly could answer.

"That's fine, Maria. I have enough trouble dealing with reality without alcohol, and I do not need anything to interfere with that."

The first days seemed to drag by, but Elly was becoming stronger. Both Neil and Maria accompanied her as she walked in the meadow. Then she tried jogging and could run almost the circumference of the meadow, she celebrated by playing with Dusty. Neil didn't approve of that. After all, Dusty was a work dog. Gradually, Neil let her have more independence, but he always had his eyes on her to make sure she was safe. Elly felt her smorgasbord of activities had shrunk to a pitiable few.

In the evening of the fifth day, Neil got a phone call from Todd. He announced that Elly's cousins were coming that Friday. Elly is excited, and her joy has sent waves of emotion throughout their small community.

However, Neil had *some mixed emotions. I am worried about the increased security problems but they are her cousins and family is important.*

That afternoon she visited Georgie's cabin to plan for the cousins' visit. Over cups of hot chocolate, they discussed the food. George was a portly man in his fifties, and he was known to have a temper.

"I want to plan a special dinner for them. I was thinking of wild boar. Is that possible?"

"Yes, I know some hunters that bring in a wild boar occasionally. I will put a call to them. That would be delicious. I could barbeque a leg or something large. I will investigate that. What would you like with it?"

"Oh, something like German sour red cabbage and baked potatoes or yams and lots of vegetables like you often do."

"Is that what these guys like?" George asked with suspicion.

She chuckled. "I really don't know them at all ... or what they like. I just thought that this sort of menu was masculine and in keeping with our setting. I know this isn't a hunting party, but we can pretend. If we have a variety of food, we should not have anyone go hungry."

"It is interesting that Todd is letting people you don't know come up here. That isn't going to put you in any danger, is it?"

Elly noted that Georgie and Neil were both wearing holsters and guns. As a caution, she used care with her answer. "They are my heroes. When I was kidnapped, they threatened someone, and the person set me free. As a result, Todd has decided that they are not dangerous."

Georgie's face turned red, and he was just barely keeping his anger in place. "Hump! We are charged with your safety, lady. Do you realize how inviting people you don't know can endanger you? They had better come with some powerful strong IDs, or they will be out on their asses," he growled.

"Well, I'm sure they will. Thank you for your help with the party that I want to plan. I know you are looking out for my best welfare as far as security is concerned. Knowing the Longacre family, I am sure that these men are ethical and that they will not cause any harm," Elly hastily said as she rose from her chair. The sun was shining brightly in the meadow as Elly walked out the door. The magical effect of nature was drawing her; however, her thoughts were still confused and Georgie's response bothered her.

That man gets under my skin, and it is most irritating. I have to trust that he means well. It is such a lovely day. I think I will take a walk and cool down. I am so bored here. The thought of someone new to talk to sounds heavenly. I wonder what they will be like. We were just little children when we met. Hank was always my friend. I wonder if he remembers those times.

***

The following chilly morning, the fog hung heavily on the ground. Elly lit the fire in the fireplace and put on an extra sweater. "Brrr, I hope the fire warms up this place fast, or our tea will be frozen before we can drink it."

In the kitchen Maria was just getting the hot drinks ready to serve. "Well, today is the big day, isn't it? I am looking forward to meeting these cousins of yours. I hope you find they are entertaining."

"Me too. This fog is so disorienting and depressing! I am going stir-crazy sitting here, playing card games, reading outdated books, having every movement monitored, and present company excluded; I need someone stimulating to talk to."

By noon the fog was lifting. Elly was out on her porch, waiting anxiously. *I feel like I am seventeen again, waiting impatiently for my first date to arrive.* She had taken special care with her makeup, and she wore a green stylish sweater over a warm turtleneck jersey. The silence of the forest was bugging her. She wanted to hear a car coming up the road. Maybe they had gotten lost. What a miserable thought. She stood there, and she was about to go back into the cabin when she heard a new sound. "Is that them?"

A few moments later, a blue Mercedes drove up to the gate. Neil with Dusty are there to check their papers. Berlin has Checkpoint Charlie and we have Checkpoint Dusty, Elly thought with amusement. After their interrogation and a sniff over by Dusty they drove in confidently.

Elly franticly waved as the car passed by her on its way to the cabin assigned to them. With youthful joy, she ran after the car.

With the car parked, the two men got out to greet their cousin. "Elinor, it has been so many years. It is a real treat to meet up with you again," Leland said in greeting her.

The older cousin, Leland, was darker and heavier set with a neat, well-trimmed beard and flashing dark eyes. Hank, the younger cousin, was blonder, taller, and thinner with a clean-shaven face and soft blue eyes that twinkled when he looked at her. Both were well dressed in expensive casual clothes. Leland was more formal and cynical, while Hank was more relaxed with a sense of humor.

"I can't tell you how much I appreciate your coming to visit. I am in this lovely nature preserve, but it can be too quiet sometimes."

"We would have had contact with you sooner, but we had no idea what had happened to you or where you were," Hank added.

Over lunch Elly loved reminiscing with her cousins about their childhood. Both Leland and Hank admired their attractive cousin. They found her vivacious, charming, open, and totally unsophisticated, which intrigued them. After they ate, they sat on her porch, spinning tales of their travels and adventures. Some of the stories they told were about their journeys to foreign countries and their safari exploits.

"You will love Paris with all the wonderful places to eat and the way it is romantically lit up at night. I can't wait to show you my favorite streets and the chocolate shops," Leland told her.

"How about Rome? That is the city where I want to take you. The history is so touchable there," Hank added.

Sitting back, Elly just enjoyed their glee in trying to outdo each other. It was just like when they were small boys so long ago. However, now she was no longer the ragged one, the bastard. Now they admired and valued her like the latest sleek new car. Something told her, she should be cautious. Hank and Leland were powerful men who were coming on with heavy quixotic notions. *Traveling with them? Did they really mean to follow through with those offers?*

*Am I being naïve to take their words for reality? It would be best if I
can learn from them, but I shouldn't let them feel they could have me
for more than a friend.*

The dinner that night was spectacular. It was served outdoors
at the fire pit in front of the large kitchen. Georgie had followed
through and had done his best. The wild boar was delicious. It hit
the mark with the cousins. They complemented the helpers and
told Georgie he was a super chef who should open a restaurant.
Secretly, Elly beamed with glee that her plans for the party had
really worked out well.

Hank and Leland were greedily eating their fill of the pork and
vegetables, but they really loved that there was plenty of wine and
scotch whiskey. However, by staying absolutely sober, Elly could
observe her guests objectively. They now amused her and gave her
insights as to their characters.

To Leland, who was closest to her, she proposed, "It would be
nice to take a hike tomorrow. With so many men to guard me, we
could take one of the trails into the forest. Would you like that?"

"Sure, every red-blooded man wants to plunge into a forest with
comely lass," Leland said, slurring his words.

Elly noticed that her guests were fading, "Georgie, maybe we
should serve some coffee and dessert. I think our guests are getting
a little overdone."

The dessert was a flan with a brandy sauce, and the coffee was
served black. It stiffened Hank and Leland enough to help them
wobble off to their cabin to sleep off their high. Elly felt a relief when
they left. She thanked Georgie and the helpers for a perfect party
and went to her cabin to collapse.

"Oh, Maria, everything was perfect, but they drank too much.
You would think they would know better."

"It has been my experience that when men are off in the wilderness, they tend to drink more because they don't have the social clues that tell them they are overdoing it. Also, many men feel insecure in the wilderness. It isn't like being home at a dining table with their friends. Here it is like a different social experience that they aren't comfortable with. They are not necessarily used to the more laid-back, rough setting that we have here, and they don't know the cues that indicate when too much is overdoing it."

"You are probably right. I appreciate your wisdom. I just hope they aren't hung over tomorrow."

***

In the middle of the night, Elly was awakened by the dog barking and footsteps running near her cabin. With excruciating slowness, she cautiously opened the curtain a little bit. All she saw was a shadow moving. It was creepy, and she waited for the next sound with trepidation. The only sound that followed was Neil. He was yelling something in the distance, but she couldn't understand it, besides, it was short. Holding the blankets to her face, she waited for a knock at her door that never came.

Sunrise was slow to have an effect because of the mist. Elly slept late to make up for the loss of sleep in the wee hours of the morning. While she showered, she thought of her cousins. They would most likely be late in rising too. She dressed in warm clothes with a red turtleneck sweater that was cozy and emphasized her feminine qualities. After that tension during the night, she was feeling vulnerable, and she wanted to invite the men over to wrap their strength around her.

When she came out on the porch, Neil was walking toward her cabin. "Good morning. Did you hear the noise in the night?" she called out.

"Yes, Dusty was barking, but I didn't see anything. Nor did I hear anything."

"I was awakened by Dusty, and I heard someone running past my cabin right near my window. It scared me to death."

"That's interesting. Did you see anything out of the window?"

"No, just wisps of shadows stirring. I was too scared to pull back the curtains very much. I just shivered in my bed."

Neil walked around the cabin and let Dusty do his sniffing inspection. "He doesn't seem to smell anything unfriendly, nothing that he hasn't smelled before. . . It might have been a deer or some other animal. He is trained to ignore those odors. Dusty is trained to hunt the bad guys and to protect people. I don't know what it could be."

This news made Elly more comfortable. "Thank you, Neil. I can see that Dusty is a real asset."

"I understand you would like to take a hike with your guests. Dusty and I must accompany you, and I want to check it out before we all get involved. Is that agreeable to you? I am available now to scope out our path, and I will return before noon."

"Yes, you are right. I am glad you are taking such wonderful precautions. After last night I am afraid of my own shadow."

Breakfast was quiet. The cousins were bravely handling their hangovers. "We are interested in the hike today. Are we doing this after lunch?" Leland asked.

"Neil is checking out the trail this morning, and we will be ready to go as soon as we eat lunch," Elly announced.

Even with his foggy brain, Leland was becoming more interested in Elly. *I like the aristocratic bone structure of her delicate face. Under all those sweaters, there must be a warm, slim, sensuous body. I can imagine her on my arm, strolling into a fashionable restaurant and having all the heads turn. Those moments are my favorite with effortless admiration and notoriety. That is what I want. She is a delicious morsel, and she will look perfect next to me.*

Hank held back. He, too, was attracted to Elly, but he had always yielded to his older brother. He knew that Leland had a short attention span when it came to women. *So all I have to do is wait. Eventually, Leland will be off with some other female dessert, and I will have a chance to move in. I will watch her, and I know that every time I smile at her, she returns my gesture with a knowing look of appreciation. Her eyes say it all. We were buddies when we were kids, and as time went by, I often thought about her and what had happened to her in those years in between. I've waited this long. I can wait some more. She is not going to yield to Leland. I know her too well. Elly has a mind that is too analytical to buy Leland's phony lines. He doesn't understand her like I do.*

Chapter 9

The Encounter

Neil arrived during the forenoon and told them about the hike they were taking after lunch. "The terrain is rugged and scenic. The trail starts at the north end of this meadow and it switchbacks up the first hill and then levels out and follows a ridge. Eventually, it comes to an old dirt road that is used rarely. It is a moderate-level trail, which means it is good exercise but not overly strenuous, and most of all, I think it is very safe."

"It sounds perfect. Thank you for scouting it out for us. Now sit with us and eat. We can leave in an hour," Elly said with a smile.

***

On a hill above the meadow in a large oak tree, a man sat in camouflage green overalls. He was scanning the meadow below him with high-power binoculars. *They have a nice scene down there. It is ironic that we are going to upset the peace and quiet, but then peace can get boring at times. That is why we are going to liven it up for them. The boss wants those men to think twice about helping the woman. He is a strange one. I wonder what he has against her. It must be pretty bad, or perhaps she refused his ardent offer that he wants to kill people. I should have been a shrink with the crazy people who hire me. I would love to know what makes them tick.*

***

"I am thrilled that we are going for a real hike. I haven't done that in years. When I was a teenager, I was always hiking with my friends," Elly said as she put on her sturdiest shoes.

"You really like exercise. That is so admirable. I need to join a gym or something when we get back to the city. I am so out of shape," Maria said as she was straightening up the cabin.

"Aren't you joining us today?"

"Hardly. I would just be slowing you down, and it isn't my gig anyway. Neil thinks he will be fine without another officer."

The small band of explorers gathered at the fire pit. Hank and Leland had swapped their wool pants for jeans, and they wore hunting jackets with many pockets. Elly appreciated the change. Now they looked less like Wall Street and more down to earth. Elly brought a small backpack for the essentials like water and snacks.

"You look ready for an expedition. We are just going up this hill and not much farther," Leland commented.

"A nurse is always prepared. I even have a mini first-aid kit in my bag for all those scratches."

"Heads up, hikers! Are we all ready? We have to walk single file on this trail, so I will walk at the rear. And I want Elinor in the middle of you guys. If we have any problems like a snake or a wild pig, I will deal with it. Just let me know what you see. Is that clear?" Neil announced.

They walked together to the trail with curiosity and a feeling of adventure. The hill was covered with wild oaks of several varieties, some had beards of Spanish moss and others had balls of mistletoe. Elly loved the Bay laurels because they smelled so good. She liked the madrone trees too with their red pealing bark.

"These bay leaves that I pick off these laurel trees are so good when they are cooked with meat."

"Do you like to cook?" Leland asked.

"Yes, didn't Shakespeare say something about food and music being the language of love? I delight in finding new ways to make ordinary food enticing."

"Oh, I know that one. It is from *Twelfth Night*, and it goes like this. 'If music be the food of love, play on.' That is one of my favorite lines," Hank responded.

Climbing up the switchbacks got them breathing hard, and the talk fell off until they reached the top. The ridge ran south to southwest. They could see the potential of nice views if they walked to the next hill, which rose up in the west.

As they were hiking through a small valley, Elly remarked, "It is always annoying to go down only then to exert yourself again by climbing up to a new altitude on the other side."

She was looking forward to the road and the carrot that encouraged her was the views she might get of the Pacific Ocean. There was one more steep uphill push to the edge of the road. Her first steps on the road were delightful.

Surly, it was going to be more pleasant walking on the soft, dusty road. Elly was filled with the expectation of the view around the next corner. Then out of the calm came the rumbling roar of a truck engine around a curve. Their peaceful silence was broken, and the feeling of solitude was shattered by a truck bearing down on them.

Neil grabbed Elly's elbow and dragged her to the edge of the road and down the embankment while he yelled at the men to do the same. Gunshots rang out, and Elly was stunned when a bullet whizzed past her. Neil pushed Elly behind a large oak tree trunk and ordered the cousins to protect her. Hank and Leland took positions behind other trees and listened as the bullets flew past or plunged into trees with a thud.

Hank slowly worked his way up to the oak where Elly was cowering between gunshots. He covered her body with his own and put his arm around her. He could feel her terror as she shivered with fear. In her ear he whispered, "Just relax, Little Rabbit." (That was his nickname for her back when she was five.) "I won't let them hurt you." Her body became softer, and she stopped quivering.

The truck had stopped just before the place that the hikers had dropped over the edge of the road. Neil and Dusty observed them for an opening. He watched the two men dismount the truck and walk along the road, searching for the hikers, their rifles ready to fire. Neil took a deep breath and then silently disconnected Dusty's leash. All his canine fury stood tense, waiting for a command. When the men were farther down the road, Neil instructed Dusty to follow him as he quietly climbed up to the road. On the road Neil drew his hand gun, and using the truck as a shield, he commanded Dusty to disarm the men. Dusty plunged forward with all his strength, knocking the closest man down. Neil ran up to grab the rifle that went flying just as the other man turned to shoot. With fury Dusty went after the other man, but the man was able to block the attack with the side of his rifle. Dusty went down, yelping. Again, the dog arose and attacked from the rear, grabbing his pant leg just as Neil was shooting at the man. At first he was stunned that his shots were having no effect. Then it dawned on Neil that the man was wearing a bulletproof vest. This worried him. The man kicked back against the dog. Dusty recovered, and again grabbed the man's leg. Turning in pain and anger, the man brought the butt of his rifle down hard on the dog's head. Dusty fell off, yelping and injured. Trembling, Neil displayed his badge in his left hand, and from his right hand, he fired his .38 special in the air as the man charged him in a zigzagging fashion to avoid bullets.

"I'm a police officer. Put down your arms, or I'll be forced to shoot you."

"Okay, okay, I'm sorry. We were hunting deer and didn't know there were humans running around. Now let's talk some sense." JR roared with his hands up. As he approached at a slower speed, Neil backed up to the truck. JR's biggest worry was about a trigger-happy officer who was cornered, so he decided to change his approach.

"Drop your rifle!" Neil ordered. "This is not hunting season for any game. You are violating the law in many ways. I could arrest you for endangering hikers with your wild shooting."

"What's this crap? You? How are you going to arrest me?" JR said as he stood towering over Neil, so close the officer could smell his stinking breath.

Neil felt a chill down his spine. *The man is right. I can collect their rifles and slap their wrists, but I know I have no authority or ability to bring them in. If I confiscate their firearms and then let them go, they can collect their firearms at the Marin County offices. And the office will fine them for illegal brandishing of weapons, hunting out of season, and endangering hikers. I can write down the license number off the truck, but I have a feeling it has been stolen. My biggest worry is that it would be so easy for them to kill us all as well.*

"This is the deal. You let us go, and we won't bother you anymore. Now give me my partner's rifle, or I'll knock your block off," JR said. As he said this, the other man got up and hurried to the confrontation. He was also large and angry. Both men glared at Neil and clenched their fists.

He hesitated. Neil did not want to fight this man ... or these two men. "Okay, here is the rifle. Put them away and leave," he ordered.

"Ah, you can be reasonable. Here we are a long way from civilization. Your power is back in the city, not out here in the sticks. There is just you and those silly city slickers. We operate differently out here. It takes cooperation and some tolerance for rednecks."

They hung up their rifles in the carrier of the truck's rear window and climbed in. The head man revved up the engine to a roar and lurched forward. Neil jumped out of the way, feeling impotent and defeated.

Neil sadly gathered up his wounded dog. He was bleeding from an injury to his head. With effort he carried him down to the hikers. "I think we should get back to the meadow as fast as we can in case they come back."

No one needed encouragement. In silence, they hurried down to the little ravine where they had passed before. Here Elly put down her backpack and offered to treat Dusty's injuries.

"Yes, that is a good idea. Thank you," Neil said as he carefully laid Dusty next to Elly.

As she worked to clean the cuts, she said, "I think I recognized that one man's voice. He might be the man who kidnapped me."

"That *is* interesting. I'm sorry I couldn't arrest them. I have no backup or handcuffs, and those guys were huge. They were dangerous, and I was afraid to push them because then they might have killed us all. I didn't want to risk that."

"You did great. I was so afraid that they would kill you. Or you would have this big shoot out, and there would be bodies everywhere," Leland added.

All the hearts leaped when they heard a truck up on the road again, but to their relief, it seemed to drive on once they realized the hikers had left.

"We have to keep moving. These guys are not predictable," Hank whispered.

Elly had just finished bandaging Dusty. The dog was looking up at her and seemed to realize she was helping him. With effort, he wobbled up on his feet. "Hurrah! He may be able to walk."

"That's an improvement. He is really heavy," Neil admitted.

"He doesn't look strong enough to climb this hill. We can take turns carrying him up this hill and then it is all downhill to the meadow," offered Hank.

Hank took the first shift lugging Dusty as they drudged up the hill. When Hank was worn out, Leland took over, and then Neil helped.

"Dusty weighs almost a hundred pounds. And he is harder to carry than a human," Neil softly said as he took back his burden.

The downhill portion of the hike was easier, and Dusty walked part of it. It was late in the afternoon when they trudged into the camp, tired, sweaty, and dragging their grimy bodies like sacks of dirty laundry.

As everyone staggered off to their respective cabins for showers and rest, Neil called out to them, "Thanks, guys. You were really super today. Now I need to call in a report of our encounter."

With tender care, Neil laid Dusty on a clean blanket in his pen and closed the gate. A wave of exhaustion flooded his senses. In his cabin he got his radio telephone and called the San Francisco PD. "This is 5773 calling. We had contact with suspicious characters that are armed and dangerous. They fired randomly with high-power rifles. I was overwhelmed with the men's supremacy and gun power. I need to request reinforcements."

The officer on the other end responded with a request for more information.

Neil responded, "We had a run-in with some out-of-season hunters, but I don't really think they were hunters. I am very suspicious of them. They had army Browning auto-5, recoil-operated, semiautomatic shotguns. They acted like infantry men, and Elly thought their voices sounded familiar. I have a license number, but I have a feeling it isn't worth anything. It is California plate BPN 483. I think when you run it, you will find it belongs to dead people, or it's a stolen truck. I really felt frustrated out there with only a pistol. I need back up. Please give this message to Todd or Jim."

The San Francisco exchange informed him that she would pass his request on as soon as possible and that he should wait for their reply.

Neil was frustrated by this and walked out of his cabin to vent his frustration to the newly showered small group at his door. After he finished telling them about his frustrating message to SFPD, he asked if there were any suggestions.

"No offense to you, Neil, but I don't think Elinor has enough protection here," Leland offered. Then he turned to Maria and said, "Neil performed admirably with those two guys with rifles. And Dusty deserves a medal too," he added.

"I assure you that I will get more help when I can get a hold of the office in San Francisco," Sergeant Fuentes guaranteed him. "Are you and your brother still planning on leaving this afternoon?"

"We would rather stay, but without a phone, we are helpless professionally. Of course, we could take Elly with us. Then you would be free to go after turkeys like those two outrageous characters we ran into on that road," Leland suggested.

"Without the blessing of my boss, I cannot let her go. Of course, I can't hold her against her will either," Maria said with a smile.

Elly felt on the spot, but in her heart she knew who she trusted. "I think it is better that I stay here and wait for Todd to call."

Later Leland came up to Elly's cabin. "I would like you to show me this lovely meadow while I wait for my brother to finish packing. It looks delightful, and we need something peaceful to think about. Are you up for that?" Leland asked.

"Sure, just let me get my shoes on," she responded.

Elly was freshly showered, and her curly dark, sophisticated haircut framed her face seductively. The clean sky-blue shirt accentuated her violet blue eyes. She fairly glided out of the door and into the sunshine. Leland felt drawn to her graceful vulnerability as well as her beauty. He wanted to convince her to come with him; however, he didn't want her to feel he just wanted to ravish her physically, even though that interested him too. They walked out into the meadow, investigating the spring flowers and birds. Elly picked some blossoms and put them in her hair. They climbed up on a large bolder to have a view and a light conversation. Then Leland decided to risk a suggestion.

"I have a proposal to make. I am concerned about your safety, and I have a big house with lovely bedrooms. I could put you up there and get guards or whatever to keep you safe. Would you consider that?"

"Please remind me where you live," she said tentatively.

"My house is in the hills above Menlo Park. There are wonderful views of the bay from my deck. I would love to show it to you," Leland said, gazing into her eyes.

"I find it funny that you just want to have me move in with you when I hardly know you. I'm not one to move in with a man just like that. I am engaged to be married in May, and I don't even live with him. So how could I just pick up and move in with you?"

Leland was not going to give up yet. "I'm family. Doesn't that make a difference? Besides, I can go to live with Hank if that makes you more comfortable. You can have my whole house all to yourself. I just want you safe."

She smiled, and he wanted so much to take her into his arms. Instead he said, "Please think about it."

Bouncing off the rock, she took his hand and drew him down from his perch. This was an opportunity he wanted, and he wrapped his arms around her and passionately kissed her. She gently shook herself free.

"Stop playing romantic games with me. I'm no fool. This coming May, I'm going to marry Todd. So I shouldn't be kissing you," she said with a pout.

"I can't help that I am falling in love with you, and you aren't married yet. I also think you liked being kissed, and you tasted so good to me," he said in a deep voice filled with emotion.

In the distance she heard someone calling.

"Hank is calling you, Leland. I'm very sad to see you go, but let's talk more about all this later. I'm not ready just now to take another lover. I'm not the kind of woman who juggles two lovers at the same time," she said, looking earnestly into his eyes.

"You don't realize how hard it is for me to let you go. After this morning's terrible experience, I'm worried that something will happen to you. I want you to marry me because I will keep you safe. Please marry me!" he stammered.

Elly was stunned by his proposal, but all she could say was, "Let's talk about it when we have more time. I need to think about it. But you are right. I don't feel safe here."

They returned to the grounds around the cabins, hand in hand. Hank was putting luggage in the car. He rose up as they approached. "Hi, Leland, I wasn't sure you were coming with me," Hank said with an ear-to-ear grin. "Is the lady coming with us?"

"You will have to ask her. By the way, do you want to drive?" Leland said with annoyance.

"I must stay here where Todd can find me. I will be safe, I think."

They turned to say their good-byes. Both hugged and kissed Elly. Her eyes were full of tears as she watched them drive away.

The afternoon was quiet as everyone waited to hear from Todd and Jim. Elly curled up with a good book. Maria knitted and worried along with Neil since they had not heard anything from Todd yet.

About the time Elly was thinking of a nap, Maria's police radio came to life.

"This is Todd. Neil requested an extra officer?"

"Yes, we had a shooting incident this afternoon."

"I will be there tomorrow ... in the morning."

"Thanks. See you then."

"Over and out."

They looked at each other with relief.

"We must tell Neil right away," Maria added.

"This reprieve must be what the pioneers felt when they heard the cavalry was coming," Elly said.

***

Leland and Hank were silent as they drove until they reached the Golden Gate Bridge. Hank finally asked Leland, "You were pretty thick with Elinor. What's up?"

"She intrigues me. I can't get her out of my head. I don't know if I just want to screw her or if I really am falling for her. I wasn't able to entice her up to my lair. She guessed it would not be a celibate arrangement. What is your take on her?" Leland asked.

"My guess is that she is a savvy lady and that you are not going to get her easily. I understand she is engaged to marry that officer we talked to the other day. He may have a hold on her she won't break. How much are you willing to give to get her, and how permanent would that liaison be? My advice, dear brother, is to be careful. Remember, she is a Longacre. She has power, although she doesn't seem to know how to use it yet. But she is smart, and she will learn."

"You won't believe this, but I asked her to marry me. I could not believe it myself. It was as if my alter ego could not resist her. Bless her heart; she said she would think about it. Now that I am away from her, I realize that was what I would like to have happen. It is the perfect match for me, and she is so gentle on the eyes," Leland said, daydreaming.

"I remember when you were dating Greta. She was just what you always wanted. Her mother loved you, and even her powerful father thought you were ideal for his daughter. Then there was the wedding, and it cost a fortune. Remember that torturous year later when you were in the divorce courts and she was ripping the clothes off your back! If it wasn't for her father, who talked some sense into her, you would be on skid row," Hank reminded him.

"Good god that was an awful experience. I need to be reminded of that every once in a while. Greta was gorgeous and a social gadfly, but she didn't have an ounce of sense. Elly is totally different personality-wise, and it's refreshing. I have grown up in the last five years too, and I think I'm a better judge of feminine flesh these days," Leland philosophized.

"Elly has two grown boys, and you haven't met them yet. Find out what happened to her last marriage, Lee. I also think she is in a lot of danger at the moment, and I think we should concentrate on that. When she is out of danger, then we both can romance her. And may the best man win," Hank proposed.

"But Hank, you have Reggie. Are you telling me you are not gay anymore?"

"I have always been bisexual. Besides, Reggie and I are not getting along very well, and we haven't slept together in weeks. I am terrified that I will get AIDS."

"And then the smell of money has a lot of power to change one ... like you are a chameleon."

***

At dinner they ate leftovers from the wild boar and other delicacies. Maria and Neil were happier. Even Dusty was acting like he was getting stronger. Elly continued to treat his wounds. He was standing more, but he was still limping. He did eat his dinner, and that was a good sign.

"What time do you think Todd will be here tomorrow?" Elly asked wistfully.

"If he goes to the 7:00 a.m. report, he should be able to get here by ten."

"How exciting! I can't wait to see him," Elly said and closed her eyes to imagine him there already.

Later as Elly and Maria were getting ready for bed, Georgie brought up a cup of hot chocolate for Elly. Maria brought it to her.

"He says you will sleep better. That's why he made it," Maria told her.

"That was generous of him, but I just brushed my teeth. Why don't you have it, Maria?"

"Well, I can't resist chocolate in any form, and I haven't brushed my teeth yet," Maria said. She took the cup to her room to read in bed, sipping on the warm liquid.

In the loneliness of her room, Elly thought about her conflict with Todd and Leland. She liked Hank too. It was nice that Hank was less aggressive, and yet she knew he was interested in her too. She decided that she loved Todd enough that seeing more of the brothers would not necessarily conflict with her wedding plans.

Chapter 10

Complications

The morning dawned, but everything was veiled in fog. Elly was up early in anticipation of Todd's arrival. Her arms ached to hold him and feel his reassuring strength. With a crying yearning for security, she hoped he would suggest that they all go back to the city. Any other choice was out of the question.

Everything was so quiet even though it was after seven. Maybe the miserable murkiness was keeping everyone in bed. Usually, she could hear the cook getting breakfast ready or Neil running Dusty and playing with him, but Dusty was probably still in pain. Maria was often up by this time too. They must be sleeping in after all the exhausting excitement yesterday. She went back to her book and decided to relax until she heard more activity.

By eight, Elly was getting desperate with concern, and then there was a knock on her door. But there was no sound from Maria's room, so she grabbed her robe and went to the door.

Neil was standing there with disheveled clothing and a look of serious despair. "May I come in?" he asked, looking furtively over his shoulder.

"Sure, good morning. It is so good to see you. Everyone seems to be sleeping late," Elly said, her words accented with worry.

"There is more going on than that. I can't find the cook, Georgie. He is not on the property, and it isn't like him to take an early morning walk. Normally, he is making breakfast at this time," Neil said with concern in his face.

"Come in. I will get Maria up," Elly said. She ran to Maria's room. Knocking on the door, she got no response, so Elly opened the door. "Maria, are you all right?"

There was a groan from Maria, who lay in a heap on the bed. "I think I have the flu. I'm very sick," Maria shakily whispered in a weak, scratchy voice.

Elly noticed the cup and saucer on the nightstand. There were a few drops in the bottom of the cup. "Maria, tell me. Were you sick yesterday, or did this start last night?"

"I had a little cold starting yesterday, but it got worse last night. I'm sorry, but I won't be worth much today," Maria feebly explained.

"I will be right back. I want to get you some breakfast," Elly announced.

"I ... don't think I can eat anything, Elly. Please don't go to any trouble," Maria whimpered.

"How about some liquids? I don't want you to get dehydrated," Elly said in her best nursing voice, full of compassion.

Outside Maria's room Neil was standing with a look of frustrated inaction. "What is going on? Is Maria really ill or—" He stopped because he was afraid they were in a worse situation.

"How do I preserve the cup in Maria's room? I think there is chance that she might have been poisoned, and I want to keep it for evidence just in case it is useful," Elly said in a strident voice. "It might sound crazy but when Georgie brought only one cup of chocolate last night my mind ran to poisoning this morning."

"Don't touch it. I will look for a plastic bag and some gloves. I'll be right back," Neil said as he went out the door.

Elly went into her cabin kitchen to look for something to eat. The refrigerator had soft drinks and beer. Franticly, Elly combed through the drinks and found a ginger ale. She opened it, poured it into a clean glass, and then brought it to her patient. "Maria, I brought you something cold and wet to drink. It may help settle your stomach and give you the strength to get up," Elly suggested.

She rolled Maria over and propped up her head with several pillows. Then while sitting on the bed, she helped Maria take small sips with a spoon and then more from the glass. At first, she didn't seem to want it. But the wet feel in her mouth was soothing, and Maria gave in. While Maria drank drop by drop, Elly took her vitals and felt her forehead because she had no thermometer. Maria didn't seem very feverish, which was something she would expect if Maria had the flu.

Neil returned after some period of time. "I was worried about you. What took you so long?" Elly asked with genuine concern.

"I had to break into the cook's cabin, and I didn't want to disturb any evidence there. But the gloves were in a drawer, and the plastic bag was in another place. I'll collect the cup, now. Why do you think that Maria has been poisoned?"

"Just using my deductive reasoning for what it's worth, last night Georgie brought up *one* cup of hot chocolate for me to help me sleep. I had just brushed my teeth, and so I offered it to Maria. Then this morning she has this mysterious illness, and Georgie has skipped out. Am I suffering from paranoia? What do you make of it? Maybe it is all innocent. It is possible Georgie's mother got ill and he had to leave in a hurry," Elly explained.

"Well, your theory is logical enough for me. Georgie's disappearance is unnerving. If he poisoned Maria, he could have given any of us poison at any time he wanted. We were all guzzling down cups of chocolate frequently. Also, with that incident on the road yesterday, that guy who hurt Dusty was coming at me with so much macho anger that I was sure he was going to shoot me dead. And then as I'm getting ready to meet my maker, he makes a joke out of it. Like he was playing some sort of game."

Elly shivered with fear. "I think they didn't want you, and they probably recoiled from killing a cop. The way it looks to me is they just wanted me!" Then she hung her head and sobbed. "This is all about my inheritance in some way, but I don't understand why someone is so hell-bent to kill me."

"Let's have some breakfast, and maybe the world will get brighter. We can have these packages of oatmeal. You get some hot water going and get some bowls. I'll collect the cups," Neil suggested.

"I have a kettle here, and that will work for the hot water. If the cook's cabin is open, I will try to find some fruit or juice for us," Elly said with more cheerfulness.

"You had better let me find the fruit. It might be a crime scene, and we need to respect that," Neil responded as he walked toward Maria's bedroom door. "Besides, I think you are safest in here. If someone is watching us and they don't see you, then they might think you have been poisoned. So I want you to lay low, okay?"

Elly nodded her appreciation of Neil's insights and went to start a kettle of water on the little two-burner stove.

When Neil returned, he brought a bag of bananas and some apples. He also had Dusty on a leash. "I got Dust because I am afraid that someone will try to poison him or kill him some other way, and with no other officers who are healthy, I need all the help I can get."

They ate their Spartan breakfast in silence, and then Elly went and tried to feed Maria oatmeal too. She only took a few bites. Elly tried to cheer her up. "Now, Maria, this is no way to lose weight. You need nourishment to get well."

"Please call Todd and tell him to hurry. I feel like ... I just want to go home!" Maria said weakly.

"I'll tell Neil to call him. Just try to drink some more ginger ale and rest," Elly said as she lifted the glass to Maria's lips. After attempting feeding and helping Maria drink, Elly decided to let Maria have a break, and she went out to the main room to talk to Neil.

Neil was one step ahead of her and had called and left a message for Todd when he was outside, but he hadn't gotten an answer yet. "While we wait for Todd, I think it is best if we all stay here in this cabin until he arrives. If we get separated, we are in a weaker position. We really don't know what happened to Georgie. He could have been kidnapped. I don't want anyone else to disappear."

"I agree entirely, and I like having you and Dusty here where I can see you. I think we all feel insecure at the moment, and we need to see one another. It's almost ten o'clock," Elly said with a wistfully sad note in her voice.

The time inched by, and with every noise outside, Elly jumped and wanted to run to the window. But Neil cautioned her not to do that. They played games together—first gin rummy and then poker without any bets. Elly tried to keep a poker face, but she failed miserably at it. Neil was much better and won most of the games.

"I'm glad we don't have any money on this. I would end up in the poorhouse. Where is Todd? He is so late," Elly lamented.

Just as Elly was dealing another game, a car drove up to the gate. Neil and Elly looked at each other but didn't move. Dusty began to growl and went to the door. Then there was a knock. "It's me. It's Todd. You can call off Dusty and open the door."

"What is the code?" Elly asked, half-joking.

"I love you," he said. He was so happy to hear her voice.

She was so desperate to see him that she threw open the door. "Am I so glad to see you! Why did you torture us by coming so late?" she sniffled.

He took her in his arms and hugged her, trying to comfort her. "I need to understand what is happening here," Todd said and looked at Neil for a report.

"Maria needs a doctor. Dusty needs a vet, and I need to get out of here. It has been too scary," Elly said, begging. "I hope you realize that this safe house has failed miserably."

Neil had written up the issues of the two days, and he handed them to Todd. "Sir, I strongly advise leaving here as soon as possible. The cook, George Collinger, is missing. Maria may have been poisoned, and Elinor's nerves are shot.

They discussed the problems from yesterday's encounter with the hunters. Neil explained his frustrations in not being able to arrest these men. "I wish Elinor could have escaped with her cousins, but I know there were problems with that."

"I got a call from Hank and Leland, and they told me they did not think there was adequate protection here, for Elly," Todd admitted. "I see that they were not blowing smoke at me at all. I think we need to get everyone out of here ASAP," Todd continued. "Let me see Maria."

Elly took Todd's hand and walked to Maria's bedroom. "There might have been something in the hot chocolate that was meant for me, but I passed it on to Maria. Neil has secured the cup for evidence."

"This drink came from the cook who has vanished?" Todd asked.

"Yes," Elly said as she looked into his eyes. She could see he was happy she had not drunk the chocolate, but he was sorry that his sergeant had taken the alleged poison accidentally.

They opened the door. Maria was lying on her side, facing the wall. Elly went to her side to make sure her vitals were holding up and she was comfortable.

"Maria, Todd is here. We are taking you back home. I think you need to see a doctor. Can you roll on to your back so you can see Todd," Elly said, encouraging her.

With effort, Maria rolled on to her back with Elly's help. "Hi, boss," she said weakly.

"You will have the best care in San Francisco," Todd assured her as he bent over the bed.

"I have had a very good nurse here, but I do want to go home," Maria whispered.

By noon they had everything ready to leave. The arrangements were that Neil was going to stay longer to secure the evidence in the cook's kitchen area. He was going to follow them to San Francisco as soon as the local sheriff arrived to take over.

They needed very little time to pack everything into the two police cars. Maria would be made comfortable in the back of Todd's van. They'd secured most of the luggage and evidence in the car Neil was driving. Todd looked over the cook's cabin and decided he wanted to lock it up for the sheriff to go through and look for more clues that could lead to finding the cook. Todd and Elly would drive back to San Francisco with Maria. After some final good-byes, and Elly hugging Neil and Dusty, they drove away. There was silence as they traveled on to the dirt road toward home.

A few miles down the road, Elly came out of her reverie and said, "Am I glad to leave that place! You have no idea what we have been put through there. I was supposed to rest and recuperate, but this was a scary place with people shooting and ... my cousins." Elly's voice trailed off. She was not sure how much to tell Todd about Leland and his proposal. "Please let's get out of this lion's den before something else happens."

"What were the cousins like?" Todd asked with genuine curiosity.

"Oh, they are your typical wealthy young men who like to rescue ladies in distress. They were fun, but ... they remind me of my childhood. Only now everything has changed. I am accepted, and in the past I wasn't so. I am suspicious of them and their motives. They felt I was not well protected and wanted me to go with them to Palo Alto or Menlo Park or wherever they live. This was yesterday before Maria got sick. Yesterday I got the feeling that Maria wanted me to leave with my cousins, but I wanted to see you, dear Todd, so leaving with them wasn't an option," Elly said with a feeling of depression that she didn't fully understand.

"How were they planning to keep you safe? It seems that they would have the same problems we've had," Todd offered.

"They told me they would hire an armed guard to protect me. A bodyguard, I would guess. They felt that getting me into an urban environment close to them would be safer. After the gunfight incident, I was almost ready to agree with them."

"Neil thinks he can identify those men. It might be the same bunch that kidnapped you. If we can identify them, then we have an easier time arresting them. Neil said you recognized their voices. Is that right?" Todd asked.

"Yes, they sounded familiar, but I was flat on my belly. And it was a long way from these men, hiding in the brush behind a large tree with Hank shielding me with his body, so I wasn't in the best position to listen to their conversations. You can't imagine what was going through my mind. I was just as fearful as when I had been kidnapped; only it was worse. I was sure we were all going to die," Elly said with a trembling voice. It was then that Elly remembered how fond she was having Hank's protective arms around her as they dodged bullets.

The road out of the rural area seemed endless to Elly. She and Todd sat in silence, lost in their thoughts as they drove over the hills on a winding road. At the top of the hill, they suddenly saw the Golden Gate Bridge and the city. A few minutes later, they were on the bridge and driving up to the tollbooth. Elly roused herself from her daydreams and started to take an interest in the scenery. "It is so nice to see the city again. I didn't know how much I missed it."

"I have a surprise for you! I want to show you something special. Also, I want a special date with my honey tonight? Will that cheer you up?" Todd said with happiness.

"Oh, I'm looking forward to your surprise. Is it bigger than a telephone? Or is it smaller than a watch?" she quizzed.

"It is bigger than an elephant! And it is both alive and dead," he teased.

Elly's smile was a welcome sight. He wanted to take her in his arms and make her forget about her experiences over the last several days.

"You are a big tormenter! I don't have any idea about what you have dreamed up. What is both alive and dead?" she said as she reached over to kiss his cheek. "I've missed you so much."

"You will see, but first, we have to take care of Maria," Todd said as he used his radio phone to call his office. "Jim, call Maria Fuente's husband, and tell him we are taking her to the hospital on Franklin."

"Roger. It is as good as done," Jim responded.

Then Todd called the hospital to inform them that he had a police case that would need immediate attention and extra security. In addition, he explained that it most likely was a poisoning and told them to run the appropriate tests. A few minutes later, they pulled into the emergency bay of the hospital. Several staff members were waiting for them, and they put Maria on a gurney and got her into the hospital with haste.

Todd and Elly were with her as they rolled Maria through the hospital doors. Todd was taking care of the paperwork. Elly was explaining to the physician the possible source of Maria's illness. She told him that Maria has possibly ingested it and recounted what she had done to make Maria comfortable. "Maria's family is coming. The security will let them see her, won't they?" Elly asked.

"We are going to run a battery of tests to determine any poisons. In addition, we will set up IVs and such so that we can hydrate and monitor her. When that is taken care of, we will put her in a private room upstairs with officers. I would say that the best time for her family to visit would be an hour and a half from now," Dr. Parker told her.

"Thank you. I will wait for them in the waiting room," Elly said.

Elly wandered into the waiting room, feeling less important suddenly. She had spent all morning worrying about Maria and her own security that it was strange to sit there and let go of her concerns. She found her mind thinking about Hank and Leland and what they were doing. She missed Leland's adoration, even though she thought it was an affectation. Hank was another matter. When they were hiding behind that tree, he was very *real*, and she was sure he would risk his life for her. This thought of him comforting her came up over and over. Could she dare to imagine a relationship with Hank?

She was shaken from her daydreaming by Mr. Fuentes, who was now standing over her. "Todd said I might find you here. I am Joe Fuentes, Maria's husband."

"Oh, yes, please sit down. They said you could see Maria in about an hour or so," Elly said as she looked at her watch.

"I am sorry your rest was interrupted by Maria's sickness," Joe said cautiously. He wasn't used to small talk.

Elly smiled at him and said, "I was more than ready to come home, but thank you. I missed my friends and the city. It is easier to be invisible in a city than in the country," she said, trying hard to keep a smile on her face.

He nodded his head as if he understood and then asked, "My English is no good. Did you say invisible? Like no one can see you?"

"I mean I want to walk around and not have people know who I am," she explained, but she really didn't want to talk about her problems. So she asked, "Do you have children?"

"Maria and I have two boys, and they speak English good like their mother."

"That is nice. I have two boys too. They are almost grown up and on their own," Elly explained.

Just then the door opened, and Todd came in. "Maria is in her room, and you can visit her now, Mr. Fuentes. She is in 532, and the elevator is down the hall on the right.

Todd and Elly walked out of the hospital, feeling lighter and freer. In the vehicle Todd said, "I have to turn in this police van, but then the rest of the day is ours."

They drove back to the police station, and Todd parked the patrol van. After transferring the luggage to the sedan, Todd took Elly in his arms and said, "I can't say how much I would have been devastated if you were the one in that hospital room." Todd opened the door and made her comfortable in his sedan. "Now I am going to take you to your surprise."

As they drove through the city, Todd told jokes and teased Elly to cheer her up. "You can be so funny, Todd, but we need to think about my security. Those men yesterday were very professional, and I was afraid that someone or all of us were going to die. Neil was extraordinarily brave. He and Dusty went after those men. I couldn't see what was happening, but I heard a lot of gunshots. I thought they would kill Neil and then come after Leland, Hank, and me."

"I wonder if they were also after the cousins. Aren't they in line to inherit this estate if something happens to you? In that case, who would benefit with the three of you dead?"

"There is no one I can think of who would want us all dead. If I died, then the estate would go to my boys and not to Leland and Hank. By the way, do you have a suspect for Jacob Mendelsen's death?" Elly asked.

"Yeah, but he is out on bail. We are working on witnesses and those with motives. There is not enough evidence that killing Mendelsen would benefit this fellow. So we think he is working for someone, and that is the direction of the investigation."

They turned a corner and stopped in front of a large building with an awning covering the path from the curb to the massive front doors. Elly's eyes were big, and she said, "This is Nob Hill, and this is one of those fancy apartment houses!"

"Yes, indeed, Elly. This is the most secure apartment I could find for you, and you are going to love it," Todd said as he kissed her forehead.

"See, there is a code to get in the door, and then there is always a guard inside to make sure only the people on the list I set up get in."

They walked into the grand foyer and talked to the guard before they took the elevator to the eighth floor. "This is perfect. Eight is my lucky number."

"Your apartment is 804. There are four apartments on each floor," Todd explained as they walked directly to it, and Todd knocked.

The door opened, and there was Ted, Elly's oldest son. "Oh, Teddy, how good it is to see you," she said as she hugged and kissed him.

"Todd and I moved everything from your old apartment here, but we weren't sure where you wanted everything. So whenever you are rested, we can rearrange the whole enchilada."

Elly looked around the room and thought her couch and chair looked so shabby in this elegant room. "Maybe it is time to buy some new chairs and such. Mine look like they are totally out of place here," she said as she strolled over to the large windows to see the view. "Oh, Todd, the view is magnificent! Look! We can see the sailboats on the bay!"

They sat on the old couch, and Ted brought Todd some coffee and his mother some tea. "Teddy, come and sit here, I want to hear about your life. How is the university treating you?" Elly said as he served the tea.

Ted came and sat in the chair with his cup of coffee. "It's cool, Mom. I have lots of friends, and I am getting really good grades."

Elly looked at her son and realized he was worried about something. "Where is Davie?"

"Mom, I want you to rest. You have had a terrible ordeal, and we can handle David when you are well."

"I am not on my death bed, so cut to the facts. What don't you want me to know about Davie?"

Ted looked worriedly at Todd. "Maybe you can tell her better than me," Ted said, looking very glum.

"Well, will someone tell me what is going on?" she said, and her voice was getting more strident.

Todd cleared his throat and said, "David keeps running away from his father's home, and we think he is hanging around with homosexual boys here in San Francisco. We—that is, Ted and I— think you should have custody of Davie to get him off the streets."

"There must be more to this. Let me guess. Is your father blaming me for Davie's gay behavior? He thinks I am still an unfit mother and somehow I am responsible for Davie being missing?" Elly asked defiantly.

"Mom, that is part of the problem, but Todd and I are worried that Davie will get AIDS by hanging around with those unsavory boys and men."

"Also, I have a social worker who thinks you could have a good chance of getting custody because you don't have to work and you could spend a lot of time with him. You are a super nurse, and that is what he needs," Todd added.

"Where in this city is he, and can we find him and then bring him here?" Elly asked.

They sat immersed in their private worlds. Each clutched their cups and thought deeply about the best way to find David. Elly became too frustrated and stood up and wandered around the room, gazing out the windows.

"Elly, come and sit by me. I know you can't enjoy this new apartment until we have a plan for David."

She came over and collapsed down on the couch like a sack of potatoes. Her face was tear-streaked, and she shuttered with sobs. "He is only fifteen and knows so little about the world. I know teens can be suicidal when they are stressed. We have to find him. There is no other choice."

Todd put his arm around her and whispered in her ear, "I have alerted the hospitals, and I have an officer assigned to the Tenderloin who is rounding up the underage kids. I hope he finds him."

"I'll go looking myself. I won't be content until I have him in my arms," she blurted out. "Please. I can't sit here when I know he is suffering out there. We must go tonight."

"That area of the city is no place for a woman, even if I am with her," Todd answered impatiently.

"If I dress like a boy and I have my big strapping Ted and Todd to protect me, we can do it. I just feel it in my bones."

"Okay, let's make some plans. I know you need to have him back, and I will do all I can to find him," Todd said with somber conviction.

***

Somewhere in San Francisco, Mike Nikcols was in a phone booth calling Arnold. "This is your lover. The cops are getting rough, and I think if you want me to stay silent, I need some compensation."

"What? Are you threatening me?" Arnold whispered into the receiver.

"Oh, come on, Arney, this is for old time's sake. I can't go to prison. I would be raped daily. The cops are offering a lesser sentence, or they may even grant me immunity if I tell them more about why I did it." Nikcols whined.

"I'm disappointed that you want to squeal on me. You know they won't believe you, and I can say you are just an employee of the bank and a rejected lover who is seeking revenge . . . Now that I think about it, maybe I can offer you something. How about if you were awarded a position of vice president at the bank, would that make you happy? I will make sure you have a really good salary with the best benefits package." Arnold retorted.

"Yes, now you are talking my language. When can we get together for a love fest to cement the deal?" Nikcols chuckled.

Chapter 11

The Two Leaks

Jim got to work early. He wanted to get the paperwork together before Todd arrived. The papers were scattered across the desk, and he was just getting them organized when Todd walked in, looking morose.

"I feel so guilty. Why didn't I do more with Davie when I had him?" Todd asked without offering a greeting to Jim.

"I have some other news that isn't too good. Maria is dying. I decided to do some busywork to keep my mind off it," Jim confessed. Then he waited for Todd, but when he made no comment, Jim tried again. "The tests came back yesterday, and the cup shows evidence of castor bean residue. The doc says this poison holds hostage the defensive systems of the body, and then all the viruses and bacteria take over and kill the victim. As I see it, the tests show intent to murder, and Maria didn't suspect a thing."

"So is George Collinger captured yet?" asked Todd.

"I would be dancing in the halls if that was true. The supposition is that he has fled the state. We think Nevada because he has some family there. Our contacts in Nevada are on the alert. They are good guys, and they will get even more aggressive if Maria dies."

"Have the FBI located JR? And then there is Mike Nikcols. Do we still have him on a leash somewhere?" Todd inquired.

"We wanted him to put him on a house-arrest charge, but the judge felt the $10,000 bail was enough. The district attorney Darnell thinks we do not have enough evidence. Then there is Arnold Smith, who gave Nikcols the ticket to Brazil. Arnold maintains it was a coincidence that the trip to Brazil came so near to Mendelsen's death. Was he rewarding Nikcols for sexual favors?"

"It's Interesting that these two are homosexuals. Last night Elly, Ted, and I went searching for David, Elly's youngest son. We thought we saw Arnold down on 6th Street, but he evaded us. If he likes Nikcols and young kids on 6th Street, then he could be hiding David. I don't like how this is working out," Todd admitted.

"Let's put David's picture and description on the missing person's list," Jim decided.

When the phone rang, it startled both men. Jim picked it up on the second ring. "This is Dr. Fowler at the community hospital, and I regret to inform you that Maria Fuentes expired fifteen minutes ago. Her family is here, and they want to know about the funeral arrangements for a police officer killed while in active duty." Jim gave him the information and hung up the phone.

"You look like you got some bad news," Todd said. Jim had a gloomy look on his face.

"Yeah, man. Sadly, Maria died a few minutes ago. God, poor Joe, he'll be very devastated by the loss of his wife. We'll miss her too. Now, I will call Nevada and Oregon to put out a warrant for the arrest of George Collinger for this murder," Jim said dejectedly. "It is very sad. I thought George was one of us. We all feel betrayed"

Then both men walked out of Jim's office and glumly went to the cafeteria for coffee. "We should inform the boss right away. He will want to send his condolences to the family," Todd said.

"There is a funeral to plan too. You and I just need to step away for a few minutes to absorb all the ramifications from this death."

***

By noon the papers were full of the news of the officer's death, and the various city officials used this opportunity to request more money for the police department. The mayor complained that the newsmen weren't even waiting for the funeral before they were knocking on the family's door.

Arnold received the news of the death of Officer Fuentes badly. He worried about Georgie, who was hiding out at Arnold's friend's cabin near the Oregon border. The cabin didn't have a phone, so he couldn't warn him. This cabin was perfect because the rednecks in the area were not very tolerant of strangers because they didn't want their pot-growing activities disturbed. He needed to contact the doer to take care of the matter. There was also the problem of Mike. If the doer could take care of both of them, Arnold would sleep better at night.

When all the meetings were ended and he had a free moment, he ran down the back stairs of the building and out on the street. Quickly, he found his way to the pay phone on the corner. He dialed the number and waited. The messaging system came on, and Arnold spoke, "I need to contact the doer. We need to repair two leaks. Call me. This is ASS." Arnold hung up and ran back to the door to the stairway to his office. Panting, he arrived in time for an appointment with a client.

Later, his phone rang, and someone said, "At the waterfront pub." And then the caller hung up. Arnold knew the time, place, and the caller by the code. He quickly scribbled some notes on a pad of paper. He must return home to prepare for the meeting.

Gathering his coat and hat, he walked out the office door. Sara, his secretary, said, "Leaving early, Mr. Smith?"

"Yes, I am not feeling well, and I need to have an early dinner and some rest."

"Take care of yourself. Will you be in tomorrow?"

"Oh, yes, I know I have several important meetings. I'll be here bright and early," Arnold said as he went out the door.

The BART train was unusually crowded going to Oakland. Most of the passengers were going on to the wider Bay Area. Arnold noted this as he got off at his station.

His car was waiting, and he quickly drove home. As he unlocked the front door of his house, he could hear the patter of feet. "David?" he called out.

"Yeah, I have been studying. You are home early."

"You need to leave, David. I have some projects to take care of and you will just be in my way," he said abruptly as he hung up his coat and hat.

"Where am I supposed to go?" David said, pouting.

"Go home, where kids are supposed to go. Like ... find your mother. I think she is back in San Francisco," Arnold said with irritation as he rushed past him on his way upstairs. "I want you out in fifteen minutes," he yelled down the staircase.

David bounded up the stairs two at a time. "I need some dough, daddy-o," he called out at the top of his lungs, but Arnold was in the shower and couldn't hear him.

A few minutes later, Arnold emerged from the shower to see David with his coat on and his backpack slung over his back. "I need some cash. Just five would do. Please," David pleaded.

"Go ahead. Take ten. It is on the dresser. I will see you later. Don't call me. I will call you. Understand?"

"Thanks. I'll be on 6th Street, so don't call my dad. I am off like a dirty shirt, daddy-o," David said with a smile.

When he heard the door latch with a *click*, Arnold watched Davie walk away from his house. "God, what have I gotten myself into? I hope he stays safe and keeps his mouth shut. Kids can be delicious bundle of trouble."

Arnold got out his old dirty overalls and dressed. He purposely didn't shave or use any aftershave lotion. He didn't want to smell like an executive. Lastly, he put a navy blue wool cap on his head and pulled it down over his ears.

He looked out the downstairs widow to see if anyone was lurking about in the neighborhood, but he could not see anyone. He put on some old boots and carefully opened the door.

The sun was a great red ball on the western horizon, and the sky was streaked with orange and pink. Arnold looked at the sunset as a good omen. This meeting would start the process of ending his anxieties. Arnold wrapped the red scarf around his face, hunkered down, and walked the two blocks to a thoroughfare where he could catch a taxi. The taxi took him to the waterfront at the Oakland docks. Arnold got out of the taxi and gave the driver a meager tip.

JR was in the bar close by, but Arnold just walked past the bar and waited until he saw JR come out of the bar. Then JR walked down to the wharf where Arnold was hanging out. They acted as if JR was asking Arnold for a light for his cigarette. Arnold said, "G is a problem, and so is M. Can you do them? That scum bag M is trying to blackmail me. And then there is the issue of E."

"Yes, I will take care of G and M. I want your help with M. You need to coax him into a situation. Okay? The price is the same. Now for E, what do you want done? She is in hiding and won't bother you for now. We can deal with that at another time."

Arnold walked away while JR had his cigarette. He walked several blocks before he found another taxi. The trip home to Berkeley required several hours because he took a circuitous route.

***

David sat in a fast-food restaurant in San Francisco, eating a burger and wondering what he should do next. *Dad will kill me if I go home. Mom will be more understanding. I could call her or Todd*, he thought. He finished his dinner and went to the payphone outside the door and dialed his mother's number, but there was no answer. He called the police department, but Todd had left for the day. Dejected, unable to reach his mother or Todd, he walked back into the restaurant and sat down. At least it was warm in the restaurant, but it was boring too. After a while he got so frustrated he decided to go back to 6th Street to see what was happening.

Walking slowly but with a purpose, Davie looked for opportunities. There was a boy he had gotten to know who lived off his cash from prostitution. *There's more to learn about getting johns and getting paid. What I need is a kind john like ASS who won't string me up by my neck and get off by choking me.* He picked his way along the dark street with boys and men milling together in small groups. Sometimes there was hysterical laughter, and other times there were screams of terror or cries of pain. He didn't hear any intelligent discussions, and he realized he missed that.

***

The new apartment was silent. Elly sat by the window, watching the city life below her. She was sad, lonely, and worried. Todd had called and said that Maria had died. She felt a sinking, crushing guilt. If she hadn't inherited this estate, everyone would be fine—that is, except Davie. She still didn't know where he was or if he was safe. The anxiety gnawed at her with a sharp pain. She would have no relief until she had him in her arms. It was silly, she thought. If she could only see him from her window, it would delight her.

The intercom was suddenly active. "This is me, sweetheart. I'm coming up. I bought some pizza and salads."

Shortly after that, he was walking in the door, loaded with packages of food. "Hello. How is my sweet thing?" he said, although his face was full of grief over his sergeant.

Elly ran to greet Todd and hugged him as she poured out her heartache because of Maria. "It could have been different. Why did Georgie want to harm us? He seemed like such a nice person. What did he have to gain?"

"Money! Just the greed for money," he blurted out, and then he buried his head in her neck.

There was a painful silence, but finally, they parted. Elly quietly said, "Let's eat before the pizza gets cold."

They ate in silence. Each wrapped up in their own silent pain. Finally, Elly said, "I would like to go back to the Tenderloin and look for Davie again tonight. I feel he is out there, and we need to get him before some awful man grabs him."

"We can, just you and me. I think we should start with 6th Street because that is where the drugs and homosexual prostitution is happening. It is an ugly place, full of nasty odors, garbage, and tragic characters. You won't like it!" Todd said reluctantly.

"It is all right. I feel safe with you. Should I dress like a boy?" she asked with hope in her voice.

An hour later they were walking down Market Street. Elly wore no makeup, a navy cap on her head, a raggedy black sweatshirt, and old jeans that she used to paint in. Todd wore all black and a hat with a brim to disguise him so the boys would not recognize him as a cop.

There was garbage on the sidewalk and in the street. Men were curled up, sleeping in doorways, and some were snoring. Hangdog expressions were on the faces of the awake members who trudged along the street without a purpose. When they turned down 6th Street, there were more. They had to step over some. The odor of urine and feces mixed with the body odors of those who hadn't bathed in months, and the smell hit them and clung to them tenaciously. Elly tried to hold her breath as she searched each face for recognition. After several blocks they encountered a group of boys. Todd said to them, "We are looking for David. Do you know a David?"

"Why do ya' ask?" one growled.

"We just want him. That's all," Todd said emphatically.

They grunted but had no information to offer; however, a young face peered at them from the group. Todd went over to the youngster and asked, "Have you seen him?"

"We shot the shit earlier, but I don't know where he is now," the kid said guardedly, slurring his words like he was high on something.

Elly observed each child and got down on her haunches to look at the bodies in the doorways more critically. In her mind she was thinking, *He won't look like I expect him to look. I have to look at each of them to find him.* As she was meticulously looking at each boy, she saw a shape she thought she knew, but when he turned around, he was not the right kid. Then in a doorway by himself, she roused a young body. When the face turned to her, there was instant recognition.

She knelt by him and softly said, "Dear Davie, I want you to come home with me."

"Is that you, Mom?" the face said haltingly.

By this time, Todd was leaning over and looking too. "David, would you like to sleep in a nice, clean bed tonight?"

"Ah, I'm fine, and too ... sleepy ... to move," the boy complained, slurring his words.

Todd and Elly reached down and helped Davie to a standing position. He wobbled between them. He was very heavy. Todd said, "Let's put him on a step with you, and I will go and get the car."

"Davie, what has happened to you? Where is my sweet, gentle, lovable boy? You have grown up so fast! What has happened while I wasn't looking?" Elly sobbed as she cradled Davie's head in her arms.

"Oh, Mom, I've missed you. I've ... become a man, Mom. I'm no longer a boy, so don't call me one. I was looking for my lover, but I can't find him," Davie stammered weakly.

"Hush, my sweet. We will talk about it later. Right now Todd is getting the car, and we are taking you home.

It was after three in the morning before they got back to Elly's apartment and got David into a hot shower. Once he was in bed, Elly took his temperature and asked him, "How long have you been so ill, David? When did you last eat something?"

"Mom, I don't feel like being pushed with questions. I just want to sleep."

"David, you are sick, and you have a temp of 101 degrees. And you look like hell. Do you realize how dangerous it was for you to be out there on 6th Street? You might get AIDS or some other nasty virus," Elly said with exasperation.

"Okay, okay, but let's talk about it tomorrow please."

"You win," she said with a sign of resignation. She kissed him on his feverish forehead. "See you in the morning."

Finally, Elly came to the living room and buckled into a heap. "I'm exhausted. How are you?"

Todd offered her a glass of wine. "I think the night provided a badly needed success."

"Yes, but it will be better if you stay the night with me, Todd. I need you close to me. I am so scared and worried about Davie. He isn't himself," she said as she spread herself out on the couch like sweet, warm butter across Todd's lap.

Todd cradled her and kissed her. "I cannot tell you how happy I am that you did not drink that hot chocolate that killed Maria. That keeps going through my head. You had such a close call. And I am so glad that it was a successful night with finding David too." Todd raised her face to his and kissed her sweetly.

"He is very ill. He is feverish, and I don't like the look of him," Elly added. "We have been through a lot this week. Can't you call in sick tomorrow and say you are unable to come in. Then we can both sleep in," she said, kissing him back.

"I love you dearly and would like to stay, but I have to find Maria's killer. Besides, you have David now, and the two of you have a lot to catch up on. You have a patient to take care of now."

She looked at him lovingly as she put down her glass on the table. Then she held his face in both of her hands and kissed him seductively as she pulled him on top of her. "David can never take your place. I need my lover now," she said as her hands slipped down his body to his groin. She felt him get aroused and then worked at opening his shirt and jeans.

Picking her up in his arms, he carried her to the bedroom and kicked the door shut. "We haven't properly celebrated getting this apartment, sweet thing, but I have to leave after I pleasure you."

"We will see," she purred in his ear.

Chapter 12

The Solution

"Hi, Mike, how are you this fine morning?" the guard at the bank greeted Mike Nikcols as he entered the heavy brass doors.

Mike was grinning ear to ear. "Is Mr. Jordan here yet?"

"No, I haven't seen him. He usually gets here about ten."

Mike went to his work area and prepared for his job as a teller.

At about eleven o'clock, Mr. Jordan came to Mike and asked him to come to his office. Mike dutifully closed his teller position and walked with Mr. Jordan to his office.

"Mike, we are having a meeting at noon to announce the new vice-president position, and I want you to attend. It would be nice if you would go down to the deli and get lunch for us."

"Sure, Mr. Jordan," Mike said with Cheshire grin.

When it got to be 11:30, Mr. Jordan called Mike and said, "The orders are ready at the deli on Market. Just go there and pick them up. It is all paid in advance."

Mike was almost bopping out of the bank on his way to the deli. He was certain that he was going to get this new position at the meeting, and he was delighted. He was so distracted by his thoughts that he didn't notice the black car that slipped up to the curb, until it honked. Arnold was driving. Rolling down the window, Arnold seductively yelled, "Mike, get in. Jordan told me you were on your way to the deli, and I thought that since I am going that way, I could give you a lift."

"Sure," Mike said as he opened the door, and without a care in the world, he got in.

"I want to talk to you," Arnold said as they drove away. "I understand they are making you a vice president today. Oops, maybe I shouldn't have let it out of the bag."

"Wow that is super!" Mike said as he snuggled up to Arnold, and in his excitement he didn't notice that Arnold had pulled the car into a dark alley.

From behind with lightning speed, a shadowy figure in the back seat rose up with a rope in his hands and quickly tossed it over Mike's head. The rope settled around his neck, and JR pulled tightly, suffocating Mike. The struggle between the two men began. Bracing himself with his knee against the back of Mike's seat, JR held on forcefully to the rope. Mike struggled vainly, thrashing and rolling in his seat. His face turned crimson, and his eyes bulged out. Those eyes pleaded with Arnold as his hands clawed at the rope in desperation. It took several minutes before Mike's body went floppy with death. JR didn't let go of the rope until Mike's body stopped twitching. When it was quiet, he removed the rope and tossed it in the back seat. They put a hat over the gray and blue face, threw a blanket over the body, covering him up to his chin, and reclined the seat.

Both men got out of the car, and JR took the driver's seat. Arnold hurriedly walked to the alley entrance. The nausea was crashing in on him. What awful thing had he done? Numb, he walked back to his office and vomited in the nearest toilet.

JR drove the car out of the end of the alley and drove north with the body. Going north, he didn't have to go through the tollbooth on the Golden Gate Bridge avoiding embarrassing questions. His companion looked like he was just asleep to those who could see in the car window.

At the bank Mr. Jordan announced that Mike Nikcols had been fired because he had been arrested for suspicion of murder and would not be back today. The bank could not tolerate this sort of bad publicity. No one seemed to miss him.

***

Elly had slept late that morning. Todd had left at about five in the morning, and Elly had given him a sleepy nuzzle before he left. Now at noon, she stretched and sleepily remembered her son was in the other bedroom. She quietly tiptoed up to his door and knocked. When she opened the door, there was her youngest son, her baby, sprawled out across the bed. "Davie," she called out and nudged his shoulder as she sat on the edge of the bed.

"Gosh, Mom. How did I get here?" he said and yawed. "I dreamed that you were talking to me, but I thought it was all a dream."

"You are so warm. Do you still have a fever?" she asked as she felt his brow. "How long have you been sick?"

"I don' know, a day or two. I remember I threw up my dinner. I think I have the flu."

"Do you feel like something light to eat? We need to get some liquids into you. There are some pajamas for you in the drawer. I will get them for you. I need to look you over to assess your illness," she said. She expected some back talk, but he seemed too sick to care.

Elly's mind was reeling from her experiences of the last twenty-four hours. *How sick is my baby? What were his experiences in the Tenderloin, and what had he caught there?* She decided to make him some broth and some Jell-O. *Just be a good nurse, and he will get well.* She stood up and went to the dresser to get the pajamas. Then she turned to her son and said, "Let me help you off with your clothes, and we will get these pajamas on."

She sat on the edge of the bed again and unbuttoned his shirt. He was wearing several layers, and they were full of sweat and smelled like an illness that Elly could not identify. His chest had a rash that interested her. Like a computer, her mind searched through her files to find the other diseases with rashes like measles. She knew he had been vaccinated for that. He didn't have much energy, and she slipped off his jeans and noticed that the rash was there on his legs too. She worried about syphilis and also HIV. When he was all tucked in bed with pillows, Elly went to the kitchen to make some broth for him and some breakfast for herself.

When the broth was ready, Elly put some in a cup and took a tray to Davie with ginger ale and tea to settle his stomach. "Davie, I want you to tell me about your friends. Todd told me you are gay. I have no problem with that, but we need to know who you are actively having sex with and what their health is like."

He sipped his broth and drank some ginger ale silently. "I have a … nice man who treats … me well. He lives … in Berkeley," he said haltingly in a small voice.

"Berkeley? What's his name and his address?" Elly asked anxiously.

"I don't know his name. He just calls himself ASS. I have been to his house … several times, but it was in the dark. I didn't notice the … house number … or street." he said, staring at his hands. "I love him."

"Are you protecting him, Davie?"

"Of course I am. He made me promise not to tell anyone because I am … too young."

"It is important for your health to find out if he has AIDS or something else so we can treat him too," she said as she stroked his arm tenderly. "I'm concerned about this because there is an epidemic of HIV going around, and we need to get some control over it. Did you and he use condoms?"

"No, I didn't think of that."

"My dear, sweet Davie, we need to take you to a doctor. I want to know what is making you sick."

"Mom, all I have is the flu. Don't make a big deal out of it."

"A rash doesn't accompany influenza!"

Just at this moment, the phone rang, and Elly went to answer it. "Hi, Elly, how is David?" Todd asked. Then he went on, "I am calling because we need you to come down and tell us all you know about George Collinger."

"Have you found Georgie?"

"No, but the district attorney wants a statement from you. So when can we arrange that?"

"Davie is really sick, and I need to have a doctor visit here or take him to the hospital."

"The DA said we had twenty-four hours to get this statement. Memory fades as time goes on. Maybe we could take David to the hospital, get him checked in, and then come over here for the deposition," Todd offered.

"Okay, let me call the doctor and see if the hospital thing will work or what he suggests. Maybe I can ask Ted to come and take care of his brother while I go and give my statement. Let me find out more, and then I will call you back," Elly offered.

When she got off the phone, she looked up the best doctor for HIV. There were no listings for HIV or AIDS, so she called the UC Medical School Hospital and asked for Dr. Mays' office. When she was connected, she asked the answering party to connect her to his office. "Hello, Elinor, this is Dr. Mays. It has been a long time. Are you looking for a job here?"

"No, I am worried that my son has AIDS, and I would like the best physician to help him. Do you have someone you can recommend?"

"Let's see. My schedule is very full today and tomorrow, but I know of a new doctor who is really interested in this one disease. His name is Larry Andreessen, and his number is ... ummm. Well, call over to the immunology department, and they can find him. He is a remarkable man, and you will like him.

After several dead ends, Elly finally connected with Dr. Andreessen. She explained David's signs and symptoms. Then she asked what the next step was. The doctor wanted to see David, and he offered to come to Elly's apartment.

An hour and a half later, a call came from the front desk. "Ms. Jones (Elly's code name), there is a Dr. Andreessen here to visit. May I send him up?"

"Yes, please."

Dr. Andreessen was in his early thirties. He had dark brown hair that was long, pulled back in a ponytail, and twinkling hazel eyes. Elly greeted him like he was her savior. "My son is fifteen, and he may have a HIV infection. He has a rash and a temperature of 100.42 as of this morning. He says he has vomited this morning, so I made him broth, ginger ale, and tea. He took it all, and he's had no vomiting since then. He has not frequently complained of diarrhea, just once or twice."

"I'll have a look at him and take a history, and then we can decide the best way to treat him. Dr. Mays says you are an RN, and the best care for him may be right here," he said.

While the doctor visited David, Elly had a chance to call Ted. "Hi, we finally found your brother, and he is ill. I will need someone to watch him while I go to the police station to give a deposition. Could you do that today?"

"Sure, I can be there in about an hour. See you soon," Ted said so cheerfully that it made Elly weep.

Several minutes passed as Elly wondered what was happening. She wanted to give the doctor and Davie the privacy they needed. Finally, the doctor came out to the kitchen.

"I think I have all the information I need. I am taking some samples and will get back to you by the end of the week. Just keep him from socializing with gays until we know the whole story."

"His older brother is coming over to take care of him while I run a few errands. Thank you for making a house call."

"Well, we younger docs think that house calls are a way to save health care costs, and I think your son's case is one of them," he said with a generous smile. "Here are some prescriptions. Try to keep him quiet while he has a fever. If he gets more ill and has difficulty breathing, then take him to the emergency room." And with that, he went out the door.

***

Arnold felt unwell. He had this queasy feeling ever since he watched JR kill Mike. The vision of Mike suffering, the pleading look in his eyes, it was all too much.

He decided to cancel his afternoon appointments and go home. Better yet, he would go down on 6th Street and see if he could find Davie. *He will give me comfort. Delicious, cozy comfort, and then I will sleep better tonight.*

The sun was shining, and this perked up Arnold as he walked down the street. His upset stomach didn't even bother him out here in the sunshine. Market Street was busy, and Arnold felt he was imperceptible in the crowds. As he approached 6th Street, the crowds diminished, and the garbage increased. He was constantly avoiding dog shit and tin cans. At 6ᵗʰ Street, he turned and looked everywhere for Davie's sweet face. He searched each door opening and every alley. Each kid was inspected, but to no avail. Davie didn't seem to be there. Finally, he asked one of the boys if he had seen Davie.

"I haven't seen him for hours. He was sick, and some men came and took him somewhere. I'll service you, ASS. I can do you good. You'll squirm with delight. Just try me."

Arnold looked the boy over. He was a dirty little snipe. "I don't think you are my type, kid. But thanks for the information." Arnold trudged away, weary, worn, and worried. He needed supportive company, so he hailed a cab and went to the Castro District, which was the heart of the gay community.

Searching the many bars and dance halls, he searched for a familiar face. Finally, through the smoke of a crowded bar, he heard the voice of an old pal. "Mark! How is my favorite drag queen?"

"It's Arnie. I haven't seen you in ages. What are you up to?" Mark Jacobs said with genuine curiosity and then gave Arnold a big hug.

"I thought they jailed you after Annette died. I am so glad to see you. I am working on a project to find a cure for AIDS, and it is costing a bundle."

"Well, I got off on a technicality, and I am free as a bird. I hear that slimy Elinor inherited my sweet Annie's wealth," Mark said in a confidential voice.

"Yeah, she was the only heir, so there wasn't any choice."

They sat and talked for several hours, drinking and sharing experiences. It was getting late in the afternoon when Mark told Arnold he had to get back to the university to teach a class. They parted like old friends and offered to meet up again in a few days.

Arnold walked to the BART station and slowly descended the stairs. It was early, and the trains were full. Arnold didn't like crowded trains. But he wanted to get home, and his needs overruled his paranoia. When the train rolled up and the doors opened, a young man who looked familiar got off. Arnold was shaken by the sight. Davie had a brother. Could this man be him? He wished he felt strong enough to follow him, but his health was not up to it. Stepping back, Arnold waited for a less crowded train.

***

Elly rushed to open the door for Ted. He had his arms full and said, "I bought some groceries for you. Some are Davie's favorites, and some are for you."

"It is such a pleasure to have you and Davie at the same time. It used to be like that all the time, but now you are grown and have your own life. How is your dad doing?"

"I told him that Davie was with you and he was sick. He seemed relieved to know Davie was safe. Do they know what sort of bug he has?" Ted asked.

"The doctor was here earlier. He took some blood tests, and he will get back to us later when he has the results. Then we will have some idea of how to treat him. I have him on a liquid diet because he was vomiting and such. What did you bring him to eat?"

"Just chips, cookies, and such. Nothing that is good in your book. I can eat them if they are not good for him."

"You were sweet to think of him. Maybe the interest in them will help him get well. We just never know what makes people want to get well."

"Is he depressed?"

"That's right. You are studying psychology, but I don't think his problem is strictly depression. He is gay, you know, and he loves this man. But he doesn't know the man's name. He calls him ASS, which sounds obscene to me. Todd is worried that this man is a pedophile who preys on boys like Davie," Elly said with sadness.

"Davie was having problems with Dad and the school. Was that because he is gay?"

Elly took Ted's hands and said, "I think so, but maybe while I am gone, you can talk to your brother and feel him out. We need more information. See if you can find out why he ran away and how he's been living this month. Was he prostituting himself? And by the way, if he gets short of breath or his temperature goes up, then call me at Todd's number. I have it right here. Thank you for coming and helping me care for him." She stood on her tiptoes and kissed her son on his cheek.

She heard knocking on the door and opened it for Todd. "Are you ready to go? I am double-parked downstairs, and we need to hustle. Oh, hi, Ted. It is nice to see you again. I have to take your mom to give a formal statement to a district attorney's office, and we have to hurry."

***

The drive to the police station was short, and Todd left Elly off at the main door before he parked the car.

Elly walked up to the desk and gave her name to the desk agent. "I am here to give a deposition to the district attorney, Mathew Darnell."

"Yes, just have a seat, and they will call you," desk clerk said without any emotion.

Elly chose a seat near a table with magazines and waited. Then a young man in a business suit walked up to her.

"Elinor Longacre DeMartini? I am Mat Darnell. I would like you to come with me."

Elly followed him to a nice office off a hallway with many offices. There she found a desk with a tape recorder and three chairs. Mat motioned to one of them, turned on the tape recorder, and announced, "I understand that you were in protective custody with several officers on March 4 to March 9, 1983, and during that time Officer Maria Fuentes drank some hot chocolate and later died. Is that true?"

"Yes, sir, the chocolate milk was offered to me by Georgie ... er, George Collinger, but I had just brushed my teeth and didn't want it. I offered it to Maria, and unfortunately, she drank it."

"Was this George Collinger one of our officers?"

"Yes, I had no reason to not trust him. We had drunk hot chocolate from him almost every day. There was no reason to suspect him this one time, when he brought the fatal cup of cocoa."

"Where were you, George Collinger, and Maria Fuentes on March 8?"

"Maria and I were in my cabin in Marin County, getting ready for bed. We were exhausted because we had had a traumatic day."

"Was anyone else there when George offered you the drink?" Mr. Darnell asked.

"No, Neil, the other officer, was not present, and my two cousins had gone home several hours before."

"Tell me. Did you sleep well that night, or were there some disturbances?"

"I didn't sleep well. I was anxious about the day before, and I was nervously waiting for Todd to come and take us back to the city."

"During the night, did you hear any noise or sounds that you could not identify?"

"Not that night, although I was listening for them. The night before on March 7, I did hear Dusty the dog barking and footsteps in the night. When I looked out, there was a shadowy figure running through the trees and then across the meadow toward the cabins. I couldn't identify the person or tell you if it was a man or woman. When I discussed this with Neil the next day, he said that he got up to see what Dusty was barking at but that he didn't see anyone. My cousins did not see anything either."

"Okay, I think that is new information. You are a nurse. Did you nurse Maria when she was ill?"

"Oh, yes, I was so worried about her. I wish we had discovered her problem earlier. We might have induced vomiting so she would not absorb the poison. I didn't become aware of her illness until about eight o'clock that next morning."

"Let's see. That was on the March 9th when you identified her illness. I don't have your cousins' names or addresses, but I understand that Todd has those. Are you still in protective custody?"

"I think so. I find it terribly boring. I had to quit my job, and I don't see any of my friends. However, I know I am still in peril, and I want to be safe."

Elly walked out the door of the office in a daze. She wandered toward the exit, but then it occurred to her she could visit Todd. Turning, she walked to the desk. Within a few minutes, the clerk came to ask what she needed.

"Could you call Todd Markam's office and ask him if Elly DeMartini can visit?"

The clerk called and then returned to Elly, "He is coming down, and he wanted you to wait for him."

"Okay, will do." Then she found a chair near some magazines again and waited.

Forty-five minutes passed before she saw his happy face. "How is my sweet lady? I am sorry to keep you waiting. How about we have dinner before I take you home?"

They walked out to Todd's car in silence, but when they entered the car, Todd took Elly in his arms and kissed her. "We have lots to talk about."

"Tell me. Have you found Georgie?" Elly asked hopefully.

"No, and to top it off, we can't find Mike Nikcols either. The bank says they fired him, and they haven't seen him since."

"Could he be hiding out with Georgie?"

"We have been scouring the state, looking for him. We have questioned all of Georgie's friends and relatives. I am afraid that the professional that abducted you is after both him and maybe Nikcols. There is good evidence to make us believe that he sees their lives as threats to him because they could squeal."

"That sounds awful. Do they want me too?"

"It is important that you lay low. I'm sorry. If that poison Maria took was meant for you, I would say you are still in danger. Let's stop this talk of death and have a peaceful dinner."

Chapter 13

Another Death

Elly was sleeping late. Something crashing woke her. "Davie?" she called at the top of her lungs as she got up and tossed on her robe.

Running into the kitchen, she found Davie on the floor, moaning. "What happened to you?" his mother pleaded.

"I think I am weak, and my head isn't working right. I tried to get a glass, and when I reached up to get it, I got dizzy and passed out. That is when the glass went flying, I guess."

Elly helped him into the chair. "I think you had better let me wait on you until you are stronger," she said as she helped him into a chair. "Today we should hear from the doctor about your tests. By the way, what sounds good for breakfast? I hear you had soup last night, and that went down well. Do you want more for breakfast?"

"Yeah, I am both hungry and nauseated, and I ache all over like someone beat me. When I pee, it is dark. I have never had dark pee before. What does that mean?" he asked, his voice trembling with fear.

She gently put her arm around him to comfort both Davie and herself. She gently kissed his forehead and cooed, "You will get better, and then we will find you a private school that doesn't discriminate against gays."

"You don't mind that I am gay? I know Dad would have a fit."

"Hmmm, your dad will come around, but it may take time," she softly said. "He will blame me and go easy on you, I think."

The breakfast went well, and Davie went back to bed. Elly curled up on the couch to read when the phone rang.

"Hello," she said cautiously.

"Hi, this is your cousin Leland. How are you? I hear you have a new address."

"Yes, up here on Nob Hill with a glorious view. Are you in town?" she said with genuine interest.

"I'm here with Hank, and we were wondering if you could have lunch with us."

"I am nursing a sick kid. But you could come here. Either you could bring lunch, or we can send out for it. Wait a minute. Todd doesn't want anyone delivering food, so you had better bring it with you."

"Not a problem, we heard that Maria Fuentes died. You can tell us what happened when we come. We don't want anything to happen to you. So we will be there at about two o'clock after our meeting, and we will come with lunch. Will that work?

"Perfect. I just had breakfast, and I won't be hungry until later, so that works out well. See you then."

***

Several hours passed before Leland and Hank could get to the deli to pick up salads and sandwiches. When they had their gourmet lunch together, they drove to Elly's apartment on Nob Hill. Parking was difficult as usual, but they finally found a parking lot within four blocks of Elly's apartment building. At the door they were interrogated by a policeman and the apartment guard. It took several minutes for them to call Elly, and she gave her approval for their entrance.

They felt relief when they finally entered her apartment. Both hugged and kissed Elly. "It is so sweet of you to come to visit me. I feel like a prisoner in this apartment even with its spectacular views."

"Well, you look charming as always. It is our pleasure to come to visit. We had so many trying experiences in our short acquaintance. We needed to make sure you are safe and well. What has made your son ill?" Leland said, holding Elly's hand.

"It is a long story. Let me set the table, and we can have lunch first. My son has been diagnosed with a HIV infection. The doctor called this morning with the unwelcome news and I think he is sleeping now," Elly said softly while she choked back her tears.

Leland gently drew her to him and comforted her in his arms. "We can set the table. Just let us wait on you."

The meal was beautiful and delicious. They had brought a bottle of wine, and Elly began to feel more relaxed and cheery.

"Does your son have a lover, and does he have AIDS too?" Hank asked, carefully not to offend her.

"He tells me his lover is called ASS, which is a terrible name or nickname. Evidently, he doesn't know the man's full name or address. This man is supposed to be an older person. Todd thinks he could arrest the man for statutory rape because my son is only fifteen and he is looking for him," Elly mechanically told the story.

After lunch they moved to the couch. Elly and Leland sat on the couch. Hank sat on the adjoining chair. Leland asked, "Have you any idea of who this older man could be?"

"No, I am so concerned that my son may be deathly ill that I don't have time to be vindictive," Elly said with anger mixed with remorse.

"I don't mean to upset you. But Arnold is gay, and maybe he could help us identify the person who is the source of the disease," Hank offered.

"It is important to find this man because he could be infecting other boys and causing more parents to suffer," Leland offered.

"Please. I would like to change the subject. What have you been up to since I last saw you?" Elly pleaded.

"We have been up to our ears in work. However, we have plans to go to the Black and White Ball in a couple of weeks, which is an occasion for raising funds to support the San Francisco Symphony. We would love to have you join us. It is a great chance for you to meet everyone who is worth knowing in this city. You can invite Todd to escort you. It is a black tie affair, and you will look lovely in a designer gown in black or white or both colors. Does that appeal to you?" Leland said enthusiastically as he put his arm around her.

"Now that does sound exciting. I love to dance, and I feel like I'm living in a fairy tale as the lowly nurse getting all dressed up to dance with the handsome men. I have always wanted to go to this ball. I will have to convince Todd to wear a tux, but I know he will come around." Elly bubbled with glee.

"Also, my sweet Elly, I was serious when I asked you to marry me. Have you thought about it?"

The glee disappeared like air escaping from a burst balloon. "I am engaged already, and Todd and I plan to marry in May, so I have to refuse your generous offer," Elly said firmly without a smile.

"Let's keep our options open. I love you, and please notice I am saying all this in front of my brother. I am not telling you this because I want to seduce you. I want you to be my partner in life. You know, Annette married a man who wasn't raised like us. He came from a poor family, and it was a problem. Annette had different values than him, and he took advantage of the fact that she would not divorce him. It would pain me to see you marry someone like that and end up unhappy."

Elly turned to Leland and looked him in his eyes with distrust, but she saw unbelievable sincerity. Still annoyed, she said, "I was married once, and I know how men are very generous before they marry. Then afterward they take control, and their wives suffer. I don't want to be told what I can and can't do. I don't want a man who finds me less interesting and then starts having affairs. You need to marry one of your other women in your life. Not me! Never me!"

He didn't want to argue with her, so he held her chin, stroking it until she relaxed, and then he kissed her gently on her lips. She liked his touch, the tickle of his short beard and the taste of his mouth on hers. Her shoulders relaxed, and she felt she was melting. He knew she was yielding, so he said, "I, too, was married to a woman. My parents and her parents thought we were the perfect match. We had a very short marriage. Her mind was vacuous. You know what I love about you? Your mind is star bright. I admire that you are a nurse with an excellent education. I also love the package you come in. Everything is lovely about you. You are so easy on the eyes, so gentle to be with. So think about my offer. You are still single, and I am eager to change that."

"This has nothing to do with the fact that I have inherited this estate? You don't want to take control of it, do you? Would you sign a marriage contract to prove that?" she said to tease him into her reality.

"That is fair. I will sign a marriage contract happily. I will do that if that makes you feel better. You have to realize I am worth a sizable amount on my own. I see us as equals, and I love you for that." And with that, Leland took her in his arms and kissed her passionately. She melted in his arms and felt ashamed that she wanted more.

They left shortly after that, and when the door closed behind them, Elly realized she would miss Leland. But she also wanted to know more about Hank. Sitting numbly on the couch, she was surprised about how she didn't feel guilty about kissing Leland or thinking about him when he wasn't there. *I really have to get serious about his offer and Todd's. If I remarry, I want the most perfect partner possible.*

***

JR and his henchman were driving north on US 101 toward Eureka in an old warn sedan. Mike Nikcols' body was slowly decaying in the trunk. They stopped at a diner outside of town, but it was full of officers, so they went on.

"Maybe we should head into Canada if this keeps up," said the partner.

"First, let's go into Oregon on Interstate 5 and act like fly fishermen. George is in Oregon anyway. There are some apples and jerky in the back. We will have to eat what we have until we can find an area without the police."

They talked as they drove. JR was ranting about how he disliked this job. "I hate these fat cats that hire you and me to do their dirty work. I got that fag to help me kill Nikcols, his lover, so he would understand what a nasty job this is. He thought he was paying us too much, but I wanted him so see that the job isn't just a walk in the park. And now we have to do another clean up job with George. After this I am retiring. I'm taking my honey and going to Canada. What are you going to do?"

"I think I'll go back to Arkansas and hang out with my family and friends. I don't think the cops know as much about me as they do you. You have to be so much more careful."

"Yeah, after we take care of the problems, I will have to go into hiding for a long while. That is the biggest drag," JR said with a resigned sigh.

They drove east toward the mountains and decided to dump their present sedan and steal a truck in Oregon with Oregon plates. Outside of Bend, Oregon, they found a van without markings parked in a diner parking lot that fit their needs. They decided that removing the license plates off the front and back was the most expedient choice. With professional ease, they removed them and put them in their car trunk in case they needed them and sped away as fast as the car would go. This would be less risky than stealing the whole vehicle. The owner of the van would not notice his plates were missing for several days. He might guess that kids had played a joke on him and not report the loss to the cops right away.

The road out of Bend had very light traffic. It was getting late, and they could see the waning moon. The air was clear and cold with light snow flurries. They turned off the road on to a dirt road that was no more than a trail used by loggers, and after several miles of bouncing through the potholes, they turned on to an even less traveled dirt logging road. In a meadow created by someone clear cutting the trees, there was a lonely cabin. This was where Georgie was hiding. It was past midnight.

Walking up to the cabin, they were cautious. After all, George was a former cop. JR pounded on the door and yelled, "Hey, George, it is JR and BJ. We are on the lam and came to see how you are."

There was some rattling and scraping in the cabin, and then George opened the door a crack. "Yeah, let me see your faces."

JR turned on his flashlight, lighting up their faces. George recognized them and opened the door wider. He was unshaven, disheveled, and holding a rifle.

"I am glad you are being careful. The scuttlebutt is that you are being searched for throughout the western states," JR said as he forced the door open and pushed George aside.

The cabin was one room with bare boards on the outside as well as the inside. There was an empty cabinet with a makeshift sink on the back wall. An oil-burning stove stood in the middle. There were three chairs scattered about and a cot-sized bed against the north wall. George lit an oil-burning lantern so that they could see.

"Hey, have you got any food? We haven't had a decent bite since we left Frisco. The roads are full of cops everywhere, so we didn't stop for eats," JR said, looking at his victim hungrily.

"I have eaten almost everything. I was expecting you to bring some provisions," George said in his defense.

"Any beer?"

"There's a can or two in the back. Would you like that?" He was uneasy with JR. He wasn't a man to cross or to trust.

"Okay, get it and make it quick. Leave the rifle here. I don't like people to walk around with heat in their hands. It makes me nervous," JR said with a sneer.

Within moments, George came back with two beers and gave them to the guests.

"Ah, that is better hospitality," JR said, and he opened the can and drank while all the time he was staring at George. When he finished, he said, "Do you know why the cops are looking for you so diligently?"

"Er, Elly died?"

"No, my stupid friend, you killed a cop!" And with that statement, JR lunged at George, grabbing his arm. He spun him around so the arm was against George's back in a painful hold. BJ seized his feet and tied them with some rope he had in his pocket. George collapsed to the floor in a screaming, fat mass until JR put a piece of tape over his mouth to keep it shut.

"I told you to just make her sick to scare her. No one was supposed to die!" he said with venom as he yanked the end of the rope he had used to tie George's arms to bind his feet. The victim's eyes said it all. Using all his strength, the victim struggled to free himself. The tugging and twisting tightened the knots and chafed his wrists until they bled, making his efforts futile. He knew he was doomed. All he hoped for now was that he wouldn't suffer long.

"If you don't scream, I'll remove the tape over your mouth."

George nodded his head vigorously. So JR took the tape off his mouth.

"Please, JR. It's hard to measure out that poison so precisely. I had no instructions. I had no idea of the right quantity or the potency. Please. I'm not a squealer," George said in his defense, sobbing.

They dragged him to the bed and forced him awkwardly on it. He was shaking in fear and smelled like he had lost control of his pee. Then they took the rifle and propped it up in front of him. They thought of making it look like a suicide. But then they needed to get rid of the other body in the car, too.

"I promise to disappear. I have friends in Wyoming where I can hide. You can make it look like you killed me, and then the cops will think I am dead. They won't be looking for me then. Please give me a chance," he begged.

"If I let you go, you will have to really vanish. If I hear anything about you, I will come and decapitate you slowly like the goons in Cambodia did with a dull knife. So tell me about this hiding place," JR said in a low growl.

"I ... know some white supremacists dudes. You know, Aryan Nation types. They hang out in a rural area of Wyoming about twenty miles southeast of Ten Sheep. Those guys aren't bothered by anybody. The whole area is full of rednecks with shotguns, ready to blast at any stranger. All the sheriffs are smart enough to never be in that part of Wyoming, especially if they are brown. You would like it. If you need a safe place to hide, it is ideal," George said, pleading.

JR rummaged in George's pockets and found his .38 caliber revolver. "Ah, this is a handy tool," he said as he checked it for bullets. He inspected the gun with an expert eye, turning it over in his hands to admire it like a precious jewel.

"It's a really nice revolver. You can have it. I don't want it anymore, but please let me live. I won't say a word to anyone."

"God damn it. Will you stop your whining and bitching!" Then he turned to his friend and said, "Go get Nikcols' body and bring it in here. Do you need help?"

"Of course I need help! He is damn heavy and smelly enough to make a maggot gag."

Together, they carried and dragged Nikcols' body into the cabin. The heavy, sickening sweet stench of a decaying dead body made it a very odorous package by now.

"Get up, George. We need the bed for this stiff. It's a narrow bed, but he won't mind. Now unless you want to die, get out to the car and sit in the back seat," JR said with black humor.

"I can't. You tied me up."

"Ah, so I have." JR nodded and loosened the ropes.

Cautiously, George got up, and then JR stepped up to him. They were nose to nose now "Lay this body on the cot.". he growled as he then placed the handgun in George's limp hand. "Shoot Nikcols in the head, you fucker."

George looked a moment at Nikcols and shot at the dead body's head. The blast was deafening, and the body jumped. "Now lay the gun in Nikcols' hand like he shot himself."

Georgie silently followed the directions and then waited for further orders.

"Don't just stand there like you're paralyzed. Go out to the car and change the license plates from California plates to these Oregon ones. That way it will be harder to trace the owner of the vehicle and where it was stolen. Then get in the back seat of the car."

Georgie followed the orders precisely.

BJ found some fuel oil and poured it on their victim and then looked at the stove. They rigged up a fuse and ran it between the stove and the body on the bed. Lastly, they poured oil all over the floor just to be safe.

"I'm taking this nice Remington rifle. It may come in handy. Georgie won't mind. Are we ready to roll?" JR asked BJ.

"Yes, boss, and my lighter is ready."

They took a rag and set it aflame, and then they threw it into the stove and made sure it ignited. The flames roared up like a monster. The fuel burned brightly and then danced across the floor to the body. Soon the whole room was ablaze. They left the door open a crack to let in oxygen.

They ran for the car, with Georgie in the back seat out of the way. When the doors slammed shut, they pulled away as fast as possible before an explosion. Lying low in the back seat, Georgie was saying his prayers. They knew that the flames would alert the fire brigade and everyone else in the county. The plan was to get far away from this place as fast as possible.

As they drove away, they looked back to see the red flames licking above the forest. "It is a beautiful sight. I hope the fire patrol is not too quick to get here."

As they drove toward the main highway, they heard a helicopter circling overhead to find the site of the fire. JR shut off the headlights and cautiously crawled ahead. The half-moon lit up the snow and made driving easier without lights. Their ears were listening intently for the fire sirens. When they reached the main highway, they heard a siren in the distance. With hope of escape, they turned the opposite direction and sped north to the open country.

All night they drove, fear keeping them awake. At dawn they stopped at a truck stop outside of Boise for breakfast. While they ate, they listened for any news of the fire. One waitress was telling a truck driver about her brother being called in the middle of the night to be on call for fighting a fire in the Cascade Forest, but whatever they saw wasn't a forest fire, so they all thought it was a false alarm. "Probably somebody's campfire got out of control is my guess," she said with false authority.

There was a pay phone outside, and JR took this opportunity to call his girlfriend in Montana. He dialed the number from memory, and it rang and rang. Finally, a sleepy voice came on. "Hello?"

"This is me."

"Oh, I am sick!" she said in code.

"Okay, hope you get better." Then JR hung up before the call could be traced.

He walked back into the diner. JR gave a flinty look at BJ and said, "Let's get going as soon as possible."

"Hey, Miss, could we have our bill?" BJ asked as she walked by.

They paid with cash and hurriedly left. They bought gas and again paid with cash. JR didn't want to leave a trail. They pulled into a deserted road and drove north.

"Barb indicated that the FBI had been snooping around, and we shouldn't go there. So what I suggest is that I drop BJ off at a bus station where he can get a bus to Arkansas, and I will head for Canada. Georgie, this is where you get off too. Try hitching a ride to Wyoming. Don't take the bus. It is too easy to track you."

The miles went by as they gradually moved north in a zigzagging path, taking minor roads. They stopped in Spokane, Idaho, at the bus station. In the early morning light, it was a ramshackle place that was deserted except for a few down on their luck guys. JR, BJ, and Georgie had not shaved for many days, and in their rumpled clothing, they looked like the other drifters. There was a bus leaving in a couple of hours for Texas that ran through Arkansas. BJ bought a one way ticket.

Georgie walked out to the highway to find a good place to hitch a ride. In his hand he had a sign with Wyoming in big letters on it and a small backpack on his back. When Georgie was out of sight, JR turned to BJ and said, "Well, he's gone, and I hope I don't hear from him again. Good luck, buddy! Spend your money carefully cause I am not doing any more jobs like this one," JR said to his friend.

"I wish you the best too, buddy. Look me up sometime, and we will go hunting or something."

BJ waved good-bye, and then JR turned around and said to the ticket agent, "Hey is there a bus to Calgary, Canada, today?"

"Sorry, but those only run every other week, and this week was one of those. But it went yesterday, so the next one goes the week after next."

"Oh, well, I was meant to suffer to get there, I guess," he mumbled to himself.

Now he had to drive, and he was alone. He could not shake the feeling that he should sleep, and he reviewed his options as he drove closer and closer to the Canadian border. JR had not shaved for days, and they had traded off driving so that one could sleep, but no one had had a decent rest. He felt that fatigue acutely now that he was alone.

When I get over the border, I am finding the first place I can to sleep. I need to stash this car somewhere, and then I think I should hike over the border to avoid prying border agents. I can get more wheels in

Canada, he thought as he drove. He found a road to turn on that was not well traveled, and after a few miles, he found a dirt road leading into the mountains. Miles later he found a place to stop. Everything was out of the car in a pile. He didn't want to leave anything in the car that could lead to him. So he filled the backpack with everything incriminating, and the rest went back in the car. Lastly, he took off the Oregon plates and brought them with him.

Exhausted, he trudged down the road going north. Several hours later he reached a cleared area that indicated the border. There wasn't a fence, just a cleared stripe across the mountains and a sign. As he stepped across the border, he felt a relief. He rested under a tree for several minutes and then dug a hole where he buried the license plates. *Now all I need is a place to sleep. In the summer I would have made a bed of pine boughs, but today there's still some snow on the ground, making it most uncomfortable. I will use this stop to eat a snack so that I can contemplate my options. The only reasonable choice is to keep walking to a highway and thumb a ride.*

Miles later he found a busy road, and his tiredness forced him into trying to hitch a ride. An old man in a truck stopped near him and offered to pick him up. The driver yelled out the window, "Where are you going, fella?"

"I need to get to Calgary. I have a job waiting for me there," JR said with as much cheer as he could muster.

"I can't take you that far, but I can take you to the next town. You can get a ride on one of the big semis that go that way. Have you been hunting this time of the year?"

"No, I just have all my belongings with me cause I'm movin, and that is why I have the rifle," JR chuckled, hoping the man would believe him. Now he wished he had left the rifle there at the cabin.

"Well, you don't look too dangerous. Just put it in the bed of the truck with your backpack."

JR did as he was told. The older man was the silent type. JR wasn't sure what to say to this kind stranger anyway.

As soon as he was in the truck, he told the man, "Andy is my name, and I am from Vancouver. I have been taking the small roads because it is easier to get rides, and most county folks don't mind the rifle."

The old truck bounced along the country road past farms and forested areas. JR was lulled asleep and didn't wake up until they came to a stop in a small town.

JR woke up and turned to the man, "I am so obliged that you gave me a ride. Would you like the rifle for payment?"

The man looked at him suspiciously. "No, thank you, but you can sell it at the gun shop down the street."

"Thank you. My mom didn't want me to leave it with her, so I have been stuck with it." He was good at being deceitful with a straight face. He worried that the man might be a lawman of some sort, but he didn't want to ask.

"Good luck to you, Andy," the man said as he locked up his truck and walked away.

JR found the gun shop and stood gazing in the window to work up the courage. *It was stupid of me to greedily take this rifle. It all comes from wanting a gun when I was a kid. My old man refused to buy me a pellet gun. I was only ten, and he wanted me to be older before I got a gun. Then when I was a teenager, I fell in love with a Remington rifle, but I didn't have the money to buy it. When I saw this same Remington at the cabin, I couldn't resist it.* Now that rifle was sticking out of his backpack, and he needed to get rid of it. Gingerly, he walked into the gun store and up to the counter, where there was an older man standing. "How can I help you?" the man asked.

"I need to talk to someone about selling this rifle."

"Let's have a look at it."

JR handed the rifle to the man at the counter. The man had a gray ponytail that was secured by a leather thong at the nape of his neck. He was a solid-looking man who had trouble smiling. He grunted, "Where'd you get this gun?"

"I bought it at a gun show in Idaho. Why do you ask?" JR asked with the wolves of worry howling at him.

The man took a deep breath and thought a moment. The minutes passed. Then after reading the numbers on the stock, he said, "I think it could be *hot*, so I can only offer fifty Canadian dollars."

"Why do you think it is stolen? I was hoping for more."

"It is a risk. I just don't like the look of you or the gun for me to pay anything more for it."

"I have to sell it. I don't have a car. I need the money, and I can't hitchhike with this rifle in my pack. It scares people and makes me uncomfortable."

"Then you will take what you can get, buddy," the man said as he held the rifle in one hand and slid a few bills across the counter with the other.

Chapter 14

The Illness

Elly sat on the edge of her son's bed. "How are you feeling this morning?" she asked gently.

"Oh, Mom, when am I going to feel good again? Every time I go to sleep, I dream that I wake up well. Then when I really am awake, it is a different story."

"Davie, you have a nasty virus that attacks your immune system, and there is no cure for it. You most likely got it from having sex without a condom," she said, choking back the tears.

"Is that what the doctor said? Do I have to live with this the rest of my life?" Davie said and moaned.

"Yes, and we can't put off calling your father about this. I want to do that today."

David pulled the covers over his head and mumbled, "He'll kill me!"

"I know it is going to be difficult. Certainly, I am not looking forward to doing this. Let's have breakfast, and then we will give him a call."

Elly fixed a fruit energy drink for both of them. It was something David tolerated, and it was full of good nutrition.

"I don't have much of an appetite. Don't you have anything better?"

"Are you putting off talking to your dad?" Elly asked him. She had been through this before, and she was tired of making meals he wasn't going to eat.

She went to the phone and dialed her former husband's office. When Jerry came on the phone, he was brisk and annoyed. "I have a class in fifteen minutes, so make it fast."

"Jerry, I have our son David here, and we have some bad news for you," Elly said, trying to present her news gradually.

"If you want custody of him, then why are you making a game of this?" Jerry yelled into the receiver.

"Our son has an HIV infection and I want custody of him because that is what he wants," she said, trying to keep her voice as steady as possible.

"Oh, come on now. I know Davie better than that. He just wants to play hooky from school. Has he seen a doctor?"

"Yes, the doctor saw him and took blood samples that turned out to be positive for the HIV infection," she said.

"Are you telling me that David could be gay?" Jerry said in a surprising low voice as if he was whispering into the receiver.

"Yes, but we do not know the name of the man who had sex with him," Elly replied, her voice shaking.

"I am going to come over and see him. I will cancel my class, and I can be there in an hour."

Elly hung up the phone and thought about how she was going to manage Jerry. He might be in one of his alcohol-fueled violent periods. Whatever the case, she needed to protect Davie from any violence.

"What are we going to do with him when he comes over? I don't want to talk to him. In fact, I am going back to bed. I feel all worn out just thinking about him," Davie moaned.

She helped her son back to bed and waited.

***

Todd sat at his desk with his feet up, Jim, his partner, and Sanchez sat in a relaxed poses as well. All were nursing their cups of coffee. Todd loved the smell of fresh brewed coffee to simulate the conversation. They were discussing JR, the professional killer, with the FBI man, Joe Sanchez.

"JR or Jason Roberts is a smart and capable man. He is amazing in that he has had many identities over the years. There are not many crooks that can forge documents as well as he can. To make it more difficult, he creates new identities for every job. So we know he is north of here. Some officers saw a person who looked like him, and he has with him another man we have not identified yet. I think the buddy is someone he has known since the days when he was in the Special Forces in Cambodia, but we might find there are too many men to check to be practical. The cabin in the Cascade Mountains may have been their way of getting rid of a body or bodies. Luckily, the freezing snow helped retard the fire. We might find the remains of George Collinger and/or Nikcols in the ashes. The Oregon police are looking over the ruins, but I think it would be wise for one of you to go up there with me to look it over," Sanchez advised.

"This is information we can work with, and we will contact the authorities in Oregon and let them know that we would like to help them investigate this fire. Thank you, Joe, for coming by to give us this information. When do you want to go? I need time to clear it with my chief," Todd said.

"If we left tomorrow, that would be good timing. In addition, we have been bugging a hideout that JR has used in the past, and we are sure that he called the number yesterday. He was too fast to trace the call. We don't have evidence, but we are sure it was him. The woman who lives at the residence has been a long-term friend or lover of JR, and we are just waiting to see if he will come to her or the other way around," Sanchez added.

All three walked to the door and down to Sanchez's car. After he left, Jim turned to Todd and said, "Let's call Bend to see how the fire investigation is going and clear it with the boss."

***

As the minutes ticked by, Elly waited for her ex-husband with mixed emotions. She hadn't seen him in several years. Ever since her sons started coming to visit on their own, their father had become a forgotten person in Elly's life. Now he was expected, but he was keeping them in suspense.

The phone rang, and Elly jumped. "Hello?"

"It's me, Todd. Tomorrow we are going up to Bend, Oregon, to investigate a fire. Can you get away and come with me?"

"I would like to. I am waiting for Jerry right now. I will look for someone to take care of Davie if he doesn't want to visit his father."

"Okay, I will see you about six. Love you."

Suddenly, the buzzer rang, and Elly answered the intercom. "Ms. Jones, I have a Gerald DeMartini down here. Are you expecting him?"

"Yes, send him up."

Jerry arrived, and with fanfare, he swept into the room and dominated it with his girth. "What a gorgeous view you have. You are almost worth remarrying for this view."

"I can't image being back with you. You are the most ..."and she stopped herself. She didn't want to fight with him. "Come and sit on the couch with me."

"No, I will take the overstuffed chair so I can really look you over. All the way over here, I was trying to understand what ended our marriage."

Elly scrutinized this man she had once loved and could not find anything that interested her. "I hope you do not have plans for romancing me because you had your chance. I mourned the end of our relationship for years. I had to leave without my boys. It took five long years and a lot of pain to get over you. You broke my heart, and now you act as if we just had a little tiff and you want to make up. Let's talk about our son instead. Why did he run away from home and hang out in the Tenderloin district with all those other throwaway boys?"

"You always had a way to destroy a man's ardor, a real ball smasher," he said in defense. He, too, had suffered, but he would never admit it. "Davie hasn't been doing well in school. I don't know why he left my nice home. He was playing hooky from school and didn't want to talk with me about it. That's why he ran away," he said, growling.

"You mean you didn't know he was bullied at school and even the teachers were not protecting him because he is gay."

"How do you know he is a fag? Maybe this is a passing phase."

"He tells me he is in love with this man who probably gave him AIDS. Let me see if he is awake, and you can talk to him. It would be nice if he wanted to visit you for a couple of days because I have to be away, and he needs someone to care for him." At that, Elly rose and left the room.

Jerry got up and couldn't keep from pacing the floor. He pulled a flask out of the pocket in his jacket and took several swills. *My flesh and blood can't be a fag. If he really has AIDS, he must have gotten it off a toilet seat or something. I think it is just a flu bug, and he will get over it,* he thought, rationalizing his denial of the situation. After all, what would he tell his fellow professors? They would laugh at him if they thought his son was a weird boy. *Why did he hang out in the Tenderloin? Why can't I talk to him like Ted?* Nervously, he took another swig of his helpful liquid confidence.

He focused his mind on the view out the window. The day was getting late, and the bridge traffic was heavy with commuters. If he squinted, he could see the traffic moving slowly.

Elly came back into the room and announced, "He is very tired today, but he has consented to seeing you for a few minutes. Please do not stress him with your overbearing attitude. He needs to rest. He can have a peaceful talk with you. Can you do that?"

"Sure, I talk to young people every day, and I know how to communicate without stressing out the other person."

"He is in the bedroom with the door open. I am going to stay with you both to make sure everything is calm. By the way, this is what he requested," Elly said in a soft voice so she wouldn't sound like she was too assertive.

"Okay, I will follow you," he said as he motioned for her to walk ahead. Together, they entered the room. Davie was curled up, hugging a pillow for comfort.

"Hey, Davie, would you like to spend a couple of days with your dad? I will set up a nice cozy room downstairs where you can be a part of everything. I will get Ted to come and stay there to help me. Would you like that? We will get your favorite food and drinks. You will like it."

David could not believe that his father was not bitching about school or his problems. He looked at his father suspiciously. He could smell the alcohol on him, and it made him ill. "Dad, I would love to come to your house if you didn't drink all the time. Can you promise that?" David said quietly in a weak voice.

"Sure, I can manage that for a few days. I think you will get well faster with me than with your mother, who is always talking about depressing medical stuff," he said with good intentions.

"Davie, I have to go up north with Todd for a few days, and it would be nice to know if you are safe. Let's call Ted to make sure he will be available."

Elly and Jerry walked back into the living area. "We need to consult with Ted to see if he is available to help you tend to Davie's needs. Davie is fragile, and if he gets short of breath, then you need to call 911. It will be an emergency," she said, looking for acknowledgment from Jerry.

"I think you are making a calamity out of nothing. You tend to always make an emergency out of a headache. Ted and I will handle all this smoothly and without any upset. You will see. We will pick him up tomorrow morning. Is that agreeable?" Jerry said. He wanted to leave to get to an afternoon lecture he was giving.

Jerry left shortly after calling Ted to satisfy Elly with the arrangement. Elly was happy to see the door shut behind him. She didn't like the smoking and alcoholism, and he was a heart attack waiting to happen. It was hard for her to understand her former feelings for this man. He was so handsome and cultured when they first fell in love. The smoking and drinking seemed sophisticated just like in the movies where the actors always had cigarettes between their fingers and drinks in their other hand. Her parents smoked and drank. Her stepfather was probably an alcoholic. But she had changed, and she was wiser now. In that moment she knew that her love affair with the father of her boys was long over, and it felt liberating.

***

From the small town in British Columbia, JR had taken the bus to Calgary. It was a long trip made longer because he sat next to a man who smelled like he had sat in a pigsty for a week. This seat was chosen because the smelly man in the adjoining seat didn't look like a talker, and he wasn't. JR had plenty of time to think about his next move. *I need to create a new identity. Andy will have to change to Bill or someone else. Maybe I can find somewhere in Calgary where I can work on new documents. I want a job in mining or oil drilling. I'll just settle down to a new life at a dull pace.*

In Calgary, he got out and stretched. He needed some exercise, so he walked around and looked for a cheap hotel. The Union Hotel interested him. The lobby was small and compact without any decoration or chairs. He got a room overlooking the street so he could watch for the cops. It was a habit of his to always be on guard. The room had a double bed and a small desk. That was all he needed.

He pulled out some paper, special inks, and tools from his pack. He carefully formed a picture of his new image. It would be *Bill Macintyre*. He decided to dye his hair red and his beard red with blond highlights. He rummaged in his pack and found some henna dye and went to the bathroom and changed his look. Later that afternoon he went back to the bus station. He had seen a kiosk there where he could have his picture taken without spending a lot of money. The kiosk was cluttered with yesterday's candy wrappers and other debris. After several tries he got an image that he liked. It was almost dark now. He liked the dark, and he worked best when he was in the shadows. He took the photos back to the hotel room and then went and had dinner.

As he entered the local diner, he noticed there were very few people in it. The facilities had that tired look with patched upholstery on the stools at the counter. There were three booths with raged seats that had seen better days. He was about to walk out when this lovely wench spoke to him, "You will be comfortable here, and we will give you good food and service."

She led him to the last booth and put him in the best seat in the place. She was so helpful. He decided to look at the menu. When she brought his cup of java, she said, "I think the chicken fried steak would suit you fine. It comes with a baked potato and all the trimmings," she said slowly like she was talking about her favorite alcoholic drink.

He couldn't complain that they were unfriendly. As she hovered over him like a mother bird, he could smell her flowery odor like heather, and he relaxed. She didn't seem to mind that he couldn't keep his eyes off of her shapely breasts. About twenty minutes later, she brought a steaming dish of food that was pretty good for a diner. He wasn't expecting a gourmet delight anyway. As he ate, he watched the waitress. She had soft light brown hair tucked under a calico cap. Her yellow gingham uniform showed a graceful figure that made his mouth water. A few patrons came in and flirted with her. It sounded like she was a new employee. When she came to fill his cup, he decided to try out his new name on her. "What is your name, cutie?" he asked.

"My name is Sally. What's yours, big boy?"

"Bill is my name, Bill Macintyre. I'm pleased to meet you."

She smiled amiably. "Are you Irish?"

"Sure, but not totally, and I have never been to Ireland. I hear it is a lovely green place full of friendly lads and lasses."

She gave him no indication that he didn't look the part and joked with him about the Irish. She told him that the breakfast menu was really good, and he asked if she was going to be there again the next day. Sally was full of sexy allure, and she seemed to be toying with him. However, he had to be cautious and wasn't ready to have her come up to his hotel room.

Back in the hotel room, he again thought about his new image and future plans. It occurred to him that maybe if he was traveling with a woman, he would look less like his old self. He went to bed, and he was sexually aroused when he thought of Sally. She was a slender lassie with green eyes and soft brown hair, just his type. He went to sleep, dreaming of her in his arms, but it was just the pillow.

He got up early and went for a long run. Then he returned, took a shower, and went back to the diner for breakfast. Sally was there just as she had said she would be. With an ear-to-ear grin, she brought him coffee. He grabbed her hand and asked, "If there is a good movie in town, would you go to it with me tonight?"

She thought a moment and then said, "Maybe. Do you have a car?"

"No, sorry I'm not a wealthy dude. But I would like to take you out."

She left to take another order, but she found her way back to him. "I think I could see a movie with you. There is a good one at the Bijou Theater. I think it starts at eight."

"Great. Where do I pick you up?" he asked eagerly.

"Here. I'll be waiting here for you at 7:30," she said cautiously.

"That will work. I am looking forward to the date," he said with a gentle smile.

In his hotel room, he worked on documents, and when they were done, he cleaned his room in case she would return with him later.

He felt like a teenager again. It had been a long time since he made love to a woman. He didn't want to rush her. He was experienced enough to know that never worked. The plan was to see the movie, and he would put his arm around her then. But he'd go no further unless she was warm to that. Then they could go to a place to eat before he brought her to his hotel... only, of course, if she wanted to come.

In preparation, he went to a Laundromat to wash his clothes. He bought a blue work shirt and new jeans. The enthusiasm for Sally grew as the afternoon dragged by. Her body was in his imagination, and he thought about how she would taste and what her curvaceous body would look like undressed. She was becoming an obsession. It was all he could do to convince himself to go slow.

Sally, on the other hand, had watched JR walk out of the diner and thought of a plan. When she had a break, she went to the pay phone and dialed an undercover number. "This is Sally," she announced. "I think I have the mark interested in me. I will keep you posted." She quickly left the phone booth and briskly walked to her little apartment to change her clothes.

In JR's room a more leisurely scene was taking place. Carefully, he dressed as if he was going to his first prom. He took a shower and neatly trimmed his beard. He put on a fresh green plaid shirt and clean jeans. When he felt truly good about himself, he walked to the diner. She was there in jeans and a sweater. He took her hand, and they walked to the Bijou, an old worn-out theater. It was a B-rated movie, and the theater had only a few patrons. He bought her popcorn, and they watched the movie like zombies. Then when he put his arm around her, she snuggled into it, and now he didn't care what was on the screen. When he kissed her on her cheek, she turned and kissed him fully on his mouth. He felt he was getting an erection and stifled it because it was too early. They walked out of the theater hand in hand. She liked the feel of his hand and the warmth of his body next to her. They had a simple meal at a local Turkish restaurant.

"How long have you worked at the diner?" he asked to learn more about her.

"Not long. I just got divorced, and I needed a way to support myself. I want to save my money to move to Montreal. I have family there," she said as if they were old friends. "And you? Why are you in Calgary?"

He was cagey at first and said, "How do you know I am not a native of Calgary?"

"By your accent, I have known lots of people from here, and they don't talk like you."

"Okay, I'm from Vancouver. It is interesting that you are from Montreal. I am on my way to Montreal. I know there are gold mines north of there where I want to get work."

She smiled as if plotting a conspiracy. "How are you traveling? And would you take me with you?"

He gave her a wink and leaned closer to her to inhale her sweet violet fragrance and said softly, "I will take the train or the bus, whichever is cheaper, and nothing would be better than your company."

They talked on about their dreams. He loved her enthusiasm. She was perfect for him. Time flew by fast because they were so engrossed in their conversation. The waitress finally asked that they could pay the bill. It was getting late, and the restaurant wanted to close.

He now felt comfortable enough with her to say, "Would you come to my place?"

Her nod was full of gentle but nervous laughter. After paying the bill, he turned to her and took her hand as they walked outside. Once in the privacy of the street, he put his arm around her shoulders, and they walked to his hotel.

The man in the lobby had seen this before. Men were regularly bringing women up to their rooms, and women were bringing men all for the same purpose. This couple at least was laughing and joyous. When they got inside the room, they fell into each other's arms with sensuous kissing and groping. He loved the feel of her body. She loved his strength and his masculine odor. He didn't drink or smoke, and that was so welcome. They fell on the bed, struggling to get their clothes off. His first orgasm came too fast. But the second time around, he waited for her, and it was beautiful. Together, they fell asleep in each other's arms.

In the morning they made love again. JR buried his head between her legs and made her squirm with ecstasy. She loved his beard tickling her clit. Then he turned his body so she could service his member. They both came together, and JR thought they could be a perfect team.

As they lay lazily in bed that morning, JR asked Sally, "Do you need to get to work this morning?"

"It's my day off, lover boy. Let's get up and have breakfast. I am famished after all that enjoyable exercise."

During breakfast JR proposed, "Let's look into train or bus travel to Montreal this morning."

"Okay, my wealthy friend. You go, but I haven't saved enough to take a horse and wagon there," she pouted.

"How much do you have, Sally? I really would like your company."

She smiled and took his hand. "I'm glad you want me. I would like to see more of you. It would be nice if we could be special to each other. I only have $95, and I have to pay my rent $65. A waitress doesn't make much, even with the tips. I barely have enough to live on." Her voice trailed off.

Calculating her worth to him, he waited to suggest, "I could pay your way."

She looked at him with wide, beautiful green eyes. "You really could? I would pay you back when we got to Montreal. My family has a business there, and I can get a better job. Don't worry. I intend to pay you back," she nervously repeated.

JR enjoyed her innocent honesty. He envied her naïve and rough-and-tumble sweet decency. "Well then, there is nothing stopping us from buying our tickets."

As they walked toward the bus station, JR thought about what he was getting himself into. The problem was that he liked meaningful sex. Prostitutes had never appealed to him. Sally was a perfect toy. He must not fall in love. She shouldn't either. She must never know what he really was like. The past had nasty ways of showing itself at the most in opportune times, and she must not see that. However, a man deserved a woman, and he liked this woman. She would be pleasurable for a while. Nevertheless, he didn't want to meet her family.

The bus tickets were for the following day. It would take two and a half days to get to Montreal. As they came out of the bus station, Sally turned to JR and said, "I need to pack my bags and I would like to know what your plans are for tonight. Do you want to romp some more? We won't get much time in a bed when we are on the bus?"

"I have to pack as well," he said with a smile. "Let's make a date to have dinner and come back to my place tonight. I like your company."

She smiled warmly and kissed him tenderly on his lips. "I need to call my folks too."

He watched her walk away with a smile. He knew she was his flawless almost too perfect a companion and this worried him.

When Sally had a chance, she called her contact and said, "This is Sally reporting again. The mark and I are taking a bus to Montreal. I used my imaginary family in Montreal to flush him out, but so far he is willing to go there. Now there are a few stops along the way, and I will try to keep him with me so he doesn't bolt."

"So you are sure this is our target? Be careful. He is a dangerous man. I will call the men in New York to be at the border when we hand him over. I can meet you and act like your brother or something. Don't do anything heroic, Sally. You won't be able to manage him if he gets suspicious."

"I promise. I know my limits. We might need another agent on that bus. Can you spare a man?"

"Sally, you don't have any hard evidence that this is the right man. How can I justify another agent?"

"I told you that he uses bottled water. Have you ever gotten fingerprints from a water bottle? He handles the bottle by the paper label. I've tried to get a glass for him, but he never touches them."

"He is a cagey bastard, isn't he? Well, my hands are tied. I can't put another agent on this without firm evidence. Good Luck, Sally. Call me if you have problems."

A few hours later, Sally was knocking on JR's door. When he opened the door, she said, "Hi, Billy, I am all packed."

Scooping her up in his massive arms, he tossed her playfully on the bed. "I have been waiting for you with a stiff pecker, and I want some relief before we have dinner," he said as he nuzzled her neck.

Sally smiled seductively and kissed him sensually on his open mouth. "I love a man who is hungrier for my body than his dinner. Kiss me, and I will be your sex slave."

By disrobing as fast as she could, she wanted to have him think how much she desired him, for her protection. When she was naked, she slowly took off his clothes, tantalizing him. Gently, she forced him down on his back, tucked his member between her legs, and settled down on top of him. He was thrilled with her response and felt safe in her arms. She relished his surrender. There would be darker days ahead, she knew. Most of the time she didn't get attached to her suspects; however, JR was gentle and fun. He was so different than other criminals. There was this nagging idea that maybe he was the wrong man.

They had dinner at a fast-food joint, and they happily walked back to JR's apartment with their burgers and fries.

Chapter 15

The game

Finally, Davie, his father, and Ted had left for Berkeley. Elly hoped that the directions and all the information she had given them would be enough. Ted would be reliable, and she could count on him. Their father was another matter. Jerry's alcoholism and smoking would not be helpful for Davie's health. In the end, she had to trust them to take good care of her youngest son. It was going to be for only a few days. Todd had said that they would only be gone three to four days at the most. Elly was looking forward to getting out of the apartment and out of the city. It had been too long since she had smelled the fragrant mountain air. Maybe she could do some running.

Elly hummed a tune as she packed a bag for herself. She loved thinking of getting away with her sweetheart even if this was a trip to investigate a possible murder. She thought about how strange it was to be happy when someone else maybe mourning. *I don't wish anyone grief. But Marie should not have died, and someone must pay. Maybe Georgie will be found alive. Wouldn't that be an adventure? Todd thinks this professional man would get rid of him because he is a witness. This professional killer is scary. I shudder to think of that so-called hunter who sounded like the man who abducted me. I don't want to meet him ever again.*

When she was all packed, she brought the suitcase into the living area. Just then the intercom came to life. "Mr. Todd Markam is here. Can I send him up?"

Elly responded with joyfulness. "Sure, send him as fast as you can."

A few minutes later, the doorbell rang, and she opened the door. There stood Todd in jeans and a sweatshirt, and next to him was a German shepherd dog. "Well, what is this?"

"This, dearest, is Fred. He is going to be your new guardian. You can run with him and take him everywhere. This time away will help you and Fred get accustomed to each other and bonded."

She knelt down and petted Fred's burley neck and back. "He is beautiful, and he is so calm."

"Fred is a retired army dog, and then he joined the police canine crew and has been doing that for the last five years. Recently, he got retired from that, and now he will keep you safe. He took a bullet a few months ago, but the vet thinks he has about five more good years of work. Neil, who manages the canine force, thought he had seen enough rough work and should be retired to a family. I thought he would be perfect for you. So here he is."

Elly knelt down to Fred's level. "Oh, you poor baby, you were shot. I will smother you with love and give you a good home with lots of runs in the park. I know I am going to feel safe too. Do I have to be trained to manage him?" She nuzzled his soft ears and kissed his forehead.

"Yes, it would be good to walk with him and get him used to you. He will heel perfectly and will growl if he senses something dangerous. If you release him in that growling state, he will attack the person who is threatening you."

"That sounds scary and reassuring at the same time. So what is the plan for going north?" Elly asked with enthusiasm.

"We can leave now. Is this your bag? If you take Fred's leash, I will take the bag. Make sure you have a warm jacket, sweaters, and boots. We will be at an altitude that will have snow and ice. You don't want a blue nose, toes, and fingers," he said in a loving way.

The three went together down the elevator and out into the street. The chimes of the cathedral were just sounding off three o'clock. "We will drive as long as possible and stay in Redding or Red Bluff tonight," Todd announced as they reached his car.

"What will Fred eat?" Elly said with genuine concern.

"I have kibble for him and some bones for him to chew on as we drive. We will give him the back seat. I have laid out a blanket for him. If the FBI fellow comes with us, then you can sit with Fred. It would be a good time to bond with him."

As they walked down the hall to the elevators, Fred healed perfectly at Elly's side. He wasn't even interested when he reached the lobby where a lady in furs had a poodle on a rhinestone leash that was barking crazily at Fred. The lady was arguing with the guard about something and ignoring her dog. Elly was amazed how the dog and the mistress sounded the same. The lady's dog continued to pull on his leash and yapped franticly at Fred, but Fred was calmly oblivious. Elly was impressed that Fred could tune it all out.

When they reached the car, Elly said, "Let me sit in back with Fred. I am really interested in getting to know him."

"Next you will be sleeping with him, and I will be on the couch!" he said, laughing.

They drove to the police station. When they parked, Todd explained to Elly that she could come to the lobby but not up to his office. They would work out their arrangements upstairs and tell her about them when they were ready to go.

***

Sally and JR were jostling along the highway going east toward Regina, Saskatchewan, where the bus would stop for dinner. There were many raucous boys on the bus. They were on their way to

Regina to be trained as Royal Canadian Mounted Police. Dinking songs were their favorite, and they kept up the singing for hours. Most of the riders joined in on the singing and laughed at the jokes. All of the riders as well the driver cheered and wished them well. However, they made JR nervous.

Chatting merrily as the bus passed the mesmerizing farm after farm and field after field, Sally talked endlessly about her family. "I am so excited about introducing you to my mom and dad. You will like them. They are so generous, and they will help you find a job. My uncle Theodore is a longshoreman, and they always are looking for more men to work. There are a lot of ships on the St. Laurence River, and they are always loading ships, and he has never been out of work."

"Sally, don't get any fancy ideas about me settling down. You don't know me. I'm a gypsy. I can't stand to be in one place very long," JR said finally. He didn't want her to get any ideas of romance leading to marriage. He wasn't the type.

As the bus rolled along, JR was lulled into sleep as the miles moved by, cloaked in boredom. While he slept, Sally wondered if she could pick his pockets or something to acquire some evidence, but it was difficult because he was sitting on his wallet.

She was silently planning the next stop. *JR or Billy had the tickets. I am not sure he trusts me, and I certainly don't trust him. When we get off, I must follow him everywhere except the men's' lavatory, which is a problem.*

The sun was low on the horizon as the bus pulled into the evening stop in Regina. There were many buses lined up in this huge bus terminal. Some were loading, and others were discharging passengers. The noise was intense and caused confusion.

"I am so stiff from sitting here for so long. We should have flown," JR growled at Sally.

Sally smiled back, but she was apprehensive about this stop. It would take all of her cunning to keep him in her clutches.

As soon as the bus stopped, the driver stood up and announced, "This is Regina. You have one hour here. I'm going to lock the bus, so take whatever you need with you. You will need to show your ticket to get back on." Then he opened the doors, and everyone piled out. The boys going to the academy were loudly laughing and teasing one another.

"Do you want your ticket in case we get separated?" JR asked Sally.

"Sure, that would make me feel secure," Sally replied, but a wolverine of worries screamed at her mind. She could not take her eyes off him, and she watched his every move. When he got his bag down from the luggage shelf, she became so alarmed that she blurted out, "Why do you need your bag?"

"Don't worry your sweet head about that. I'm only going to trim my beard and maybe change my shirt to look more presentable for you," he said with words that were gentle and saccharine. He kissed her with feeling and held her until she relaxed. "Now let's get organized, or this break will be gone before we know it. I want to use the bathroom before dinner, and while I'm in there, I want you to pick out a place for us to eat."

"Okay," she said, not sure she should trust him very much. However, as they walked to the restrooms, she wondered if he really was Bill. This trip to the WC would tell a lot about him.

The gents and ladies WCs were side by side against the north wall of the station. At the entrance, JR suggested, "I'll meet you out here in about fifteen minutes, okay?"

Sally nodded, but she hid her face because she was afraid it would reveal her concern.

JR waited for Sally to disappear into the women's side, and then he walked briskly to the entrance of the station and out the door. On the street he looked both directions and decided to walk up the street to the north, following the boys going to their school. After a few blocks, he got to a main street called Victoria Avenue with stores. He desperately needed to escape. He looked for a city bus or a taxi. Then down the street, he saw a city bus coming on the opposite side of the avenue. By running across the street though traffic, he managed to catch the bus before it pulled away from the curb.

Catching his breath, JR asked the bus driver how to get to a cheap hotel. The bus driver assured him that the bus would go by the neighborhood where there were cheap hotels. Walking unsteadily down the bus aisle, he found a seat and stared out the window watching for Sally or the cops. He took a deep sigh of relief when he saw no one. *I need to find a hotel where I can create a new ID. They might be checking the airport and other means of transportation for me.*

Back at the bus station, Sally was waiting outside the men's room. The fifteen minutes had gone by, and she was suspicious that he had pulled a fast on her. She walked up to a young boy and asked, "Would you please go in the men's room and ask if Bill is there? I'm waiting for my husband, and he's taking too long."

The boy agreed and went in to check, but when he came out, he said, "Ma'am, there's no one in there. I checked all the stalls, and there isn't anyone."

"Damn him to hell," Sally mumbled to herself as she received the news, cursing her trust in Bill or whatever his real name was. She was also angry at her boss for not sending another agent to help her. Now she had to call in and tell them she had lost him. She despised failure in any form.

***

The day had been a long one for Elly too. She sat in the back seat with Fred's head in her lap for hours. Todd was driving, and the FBI agent Sanchez was telling them all about the professional killer.

"We have had contact with a Canadian agent," Mr. Sanchez explained to Todd. "We think JR has gone to Canada to hide. This agent thinks she has identified him. She has been trying to gain his confidence and then bring him in. The plan is to get him to Montreal. There, our agents can just pick him up at the border."

Elly was fascinated by what she heard. They arrived in Redding at about late dinnertime. The three of them were starving by this time. First, they located a motel. There were not that many, but they took one near a reasonable restaurant. In Todd and Elly's room, they set up an area for Fred with some chow and bones for him to chew on. After he was watered and fed, they all went to the nearest place to eat, which was just a few steps away. Todd and Mr. Sanchez were deep in thought when a call came in on Sanchez's phone. He found a private place to talk and conversed accordingly. Todd and Elinor looked at each other and hoped there the authorities had captured the killer. It was several agonizing moments before Sanchez returned to talk to them.

"Well, the news isn't great. It appears he got away. He is a slick and cunning one. I wish I was up there to manage the search, but it is out of my territory."

"Perhaps he will come back into the United States in another disguise," Elly offered.

"That's true. He could. He is a difficult man to capture as he is always one step ahead of the officers. I had to explain that to the Canadians because they doubted they had the right man. The agent who identified him was uncertain, but she at least followed him to Regina, Saskatchewan. They are checking the airports and train stations in Canada. We will keep an eye on outgoing carriers too like hitchhiking targets. He is probably at this moment is reinventing himself, but he can't do that forever," Sanchez dryly answered.

They ate a simple dinner of chili with beans and rice. The salad that came with it was mostly greens with a little carrot and one lonely cherry tomato. The dinner matched their dumpy mood.

Elly spoke up, "I am going out to use the pay phone to call my son and give Fred a walk. You enjoy your dessert, and I will be back after my call."

She stood up, and the men looked up at her with sympathy. Quietly, Elly left the restaurant with Fred and walked up the block to a pay phone. In the cramped, suffocating space, she dialed the phone and waited. The operator came on and asked for money, and Elly put some in the phone then. On the receiving end, the phone rang several times before it was picked up.

"DeMartini residence. This is Ted."

"Hi, sweetie, is Davie settled in, and is he comfortable?"

"Oh, Mom, it is so nice to hear your voice. Davie is right here and can talk to you."

There was a slight pause, and then Davie weakly stammered, "Hi, Mom ... I'm okay. Ted made me a bed downstairs so I ... can watch ... TV ... and the phone is right here ... so if I need help ... I can call."

"You are so breathless. Are you feeling okay?"

"This is Ted again. Davie is weak, and he has these red splotches on his face and on his chest. Is that new? I called the doctor that you gave us, and he said if Davie gets weaker and more short of breath, I should take him to the local hospital. Do you agree with that?"

"I'm glad you called the doctor. I had noticed one or two patches, but maybe there are more now. Please follow the doctor's directions. I feel so helpless way up here in Redding. We will be going to this area up north, and there won't be any phones up there. If there are any emergencies, please call the police department in SF and tell them to contact Todd. Is that clear? I can't just come running to the rescue, but at least I can call you back and give advice. Call 911 if his respiratory rate is more than twenty and labored. Please."

"Yes, Mom, I understand. I am going to spend time with Davie tomorrow, and I will be right with him."

Uneasy, Elly concluded the call. In the privacy of the phone booth, she wept uncontrollably. She stayed in the phone booth until an older woman came along and acted like she wanted to use the phone. Elly dried her eyes and blew her nose. Fred gazed up at her with compassion. When she felt presentable, she opened the door out of the phone booth. She was in no hurry to return to the restaurant because she wanted to recover so that she wouldn't have to explain her sadness.

When she returned to her seat at the table, Todd and Sanchez were deep in conversation about the crime scene they were going to be visiting in the morning. Quietly, Elly slid into her chair. Todd reached out to her and held her hand while he continued talking to Sanchez. The table was full of coffee cups and plates with half-eaten pie of some variety. Fred sat faithfully by Elly's chair.

"I think we are ready to go," Todd said as he pushed back his chair. Elly sniffled quietly coving her face to hide her pain. This prompted Todd to say, "Are you okay, Elly?"

"I would rather talk about it later," Elly said as she turned her head to hide her tears.

Outside the restaurant the cool air caressed Elly's face, and she felt comforted by its tender touch. They walked to the motel in silence, even though Elly would have liked them to talk. They were all silent in the elevator. Sanchez left them at his room, and then they walked several feet down the hall in silence to their room on the same floor. As soon as they were in the room, Elly ran into the bathroom, slammed the door shut, and burst into tears.

Fred was immediately at the door, snuffling and cocking his head to one side. He looked at Todd and then the door. When the door didn't open, Fred whined at the door in sympathy.

Todd was surprised, but he knew Elly was upset from the moment she sat down at the table after her phone call. "Elly, tell me what happened when you called about Davie." He waited a moment and then said, "I want to comfort you." The whimpering slowed down. "Do you want to go home?"

When he didn't expect it, the door flew open. "No, I want to get the man who gave my son AIDS because— I know this is going to sound like I'm paranoid, but could it be a way to get at me like all the other attempts?"

"Elly, you are not paranoid. That idea has crossed my mind too." He gently took her in his arms. "Tell me about your phone call."

"Davie sounds much worse. Ted is there and said he would stay right by him. He knows his father is not capable of caring for his son and I feel guilty because I have gone and left him."

Todd scooped Elly up in his arms and carried her to the bed. As he carefully laid her down, he said, "You can fly home tomorrow if that makes you feel better."

"I have given that idea a lot of thought, and I think being here with you is good therapy for me. And I will get to know Fred better." Fred eagerly waged his tail at the sound of his name.

***

After looking at several dumpy hotels on skid row, JR found the perfect hotel. It was a 1920s building called the Queen's Rest. This building needed repairs and a face-lift, but he liked the feeling of the place. When he entered the lobby, which was a short hall with a desk and a stairwell at the end, he also saw the man at the desk, a very tall fellow with a long brown face and large sad eyes with drooping bags. He had a tuft of kinky gray hair on his head and strong, massive hands. The recognition was immediate. JR and Danny had both been in the Special Forces, fighting the Kamer Rouge years before. There JR had learned to kill, and Danny had become a heroin addict. Both returned to their homes with an inability to adjust to a normal middle-class life. Now they were exiles, and JR wanted a different life. But could he find freedom?

"Well, yo' is a vision fo' so' eyes. Where have yo' been, and what brings yo' here?" the man said.

"Danny, I didn't know you were in Regina."

"I moved here about two years ago, running from de feds as usual. I heard de drug trade is heating up in Regina, and so I slipped over the border, and here I is. And is yo' escaping something too?"

"Yeah, you don't happen to have a room for me, do ya?"

"For yo', I've got de best, the queen's suite. It's the only one left, to be truthful. What name is yo' goin' by des' days?"

"It's Billy for today ... if you know what I mean."

"Wha' is yo' go'in to change it to?"

"I haven't worked that out yet."

"Let me give yo' a name, how about Harry?"

"That will work fine. I will scribble a signature that is not decipherable anyway."

"Here is de key. It is up two flights of stairs and numba' 207," Danny said as he passed over the key. "Der 's a deadlock. Be sure yo' keep it loc'd. We've some creepy dudes who might wander in when yo' leas' expect it if yo' know wha' I mean."

"Thanks for the advice," JR said as he took the key.

The staircase was creaky as he climbed up to the second-floor landing. Room 207 faced the alley, and it smelled like a giant ashtray. JR went to the window and opened it. The fresh air came in like a hurricane. He flopped down on the double bed on top of the ragged, faded green bedspread. He thought about his luck at finding a dive that had someone he knew. *My luck is picking up. I may yet get out of this scot-free.* JR decided to celebrate.

Just as he was feeling secure, he got a call on the phone. It was Danny. "I just want you to know dat a pretty young lady was in ask'n for a Billy Macintyre. Is that you? Also, I dink dat woman's a dick. I c'n smell dem a mile away."

JR was glad he was sitting down. "Was she about five feet six with brown hair and green eyes with an innocent look about her?"

"Yeah, do yo' know dis dish?"

"I wish I didn't. So you think that she is an officer of some sort."

"Yaw', sir, she be bad news. I just want to warn yo'."

"Thanks. What did you tell her?"

"I tol' her I hadn't seen any dude of yo'r description. And she seemed to buy it."

"Where can I go to get some dinner that is safe around here?"

"Dere's a dive down on de corner of dis street and de cross street. By de way, if yo' pick her up and bring her here, I'll be gone, and my assistant will be here. If dere's any trouble, he'll help yo'. Okay."

"Do you know where I can get some drugs?"

"Yo're at de right place, buddy. What do yo' need?"

"I want a heavy tranquilizer. I want something I can inject."

"Will H do yo'?"

"Yes, that will work. Can you have it in my room? Put it in the medicine cabinet."

"Yo' just want to put her in an agreeable state or kill 'er?"

"I don't want to give her an overdose. I don't like killing cops, but I want to put her out."

"Okey-dokey. We'll assume she's not an addict. Doc' Danny will handle it. Do yo' want ma assistant to help yo'?"

JR smiled. "Yes, you see the picture perfectly. Tell your assistant to come to my room about an hour after we arrive. After all, I may not run into her. Then I will have an even better dinner."

Chapter 16

The Ashes of Death

"Good morning, boys! It is so nice to have both my boys here with me again. I can't tell you how much that pleases me." Jerry DeMartini was cheerful this morning.

Ted was sprawled over the chaise in a chaotic mass of blankets and pillows. He stiffly picked himself up and shook his head to clear it. "That chaise lounge is nice for a lazy afternoon nap, but when you really want some sleep, it is a loser."

"Well, I am sorry this hotel isn't as luxurious as the Claremont! However, I do appreciate you looking after Davie. By the way, how is our Davie this morning?"

The shades of sleep hung on his slender frame, Davie stretched his stiff body to wake up. "I am breathing better today, and I am actually hungry."

"Really? What can I get for you? Bacon and eggs or cereal?" his father asked.

"No, some fruit and a piece of toast with nothing on it." Just this little request seemed to exhaust him and sent him into a coughing fit.

"I will take care of Davie. You don't have to worry about him, Dad," Ted said softly.

"Well, fine. You take care of the sick, feeble one. I for one have no time for lying around. I have a job and a lecture this morning," Jerry said with distain mixed with disappointment.

"Oh, Dad, you are very important to us. While you are here, I want to go to the store and get some supplies for Davie. Is that okay? You don't leave until ten, and I will be back by then," Ted said brightly to counter his father's sour mood.

Ted went into the kitchen and brought back a small glass of apricot nectar for Davie. In the kitchen Jerry was preparing his breakfast of eggs, sausages, and potatoes. When Ted came back into the kitchen, Ted announced, "I'm off to the store. Is there anything I can get for you?"

"No, don't be gone long. Davie makes me nervous."

In the living room where Davie was propped up watching television, he was rummaging in his knapsack for a piece of paper. Finally, he found it. On the paper he had the scratchings of a phone number. He dialed the number. It rang and rang. Then someone picked up the phone. "Hello," the baritone voice said.

"This is Davie. Is this ASS? I miss you," Davie said in his weak, squeaky voice.

"Oh, Davie, where are you? I have been so worried, and I need you desperately," Arnold said with genuine passion and longing.

"I want you to know I have AIDS, and I am upset that I might have given you this nasty virus. I am really sorry to tell you this," Davie bravely confessed.

"My dear Davie, don't worry. I have AIDS too, but I am fighting it fairly well and you can, also. Are you with your mother?"

"No, I'm at my dad's place. My mom went off with her boyfriend, Todd. They are looking at a cabin in Oregon."

Arnold was startled by this news. "I can't talk long, but I want you to know that I have been funding a project to find a cure for AIDS. I am sure they are going to conquer this like they eradicated smallpox. You hang in there and call me again sometime. And Davie,

I love you. Please don't give this number to anyone, okay? Bye." Then there was a click, and the dial tone came on.

Davie put the receiver down with soundless skill and smiled. *I feel like I have gotten something momentous off my back, and it was such a relief to hear he loves me. The sound of his voice arouses me. I can almost taste him. I want him so much.*

***

Elly awoke, all excited about the interesting day ahead. "Todd, how soon can we get going. I'm famished, and Fred needs a walk."

"I'm awake, my love, and I think when we are finished with the essentials like breakfast, we will go to a store and buy a Frisbee for Fred. You can play with him while we sift through the ashes."

"I have thought about Davie all night. Some people with AIDS live many years with it, but others are different and I must prepare myself for his eventual death. Last night was just the beginning of that process. There is going to be more," she said and sighed. "I have to understand that he found someone to love and gave his all for that experience. That is what all the rest of us want and strive for. It is just that he will pay the ultimate price at a very young age."

"I want to catch the man who gave him AIDS and the man who is harassing you and killed Maria ... and Jacob ... and so many others. We must catch and convict these people. Our lives will not be peaceful with them running loose. They seem to be linked. I am hoping this burned cabin will offer clues to a couple of characters, Collinger and Nikcols. I am so glad you are feeling stronger. I need you, Elly. I need you at my side."

"Todd, I want to help you in any way I can, but this case is so confusing. I don't understand anyone's motives for killing. Do you have motives for these people? Another thing is I am worried about what you are going to find at this cabin."

"It's okay. The more information we get, the clearer the picture will become."

"Keep a stiff upper lip, as the British say. Let's go and have breakfast," she stated as she locked her right arm in his and held the leash for Fred in the other hand, guiding them both to the door.

***

It was midmorning in Regina. JR was having breakfast at a local diner. He had chosen a table in the back, and he wore a large-brimmed, straw, farmer's hat so that he would blend in with the others. He was just finishing a plate of pancakes when a woman walked in.

God, is that Sally? She is hiding her face while talking to the men at the counter. If I can somehow pay my bill and sneak out, I will stand a chance. Then again, if I stay in my seat and keep my head down, she might go away. I'm taking my chances by holding tight.

He kept his head down and didn't hear the waitress come up to him. "Sir, do you want more coffee or the bill?"

It surprised him. "Yes, just the check will do. I'm sorry. I was deep in thought."

"Everyone seems to be worried about something these days," she mused as she offered the check for the food.

When she left, he chanced a look to see if the woman who could have been Sally was still there. She appeared to be gone, but he automatically looked out the dirty window to see if she was waiting outside. He turned and motioned to the waitress to come over to his table. "I changed my mind, waitress. I'll take that fill-up of coffee!" he bellowed louder than he wanted to. *I need to stay here a little longer as this seems to be a safe place.*

An hour later he was walking briskly to the Queen's Rest. Danny was happy to see him.

"Sally was here ag'in. She wanted to check de guest list, but I says she couldn't 'til she had a court order. Dat's my usual routine. So she was not suspicious at dat. Jist annoyed."

"She's really combing the neighborhood. She knows me too well. Thank you for suggesting the hat. It is a great way to hide my face. It helped me avoid people at the diner. I think the way to avoid her is to come right at her."

"To avoid her yo's going to come right out and greet her like a long lost friend? Dat sounds like a good way to get in jail. Tell me more."

"She is so hot to get me that I thought I should lay a trap for her. Either I can go out and be perfectly available, or I can wait in my room. The next time she comes, you send her up to my dump. This is assuming she is alone. I will use my Bill personality and entice her into a snare. Any advice, Danny?"

The hotel manager scratched his thin head of hair. "I'd be careful. I hope she don't come back wid a warrant. She might be carrying heat. It might be better to go out and see if she engages you. I take it that she don't have any firm evidence. And maybe if yo' play it cagey, she'll come back here wid' yo', but she's comin' to see your room for evidence.

"Interesting. But I like that plan. Let me think through the options, and I will get back to you."

***

The drive up to the area with the cabin was complicated since it was covered by a maze of dirt roads. After an hour of twists and turns, Elly thought they must be lost, but if she had said that, it would not go over well. So she quietly concentrated on loving Fred by rubbing his ears and his neck.

In the midmorning, they came to a stop in what appeared to be a meadow, but in reality, this was a clear-cut area in the forest that was covered with a thin layer of snow. There were several Oregonian police cars parked in a makeshift lot. A couple of the officers came over to their car.

"Hi, nice to see you, I'm Doug Cartwright, and this is my buddy Terry Draper. We are officers from Eugene," they announced through the car window.

Todd and Mr. Sanchez got out of the car and introduced themselves and displayed their badges.

"The fire destroyed most of the evidence. Our coroner said there might be few slivers of bone fragments that we might turn up for samples. There are also the remains of a handgun and a stove. We do not think this fire was anything but arson. The pattern of the burnt floor indicates a flammable substance was in a path on the floor to a bed. It is an iron bed. The flammable substance probably connected to the bedding. We think there were one or possibly two bodies on the bed. We found a handgun and one bullet, but both are so destroyed by the fire that we can't read any serial numbers."

"Thank you for the overview. Let's go look for ourselves, but let me take care of the woman in the car," Todd said to the officer. Then he walked over to his car and opened the door for Elly.

She looked up at him with one of her ground-trembling smiles, "I know. I will stay out of the way and play with Fred. If I take a walk with him, when do you want me back here?"

"Give us at least three to four hours. We have a lot of ash to sift through. Please stay near this clear-cut area so you don't get lost."

"I will be careful, and Fred will know the way back," she assured him.

The clear-cut forest was about as wide as the length of two football fields, and it went on and on for miles toward the south. Elly ventured out of the car, bundled in a down jacket and warm gloves, hat, and boots. She carried the Frisbee in her gloved hand.

"Well, Fred, we are on our own. Let's see what we can discover about the forest." She released Fred from his leash and flung the Frisbee as hard as she could as she said, "Go get it!"

The powerful dog lunged forward and ran after the Frisbee with Elly running after him. Fred was happy, leaping into the air to catch the toy. They did this over and over for about an hour. When Elly felt exhausted, they wandered down to a creek that ran along the far side of the clearing.

The water came through a narrow canyon, colliding off of an assortment of rocks in a pinball pattern, creating a formidable array of waves and class-three rapids. The roaring creek was full of melted snow as it crashed against the boulders and whirled in the eddies. Gallons of water surged like a wild animal thrashing among the rocks while throwing white foam into the frigid air. When Elly looked into the rapids, the water was crystal clear, and as they walked along the edge of the maelstrom, Elly noticed that the creek twisted through the trees, taking the path of least resistance. At times it was difficult to come down to the water because of the treacherous rocks and tree stumps, so they had to walk around them and look for an opening. Finally, Elly found a place without snow or inconvenient rocks to settle down. She found a boulder at the edge of the creek that was dry and sat on it. The torrent of water was deafening, but Elly found the sound relaxing, numbing her concerns.

Fred loved the creek area as it was full of interesting smells. As he leaped among the rocks, he searched for little animals to chase. Elly let him wander as long as he was in sight. She also loved the serenity of the uncut forest on the other side of the creek. The book in her pocket was calling to her, so she pulled it out and started to read. Fred was exploring the boulders and pools in the water. Off and on, he would do some wandering, but he would return to Elly to make sure she was safe. Elly delighted in his loyalty to her and each time he came back to her, she would give him a treat that she kept in her pocket. Sometimes she would throw the Frisbee, which he would dutifully return to her even when it meant he had to enter the ice-cold water.

On one of Fred's explorations, he found a bottle caught wedged between two rocks in the water and brought it to Elly in his teeth. At first, she ignored his gift and threw the Frisbee to reward him. As she read her book, a strange feeling came over her. It was as if the bottle was begging for her attention. Laying down the book, she took another look at the bottle. When she turned the battered bottle over in her hand, she could see something inside of it and realized there was a note in it.

"Wow, this is wonderful, Fred. You have found a treasure. The only problem is the lid is stuck tight with corrosion."

While struggling with the bottle, she felt frustrated and smashed the top off with a blow, on a rock. Fred watched and wined, but when the note was released, he growled.

"What are you trying to tell me, Fred?" she mumbled while she unwrapped the note. Then she read it.

To whom it may concern,

I am writing this so that I can tell you information about me if something happens and I die. I am George Collinger, a member of the San Francisco Police Department. I was hired by a man called JR who said he was hired by someone in SF to poison Elinor Longacre so she would get ill but not die. I was sent to this cabin to wait for further orders, but I fear for my life. —GC

Elly's hand shook as she read the note with her name in it. A lump in her throat was choking her. She put her arm around Fred and buried her head in his fur to sob. *This man is dead, and now he is speaking from the grave.* Then it dawned on her that possibly she should not have opened the bottle.

"I should have listened to you, Fred. You knew I shouldn't have broken that bottle and taken out the note. Todd may think I have contaminated the evidence. He may even be angry at me for ... half of a dozen problems associated with this note. We are going to spend another hour exploring, and then we will go back to the car and suck on our bitter pickle."

Using utmost diligence, she picked up each and every shard of glass. The note she tucked into a pocket, and she collected the splinters of glass in the bottom of the bottle. With caution, she placed the broken bottle with the slivers of glass on a flat rock she found. Then she placed the rock at the base of a tree that was standing alone. When she thought it was secure and they could find it again, they went off to play. The hour crawled by so slowly. Elly's arm was getting sore from tossing the Frisbee. Fred was too fast with returning it. Elly felt tired and sad. She just wanted to return, but she had to let the men do their investigation. Her watch hands seemed to move terribly slowly. Finally, it was four o'clock.

"Okay, Fred, we can get the bottle and return to the car and see what the men have discovered."

Fred helped Elly scout out the tree. Gingerly, she picked up the broken glass bottle, balancing it with the Frisbee and leash. The care of the bottle was difficult because of all the prickly shards. The walk was over uneven branches and new trees coming up made the return slow. It was full of traps made by stumps and brush covered by snow, to snag a foot and bring one down in a heap. Finally, she reached the car park area, exhausted and worried.

Todd was talking to the Oregon police officers and Sanchez from the FBI. When he saw Elly, he motioned her over.

"We're just making plans to drive into Eugene to talk to the coroner, and then later we'll have some dinner. What do you have in your hand?" Todd asked.

"Fred found this bottle, and I was like a kid who found a treasure. I broke the top off so I could see what was in it," she said as she handed over the bottom with the splinted pieces of glass. "I couldn't open it any other way. I am sorry if I destroyed the evidence."

"What *evidence?*" Todd asked with sudden excitement.

"There ... there was a note in it," Elly stammered. "Here!" she said as she handed him the note.

He briefly read the note and then took Elly in his arms and kissed her affectionately. Then he turned to the other officers and said, "This woman is worth her weight in caviar. She has found evidence of the identity of one of the bodies! And George Collinger left this note confessing to the poisoning."

"I take it that she has helped with investigations before," Mr. Sanchez exclaimed.

"Yes, she is the smartest and bravest woman I know," Todd bragged.

"Well, let's go and get dinner in Eugene, and we will celebrate," said one of the Oregonian officers. "Thank you for the boost, Ms. Longacre. We were pretty glum without any identification."

$$***$$

JR walked slowly toward the hotel he was staying in. He had been playing cat and mouse with Sally all day, and he was so depressed by it. By using the side door, he entered into the hotel through the door that the hotel workers used for security. It entered into the staff break room. Danny was waiting for him there.

"Wall, look who's here. Dat lady has been hounding me all day, and I'm dog-tired of it," Danny said and chuckled.

"Yeah, I know. I want to talk to you about her. I have some plans, three of them to be specific, and if you have a moment, we can talk about them."

"Take a seat. I'm all ears, says de moose, so pour forth," Danny said with a twinkle in his eyes.

"My first plan is to invite her up to my room and get her into a compromising position so I can tie her hands. Then I'll shoot her up with the big H. Once she is subdued, you and I will take her down to the basement and stash her in a closet. She'll be well tied up, and I'll tape her mouth with duct tape and blindfold her. If you keep her dosed on H, she will sleep for days. This will make it possible for me to escape."

"Damn God's balls to hell. Dat means I get left holding de bag. So what do I do wid' her when yo's gone? I'll have the cops swarming de place, and I'll compromise my uder customers," Danny objected.

"Okay, that may not work. The next plan is to change my identity and slip away somehow. I am really tired of doing this, but if it is necessary, it is what it is. I have thought of dressing like a businessman. I would need a ride to the airport from you and a ticket. Maybe you could call for the ticket from a pay phone."

"Dis one's better, but why do I've to call for de ticket? I wan' a plan where I stay clean. So let's hear the last plan."

"This one I play it straight. I walk out into this city as if I didn't have a care in the world. This will attract my little shadow. I will sit down somewhere, and we will have a talk. You see, she doesn't have fingerprints or anything solid to charge me. I will insist that I am really Bill, and she will have to buy it. Once I convince her to leave me alone, then I will be free to go where I please and even leave Canada. This is the most satisfying plan because it gives me a feeling of freedom. What do you think?" JR leaned forward and looked expectantly at Danny.

Danny sat back and stared at the ceiling. "Dis one is full of monkey business. Sally's spent almost dt'ree days on your tail. What makes yo' d'ink that she's goin' to believe yo're Billy and not JR?" Danny asked.

"Because I think she is ... she is soft on me. She would be delighted to have me convince her that I am Bill, someone she can feel good about loving. Of course, my feelings are not the same, but I can put on a good act."

"I dink yo' like to play wid fire, my friend. When she has visited me, she's all business. She's certain yo'is her prey, and she won't give up on dat easily. Have yo' ever dought dat she has talked to her boss and has said she's determined to bring you in? If dat's true, she'll feel compelled to come drough wid' de goods."

"Okay, it's risky. However, in the United States, there's no substantial proof like fingerprints or weapons that show I have murdered anyone. I think it would be difficult to convict me of anything anywhere. There are no bodies or signs of violence. So they don't have a case at all."

"Yo'is certainly sure of yo'rself. I wish I felt de same way fo' yo'. I don't wan' to visit yo' in jail, but I understand yo' craving fo' freedom."

"Danny, you underestimate me. I can charm the nuts off a bear!"

"Yo're a good friend, and I'll miss yo' when yo's gone. But get goin' now. I've to mind de desk."

***

The restaurant in Eugene, Oregon, was a simple diner with a limited menu, but there were lots of beer, which seemed to interest all of the officers. The five of them squeezed into a narrow booth and waited for the menus. As soon as the ample waitress arrived, the men all asked for their favorite brands of beer.

Elly declined the beer and studied the menu, searching for healthy dishes."You may fill your guts with beer, but I am hungry. An alcohol high is the last thing I need. By the way, the corned beef and cabbage looks safe to eat."

The officers were only politely interested in Elly and were more interested in watching the football game on the TV or talking shop. Elly decided to stay silent for a while and let them wind down and start to talk about important issues.

When they had a half pint of beer each and started into their dinner, Elly felt they were ready to discuss the burned area they investigated today. She decided to direct her questions to Mr. Sanchez, the FBI officer, at first. He was a tall brown man with graying hair and a lined face. He was sitting there quietly, and that gave him an air of strength. Also, his mouth fascinated Elly. Most Hispanic people had slender lips, but Sanchez's were a full. However, he pulled them tight like a stripe across his face. The beer was loosening him up though, and that stern mouth revealed some curves that made him more approachable. He was also sitting directly across from her, which gave them both a chance to study each other.

"Mr. Sanchez, sir, what do you think the DNA is going to tell us when the analysis comes back?" Elly asked.

He paused with the fork almost to his mouth and said in a soft voice, "Miss Longacre, you may address me as Joe, and may I call you Elly? Your question is interesting because there are several theories as to what we may uncover. We only found badly burned bone fragments, and they may not have any DNA. Or it may not be human. There are so many other theories that may never reveal an answer. If we *assume* that this really is a bone fragment and it is human, we have to be careful. The man we think is at work here is a real trickster. Maybe he took the body of an animal and burned it so that George Collinger and Mike Nikcols could go free because society thinks they are dead. Or the body could belong to one of these men, but the other may have left his gun there to make it look like he had died when he really didn't. Then we will have to find the one who got away. There is a third scenario. What if there are two bodies there and JR was just cleaning up the evidence? This man has acted out these plans in former cases. Does that seem logical to you, Elly?"

"Joe, are you saying that he often burns the evidence, burying the secrets in the cold ashes?"

"Exactly, Elly. You put it so well, and by the way, thank you for suggesting the corned beef and cabbage. It was very good."

Later Elly waited to use the pay phone outside the restaurant. The lady in it finally opened the door and gathered up her belongings as she exited. *It took you long enough!* Elly thought as she made way for the woman to leave. Then with trepidation she dialed Jerry's number. She was too fast in responding when the call was answered, "Hi, Ted, how is your sweet brother and my darling son?"

"Your darling baby son had a relapse today, and he is now in the hospital," Jerry gruffly barked, ending with a choking cough.

"Oh, how sad! Are you all right? You sound a little under the weather yourself. Which hospital and what were his symptoms?"

"Elinor, you are the nurse, not me. Ted got worried about Davie and said that he was having too much trouble breathing and that he needed to get him to the hospital. So he took him to the closest one here in Berkeley. I can't remember its name."

"Is that possibly Herrick Hospital? I will call them and see if Davie is there. Jerry, aren't you drinking too much?"

"Just leave me alone. You deserted me, so I need to console myself."

"Thank you for the information, and I am sad you are alone and feeling sorry for yourself."

There was a loud click, and the dial tone came on. Elly called information and got the hospital's number. It took several minutes before she was connected to David's nurse.

"Is this Ms. DeMartini? This is Angela, and I am the nurse caring for David DeMartini. He is resting well now. The doctor was in just an hour ago and said it might be possible to discharge him tomorrow. Are you planning to pick him up?"

"Yes, I am Davie's mom. The problem is I am up in Oregon tonight. We are planning to return tomorrow, but I don't know what the timing is. I can call tomorrow about noon and see how things are moving along. Would that work?"

"We try to get our discharges done in the morning. I have a number for Ted DeMartini, and we could call him. Is that agreeable?"

"That is my son and David's older brother. He is authorized to take care of Davie until I return. I am so happy he is feeling better."

"Madam, Davie is gravely ill, and the doctor thinks it is better if he is home with his family. I would have liked to have given you better news. We can support him but not cure him. We are sending him home with an oxygen service and medicines to make him comfortable."

"Oh, dear, I live in San Francisco, and I am a RN. I will care for him there. If you discharge him in the morning, he will go to his father's home. So the oxygen service can go there first, and then I will make the arrangements to transfer the service to my home. Thank you for the information."

Elly felt weak and leaned against the phone booth. Tears ran down her face as she clumsily pushed the door open. Todd was a few feet away, waiting with Fred. He saw the door open and rushed to be with her.

"You are as white as a sheet. Did you get some more bad news?"

"He's seriously ill, and the doctor is sending him home for comfort care. I am so worried about him. When he was born, I thought he would be caring for me in my old age," she cried out.

"Start from the beginning. I am confused."

"Ted put Davie in the hospital because he was having trouble breathing. Now they want to discharge him tomorrow with oxygen. I can take care of him, but I am so far ... away." She choked and burst into sobs.

Todd wrapped her in his arms and cooed in her ear, "We will be back before you know it and Davie will be returned to your tender care."

Chapter 17

The Agent or the Mark

Margot glided into her office with an air of triumph. "It is a magnificent day! The sun is shining. And I am going to look like the most beautiful queen." She grabbed her pink flamingo phone and dialed Arnold's number.

"Hello, Arney, how is my pal?"

"Not bad, could be worse. What is up with you?"

"I am going to be the most gorgeous woman at the Black and White Ball. And I want you to escort me," she said in her most sexy voice.

"I think we can arrange that. I was planning to go myself."

"Guess who had her surgery last week. Me, of course, I'm so excited I could burst. They are magicians. I got the very best artistic job you can imagine. I have the most luscious breasts and a real vagina. I can't believe how long I have wanted to feel and look like a real woman. Now my designer has made me a stunning gown that plays up my best qualities perfectly. You will be very proud to have me on your arm. We will make a super impression on everyone."

"I am pleased you are so happy with the results of your surgery. If you don't mind telling me, how did they do it? That was a huge step to take."

"Are you sure I won't gross you out? It was like this. The surgeon took my penis and used the flesh to make the vagina and clitoris. Then he used the bag that held my balls and made labia out of them.

I love the result, but I can't have any sex for at least a month. He says sex would just slash up his beautiful work. It's pretty tender right now, so it doesn't feel good most of the time. But it is healing, and I'm willing to be patient. I hope I'm not keeping you from something. I'm sorry I'm so wrapped up in myself. How is your health?"

"I have my up days and my low days, but I'm bearing up quite well. I hate going to funerals. I went to four last month, and this month I'm sure that it will be worse. It's so depressing to watch our friends drop one by one like fruit falling from the tree."

"I know how it is. My dear, dear designer has HIV, he told me. And my beloved hairdresser told me the same. I don't know what I'll do if they die. They are so dear to me and it's all so tragic. By the way, what has happened to that nice man you always had with you? I think his name is Mike?"

Hearing his name sent a shiver of remorse and fear down his spine. "I think he died of AIDS. I think I read about it somewhere. Very sad. I was fond of him."

"Hmmm. I thought you were so close to him that you knew his every heartbeat. I should think you would go to his funeral if he died. I thought you two were really tight."

"We had a falling out after Jacob died. I really have to go now, Margot. I'll call you when I get some details handled about the ball."

Arnold was sweating like a wrestler. *God*, he thought, *I miss that rascal. He is gone, and I hope JR has gotten rid of that body. I don't want it coming back to haunt me.*

"I'm putting money into a company that is working on a cure or a solution to AIDS. You would think after landing on the moon, it wouldn't take years to find a treatment for this disease that's killing so many fine young men," he said to change the conversation.

"Just a minute, Arney, Tell me why you and your fine young friends didn't practice safe sex all those years?"

"Back before AIDS, it was a magical time. We were so high on coming out of the closet. The parties—oh, those revelries we had—were full of delicious thrills, daisy chains, and free love. During that orgasmic time, if any of us had mentioned a condom, they would have been laughed out of the city."

"They aren't laughing anymore! And the parties have turned into funerals," Margot said sarcastically. "Was all that unrestricted love worth it? If you could relive those times, would you change anything?"

"Oh, there're plenty of preachers of morals out there. I don't like hearing it from you. Yes, we could have been less joyful and free, but we had come from a long history of shame and undercover love. The energy had been pent up so long it was like a balloon that suddenly popped. We were so tired of that careful life, and we needed to stretch our wings. There's no other logic to it. In a perfect world, I might have married a young man and lived happily ever after, but it doesn't work for the straight people. Why should it work for us?"

"I am a romantic, I know. I have never been wild. Maybe that is due to my feminine side. I never went to those parties. Maybe I am grieving that timidity as well as all the deaths. Some of us need to walk on the wild side once in a while, and others just watch from a distance. I am a spectator, and it is sad when I see what I missed. I love you, Arney, and don't you forget it. I know you have a busy day planned, so I will talk to you later."

***

Danny was folding towels when JR quietly came down the stairs. "Did yo' sleep well?" Danny asked with as much carelessness as he could muster.

"No," JR said and growled. "I kept dreaming of being lost and forgotten. I hope that isn't a hint of what my day will be like."

"Are yo' takin' to Sally today?"

"Only, if I can't avoid it. I don't feel much like playing like a sap so I can charm her."

"I got yo' some vittles in the back dat you can have fo' breakfast. It'll save going out and running into her."

"That's mighty nice of you. I'll take you up on that."

JR walked to the doors that led to the back offices. In a small kitchen area was a wrapped sandwich and coffee on the hot plate. He took the sandwich and a cup of coffee to the table and sat down to eat. Opening the sandwich, he found it was egg and sausage with some onion and relish thrown in. Quietly, he ate the food and felt better when he was finished. *Maybe my unhappy mood was due to hunger. I will drive myself crazy if I don't get out of this city. If only to be free so I can sleep better and worry less. The only way to do this is to convince Sally that I really am Bill. There is no better way. I have to internalize that so I can put on a convincing act.* When the last drop of coffee was drunk, JR carried the cup back into the kitchen area. *I should never have flirted with her back in Calgary. I was just so horny and wanted a piece of ass. I can't let myself get into messes like this. It will be my undoing.*

When he walked through the door, he heard a woman talking to Danny. That voice made the hair on his head stand at attention. JR backed into the break area and waited behind the closed door. *God damn, I am not ready to face her.* Inch by inch, he nudged the door open a crack and listened. He heard a woman's voice and the sound of her shoes tapping across the floor toward the front. The door opened, and then there was silence. He could see Danny coming toward him, and he backed away from the door.

"De coast is clear. Yo' can come out," Danny announced. "She was suspicious of de sounds coming from dis room, but I tol' her de cleaning lady was working in dere. She bought that. I think yo'll find she's as jumpy as yo' is, ol' friend."

"What do I owe you for all your kindness? I would be a bundle of nerves without your help," JR said with sincerity.

"Buddy, I's pleased as a rat wid de cheese dat yo' is not goin' to involve me in yo'r schemes. I don't want to go back in de slammer again."

"I feel the same way. I think I will go to my room and pack my bags. I will think about how I can use her jumpiness to my advantage," he said as he started up the stairs.

***

Elly sat up in bed and stretched with a hardy yawn. Todd rolled over and looked at her half-naked body with awe, but it was too late for lovemaking. He took her in his arms and said, "I would love to make love to you, sweetie, but we must get back to San Francisco."

"Yes, I know. I dreamed about Davie last night. He was laughing. But then I fell out of my chair or something, and he vanished. It was a nightmare."

Fred stood on his hind legs and put his forepaws on the bed and wagged his tail.

"I think this friend of ours wants to be taken for a walk. He probably needs to take a pee," she said as she wiggled out of Todd's grasp and jumped out of bed.

Within a few minutes, she was dressed in her jeans, a sweater, and her boots. Throwing on her jacket, she said, "I'm taking Fred for a walk. We will be back before you are dressed."

After breakfast Todd packed the car while Elly took Fred for another walk so he could rest easy in the car. She loved walking him. It was a time to think and sort out problems. It was always refreshing to walk among the tree-lined streets and see the people admire Fred. He would stand stoically while children hugged him and pulled on his ears. When he met a female dog, he would look, but then he would turn toward Elly. Then he would walk stoically along as if the female didn't interest him. It reminded her of Todd when he saw a beautiful woman while he was walking with her. The thought made her smile.

∗∗∗

JR sat on his bed next to his open suitcase. He was putting the last items inside it. Feeling the relief of another job done, he walked over to the window to look outside. He knew he was looking for Sally, but he really didn't want to see her. The street was almost bare. Returning to the middle of the room, he went to the bathroom and looked at himself in the mirror. He said a silent prayer to himself, *If I can trick Sally into believing I am Bill, then I will promise to punish the man who hired me to mess up that poor woman and kill that guy in California.*

He found himself pacing the floor, bemoaning his role as the frustrated fixer or doer. It was like he was losing control. Normally, his options were broader, and now they had come down to one puny choice. There had to be another solution. He had to think. He had to find a way out of his dilemma. In Cambodia, he would find a woman who knew the black arts. He would go to these shamans and ask if he would survive the mission he was on. The woman would rattle some chicken bones or read the tea leaves and give him an answer. Never did he find their advice was wrong or misguided. Regina must have psychics too. Maybe …

Later, on a whim he decided to solicit the advice of a spiritualist he met nearby. Walking to the door, he felt strong like he was more in control of his nerves now. He was so happy that he was taking two stairs at a time.

Danny looked at him warily. "Are yo' okay, ol' man?"

"Yes, I'm in fine shape. I'm going to meet Madam Sophie down the street and see what she says about my future."

"Yo've gone completely off de deep end! I can't believe wha' I'm hearin'."

JR simply smiled and carelessly boogied out the door. On the street he looked warily for Sally, but she was nowhere in sight. *Well, that is a good omen if I ever saw one. Maybe I am on to something.*

He paused at the clairvoyant's door before opening it. "Hello, Madam Sophie, are you free?"

"Darlin', for you I am always available. Come into my divining room. I have watched you walking up and down the street like a lost lamb."

Madam Sophie was a tiny older woman wearing a bright red, green, and orange dress. Her horn-rimmed glasses with red sequined frames made her eyes look large and luminous. Her graying hair was swept up in a bun, and her wrinkled pink face twinkled with mischief.

"I'll tell you all about your life, romance, and fortune. Just sit in this chair, and I'll transport you with supreme knowledge."

JR obeyed. She reminded him of his grandmother, and he felt he was in safe hands.

"Mother Sophie, tell me. Will a certain woman be kind to me?"

She took his hands and studied his palms. Then she took her cards and one by one laid them out on the table like they were the most precious jewels. Nodding her head, she said, as she pointed to a particular card. "This is an excellent day for revealing your true feelings for someone special. You'll enjoy creating a sense of intimacy and trust with her. Then you can enlighten your soul or share your most secretive thoughts."

Transfixed, JR was stunned by her pronouncement. "How do you know so much? You are truly incredible. Tell me more."

"Don't get mixed up in situations that surround you with people. Stay with small groups where you can be happiest. Then at some point you'll appreciate enjoying some peace and quiet by yourself."

JR hoped that didn't mean jail. "Will I be free to go where I want without restraint?"

Sophie's eyes narrowed and examined him critically over her glasses. "You want to be free of this woman, or do you want her without restrictions?"

"I would enjoy having a loving relationship with this woman, but is she dangerous?"

"You look like a man who can defend himself from a woman— unless she is dangerous in an intellectual way. I still think this is a good day to reveal your true feelings, and I don't have any negative psychic feelings that you are in any danger."

This was just what JR wanted to hear. "Thank you, Mother Sophie. You are wonderful. How much do I owe you?"

After they said their good-byes and he generously compensated her, he walked out of the door, feeling invulnerable. He even whistled to himself a song he had heard so long ago.

At the hotel JR was glowing with self-confidence as he walked in, and Danny noticed it.

"Well, yo' look like a new man. What did she do to make you glow like a teen dat jist got his first piece of ass?"

"She is worth every penny. I even gave her a big hug. I like the older ladies like her. They have so much passion for their art and invaluable experience. I used psychic old women in Cambodia when

I was scared shitless. They always gave me the strength to go on. I don't think I would have survived without them."

In the afternoon JR stood in front of his mirror and combed his hair. "Hmmm, I had better touch up the color in my hair a bit." He reapplied the henna to his beard and the hair on his head. He got his red plaid shirt out of his suitcase and put it on. He worked very hard to make himself look like the Bill Macintyre he'd imagined. The last touch was a Saint Christopher metal on a silver chain that he put around his neck. Before the mirror he looked perfect in his eyes.

JR walked confidently down the stairs and stood in front of Danny. "I'm ready to take on Sally! What do you think?"

"Wal don't yo' look good. Too good to go to jail! Good luck to yo'."

It took at least fifteen minutes to walk down to the park that was adjacent to Lake Regina. This was the perfect scene. There were very few people, and the trees were just showing some green as they were just waking up after a long winter. On the water were a few pairs of geese and ducks swam. They were the first migratory birds to have arrived from the south.

Halfway around the lake, he found a bench to sit on. He sat down and waited. An hour went by with no sight of Sally. Then in the distance he saw a woman by herself. *That could be my nemesis,* he thought. She was dressed in an overcoat and wool hat, and she was walking at a slow pace as she came closer. JR braced himself. He sat with his elbows on his knees and his head in his hands. As planned, she slipped up and sat down beside him. They sat in cold silence together for several minutes.

Then JR said, "Why didn't you continue on to Montreal when you had a chance? I thought you were so interested in visiting your family. Instead you have been following me around like a lost puppy."

"Let's drop the crap, Jason Roberts. I am an officer, and I want to bring you in for questioning," she growled as she flashed her credentials.

"You are a what! And who is this Jason Roberts character?" he said in feigned surprise and raised his head to face her.

"Don't tell me you don't know who I am, and don't act like you're not who you really are," she said with conviction as she put away her badge.

"So what has this man done that you are so hot to bring him in?"

"You are wanted in the States for several murders."

"I think you are mistaking me for someone else. The worst thing I have done is shoot a dog once," he said, frigid as an ice cube.

"Do you have some ID on you?"

JR got his wallet out of his back pocket and slowly took out his forged driver's license and handed it to her.

"You know, I don't think you think I am really some wild killer. You went to bed with me several times, and if I was a killer, would you do that? You would have refused to let me touch you in all those intimate places. Didn't you enjoy my caressing you? Would you have slept in my arms without a care, if I was dangerous?"

She was shaken, dumbfounded by the statement, and she looked at him with wide open eyes. "You are right. I trusted you, and I enjoyed it," she said shyly in a small feminine voice.

Then she recovered and snarled back, "I checked all the Bill or William Macintyres in the United States, and the only one who fits you is in Connecticut. But this license is for Arkansas. Explain that."

"I did live in Connecticut, but I left my wife and family there. Now I am running from a divorce court that wants to get me for spousal support. But that is a long way from murder. I swear I'm no angel, but I don't think it is worth an arrest."

Sally took a long look at him. "A side of me would love it, if you really were Bill," she said in that same feminine voice.

He moved closer and put his arm around her. "Let's go to a coffee shop and continue this conversation. It's getting chilly out here. I can feel you shaking."

She turned her face to his and kissed him on his cheek. "I find it very hard to resist you," she said with a smile on her face. "And you are right. I didn't think you were the right man when I went to bed with you. It is just my boss who thought I should follow you."

When they stood up together, JR took Sally in his arms and kissed her sensuously. He whispered in her ear, "I have missed you, babe."

The coffee shop was a few blocks away. JR was acting his best as a lover of women. He and Sally talked and laughed at their own stories. In his head he thought, *If I take her to my hotel room and screw her, then how do I get rid of her later.*

"Where are you going next?" she asked as if she could read his thoughts.

"I think I will go back to Arkansas. I have a lot of friends there, and I need to deal with the courts in Connecticut."

"Would you like to have a companion?" she said with a hopeful smile on her face.

"No, baby, you have a job here, and I am a drifter. You would not like my lifestyle. I have a divorce to go through, and if you were with me, it would complicate matters. My ex-wife would have a fine time raking you over."

Sadly, she sat there, and he almost felt sorry for her. "We could have a farewell dinner together and then go to my apartment for a nightcap?" she said.

He could not resist the invitation. It had been more than a week without a woman in his arms, and it was difficult to resist her. *At her place I could slip out in the wee hours and leave town without the teary farewells.*

They walked close to each other to a restaurant, and he had the best dinner he had had in months. Sitting across from Sally gave him a chance to look at her, and what he found made his member uncomfortable. He desperately wanted to have her then, but he could only verbally tell her how much he wanted to make love to her. She also wanted him. She licked her lips and touched his feet with hers. Under the table he caressed her warm thighs, and his fingers slowly inched up under her skirt. But he couldn't reach her sweet zone. Sally slumped in the chair, trying to let him touch her crotch. Halfway through the dinner, they asked for boxes and hurriedly left the restaurant, walking to Sally's apartment.

Once inside the apartment, Sally led JR to her bedroom, and they franticly started disrobing each other. They didn't catch their breath until he was on top of her, licking her breasts. She moaned her need for him while reaching desperately for his erect penis, and he teased her pubic hair to excite her and then licked her clit until she climaxed.

"How could you think I am a nasty criminal?" he whispered in her ear as he plunged his penis into her. She arched up to meet him so he would hit her G-spot, and she purred with every stroke by him.

"A woman never really knows a man until he is in bed with her, and I know you very well," she cooed in his ear as they both rested from lovemaking. "Every inch of you is full of manly warmth and love."

"Women are such wonderful creatures. They can have an orgasm and then plunge right into sex again while men have to rest in between. You are such an amazing, luscious being."

They made love for several hours and then fell asleep. JR did not wake up and leave as he had planned. In the morning he was torn between staying with Sally or leaving.

Over breakfast they discussed their future. "I must go, Sally. There are too many raw ends to tie up, but I can come back later." He wanted to give her hope of his return.

"I love you. You know that. In my profession I don't meet men I think I could spend my life with. They are like you, sort of transient lovers or real dorks I don't want to allow in my bed unless I am desperate. Maybe I need a new profession. I was educated as a barrister in England. But it is a very competitive profession, and I didn't do well. Now that AIDS is running around, my friends are getting married because they are afraid of sleeping with strangers. Have you considered that, or do your friends talk about that?"

"My male friends are concerned about AIDS too, but we just look at it as a time when we should use condoms."

"Safe sex doesn't sound too exciting to me," Sally admitted. "Oh, it is getting late. I need to call my boss and fill out a document that you can use to safely exit Canada. So excuse me for a moment."

While Sally made her phone call, JR sat and thought, *God, this woman is a gift. I have never been so unconditionally loved. Even my old mom did not love me so unselfishly. I don't want to harm her, but I never can see her again. Why did I come home from the war with such a chip on my shoulder? I could have gotten therapy, or I could have been retrained to do something legal. But I was crazy. I was taught to kill, and that is what I do best. I didn't value love, and now that I know what it is like, it is something I really desire.*

Sally came back to the table. "Well, that's taken care of, and I will get a new assignment later today. Here is the document you need to exit the country," she announced as she offered him the paper.

JR took her hand with the paper and drew her to him. "I am so sorry to be leaving you. I have never met a woman I would want to spend the rest of my life with. So I will try to contact you later." He kissed her passionately and held her close to him. "I love you, and I will never forget you. It is so hard for me to go, but I must."

A few hours later, he was walking into the lobby of his hotel.

"Christ, look what de rats drug in. Did yo' spend de night in de slammer?" Danny asked.

"No, I even have a plane reservation for late this afternoon to Chicago. So life couldn't be sweeter."

"Yo're utterly amazing. Next yo'll be tellin' me yo' were screwin' her all night!"

"She is an angel. I couldn't ask for a better woman in my life. However, she's in love with Bill, that man who is in her imagination. This life of mine, in reality, is a real inconvenience. I feel like Dr. Jekyll and Mr. Hyde."

$$***$$

As the car sped along the highway, Todd, Mr. Sanchez, and Elly talked about the scene of the fire in the Cascade Mountains of Oregon.

"Someone must be hiring this man, JR, that you think is doing the killing and all. You said that the killer was a professional, so who is he working for?" Elly asked from the back seat.

"We have less evidence to go by, but those with good motives are your two cousins, Hank and Leland. In addition, we are concerned about some of the board members, especially Arnold Smith and Margot Carter," Mr. Sanchez told her.

"Hmmm, Todd and I are going to the Black and White Ball coming up in a few weeks, and that will be a good time to observe all these suspects. I am certain they will all be there," Elly suggested.

Todd looked at her through the rearview mirror and said, "This is news to me. When is this ball? Do I have to wear a monkey suit to it?"

Elly looked up at him and said, "We have been talking about it, and one of the activities for this coming week is getting a gown for me. I will be happy to get a tux ordered for you, too."

Mr. Sanchez chuckled at his companions and said, "Elly, if you need an escort to the ball, then count me in. I love the waltz, and the intrigue is interesting."

Chapter 18

Research into a Future

The sun had set almost an hour ago. Todd and Elly eventually reached the DeMartini house. Jerry welcomed them and offered them drinks.

"Will it be scotch or whiskey straight?"

"Neither thanks. Where is Davie?" Elly said as civilly as she could muster.

"What boring drips you are. Davie is in his room. He was down in the living room, but I decided I wanted to reclaim the use of that room for myself."

Tired of Jerry's alcoholic behavior, Elly ran up the stairs to Davie's room. First, she knocked, and then she opened the door. The room had one small lamp lit, and the oxygen extractor hummed in the corner was the only sound. Davie was lying on his back with his oxygen cannula in his nose.

"Oh, my poor baby, mom's here. How is my Davie?"

"Missed you, mom. Please take me to your house. Dad has been—"

"I know, Davie. He can be insensitive. I think he is having trouble realizing that you are so ill. He is afraid of losing you, so he drinks more."

At this moment Todd opened the door. "How is my brave young man?"

"Sorry I ran off and left you with your Dad," she said then turning to Todd, "We need to get Davie and his stuff into the car so we can leave as soon as possible. I'll transfer the oxygen to the portable tank. Then you can hustle that extractor machine into the car. When you come back, we can help Davie down the stairs to the door together and then out to the car," Elly said in her best nursing voice.

Then turning to her son, she asked, "Did you have something for dinner, Davie?"

"Dad brought me some Jell-O and pudding. I am not hungry, Mom."

She smiled to reassure him and said, "I will make you some yummy chicken soup when we get home. Would you like that?"

It took many trips and rearranging to get the car loaded, but finally, they were off to San Francisco.

***

JR got into Chicago after dark. He got a taxi to take him to a cheap hotel. Once he was safely inside the room, he started to work on a new identity.

I need a persona that will work with the white-supremacists. I can bleach my hair blond. I can wear blue contact lenses, and my name can be Bjorn Ericson. That's it—a Swede. Thank you, Georgie, for giving me such a good idea for a hiding place. Now I need to investigate the white-supremacist groups so I can behave properly around them. The library is a good place to begin.

When his hair was blond enough and the paperwork was under control, he decided to find the library. He walked slowly down the stairs to avoid other guests while he decided what to ask the woman at the desk in the lobby.

The large rotund lady at the hotel desk had a crooked mouth that held a half-burnt cigarette. Her stringy brown mop hung limply at the sides of her head. As JR approached, he saw she was reading the newspaper.

"Howdy, how is your day going?" he asked the woman at the desk.

"It's fine. Do you have any more earthshaking questions to ask, or can I get back to doing my work?" she said with undisguised annoyance.

He looked into her round, puffy face and asked, "Do you have a street map of Chicago that you can give me?"

"Yeah, it's here. Where do you want to go?"

"I'm interested in the main library."

"Ha! I never, ever would have pegged you for the bookish type."

"I want the books to block my door so that lovelies like you can't barge in when I don't want you."

"You aren't my type, and if you were, I am not for sale. I have a nice man in my life, and I have no interest in opening your door," she hissed at him.

JR took the map and sat in one of the two worn chairs in the lobby. It wasn't difficult to find the library and the location of his hotel. He decided that since the library was only a few miles away, he could walk and get some exercise.

Each block had a different personality, and as he approached the main part of the city, the stores looked more prosperous and better maintained. Carefully, he followed the map to the steps of the library.

The doors were heavy with brass trim and handles, inside it looked like a palace of marble. Everywhere he looked, there was a display for children or adults with different themes and the appropriate books. Finally, he found the main desk and stood in line to ask a question. When he got to the desk, a young black woman dressed in a blue suit asked him if he was ready to check out his books.

"I need directions. I am doing some research, and I don't know where to start. Can you direct me to a place I can get help?"

"The elevator is right over there, or you can take the stairs. But you need to go to the third floor and talk to the reference librarian," she said sweetly.

He thanked her and went to the stairs. The broad staircase with its brass railing was a pleasure to walk up. Each step added excise to his body.

The young fellow at the desk looked too fresh with his rosy cheeks and red hair to be a librarian. However, he asked to help him, and JR obliged. *I'm so glad that the reference librarian is not black. It will make it easier to ask questions about white-supremacists.*

"My mother thinks my brother has joined a neo-nazi group and asked me to find some information on them. Can you help me with that?"

"Yes, let's look on the computer about your subject," he said in a businesslike manner.

JR was pleased that the man wasn't looking at him like he was a sociopath.

"Look, here is some information, and you can scroll through it to find the information you need," the librarian said, and then he went back to his desk.

Gingerly perched on a stool, JR explored the computer and found a magazine in the stacks titled *American Renaissance*. He thought, *A magazine might have a section of ads for different groups.* In the stacks he found the magazine with several articles. In one article he found a group in Texas called the Aryan Nations, which was founded in 1970, but it seems the FBI was interested in them and that wasn't good. *I need to look at more issues of this magazine.*

At the reference desk he asked the librarian where he could find more issues. The librarian took him to the shelves where past issues were kept. After some searching, he found the magazine with articles he could use.

Looking through the pages, he found an article on White Pride and JR found this information interesting. He figured it may be valuable in the future. In the back few pages of the magazine, he found a list of groups around the country. The one he was looking for was there with a phone number. He wrote down all of the information that he would need to find the group in Wyoming.

Walking confidently back to the librarian's desk, JR paused to thank him for his help. The young librarian was pleased with his success.

When he came out of the building, the sun was shining, and the clouds were parting. He felt it was a sign of good luck. Now he needed to find a way to get to Wyoming. The train system would be a good place to start.

***

It took several hours to move Davie back into Elly's apartment and get him settled comfortably. Elly didn't rest until she was sure everything was in its place and he had a warm bowl of chicken soup. She had planned ahead a week ago by making the soup and packaging it in serving-sized portions. Then she froze them. Now all she had to do was defrost them and serve. Even with all her planning, she felt exhausted this night. It had been a long day. When she walked into the living room, she flopped down on the couch next to Todd.

"How is my baby?" he cooed in her ear.

"I am not discouraged, but I'm sad that there is no evidence for convicting this man who has done so much harm."

"I am sorry the wheels of investigations are not perfect and we don't always get our man. Sanchez was counting on this detective in Canada, but she said that she was sure this man was not the person we are looking for. He was just a bloke running from a divorce court. The trail has become quite cold now. I feel as frustrated as you. Let's put our energies into finding out who hired this professional killer and whose ashes were in that cabin. I am very proud of you finding that note in the bottle. It is all we have, except for a few bone fragments."

"Tomorrow I am going to get serious about planning for the Black and White Ball. It is fascinating that Sanchez wants to come to it. He will be good company for you. I am interested in meeting his wife."

"What do you think about Davie's health?"

"Yes, we should talk about that. He is not doing very well. In fact, that's an understatement. The doctor said that because of his youth, Davie's immune system wasn't well established and that is why his disease process is developing so fast. Tomorrow I am going to call Dr. Andreesen and have him look at Davie again. I don't know what else to do. I feel so helpless."

"He sure didn't look good tonight. It was such a shock to see him so pale and ill."

Elly cuddled closer. "It is not a good future to look forward to. I wish I knew what was next. I just can't imagine losing him."

"Jerry's alcoholism is getting out of control too. I don't think we should let him have Davie at his house in the future. I don't consider him responsible," Todd acknowledged.

"Oh, you are so right. I was feeling rather guilty letting him stay there while we were up north," Elly mumbled.

Todd felt like talking. "Alcohol is one of the worst drugs this country deals with. Not that I am advocating bringing back prohibition, but it is a problem nobody wants to manage. Sometimes I feel so helpless. You can't arrest a man in his home if he is drunk. We can get him for assault and abandonment. However, it is hard to prove abandonment unless there is real measurable harm. Like Jerry, he was in his home. Davie was safe in bed but isolated. Remoteness is not a crime, even when it is caused by alcoholism, unless he locks him in a closet. It is just his drunkenness that is the problem. He was not there next to Davie if he needed him. That really angered me," Todd confessed.

Elly turned to Todd and kissed him lovingly on his lips. "I am so glad you are in my life. What would I do without you?"

"I love you too. Let's get to bed. We both have a big day tomorrow, and we need our rest. Besides, I love to hold you in my arms all night." With that, he scooped Elly up in his arms and carried her into the bedroom. Fred trotted behind them.

After the door was closed, Todd laid Elly gently on the bed. "I want my baby to sleep well tonight. Do you want me to stay or go home to my own apartment?"

She looked up at him with an earthmoving smile and drew his head down to hers so she could kiss him sensuously. "I need you in my arms and in my bed. I can't face the future without you right here."

He smiled and cooed in her ear, "I want to accommodate my honey in any way I can. And if keeping your bed warm is what you want, then I am willing to do that. However, I may want to make love to you too."

"Well, if you want to do that, we had better get our clothes off," she answered as she started pulling his shirt off.

Chapter 19

The Aryan Nation

"Good morning, Ms. DeMartini. This is Dr. Andreesen's exchange. I will have him call you when he is available."

"This is so frustrating. I think I will call Clair and see if she is interested in shopping for evening gowns."

While eating his breakfast, Todd looked up at his woman and smiled. "I hope your day gets better, love."

"On the top of my list is calling about getting a nursing assistant to help me with Davie's needs. He is requiring more care, and she or he can watch over him when I am not here. Then after I talk with Andreesen, I will have a date with Clair. So I have a busy day. Are you going to find a criminal to catch today?"

"Very funny! By the way when you go to get your gown for this ball, please get some information as to where I get my monkey suit. Meanwhile, I will work on who killed who."

After Todd left, Elly went to Davie's room and gently knocked on the door. "Davie," she called. There was no answer, so she opened the door.

Davie was making an effort to sit up, but he was so feeble that he could barely move and flopped back on the pillow. "Mom, what is happening? I am so heavy I can't move."

"Sweetheart, you're just weak. I want to talk to your doctor about how we can make you stronger. Right now I want to give you some breakfast, and I've some hot cereal. Would you like that?"

"Yeah, that would be nice. Not much, just a little. I get nauseated when I eat too much."

Elly set up the tray and brought it to Davie. She had just finished with setting Davie up to eat when the phone rang.

"This is Dr. Andreesen answering your call."

"Thank you for calling. Davie is worse. He has red and purple splotches on his face and torso. He is so weak he can't lift himself, and he is on oxygen at three liters. I am worried about him."

"The red and purple lesions are Kaposi's sarcoma, which is a tumor that we are finding is only observed on persons with active HIV infections and immune-suppressed patients. When their immune system is so compromised, this carcinoma takes over. It is a type of cancer that attacks the capillary walls, especially on the skin. They are ugly, but we don't want to tell Davie that. Has he lost a lot of weight too? Is his fever back, and does he still have diarrhea?"

"I haven't been able to weigh him, but he looks thinner and frail. He has a low-grade fever and some diarrhea and vomiting when he eats too much. He doesn't have a good appetite, and after a few bites, he is exhausted and won't eat more."

"Hmmm, if the diarrhea persists, then he should be admitted where we can support him with intravenous therapy. How is his breathing?"

"His respiratory rate is fifteen to eighteen, and he panics if we move him and his cannula falls off. He is drinking water well. I keep a bottle at his side, and he drinks it."

"So I want you to keep him drinking water. It sounds like you have things under control. I will call tomorrow again to check on him."

"I am going to hire a caregiver, and I want to get him a hospital bed so that he can be out here where the family is."

"Good. I will talk to you tomorrow."

***

The train to Denver left Chicago about ten at night. JR found an empty seat and settled in. He had one thin blanket that he had lifted from the hotel where he had been staying. By wadding up his jacket, he made a pillow. There was nothing comfortable about his position, but he was inebriated and exhausted enough that he fell asleep. All night long though, he awoke when the whistle blew and when the train stopped on a siding to let another train go by. When this happened, he would open his eyes and stare out the window at the blackness. The night seemed endless as the wee hours crept by like a sloth in a tree.

In the east at about 7:45, the sky was turning pink and gray. The rows and rows of fields were changing to suburbs and then business buildings and then finally the station in Denver.

JR had drunk a pint of whiskey to make himself sleepy. Now he had to get his possessions together to get off the train in his wobbly condition. The train station was large with a café for breakfast. JR decided he needed food before he could move on to the next means of transportation. As usual, he chose a table in the rear corner. It made him nervous to have anyone behind him. You never knew who could be there waiting and able to recognize him. He chose a simple breakfast of eggs with hash browns and bacon. Taking his time, he ate slowly and watched the people. The meal helped sober him up, and his mind became sharper.

Two hours later JR was on a bus to Wyoming. The seat he chose was next to another empty one, so he could spread out. As the bus bounced along, he tried to sleep again. The miles rolled by like a slow-moving tortoise. The hills leveled out every once in a while and revealed snow-covered pastures. It was a mesmerizing landscape dotted with farms and ranches. Then it switched back to dry hills the shape of the humps on the bison that once roamed there so free. The occasional tree dotted the landscape; they were starting to burst forth with new green leaves. Spring was shaking off the snowy coat, and the blades of grass peaked through.

JR was optimistic with a cold lining of worry. *I have known white-supremacists in the past but only as individuals. Together in a group, they could be dangerous. My anxiety is that they may not accept me, and I may not be able to hold my tongue when they rave about the various ethnic groups they hate. When I was in Alabama, I met some KKK members who arrogantly told stories of harassment of black people and they even hanged them. Many of my friends are black. Danny is one of them. He would not be happy to know where I am going. I have had some ferocious, gut-wrenching arguments with the KKK, and I have no interest in repeating that experience. Keeping quiet is the best defense though, and I do have Georgie to help me get oriented to these people. I just hope they don't attract the Feds.*

The bus stopped every four hours or so. They were limited to find places where the riders could eat and use the facilities. One of these breaks was in the city of Cheyanne, where they stopped for lunch. JR called George to check on his arrival arrangements.

"Hi, George, I am here in Cheyanne, and we are leaving in a few minutes for the north. What is planned? Is someone meeting me in Kaycee?"

"The head wizard here is going to meet you at the bus stop in Kaycee as planned. He may bring someone with him, but when I came, just Wiz was there. They will be on motorcycles. You can't miss them. They will be in black from head to toe."

"What are their names?"

"The head wizard is called Wiz, and his sidekick is called Bud. They will put you on one bike and your bag on the other one. They have already gotten some information on you, and they are going to be interested in more."

"I have to go. The bus is loading. I will see you soon."

***

By lunchtime Elly had arranged for a hospital bed and a wheelchair, and they were scheduled to arrive in the afternoon. She especially wanted the nursing assistant there so she could go shopping. Just then the doorbell rang. Elly rushed to the door so the bell would not wake Davie. Fred followed to protect her.

"Mrs. Jones? I am Grace from the agency. You have a need for a caregiver?"

"Yes, please come in. My name is Elly, and my son is Davie. He is the one you will be caring for. At the moment he is sleeping. Also, this is Fred the dog. He is very protective."

"Is Davie an infant?"

"No, I thought the agency told you. He is fifteen with an HIV infection, and I have gloves for you when you are cleaning him or doing anything that might involve bodily fluids."

"Oh, I see. I have heard so much about HIV. Is there a separate bathroom I can use?"

"The doctor tells me it is a virus that you can't catch easily unless there is blood-to-blood contact. I am providing gloves that will protect you. The one bathroom should work. You can ask me anything, and I won't feel uncomfortable answering any question."

Grace didn't have a chance to answer because just then the doorbell rang again.

"That must be the hospital equipment people with the bed and wheelchair," Elly said as she walked with a purpose across the room and opened the door.

"Hello", Elly directed them to put the hospital bed by the window so that Davie could have a nice view. "Grace, if you could please make this bed, I would appreciate it. I will get the bedding. I want you to meet my son too."

Grace cautiously followed. On the bed was a very thin boy not much younger than her. He was colorless except for the red and purple splotches on his body. She had never seen anyone as ill as this boy, and her heart went out to him.

She sat down on the chair at his bedside and called his name. He opened his eyes.

"This is Grace, Davie. She is going to help you up into the wheelchair and bring you into the living area." Elly covered the wheelchair with a sheet and a towel to make it softer.

As they wheeled Davie into the larger area, Elly was giving directions to Grace about food and water for Davie.

When everything was settled, Elly changed her clothes into a stylish suit and called Clair. "Hi, I'm ready. Can you get away?"

"I can meet you at Margot's store on Maiden Lane in an hour or less. Take care. Are you driving?"

"No, I am going to take a taxi with Fred."

"With whom?"

"Todd got me a retired police dog to protect me, and his name is Fred. I'll see you there."

Elly slipped on her fashionable high heels, and with Fred on a leash, she slipped out the door. The taxi was waiting at the main door. While riding downtown, Elly thought about her son and wondered how long he could live and if he would get along with Grace.

Margot's store was full of women. Elly walked stately to the counter and told the woman there that Margot was expecting her in the display area.

"Darling Elly, how pleased I am to have you in my store. I understand you want a gown for the ball," Margot purred like an overfed cat.

"Clair is coming too. We both want to look smashing. I hope you don't mind Fred. He will be a perfect gentleman."

"We don't usually allow animals in here, but we can make an exception for you."

Elly could not help noticing that Margot was being nice to her for a change. "You seem so happy, Margot. Is your business doing well?"

"Yes, exceptionally, and I have a lot to be thankful for. I have a wonderful man in my life," she said as she twirled her scarf over her left shoulder. "Do you want to wait for Clair before I bring out my amazing collection?"

"I can wait for Clair. Do you have something to drink like a cup of coffee?"

"Why yes, how selfish of me not to offer. Please forgive me. Do you like cappuccinos?"

"Oh, how divine, Margot! You know your customers."

However, as Elly waited, she worried. *That is how Maria died. She drank a poisonous potion that was meant for me. Maybe I should sip it once and leave it.*

Just then Clair waltzed in with a smile on her face, wearing a gorgeous iridescent white silk suit. "You know, Elly, I love shopping with you. I enjoy it better than I did with your sister. I always had to be careful what I said when I was around her. She was so suspicious, jealous and lacking trust... Hey, you have your friend with you. I just love dogs. They are excellent companions."

"This is Fred. He is so smart and protective of me. I know about mistrust. I got this cappuccino, and the first thing I thought of was Maria dying from drinking that poisonous hot cocoa. . . Let's tell Margot we are ready to see her creations."

***

Todd was just going through some paperwork when Jim came into his office. "Are you ready?" Jim asked.

"Righto! I hate keeping the boss and everyone waiting."

As they walked to the elevator, Todd told Jim about Elly finding the note from George. When they reached the conference room, they put aside their conversation.

"Greetings, everyone! I know you all want to find Maria's killer. We found some evidence that George Collinger may have died in that burned-out cabin in the Cascade Mountains of Oregon. This is all speculation at this point. However, a note was recovered that was written by George." Todd waved it in front of them all. "We have verified the handwriting. I am putting it on our board right under George's picture." Turning back to his audience, he added, "We are looking at some burned bone fragments to identify the DNA. It'll take several weeks to get the report.

"Now, on to the investigation of the killer, Jason Roberts, known as JR. The FBI is on his tail. They thought they had him in Canada, but that didn't work out, although Sanchez is questioning the thoroughness of the Canadians. So when we hear more, we will let you know. Jim is going to tell you about searching for the person who hired JR."

Jim marched to the front of the room and took the microphone. Pointing to the board with Mike Nikcols's name on it, he said, "We have set up an investigation to try to find Mike Nikcols. We are checking all the flights, buses, and trains, but we haven't had any luck. I am assigning John and Pete to find the last person who saw him. I also need volunteers to investigate and stake out a watch on various members of this Longacre board of directors. We need to know who they talk to and when. We will meet when we have more information. Are there any questions?"

Several officers offered to investigate the board members. Jim had them come forward, and he took their names down for the record. In addition, he assigned each one to a suspect.

***

The wretched red sun was just setting on the western horizon. JR had been waiting for his ride for a couple of hours. He shuttered as the creeping fingers of night spread slowly across the plain. As he paced impatiently back and forth for the fiftieth time, he saw in the distance a plume of dust and two motorcyclists roaring his way. They pulled up one on each side of him. As the cycles purred, the bigger guy took off his helmet. They were both dressed in black from head to heel, but everything was covered in fine reddish brown dust.

"What's your name, mister?" the man without his helmet barked.

"Bjorn Ericson. I am a friend of George Collinger."

"Then give your bag of crap to my friend here, and you hitch a ride on my bike and hang on. I don't need any bodies to round up."

It took a few minutes to tie JR's bag on the motorcycle. When JR jumped on the cycle, the driver lurched forward so suddenly that JR almost slid off. Clinging on desperately as they flew down the dusty road and across the barren landscape, JR wasn't sure he would make it to the destination, wherever that was, in one piece.

It was dark when they arrived at a ten-foot-fenced compound with a huge gate. Inside the fort were several buildings with their lights on. His clothes and face were covered with grimy dirt like the bikes.

"Ya look like a fucking nigger. I should just shoot you, but I guess you will clean up decently," the first bike rider said in a menacing growl.

JR recoiled at the sound of that term. It boiled in his brain as the symbol of hate.

The man turned abruptly and went to a water spigot with a hose and turned it on. The blast hit JR and nearly knocked him over.

"Hey, cut that out. You're drowning me," he screamed as he shivered in the cold air.

"Well, we can't have you walking around looking like a dirty nigger," the man said and laughed.

When the man turned to shut off the spigot, he noticed that their leather jackets had the "white power" sign on the backs. JR trembled and wondered what he had gotten himself into.

The two men dragged him to a wood building with a porch. His teeth were chattering in the cold, and he longed to be dry and warm. He prayed they would not leave him out on the freezing porch.

One man pushed the door open, and JR made an effort to enter it. But the two men blocked his way. In cold anger JR pushed his way in with force and was immediately rewarded by warm air. The larger of the men lashed out with a blow to JR's back shoulder. In a fury JR spun around and leveled the man viciously with a well-placed blow.

"Stop your damn fighting!" said a gruff voice from the other side of the room. The whole room became silent.

"Who the hell are you that you think you can come in here and start a fight!" the large man said as he briskly walked across the floor toward him.

JR stood there, shaking as the water dripped off him, and he stammered, "Do you always greet your new men this way?"

The man who seemed to be in charge was clean-shaven with a bald head and a solid, square body. He scrunched up his face with a hate-filled look as he circled around JR, looking him over and sizing him up like he was a bull he was buying.

"I have a lot to offer you," JR started but was cut off by an arm that came across his neck, strangling him.

Wiz said, "I don't give a fuck what you are or who the shit you have been. Here we all start at the bottom, so as soon as you are dry, you can clean the latrines for a start tonight." Then when he felt JR relax, Wiz let him go.

Tentatively, JR walked over to the wood burning heater in the center of the room and stood there, sucking up the heat. As he stood there in this cabin so far from everything he knew, all he longed for was peace and freedom. Sadly, this place wasn't starting out well, but he hoped it would get better. He was famished and yearned for hot food. It was like he was a caged beast that required feeding, but no one was not interested in doing that. Could he ask for food, or was that out of the question?

As he sucked up the heat, he looked around the room. He was not surprised at seeing the red banners with a black swastikas burned across them. *My dad fought in WWII, and he taught me that was a symbol of hate. The old man hated the Nazis and all they stood for.* At the other end of the room, there were Confederate flags. Both banners and flags were interesting. *These people are from the past and lost in the gruesome old world of unforgiving racial hate. I fought against the Khmer Rouge and the Vietcong, which were both hate-filled groups, and now in this democratic country, there's this group of mad men. Hopefully, these men are more reasonable than the Nazis, communists, and other dictatorships. I learned to kill, but not because of hate. I killed for money.*

It was almost midnight by the time his chores were done. In the process he had learned about the layout of the cabins and had become oriented to some of the men and women who lived there. No one went by their real names. All of them had nicknames. The leader was Wiz, and they called JR ... Bee. All that knowledge was good, but on the sour side, he still was not given anything to eat. Exhausted and starving, he finally found a bunk that wasn't occupied. He collapsed on it and instantly fell asleep.

Chapter 20

The Offer

"Hello, Elly," Hank's deep voice sang out. "This is Hank Dreassler. What are you doing this fine day? Would you have time to have lunch with me?"

"Sure, what brings you to San Francisco?"

"I have a case at the courthouse, and I will have a break around noon. The case is simple and should be over this morning. I can come and pick you up or meet you downtown. Which works better for you?"

"I think it would be best if you picked me up. That way if you are held up, I wouldn't be stranded in some restaurant, drumming my fingers, wondering what happened to you."

"That's great. I have to go now, but I will see you about noon. I will call before I come."

Putting down the receiver, Elly realized her delight at hearing his voice. He was much different than his brother, Leland. Where Leland was aggressive, Hank was more reserved. He reminded her of her father. As she reminisced over her father, she remembered he was considerate, kind, generous, loving, and aristocratic. Did Hank have all of these attributes too?

Like a teenager waiting for her special date, Elly watched the traffic in the streets below her windows, looking for a familiar shape. She decided the time would fly by faster if she concentrated on her chores. She started with feeding Davie and getting him up in the wheelchair. And the time did go faster. When he was settled, she went to her own room and surveyed her wardrobe. After she discarded several garments, she chose a blue and purple dress that was very feminine and accentuated her lavender eyes. By noon she was dressed and ready for his arrival. When she emerged from dressing, she was pleased to see that Grace seemed to have everything under control. She was even able to gain Fred's confidence, so Elly felt comfortable leaving Fred with Davie.

It was shortly after twelve when the call from the guard in the lobby came. A few minutes later, she opened the door. Hank was clearly happy to see her, and he kissed her lightly on the cheek.

"God, it's nice to see you. Let's have a nice afternoon. Do you have the time?" he said as he gazed at her face with affection.

"Yes, I would love to spend the day with you," she confessed.

This was the first time they had been alone with each other. Both of them felt the magnetism that was drawing them together, yet each respected the other and didn't want to move too fast. They had lunch at a small intimate restaurant. He explained his case to her, and she told him about her trials in taking care of a child with failing health. None of this was romantic, but they both appreciated that they could share freely their individual challenges.

After lunch, they drove to the Palace of the Legion of Honor, where they could walk and take in the sweeping spectacular views of the bridge and the coastline. The salty air was sensuously soothing. Hank felt protective and took Elly's hand as they walked. She liked his warm hand in hers. He liked having her close to him so he could inhale her perfume.

"Are you coming to the Black and White Ball?" Elly asked.

"If you are there, I will be wherever you are too. You know, I want to dance with you and hold you close to me."

"You can do that here now," she replied with a chuckle.

He stopped, turned to her, and hugged her. "I don't want to rush you. You are very special to me, and I want to get to know you slowly like a graceful waltz. I have waited a long time to have you alone, and I don't want this experience of discovery to be short."

With this, Elly could only hug him back. "You are dear to me, and I, too, would like to know you better."

"You know, I would love to show you the ancestral home that's all yours now. In fact, you need to come to San Mateo soon and sign some papers that transfer the property to you."

"Wow, there is so much I don't know about this estate."

"Arnold is not doing his job very well. I don't think he has been very healthy. I will keep you informed of the signing that's coming up."

"Thank you, Hank. It's nice that you are looking after these legal transactions for me."

"I don't have any power. I just wanted you to come to my part of the Bay Area to sign these papers. You could do the signing here in San Francisco, but I thought it would be more fun for you to see the property again. Elly, you have not been there as an adult. What I am proposing is that you come down and stay in a hotel room so that you will feel safe from my brother. Then we can show you the property at your leisure ... and wine and dine you as well."

"Yes, I would love to do that." She looked at him seriously. She marveled at his finely chiseled face, his warm blue eyes, the dimple in his chin, and the way his hair flopped over his forehead in a comical way. Most of all she liked his goofy, sweet smile. She imagined that he would easily win over a jury with his charm.

He couldn't help himself from nuzzling her neck. She kissed him on the cheek, and he held her close. "It would be delicious if I could see more of you. Is that possible?"

"Yes, yes," she breathlessly said as she cuddled closer to him. "You can call me anytime. I am home, nursing my son, and I would love to talk to you. I get depressed and lonely, and any time you are in San Francisco, I want you to tell me so that we can have lunch or dinner together."

"What about Todd?" he said, pulling away from her.

"I don't know. Before today, I didn't know you had any interest in me. I love Todd, but our lives are going in different directions. I know Todd's intentions, but I don't know yours. I cannot have relationships with you both at the same time. So as you say, we must go slowly so that no one gets hurt. The real question is what sort of relationship we want to have together."

Hank looked at Elly seriously. "I could love you, but you are the boss. I will be a good loser, or if you chose me, I will love you with all my heart, my little rabbit. I firmly believe that we should not taste the fruits of love until we are sure this is a lasting relationship. I will be patient and never force myself on you. I am in love with you, but I have been keeping that rose under my hat for a long time. You are in charge of my soul and Todd's too. He is a nice man, so may the best man win." As he looked at her so intently, he wanted to kiss her sensuously. It took all his strength to resist her.

"There you go, calling me that little rabbit name again. You did that when we were in the woods, and my whole body responded with relaxation. Where does that name come from? It seems so familiar, but I can't remember its source."

"When you were a little girl and you were frightened by Annette's bulling, I would always protect you, and I called you my little rabbit because you reminded me of my pet rabbit, with big soulful eyes that spoke volumes. Today I am a man, and you, Elly, are this beautiful woman. But you will always be my little rabbit."

"Oh, Hank, now I can remember you and me. You were the only sweetness of those days," she humbly said and reached up and hugged him with a new feeling. In his ear she continued, "I will think about my choice, you or Todd. Please keep in touch on a regular basis. I need you close to me to understand my path through this darkness. First and foremost, I have to focus on my son and his failing health. I want you to know that I have strong feelings for you too, Hank. I thought I would never get you alone to tell you that. I want so much to have a happy life. The problem is that I don't know the best man with whom I should spend that life. I am fortunate to have a choice. My heart must guide me."

They walked back to the car, feeling lighter as if each had unloaded a heavy burden on a person they trusted. They were old childhood lovers with barriers to still surmount before they could really be intimate as adults. He first held her hand and then drew her toward him by putting his arm around her. The sweet warmth of her yielding body was intoxicating. She was the woman he had always dreamed about, and now he wanted her and was not going to lose her.

***

"Get up, ya' lazy bum," said the man gruffly as he shook JR.

Dragged up from a deep sleep, JR awoke, startled and ready to defend himself. He came up lashing out with his fists ready.

"Whoa! I'm just the cook, and you're assigned to help me. Now git up! Time is a wastin'.

Numb, JR dressed and followed the man to a shed where the cooking was in progress. It was before dawn, and the sky was streaked with orange against the black clouds. The air was crisp, and the ground crackled with ice.

"I'm putte'n you in charge of the tatters over there. Keep dem move'n so they don't burn."

Laboring all morning raised his anger because his blood sugar was low and he had no control. Maybe they wanted him angry so they could kill him. He had to be patient and wait for an opportunity to show them he had value. George was cooking too, but neither could communicate with the other. Finally, everyone had been fed, and now the work crew could eat. It was only eggs and spuds, but it tasted like the best meal he had ever had. He also got to talk to George, who now went by Pot. That was his name they called him, and Pot called him Bee.

"Just hang in, and you will get along with everyone in time."

"It is nice to really talk to someone I know. Most of the time I am doing forced labor and not allowed to talk to anyone."

"That will change. Right now they are super worried about security, so they think every new guy is a fink. They won't trust you until we do a raid, and they will be watching you to see how you conduct yourself."

"Are they going on a raid coming up in the next week or two?"

"Yeah, there is a ranch in the valley where some black men live, and that is prime picking for this gang."

"Do they ever get caught?"

"The sheriff doesn't like these colored guys either, so sometimes he joins us."

"Have you heard of any FBI activity?"

"They only come when they are looking for a high-profile killer who goes after federal offices or people."

"Well, I hope you are right and no one finks that I am here."

***

In the afternoon Elly took a nap on the sofa and dreamed of Hank. They were little children again, and he was teaching her how to throw a ball. She awoke and felt like she could remember him always being kind to her even when it wasn't diplomatically good for him to do so. *I am not ready to break my engagement to Todd, yet the Black and White Ball may change my mind. Todd doesn't have any interest in it, and if I get there and see it his way, then he is my man. However, I should not use anything as trivial as a ball to shift my alliances. Todd is so good with my boys. They really like him. But they are growing up. At least one is. And I don't want to marry him just because he is a good father. The real question is which man has the same values and interests me. Which one is someone I can talk to about art and music with ease? Maybe I should not be engaged. I am still evolving into a new person who will soon own a mansion. I need someone who will look good in that house. He must be important-looking and imposing like my father and grandfather.*

She got up and stretched. "How are you, Davie? Would you like some ice cream or something?"

***

Dr. Andreesen was just dictating a report on one of his patients when his receptionist buzzed him. "Yes?"

"Doctor, Mr. Smith is here and would like to talk to you."

"Very good, please send him in."

Larry Andreesen stood up to welcome his patient and friend. "How nice to see you, Arnold. Are you still taking that medication I gave you?"

"I wanted to ask about your research and how it was going."

"Well, we have done some tests, but we still do not have a vaccine or a real cure. We need to establish how the virus dismantles the immune system. That is a key to finding a treatment."

"Are you treating the DeMartini kid? How is he doing? I am worried about him. Is he dying?" Arnold asked with unease.

"I was not aware that you knew this family. I really can't talk about my patients with you. That is not ethical. What you need to do is call them yourself and ask about him. Just because you are my secret benefactor, I cannot discuss what I don't divulge to my colleagues or my partner. I don't talk about your medical history with anyone either."

"I'm worried about this boy, and I can't go to see him. It is out of the question," Arnold said as he paced the floor and wrung his hands. "I was his lover, and I think I gave him AIDS," he cried out.

"I'm very sorry, and I will not tell anyone what you are telling me. I am bound by my oaths. However, do you realize that child is underage? In a court of law, it could be construed as statutory rape."

Arnold was visually grieved for himself and for Davie. "I know," he said in a small voice. He sat down heavily in the nearest chair. "I have no one to talk about this. I can't talk to the family, and Davie has not called me for several days."

"I am sorry. It is such a painful tragedy that HIV came along and disrupted so many lives. My partner and I have been monogamous since we teamed up. We met in medical school and have been living together ever since. If more gays had wired up their lives this way, we would not have the crisis that we have today. Young men and boys would not be dying. Lifestyles do make a difference."

"Some of us do not meet the perfect partner and settle down so easily. It is not just about lifestyles! You do not have to be so sacrilegious with me, Larry Andreesen."

"It grieves me that you are suffering with this disease, and I think you are doing a good job of righting the wrongs with your generous contributions to research."

"That's what I came to talk to you about."

***

The phone was ringing in Elly's apartment. Elly ran to answer it. "Hello?"

"Hi, love, I have to work late tonight, so unless you want a late dinner, we should plan to not see each other tonight," Todd said.

"It is okay. I will spend the evening with my boys. I hope your work goes well. If it changes, then call me, and maybe we can get together," she said with a voice dripping with disappointment.

"Okay, I will call if things change. Love you. Bye."

Elly sadly put down the phone receiver. She loved her son, but he was getting weaker and fragile. He was never a big conversationalist, and now it was even worse. Diner was made up of leftovers, and Elly dragged herself through the motions of tending to Davie. Later that evening they watched a movie on television, but it bored both of them.

At about nine o'clock, the phone rang. Elly thought it was Todd again, but she was delighted when she realized it was Hank.

"Hello, sweet cousin, I am surprised to find you home tonight. I just wanted to call and tell you how much I enjoyed having you all to myself today."

"I thought it was so nice for you to ask me to spend some time with you."

"Elly, you sound so sad tonight. I want to cheer you up. Let me tell you a story. Do you remember when we were kids? You were around four or five, and I was seven. We were the odd kids. Our siblings, your sister and my older brother, were idolized by the parents. This left you and me as the spare children, and we stuck together because of it. My dad thought I wasn't his because I was a blond. He thought my mother had had an affair and I was the bastard. When much later my father had our DNA tested, he relented and accepted me, but by this time, I was thirty years old and couldn't care less. But I am getting off my real story. I always liked you. When I was seven, I grieved when your mother took you away. Over the years I thought of you, but I couldn't find you. Now here you are, a gorgeous woman. I can't tell you how joyful it has made me to have been with you alone today. You have given me hope that someday we may share our future together."

"Oh, Hank, I also have been thinking of those days when we were little children caught up in the lives of our parents. You were always kind to me. I am sorry you suffered because you were blond. I am looking forward to seeing you again. I want to feel you near me and hear your voice in my ear. I think you could be the soul mate that I have always longed for."

"Next Saturday is the Black and White Ball. I will be there early so I can grab you and waltz all around the ballroom with you. I can't tell you how much I want to take you in my arms. I love you, and I can't wait until you break that engagement. My hands are tied until you act."

"I feel I shouldn't change my life as long as my son is so ill."

"Look, I will be patient. I have waited thirty long years already. Another year or two won't matter. The most important point is that you need to be happy."

"You are so kind. I don't think he is going to live that long, unfortunately."

"Would it be appropriate for me to visit him? I would like to meet your older son too."

"Yes, yes, I would love to have you meet both boys. They are very dear to me."

"Okay, we have a plan. First, I dance all night with my beautiful darling, and then we plan to meet your young men. Good night, dear one. May I call you every night?"

"Sure, I can always use a boost."

***

On Friday night, the White Aryan Power members were having a meeting. JR hung around the back of the group since he was not an integral part of them yet. It happened after dinner, and he had actually had a decent meal that night for a change. He hadn't eaten a lot and only what was left over, but it was satisfying. He was adjusting to the routine, and he always obeyed every order. He had always been a good soldier.

The wizard was talking about the various groups they felt were not controlled enough by society, like the so-called minorities. They used so much hate-filled language that JR wanted to cover his ears or walk out. Unfortunately, they would not tolerate that behavior, and he wasn't ready to rebel.

After the meeting, they cleared the floor, and two men with guitars started to play bluegrass music. Many of the couples began to dance. The rest of the men and women clapped their hands. Most were smoking pot and drinking beer. One of the matronly women who seemed high on something came over to him unsteadily and said, "How about dancin' wit me, boy?"

JR felt he could not refuse. Who knew who she was connected to? He did his best to imitate the other dancers, and she wore herself out before him. Next a younger woman asked him, and she had more endurance. This one had a sense of humor and laughed at his mistakes. He had never thought of himself as a dancer and didn't take the ridicule personally, but he tried to laugh too. A blonde with big tits tried to tease him by forcing his head down on her breasts, but he resisted. When she grabbed for his crotch, he deftly moved aside. One by one, the women attempted to seduce him, and he knew if he flirted back with the pretty ones, he would be punished. At around midnight the party broke up, and JR was given a rest. George gave him a smile of approval, and everyone slept well that night.

Chapter 21

The Ball

"Good morning, Todd. I just wanted you to know that I have your tux here, and you can pick it up today or tonight," she announced over the phone.

"Thank you, my sweet. You know I am only going to this shindig because I know you want me to and you need an escort you can trust."

"Oh, come now. You know you are going to size up the characters on the board with Mr. Sanchez. I am sure they are all going to be there, and when they get a little liquor under their belts, they will say things they would not say in the board room."

"Sanchez is certainly interested, and he likes to dance, which is not one of my talents."

"Never mind, You will look handsome, and that will be good enough for me. So I will see you at five?"

"So early? The ball doesn't start until eight or nine."

"Suit yourself!" she said, and her voice was full of disappointment. "I want you here so we can have a light supper before we go, and I need time to prepare it and eat it. I should not have to explain why I want you here early. I just need you!"

Elly hung up and sat steaming about Todd's reluctance about going to this dance. *Maybe he senses that I want to dance with my cousins and everyone else and not really with him. I do not want to get out on the floor with everyone looking and have to teach him how to waltz. Maybe we are growing apart. Maybe marriage to anyone is a bad move at this time.*

Davie's bed needed changing, and she went over to urge him to get up into the wheelchair to free up the bed. He was so light these days that she could pick him up and place him in the chair unaided. She kissed him tenderly and cuddled him as she picked him up.

"Would you like to sit by the window this morning? The sun is out, and the view is very nice."

"Mom, I would like to call my lover," Davie squeaked.

"Do you have his number?"

"I think ... it is in my ... backpack," he said with some effort.

"Okay, I will get the backpack. I think it is in the bedroom. I will find it as soon as I make your bed. Dr. Andreesen is coming today to see you, and I want everything clean and neat so he knows I am taking good care of you."

She tucked a warm blanket around him and after combing his hair, she placed him in front of the huge floor-to-ceiling window with a panoramic view of the city.

It was several hours later when Dr. Andreesen arrived. "Good afternoon, Ms. DeMartini. How has Davie been?"

"He seems to be a little weaker, and his breathing is more labored each day. His heart rate is ninety-five to hundred. Respiratory rate is twenty-two. His BP is 124/96, and he is on three liters of oxygen."

"Thank you. Let me examine him. I will need him in the bed."

"Yes, I will assist you," she said as she started wheeling him over to the bed.

Later after he had finished with his examination, he suggested to Elly to find a quiet place for them to talk. Elly took him to the bedroom that she had converted into an office.

They sat facing each other, both feeling uncomfortable.

"I want you to know that Davie doesn't have long to live. I also wanted to know if you knew who his lover was. I don't like to see young teenagers with AIDS, and it could have been caused by a pedophile."

Elly cringed at the statement. "I don't have a clue who this man or boy was or is. He calls him ASS. I don't know if that is a nickname or the initials of someone. Does it really matter whether or not we know his name? The damage is done. Nothing will bring back my joyful, lighthearted, sweet child. He was so filled with potential," she said as the tears ran down her face.

In his mind, Dr. Andreesen wrestled with the problem of knowing the man who did this but not telling her. *Maybe I should call the police, but then she may not really want to know. Maybe I am fighting an old wound of my own, and I'm projecting my experience on this child.*

"Does Davie have contact with this man, his lover?"

"He wants to. Just this morning he asked to call him, but I could not find the phone number that he said was in his backpack. I have no problem with them communicating even if it looks like a criminal rape or something. That's one way we could find out who this man is. If he has AIDS, then he may be the cause, but I am so afraid that we may accuse the wrong person. I would feel very badly if that happened."

"That is all I wanted to discuss with you today. I must be going."

***

It was a cool evening for March. The ball participants were covered in furs to keep warm as they entered the ballroom. The coatrack concession was doing very well that night. Elly and Todd were some of the first to enter the ballroom, which was festively decorated with hanging balls of mirrors that glittered in the colored lights and black and white streamers hung from the ceiling.

They had been arguing all the way there, and they were exhausted by their disagreements. Elly felt let down on this occasion that she had looked forward to, as it was starting out on the wrong foot. Todd dragged her over to the bar and ordered some cocktails for them to help them relax. Elly protested because she never looked at alcohol as a way to cure her problems. Deep in her heart, she knew their stress was coming from Davie's illness. But it was a full barrel of liquid turmoil, and when it moved, it splashed out into other areas of her life. She stood limp with a frown on her pretty face. Even her gorgeous gown could not hold up her mood. In her hair was a headdress of sparkling white abstract forms that matched the beaded embroidery of her black gown. She tried to raise her head and pretend nothing was wrong. Todd brought her a margarita, her favorite drink. He led her over to a table and commanded her to sit down.

"Please perk up. You have looked forward to this stupid ball for weeks. I am so sorry you got some bad news today. We will deal with it, but tonight let's try to have some fun."

She didn't answer, and instead she slowly sipped her drink as she gazed blindly out across the dance floor. Since they ate before the ball, the alcohol was less numbing than if they had had empty stomachs. Todd had never seen Elly so despondent. He wished that Sanchez and his wife would arrive soon so that Elly would have someone else to talk to and dance with.

At about 9:30, the place was beginning to look crowded. The air became filled with fragrant perfume and sound of silk gowns whirling with excitement. The orchestra was playing all the favorite waltzes as the dancers glided across the floor. The Sanchez couple arrived and was dizzily dancing like it was the most beautiful activity in the world. Elly sat sadly with her head in her hands, wondering when she would start to enjoy herself. Todd was on his second round of drinks when Hank and Leland arrived.

"Hey, what is with you two? Why aren't you out there dancing? Come on, Elly. Let's see that stunning dress you are wearing. Come dance with me so that I can see it," Leland said as he took Elly's hand and helped her up. "You look like you lost your best friend. Tell me about it."

They glided out across the floor with ease. As they pirouetted, he whispered in her ear, "What is wrong, beautiful? You are usually full of joy, and tonight of all nights, you should be dancing every dance."

"You are right. I shouldn't let my failing son interfere with my social life," she blurted out and her eyes welled up with tears.

"I'm sorry. Hank told me he was critical, but in the abstract it is not as real as waiting for ... We want to support you in any way that we can," he whispered in her ear and then decided to change the subject. "This is a wonderful dress you are wearing. All this beaded embroidery from your shoulder to your hand shows off those graceful arms of yours. Then there is your exposed back down to your waist. Oh, I know there is sheer fabric there, but it is attracting a lot of looks from other dancers because it shows off your elegant back."

This got a big smile from her. "Thank you. I needed that. Please dance on. I love your hand on my back. You guide me so perfectly though all the rotations of this Viennese Waltz."

Several dances later Hank tapped Leland on the shoulder and asked to take Elly for a few dances. Hank gently took Elly in his arms, and he danced with similar skill as his brother, but with maneuvers his brother didn't try. Gracefully, he turned her away from him so that her dress flared out and showed its fullness. He dipped her close to the floor, and his face was close enough to kiss. Then he would bring her back to him as if he was making love to her.

With grace, they moved about the dance floor like well-matched gears that meshed together with each note of music. Hank whispered encouragement in her ear. "You are definitely the most beautiful and well-dressed woman here. I love looking in your eyes and watching that smile creep across your lovely face. I can never get enough of you, my dear. I know while we are out on this floor, you are all mine, and I have you lovingly in my arms."

This inspired her to kiss his neck. "I love being in your arms. I feel your inner strength, and that makes me strong." She snuggled close to him and whispered, "I feel so safe in your caress. It gives me gentle comfort. I hope you really adore me because I feel myself slipping into that sweet place myself."

This prompted him to hold her tighter, and he kissed her hair. "Yes, I love you. I have always loved you. I am waiting for you to let me make love to you."

"I think you are ... right out here on the floor. In front of God and all the people at this ball, you are making love to me. I have never danced with a man who was so sensuous that held me so securely in his arms. I am swept away by your charming grasp of me. I would love to have it go on forever."

Hank chuckled and said, "Baby, when I do really make love to you, you will feel the thrill down to your toes."

She smiled wholeheartedly and squeezed his hand. Bending down, he kissed her passionately on her lips, and ardently, she kissed him back. They were breathless as they slipped out the back entrance. The fresh air cooled them off, and they talked and laughed together like they were long-standing lovers.

"I told Todd tonight that I didn't want to be tied to an engagement. He told me I was upset about my son. But it is different, and it isn't all grief. My life is changing, and like waltzing, I am whirring through a world I still do not understand. When my son dies, I am going to Europe, and I am going to travel until I know exactly who I am and what I want in life."

"Let's go back inside so you don't catch cold."

"You are so thoughtful. I am a little chilly."

With a loving skill, Hank slipped his arm around Elly's back and drew her to him. "I never want to let you go."

They glided over the dance floor with expert ease for several waltzes. Elly felt so proud to be dancing for the first time with a man who knew how to actually dance. He knew how to make her look elegant. She loved every moment of feeling like a real-life fair lady.

"When you go to Europe, may I visit you? I would love to show you the most romantic city, Paris. There are so many dreamy places we could explore together."

Elly smiled up at him. He was a glorious, elegant man. *I have never been in the arms of such a cultivated, intelligent man who is full of so much romantic passion. Is he for real? Does he want me for my money, or is he genuine and falling in love with me? I certainly see so much I could love about him.*

"Yes, I would love to have you show me Paris. I have always wanted to see that city and get to know some French. Do you speak French?"

"Oui, madam, I will teach you how to make love in French, how to cook their cuisine, and generally everything about their culture."

"You are going to make it hard to spend any time away from you. You would make it so much fun, and I could play the part of the naïve American who is experiencing her first romantic visit to Paris. . .Oh, I just saw Arnold Smith. He is dancing with Margot."

"Elly, why do you sound so fearful?"

"He is an awful man, a moral eunuch. They don't have any proof, but I blame him for the death of Jacob at my bank. I'm suspicious of him. He made me feel like a cockroach at the board meeting I went to, and I have not been back since. Nor have I forgiven him."

"You are too uncomfortable to go to the board meetings? Dear Elly, I can help you with that. We can go to the next one with Fred on a leash and you on my arm, and we will take control. Why didn't you tell me about this sooner?"

"I was ashamed that I was not ... powerful enough. Annette didn't have any trouble because she had gone to those meetings since she was a little girl. I didn't have that training."

Hank looked at Elly's doe eyes, large and fearful, and he said, "Little rabbit, we will go over every move before we pounce on them. Unfortunately, I think the board members have been skimming off the cream of this estate, while no one was looking. Then you came along, and they didn't want you interfering. They didn't want to stop living sumptuously on your wealth, so they scared you away. You need to get an independent audit. I can be your legal counsel without charge, and we will clean their clocks."

Elly hugged him with delight. Hank knew that he had found the key to Elly's heart. "Maybe you will realize how valuable I am," he said, laughing.

With that, he waltzed her around the floor a few more times just because he loved having her in his arms and having her smile up at him.

"I would so enjoy dancing with you for hours more, but if you only dance with me, the gossips will think that we are in love and that we can't let go of each other."

Hank laughed and said, "We are, sweetheart, but I know what you are getting at. And you probably need to get back to your son. I will call you tomorrow if we don't dance anymore tonight."

"Sweet Hank, please come back to ask me to dance later. I would rather be with you than anyone here, and you know that."

He left her at the table where she was sitting before. Todd did not look at them. He was deep in conversation with a brown man. Hank gave her a conspiratorial smile as he left.

When Hank was a safe distance away, Joe Sanchez got her attention. "Is that your cousin you were dancing with?"

"My cousin and childhood friend, I must apologize. I should have introduced you to him."

"He is an excellent dancer, and you seemed to enjoy his company."

"Yes, we talked about various family members and such. I played with him and his brother when we were in grade school. They were with me in the mountains of Marin County when we encountered that awful man who shot at us." She turned away to hide her tears as she recalled that painful time.

As Elly was recovering her composure, Sanchez got up and came to her side. "Elly, may I have the next dance with you?"

"I think that would be very nice."

Mr. Sanchez was an easy-to-follow, gallant dancer. He knew the waltzes and how to lead a woman so she would look her best.

"Elinor, I want you to identify the various board members here."

"Sure, right behind you is Clair Minix and her husband, Dr. Darrel Minix. She is wearing a lovely white dress with black ruffles. Clair runs my cardiology clinic. She is a good person and my friend. I don't worry about anything she has done. But no one has questioned her about the other members, and that needs to be done. She may have experiences or observations to offer."

Joe maneuvered her around so that he could see this couple. They were a handsome pair, and they seemed to enjoy each other.

"Over by the bar is Margot, who is an excellent designer of clothes. She made Clair and my gowns. She works in a high-end clothing store I own. Margot is with a man you need to really investigate. He is Arnold Smith. I loathe that man. My cousin Hank, who is a corporate attorney, offered to help me put him in his place with legal action."

"Be careful, Elinor. If he is as big a problem as we think he is, you should stay clear for now. If he feels threatened, then someone else may die."

As they waltzed around the room, Elly identified various people he might be interested in. Around midnight Mr. Sanchez brought her back to the table where they had started. Leland and Hank were sitting there, but Todd was nowhere in sight.

Mr. Sanchez was introduced to the cousins, and then he walked toward the bar to ask Margot to dance.

When he was far enough away, Leland announced, "You missed the fireworks. Todd gave Hank a dressing down. It was like Todd was acting the part of the cuckold. He has a temper!"

"The main complaint was he felt I was monopolizing you," Hank said and motioned her to sit by him. "Let's do some more mon-op-oliz-ing!" Hank said with a smirk.

"We shouldn't be too hard on him. He is a good man, and he is realizing he can't compete with you," Elly offered with a laugh.

"By the way, he said we are to take you home, and then he left in a huff," said Leland.

"Now, does that mean your home or mine?" Hank teased.

＊＊

Todd, still dressed in his rented tux, glowered at the paperwork on his desk. He had gone to his office because it reminded him less of Elly and his problems. Reluctantly, he started to go over the paperwork and started to sign off on important pages. He was drained, but he didn't want to go to his apartment and lie wide awake in his empty bed.

By four in the morning, sleep overtook him. Three hours later Jim was shaking him awake.

"Hey, buddy, you are still in your monkey suit."

Todd yawned. "I didn't want to go home."

"Tell me about it. I am sure that you need to get something off your chest."

"We had a fight, and when we got to the ball, she danced for a couple of hours with her cousin Hank."

"Did you get to dance with her?"

"I'm just not good at that waltz crap. She danced one dance with me and dozens with her cousins." He paused to get his thoughts straight "She and Hank looked like they were ... enjoying each other too much. Then she is off dancing with Sanchez, which was okay, but while they were gone, I got in a steamy argument with the cousins over them taking up all of Elly's time. That was sour apples, I know. I lost control of my temper."

"And I bet you were drinking too. If you want Elly, you have to learn how to dance and all that upper-crust business. And most importantly, you need to learn to like it without the alcohol."

"Before the dance we were fighting over my not wanting to go to the ball, and she tells me that she wants to break our engagement. She had some bad news about Davie, and she was very upset. I thought we should not go, but she was hell-bent on dancing. Later

I thought she wanted to be there just to be with Hank. He made her happy again."

"You need to give her some space while she is dealing with a dying child. That can't be easy. I can't imagine losing one of my kids. I would go out of my mind. See, you talk to her about the investigation, and Hank can talk about subjects not connected with her problems. I can see how she might find that comforting."

"Yeah, maybe you are right. I will give her a few days to recover, and then I will start a new approach to win her back."

"Try taking her out to a nice place with soft romantic music. Take some dancing lessons. Win her over with loving support. She didn't say she never wanted to see you again, did she?"

"No, nothing that harsh, just that she did not want to marry me in May."

"Well, it doesn't sound like a lost cause. She needs to focus on her son, Todd. I know in my family the kids come first. You just have to adjust to that," Jim advised.

Then he shifted the conversation to addressing Todd's exhaustion. "Buddy, I think you need to go home and get a shower and some sleep. I can take care of any loose ends. And cheer up. The world hasn't come to an end."

Chapter 22

Several Days Later

Wyoming mornings were full of birds, and one could enjoy the sweet smell of spring after a cold, dark winter. JR had just finished his chores and had stepped out to refresh himself. He felt he was adjusting. It was reminiscent of the military. There were the same chores and discipline, but he didn't miss marching around. However, what was really different was the sex. The women smelled like they had been screwing all night. It both turned him on and made him frustrated. The women didn't interest him, but they just made him lonely. He realized he missed Sally.

He lit up a cigarette and took a big drag. The smoke curled up in the air, and made him feel less solitary. Shattering the peace, out of the cabin came Fetchit, the wizard's messenger boy.

"Hey, Bee, the wizard is having a meetin' at noon. He wants you there."

"Okay, what are we all discussing?"

"We're havin' a raid comin' up. I'm realla' excited 'bout it, ain't you?"

***

"Hi, love, I miss you. Call me when you can," Todd said on the answering machine. Elly stood in a trance, listening to the message. She was screening her calls this way. Todd was not someone she wanted to talk to quite yet.

The phone rang again and went to the answering machine. "This is Hank calling."

She hastily answered, "Hi, Hank, it is so nice to hear your voice."

"Were you so busy that the answering machine took over?"

"No, I was screening my calls. There are so many salesmen asking me to buy something."

"I know how that can be. I am calling because I have those papers for you to sign. When can you come to San Mateo for a signing date?"

"How about tomorrow? Ted can be here, and I can come to see the property too."

"Wonderful. I was also wondering if you would like to meet my mother."

"That would be very nice. I will dress accordingly."

"So you can be here by noon? Are you taking the train?"

"Yes, I don't have a car at the moment. I will need a hotel room too."

"Hmm, I like the sound of that. I will plan dinner someplace romantic with good food to give us plenty of energy. By the way, let me pick you up at your apartment. That is safer than you taking the train."

"Thanks. I would feel better driving down with you. That way we can go directly to the property. And don't let yourself be too presumptuous. I would love to sit by a warm fire, cuddled in your arms. That's what would really please me, but we can let nature take its course."

"Then you shall have it. I have something to show you too. It's a surprise."

"Now you are making me curious."

"I will see you tomorrow."

Hank hung up the phone and then nervously dialed his mother's number.

"Hi, Mom, do you mind if I come over and bend your ear a bit?"

"Why, darling, what is this occasion that you want to share it with me?"

"I'm thinking of getting married."

"Oh my, I never thought I would hear those words from you. What does Reggie think of this? Or are you marrying him?"

"I haven't told him my plans. I wanted to get your advice first."

"It is the first time you have asked for my advice," she said and chuckled. "When can I expect you?"

***

Charlotte Davis Dreassler always primped before guests arrived, even when it was one of her sons. She was a tall, elegant, older woman who had had many plastic surgeries on her delicate face, and she showed off her youngish face with a stylish hairdo. She plumped the brocaded cushions, straightened the books on the table, set a vase of flowers in an empty spot, and applied her lip stick. Then she perched like a bird on her nest as she anticipated her youngest son, Henry James.

At two o'clock the doorbell rang, and the maid answered it. "Madam, it is your son, Henry. May I show him in?"

"Yes, Georgia, I am expecting him."

Her gray eyes twinkled at seeing him. At one time she had been a great beauty, and all the young men of means had flocked like crows around her, fluttering their wings in excitement at the chance to talk to her. Now she seldom was in the company of men, and she missed them.

Hank strolled into the room and approached his mother. "Mom, you look ravishing today. Isn't that a new perfume you are wearing?"

"I think you smell the flowers. Come sit by me and tell me about your plans."

"Well, I would like to marry Elinor Longacre. She is a sweet, very real person and a good match."

"What does Reggie think of this proposal?"

"He doesn't know about it yet."

"Surely he saw the papers. The fashion page had your picture with Elinor all over it. And you looked like you were very friendly."

"I hid the paper from him."

Charlotte got up and went to the window to clear her mind. "You are asking for trouble, Hank. It was only five years ago when you came out of the closet and declared that you and Reggie were lifelong lovers. Now, I know you want to argue the point, but he has feelings that you are trying to avoid. Do you want to marry Elly for her money, or do you have some interest in a real matrimonial arrangement?"

"If possible, I would like to marry and have Reggie too. I can send Elly off to Paris once in a while and then play with Reggie during her absence."

"Have you ever thought they might both object? Let me tell you a story. David Longacre loved Elly's mother, but his father refused to sanction the marriage and forced David to marry my sister. David tried to love Elly's mother and keep his real wife at an arm's length. We all thought it was so horrid. As a result, we didn't like Elly's mother, and we didn't like the way he treated my sister. So it was then Elly and her mother were driven away. David was left with a wife he didn't like, let alone love. It shortened both of their lives. I now realize that my sister should have married someone else. I miss her. . . I don't have any ill feelings about Elinor. I was privately pleased when Elly inherited the Longacre estate."

"Would you like to meet her tomorrow?

"You are not getting the moral of my story. One man cannot give his love to two people. I firmly believe that. You are going to regret this if you don't really love Elly enough to give up Reggie!"

"I will talk to Reggie!" he said in an overly loud voice. Then in a softer voice he said, "Elly is coming tomorrow to sign some papers. I would like bring her to visit you. I want to offer to her Grandmother's necklace. Do you approve of that?"

"Now I understand you truly are serious about Elinor. I hope it doesn't blow up in your face, love. Yes, of course, I would be delighted to see her. I imagine she has grown into a beautiful woman. She showed beautiful potential as a little girl. However, I feel I can't bless this union unless you give up Reggie. By the way, does she know about him?"

***

An hour later he was in his office, which was adjacent to Reggie's. Reginald Sloan came from a respectable family. His dusky complexion and his arched eyebrows gave him a look of a man who liked to always have his own way in everything. He was a Stanford graduate. His skill with witnesses was well known in the corporate world. It was his penetrating glare that reduced his witnesses into confessing anything, and that made him well appreciated. Hank and Reggie met in law school, where they became roommates and eventually lovers. Reggie appreciated the way Hank could spell out intricate logic, effortlessly and Hank coveted Reggie's abilities to manipulate people. They made a formable professional team. Whenever they won a big case, they would celebrate with wild sexual parties with just men. Leland, Hank's brother, never came to these bashes. At this point in time, Reggie and Hank lived in separate homes but shared the keys and had an understanding that either could drop in at any time without calling first.

Now, Hank had to tell Reggie that tomorrow he was tied up with a ... client and needed privacy.

"Okay, so you don't want me dropping in?" Reggie said. His face was deadly serious with his clenched teeth. "What is up that you are not telling me?"

"It is just a family thing. This heiress is coming to the office to sign some papers, and then I thought I would take her to dinner and bring her back to my house for a nightcap."

"You have never kept any of your family from me before. Did you ever think that this little meeting might hurt my feelings?"

"This is Elinor Longacre, a cousin of mine, and she doesn't know I am gay."

"Oh, God, I thought you lost your fear of being gay years ago."

"I want to marry her ... for her money," Hank mumbled under his breath.

Reggie slammed the door shut and marched across the room and yelled, "I heard that. What the hell are you pulling off? Are you going to tell her about me? Or do I get swept into the closet? I am not going to share you!"

"I don't want to upset you. I want to continue our relationship both personally and professionally. I still have feelings for you, Reggie!"

"Are you suggesting one of those ménage à trois? If you are, then I want to know her really well."

"I hadn't thought that far ahead. I don't know if she will agree to a threesome. Nor do I want to share her that way. She is a cool lady, and I admire her."

"And more importantly, she is worth a fortune. Can we get her to sign over her wealth and then conveniently drop dead?"

***

JR walked slowly to the meeting. He didn't want to get there too early because he wanted a place in the back row out of sight and out of range for volunteering. Inside the meeting room, there were several men and women standing around, chatting with one another. In a corner some were sitting, and others were standing. They were telling jokes, JR figured, since they were laughing. He looked around for Georgie and saw him in the back. That was a perfect excuse to move to the back of the room.

"Hi, Pot, what's up?"

"They want to plan a raid. . . Sounds risky to me."

JR leaned over to Georgie and whispered, "Do they know I was in the Special Forces?"

"No, I just told them you were running from the law because of a murder."

"Oh, thanks! I didn't need that introduction. Maybe that is why they don't have much respect for me. . . Like you, I'm worried that they will attract the Feds."

The grand wizard entered the hall, and all got silent. He walked in with an air of authority and sat himself at the table in front of the members who were all scrambling for their seats. Most were sitting at attention.

In a loud voice, the wizard announced, "We are going to make Wyoming white again!" This was followed by a big cheer. "We have planned a raid on a nigger ranch up north." This announcement brought more cheers with foot stomping and clapping as the group shouted over and over again, "Make Wyoming white again!"

When they had finely quieted down, the wizard gave them his plan. "I want you new people to know that no one refuses a raid and nobody squeals. We shoot finks and deserters. Now let's get organized. This is a raid on some uppity niggers who live on a ranch north of here. As you know, the Aryan Nation wants to cleanse this state of any colored persons, and tonight we are doing our part. Our plan is to have an all-white state like Idaho. We are going to make them think that the wrath of hell has come to make them feel unwelcome.

"So now I am going to tell you how we are organizing this raid. I want all you guys who are new and have military experience to line up on the right side of the room. Then I want all those with experience with raids to go to the left side of the room."

Getting up slowly, JR took Georgie's hand and dragged him to the right side of the room.

"What are you doing?" mumbled Georgie.

"You can't hide. You were in the army ten years ago. If I have to go, I want someone with me I can trust."

"*Quiet!*" the wizard commanded. Then he counted the numbers in each group. "Okay, we have thirteen former servicemen. They are group one. And the ten who have experience with raids are group two. Now I want the members of group two to select one or two from group one to orient to our procedure tonight."

With this order, the men of group two surged across the room to the men in group one and paired up with them. JR tried to keep a low profile, but several men gathered around to share their experiences with him.

"It's easy as sliding off a roof," said one man with a chuckle.

"Yaw," said another. "Most of the time the dudes just scatter in fear when we arrive."

"So what do you have to offer us, mister group one?"

"I can show you some martial arts, if you are interested," JR suggested.

"On the raids I have been on, you don't need any fancy arts 'cause they just run as fast as they can if they know what's good for them."

"So you don't carry guns or any ammunition of any sort? How do you scare them?"

"We come bursting in, yelling, and carrying on like wild tigers. It scares the socks off of most of 'em."

"Do you cover your face so they can't identify you?"

"Yeah, ski masks, and we all look alike. Wiz says if we all look the same, it will confuse them and make them more nervous. He says in the old days, they wore hoods of white and burned crosses on people's lawns. Now we just burn the crosses and yell at the niggers."

"When are we doing this raid?"

"Soon. When Wiz says go, then we get gowin'."

Chapter 23

The Proposal

Elly preened in front of the mirror and wondered how Hank's mother would receive her. She was still of childbearing age. There was no fat on her, and she dressed conservatively in a black suit with a red silk scarf. The red heels matched the scarf and were worth considering, but they were too flashy. So she chose some sexy black creations with gold heels. They added six inches to her height and made her slender legs look elegant.

She was startled out of her reverie by the doorbell chiming. Carefully, she hurried to the door. The last thing she needed was to slip and fall. Her designer shoes were not for running. Fred followed her to the door as he always did.

"Hi, Mom, wow, you look good. Where are you off to?" Ted asked.

"I have to go down the peninsula to sign some papers for a piece of property I inherited. I wish you could come with me, but I won't be back until tomorrow. I need you to watch over Davie."

"How is Davie?"

"He is stable. He likes having Fred here, so I am leaving him with Davie to keep him happy. The attendant is here too. Her name is Grace. There is food in the fridge and snacks for you. I will be home early tomorrow."

"How are you getting down there and back?"

"My cousin Hank is picking me up and bringing me home. I am in good hands. By the way, there is a number for you to call if there is an emergency with your brother."

A few minutes later, the doorbell rang again.

Elly opened the door and greeted Hank. "So nice to see you, Hank. Please come in and meet my sons, Ted and Davie."

***

As they drove south, Hank told Elly about the house. "It has been years since you have seen it. It is now on the national registry of historic houses, and for several years the estate has offered tours to groups. However, I asked them not to have any tours today. I didn't want them to distract you from the experience."

"All I remember is that it was a big place and I was always getting lost."

They were driving up into the hills into very nice neighborhoods, and then they came to a driveway with a gate. Hank used a code on the keyboard at the side of the gate, and then it swung open. The large house in the distance was more than a hundred years old. In the foreground was a beautiful formal garden. As the gate exposed the scene, the gardens opened up to French gardens, with hedges, roses, small manicured trees, and fountains.

"Oh, it is so lovely. I don't remember it this way."

"When we were little, this area was one great lawn. But in later years, the board decided to save water and mowing charges. This garden actually uses less water."

"That is fascinating. It is much more beautiful and in keeping with the house."

"Over there are the parking lots for those groups I was telling you about, but we are going to drive right up to the door."

As the car approached, a man came out to greet them, opened the passenger door, and announced, "It is my pleasure to welcome you, Elinor Longacre, to your ancestral home."

Elly took the hand extended to her. "To whom do I owe this welcome?"

"My name is Jackson, madam. I am in charge of running the staff at your home."

"Thank you, Jackson. The garden is stunning, and I am sure the house is also well maintained."

Inside the door in the grand foyer, the members of the staff were lined up. Elly slowly went and met each member and said something nice to each individually.

Hank stood at the head of the line and beamed in pleasure at Elly's manners. He was very proud of her. When she finished, she dismissed them to go back to work. This left Hank and Elly alone. Elly noticed a large portrait of a woman on the entrance room's wall.

"Who is this lovely lady in the picture?"

"That is your great-grandmother, Elinor. She is your namesake, Elly. Do you know you were named after her? She is your grandfather's mother."

"Is that why my name has a different spelling? I can't tell you how many people and institutions misspell my name. Now I can be proud of it and the spelling. She is lovely, and she has my hair and eyes. I suddenly feel more connected to this family and feel their love even though—"

"You have made your grandfather proud of you today. Here you stand, taking command of your ancestral home. Don't worry about your birth. I am sure they are looking down on you and loving every moment of your discovery."

"Let's see the rest of the house. Isn't this the library?" Elly asked.

They toured the ground floor and then ascended the stairs.

"I can't wait to show you the nursery."

"Oh, Hank, that is not my favorite room. Annette would lock me up there and accuse me of locking her out. As a child, I hated that room. It was a symbol of my pain."

"There is a picture I want you to see, and it is in that room."

As they entered the nursery, Elly hung behind Hank because this room had so many aching memories. The nursery was large with various toys on display and a wicker daybed near the window. On the dresser Hank took a large picture and showed it to her.

At first look, Elly recoiled. It was an old photograph of Annette, the nannie she despised, and some other children.

Hank saw her discomfort and said, "Elly, don't move away. Please look here where you and I are standing."

"That scrawny little girl with the pigtails is me ... and this tall boy with his arm around me is ... *you*?"

"You're so right. I have wanted to be close to you all my life," he said as he took her in his arms and kissed her sweetly.

Elly beamed up at him and took his head in her hands and kissed him sensuously. "It's so nice that I no longer have those braids and you don't have braces on your teeth."

"It is better than that, dear one. You now own the house, the furniture, the paintings, the grounds, and me ... if you want me."

"Would you live here with me?" she teased with a wink.

"Would you be my bride? Then I would share this house with you. Let me show you the bedroom the ladies here call the bridal suite."

When they left the nursery, Elly clutched the photograph in her hands. They walked down the hall to a door, and Hank showed her in. The room was all done in white with pale pink trim. On the large bed was a silk cover that had pale pink roses scattered on it.

"You know whose bedroom this is, don't you?"

"Annette? Her mother? Who?"

"For a while your mother and father used this bedroom. That was when this room was full of love. You were born here. Then when your father married Annette's mother, he never slept another night here. From then on, this room was just for the women."

Elly wandered over to the window and looked down on the garden. "It is very sad room of lost love," she said wistfully.

"I have always thought of it as your birthplace, and that isn't unhappy at all. By the way, while we are here, I want to walk in the garden with you. I really need to talk to you, and I think that is the best place to do that. However, the ladies have fixed a lunch for us now, and they are serving that on the veranda."

They had a simple light lunch of tiny sandwiches and miniature fruit tarts with tea. The table had a nice linen tablecloth and a bouquet of flowers. The beauty of the setting cheered Elly up, and she was smiling again.

"Did I tell you today that you look ravishing? I love that red scarf against your face. It brings out the sweet rosy colors in your skin. You know I love just looking at you."

She smiled coyly. "Did you make that hotel arrangement for me, or do you want me to stay at your home?"

He smiled. "I would love to have you sleep at my home, and you may do that. But I have a reservation as you requested at a quaint little hotel I thought you would like."

Smiling, she reached for his hand and held it. "You know, no one has treated me so respectfully. If I slept at your house, could I sleep with you?"

"Yes, I think that could be arranged, but first, I want to walk in the garden and tell you my story."

"Okay," she said, but her look was full of unspoken questions.

When they finished the last crumbs of tarts and the last drop of tea, Hank took Elly's hand and guided her out into the garden.

"I want to talk to you out here where we have absolute privacy."

There among the flowering trees, winding paths, and sweet roses, he told her his story. "As a boy, I was shy with girls. I was taught ballroom dancing and was forced to dance even though I felt awkward. When I got into college, I buried myself in my books and studied all through the frat parties. In law school I met a man who changed my life—Reginald Sloan. He became my roommate, and he was gay. He taught me how to be assertive as a student of law and how to make love. It was only natural that we would form a law practice together after we graduated. Reggie could manipulate people, and I was good at organization and the logic of law in its application. Together, we started a practice by buying out an existing one. We came out of the closet five years ago. Now Reggie is a problem, if I go heterosexual. I don't know what to do?"

"Please, dear Hank, I don't judge you. I went through a homosexual period of my life too. I needed my friend. She was a lifeline for me when I needed it the most. I know how dependent one can be on someone who really understands you. I don't want to mess up your life. We can just be friends, and I will still love you."

"But I want you. I want to make love to you. I want a normal life with the woman I feel is best for me. However, Reggie is determined to not let me go, and that makes me a little crazy."

"You two have had a long relationship. You don't just wake up one morning and decide to change your life. So what is really going on?"

"We have had our arguments long before you came on the scene. He likes parties with lots of sex going on. I don't like having sex in public with complete strangers, and now with AIDS, it has become terrifying. Suddenly, this lifestyle has become dangerous to our health. In addition, I want to be tested for HIV before I make love to you. That is the only reason I didn't show absolute excitement at the thought of sleeping with you."

"Reggie probably feels betrayed. Is he a violent man?"

"He can be. I have seen him really mad at someone, and it was all I could do to calm him down."

"That sounds like we need to talk to someone who can give us some helpful advice."

"Yes, let's not worry about it now. Right now all I want is to take you to my office so that you can sign the papers. In addition, you will meet Reggie there."

"What does he know about us?"

"I told him I wanted to marry you."

"And?"

"He was upset, but by now he has probably calmed down."

"When did you give him this earthshaking news?"

"Last night. I had to tell him before you came, and I am sorry I have put it off. But I needed to be surer about you."

"Well, I think we should go and take the tiger by his tail. With luck, we will turn him into a tomcat with purr-fect charm."

Hank laughed and said, "I love your way of dealing with the rocks in the road, sweetheart. You just smooth them into a sheet of glass. Let's go have a signing party."

The drive to Hank's office took only about twenty minutes. They parked in his usual reserved spot. Both were silent as they drove through the city of Palo Alto, but when they parked, Hank said, "He can be intimidating, so I want you to let it all flow over you like water. If we give into him, he will think he has won."

"Aye, aye, captain. I have dealt with difficult people before. Trust me."

He smiled and kissed her gently. "I more than trust you, Elly. Dear one, you are like my alter ego, the person I always wanted to be like. You are the rock that sustains me."

They walked into the office with a lively attitude, which surprised the secretary. She was not used to seeing her boss so animated. On any normal day, he was so serious. Hank stifled his grin and introduced Elly to the secretary. Then he explained that she needed to bring the paperwork for the Longacre estate into his office for signing, and he wanted her to notarize the signatures.

Then hand in hand, they walked into Hank's private office, leaving the door open for his secretary and Reggie. He knew Reggie had heard them come in. Hank moved a chair to the side of his desk and offered it to Elly.

Elly scanned the office with the cherry wood paneling, plush white leather chairs, and beautiful original modern art on the walls.

In Hank's office there was also a stunning seascape hanging on one wall.

"Oh, I like that one. Where did you get it?"

Reggie entered the room then and said in a booming voice, "I bought that for Henry in Carmel one day when he loved me and we were a couple."

He glared at Elly with his penetrating glower, with which he meant to melt her. However, Elly looked up at him with a bemused smile and said, "How generous of you. It is truly beautiful. You have excellent taste. By the way, I am Elinor Longacre. I didn't hear you introduce yourself."

Recoiling, Reggie felt taken aback by Elly's immunity to his aggressive manner. "I am Reginald Sloan Esquire, Henry Dreassler's partner and lover."

"Please take that other seat. You look tired," Elly said in an effort to bring Reggie down to her level and make him feel as if he was a part of the transaction.

"I just came in to meet you. I am going back to my office as I have other work to do." And with that, he turned abruptly and walked out of the door.

Hank winked at Elly. "Here are the papers. I want you to read them, and then I will get the secretary to explain the notarizing process."

It took slightly more than an hour for the whole ritual. To complete the process, Hank concluded by saying, "The deed will be registered early next week, and that will complete the transaction."

"Thank you, Hank. That was the nicest legal transaction I have been involved with. When Arnold went over my inheritance, he was really brief as if he was talking to a child. I resented that, but this has been a very pleasant experience."

"Let's get out of here and visit my mom."

Out in the car, they both relaxed and gave great sighs of relief. Hank reached over and squeezed Elly's hand. "You were magnificent! I have never seen anyone keep their cool and stand up to Reggie quite like that."

Elly smiled. "He was a pussycat in lion's skin, and he can't hurt me."

Tall with thinning dark brown hair, Reggie had his firm chin thrust out in a scowl. His arms were akimbo with his hands on his waist as he stood at his office window, watching Hank and Elly. He could not hear them. But he saw their intimacy, and it made his stomach churn. He thought, *I love you, Hank. Why are you torturing me? What have I done to deserve this betrayal? Elinor will have to suffer for this. She is the cause of my pain. That witch has Hank under her spell.*

He grabbed the phone and dialed a number in San Francisco. "I am Reginald Sloan, and I would like an appointment with Arnold Smith as soon as possible."

***

Hank was driving them up into the hills of Palo Alto to his mother's charming English cottage. She was expecting them.

"What an attractive home. I would love to live in something like this."

"No mansions for my baby? I was hoping I could give you a palace somewhere."

Charlotte was charmed by Elly. "Please come and sit by me. It has been a long time since I last saw you. And look at you—all grown up and now an elegant lady. Tell me about your family, dear. I found some pictures of you and your mom. Here, you may keep them."

"Thank you. These pictures are a special surprise for me. My mom died a few years ago, and I miss her. But now I have two sons by a previous marriage. One is nineteen, and the other is ... fifteen."

"What does your former husband do?"

"He is a professor of sociology at UC Berkeley.

She asked if Elly had met Hank's friends.

"I have met Reggie. He was a bit distant but well mannered."

"Be careful. I don't trust him. He loves my son too much. He is not going to let you take his place without a fight."

Elly was astonished by this comment, and it worried her. She swallowed hard and asked, "How do you think he will respond?"

"Elly, dear he is not to be trusted. He is a course man with poor deportment."

"Mother!" Hank protested.

"Henry thinks he is great because they win so many cases together. I appreciate that he is a good fighter and is very good at making witnesses cooperate. However, he does this with intimidation and by being a bully. He doesn't do it with clever phrasing or his ability to quote prior judgments. There is nothing ingenious about him."

"Mother, we need to get moving. I made a reservation at Chez Nicole, and you know we can't be late."

"Yes, I know. Just as we get comfortable, you have to go. It has been a wonderful pleasure to see you, Elly, after so many years. Please come again."

"I would love to come another time when we have more leisure time to talk. Hank is in charge of our agenda today. He knows how to schedule everything so nothing gets left out."

Back in the car, driving to the restaurant, they had a chance to be alone.

"Do you think Reggie will be a problem?"

"Elly, what can he do? The worst possible act would be to destroy our law partnership, but I don't think he will do that. And if he did, I can join up with many other attorneys easily. Let's just forget about him and enjoy ourselves. Tonight is our night. I love being with you and having you all to myself. I want to give you something too. My surprise is so near you."

As they pulled into the parking lot and parked the car, Hank reached into the glove compartment and drew out a rectangular velvet box. "Here is your surprise."

"Well, the box is too large for a ring and too small for a book. What is it?"

"Would you like an engagement ring? I want to give you one, but for now please open the box."

Taking a deep breath, she slipped the blue velvet box out of the cardboard sleeve and opened it. There glittering in the lights of the parking lot was an exquisite sapphire and diamond necklace.

"Oh, it is so gorgeous," she purred with awe.

"It was my grandmother's favorite piece of jewelry. Please let me help you put it on. Those sapphires make your eyes light up."

Elly removed her scarf and held up the gems. "Yes, attach it in the back please," she said as she turned around.

"Will you marry me, sweetheart? If so, we can shop for a ring together anytime you are ready," he said in a serious tone.

"Dear, generous Hank, marriage is not in my thoughts these days. And I have never had an engagement ring. That would be a tender token of a union, and in my fantasies I dream of such luxuries. But I need to know you better. I can't get my mind wrapped around a commitment like that now. I have a son who hangs on to life by a thread and an estate I need to learn to control." She paused to see how he received this news and then said, "Right now I think you are famished, and we need to get into Chez Nicole and see what gourmet surprises they offer us."

Inside the restaurant they walked linked together, turning lots of heads with the glittering jewels at Elly's neck. "I feel like a queen," Elly softly said as she snuggled closer to Hank's shoulder.

Hank felt elevated by having a beautiful woman on his arm. He liked the attention and the appreciating looks from the other patrons. The necklace looked perfect on Elly. It was as if it had been designed just for her. Her eyes matched the sapphires and lit up her face.

The receptionist put them in a corner at Hank's request. It was a small intimate table for two. Elly felt the thrill of being pampered, and she loved it.

Hank looked at her with his soulful eyes and said, "Elly, you are the most elegant and attractive woman in this room, and it is such a pleasure to treat you."

They made their choices from the menu, which were very much the same. Neither wanted wine. They didn't want to dull their senses.

"I meant it when I asked you to marry me. I will get down on my knees whenever you say you are ready. Do you want to pick out the ring or leave it to me?"

"I think we should shop together, but you need to be patient, dear Hank. I also meant it when I said that I need to know you inside and out. However, I also need to deal with my son dying before we make any plans. I don't want to mix my joy with my grief at the same time. Does that make sense?"

As they enjoyed their dinner, Hank asked the waiter for some champagne to toast their love. Hank said with an amusing grin, "I want you to know that I have been working with my shrink on the fact that I have never had sexual relations with a woman. He says that if I feel sexually attracted to you—and I do—then it is just a matter of experimenting in a loving way."

The wine expert came at his request and took his order. When the waitperson brought the champagne in an ice bucket, he poured their glasses and Hank offered Elly a toast. "To us, may we love joyously and dance to the best music always."

She returned the toast by saying, "To my sweet boyfriend, from the past who now is a man that charms me in the present. May he always be by my side."

"Oh, I like your toast. It gives me hope."

Elly smiled. "Yes, now let's get back to what your psychologist said. I am willing to guide you and even teach you every sweet step. I think that is a very sumptuous way to get to know you," she purred, licking her lips.

The twinkle in her eyes and her sensuous lips parted just right to excite him. "My darling, I want to explore you from the tip of your sweet nose to the ends of your pink toes. I will explore each nook and cranny with my wet tongue, and my fingertips will massage your erogenous zones. Every crease, each mound, all your curves and valleys will dance in a mutual rhythm. I will discover new gems of love to lick and taste. You are my goddess, and I will worship you. Then my member will explore your inner recesses wet with arousal, and we will learn to come together," he replied, panting, his eyes locked on hers with an amorous look and caressing her hand seductively.

Her body could not resist reacting to these words he'd uttered from across the table and to his warm, gentle hands in hers. His face was shiny with perspiration. He whispered intimately to her, "I have an erection, and we can't leave here until I am presentable, so we need to order some brandy."

She smiled, empathically. "You won't have a problem pleasing me, sweet Hank. I will return the favors with joy. I like to tease and play. Whatever you do to make love to me, I will give you back with an equally sexy response. I can't wait to be in bed ... with you."

The drive to Hank's house was fairly short. Hank felt dizzy from the champagne, brandy, and the stimulating talk. He wanted to collapse on the couch in front of the fire with Elly in his arms. The house was a ranch-style perched on a hill with a view of the twinkling lights below. Elly was transfixed by the panoramic vista spread out below them.

"Come. Let's hurry and get in out of the cold. I have a gas fireplace that will give us instant warmth."

As they entered the house, Elly looked around the room. The couches were dark blue leather, and the chair was striped dark green and blue. The shag carpet was white and spotless. The coffee table was green marble, and there was a bronze figure of a young woman trying to cover her nakedness.

"My mother let her decorator loose on this room, and I would not mind if someone else wanted to change it," Hank said apologetically.

"I like the sculpture. By the way, where is your phone and answering machine?"

"Yes, I will lead you to it."

The answering machine was lit up like a carousel. As they went through the messages, they listened to one from Ted. "Mom, Davie started gasping for air. So I called Dr. Andreesen, and he is coming to see him."

The next message said, "This is me again. Davie was taken to the hospital, and that is where we are now."

In shock, Elly sat on the nearest chair. "I have to go home tonight. I'm sorry. We had such a nice day. Please forgive me."

Hank put his hand on her shoulder. "I will make some black coffee, and we will take you wherever you need to go."

***

As the darkness descended on the plains of Wyoming, the men were preparing for the raid. Stacks of black clothing were laid out on the tables of the great room. They were ranked small, medium, large, and extra-large. JR chose the largest size. He wanted to wear several layers under the black garments for warmth and security. *This raid is dangerous. I am afraid it will attract the authorities, and they will have their own invasion.* He wanted to be alert to any change in the plan. As the men were dressing, the wizard came into the room. Instantly, the room became silent. JR was impressed with the wizard's power.

"I know you are all nervous about tonight. We haven't done a raid in more than a year. It has been very peaceful around here. Now we have this vermin living down the road, and like all pests, we have to eradicate them!" he said in a thunderous voice.

Every one clapped and stomped their feet to show their support.

"Are them niggers bad?"

"Yes!" the men roared back.

This rabble-rousing speech went on for at least an hour. He was good at appealing to their emotional needs like many who had come before him. He didn't want them thinking for themselves. When the crowd was at a feverish pitch, he led them in a mindless chant, yelling and thumping their feet on the floorboards and fists on the table. It was a jumble of deafening, hate-filled sound.

"Your assignments are on the board. If tools are required, the man who's assigned the job must gather them and put them on the truck," he screamed.

JR read the list and saw that he was assigned to dig a hole three feet deep and one foot wide. Then he went over to where the tools we piled up. He looked for a posthole digger and a shovel. As he was carrying them out to the truck, a man stopped him and said that each man could only take one tool. JR liked the shovel because it could be used as a weapon, but he knew the posthole digger would be faster to dig a narrow, deep hole.

"What do we need a hole for anyway?" JR asked out loud to no one in particular.

The answer came from a voice nearby. "It's for the flaming cross, you nerdy dope!"

JR decided to pack up as many items he possessed, in his pockets, under his shirt, and in his pant legs. *I don't trust these neo-Nazis. If they attract too much attention, then I will suffer for it. I won't tell Georgie my plans. He would most likely squeal when they discover I'm missing.*

The hours ticked by as they waited for the moon to set. Around midnight they clambered into the back of the four trucks, each man with a tool. JR scanned his truck mates to see if they noticed him. He hunkered down and hid his face in the darkness.

The ride seemed endless, but finally, they came to a stop in front of a neatly maintained ranch house with a barn in the back. Silently, they all crawled out of their trucks. Wiz noiselessly led JR to a spot and coarsely whispered, "Dig like your life depended on it!"

The ground was hard. But they had had a recent rain, and that helped with digging the hole. Several minutes passed, and JR hadn't made much progress. Wiz stomped over to JR and kicked him.

"What was that for?" JR wailed.

"Shut your fuckin' mouth, you stupid son of a bitch, and dig faster!"

JR found that the posthole digger would loosen the dirt, but it was hard to pull the dirt out of the hole without a shovel. Finally, JR got down on his hands and knees to scoop the dirt with his hands as fast as he could.

The sweat was dripping off his face as he slowly rose to his feet and announced, "It seems to be three feet deep or more now."

"It's about time, you stupid dickhead," said a man who then shoved him aside with the end of the cross he was helping the group carry.

It was a struggle, but five men righted the massive cross, which was coated with tar and grease. When it was fully erected, the wizard lit the cross. Immediately, the flames licked up the pole to the cross piece, and in a ferocious whoosh, the cross was fully aflame.

A whoop of joy came up from the men as the flames enveloped the cross. When the cross blazed and lit up the world, they danced around its base like wild men. They chanted, "Make Wyoming white again," over and over as they pranced and jumped and yelled obscenities at the house. They dared the occupants to come out for a roasting, taunting them by calling them fags and niggers. While they jeered, they yelled that real men wouldn't pass up the chance to fight them. Then the men in black raised their right arms in a Nazi salute. "*Heil* Wizard!" they cried in unison. "*Heil*," they screamed at the house. "Get out of this county, you fucking niggers!"

With soundless stealth, JR shrank from the melee into the shadows. First, he put the posthole digger in one of the trucks, and then gradually one step at a time he moved to the edge of the group. Here he yelled some obscenities with the group. When the brawl was at its highest pitch, he stepped out of the group. When they were yelling really loudly, he dropped and rolled away from the cluster of men. In the darkness he scrambled into a ditch. Among the bushes in the ditch, he hid, waiting for them to leave.

Chapter 24

The Informer

In the wee hours of the morning, an African American cowboy sat on his tired quarter horse on a hillock, looking down on the horror below him. He had been out late because some his cattle had gotten out through a break in a fence. Now he was returning to find this hellish rampage right in front of his house. The blazing cross lit up the night sky. *Is this the KKK Wyoming-style?* Men in black were dancing and yelling at the top of their lungs like demons. He watched this mayhem for about an hour. Then when the intruders were packing up their tools, he had an idea. *I can follow them undetected and find out where they come from.*

As he watched the trucks move out of the drive to the main road, he noticed they didn't turn their headlights on until they reached the highway. Every paved road with a line down it was called a highway in Wyoming. This was a narrow road that followed the property lines. The whole train of trucks turned left and slowly moved west. Like an evil snake, they slithered along the slender road. Carefully, the cowboy steered his horse in the same direction, taking the cow trails that laced the countryside. He knew them like the lines in the palms of his hands. The horse moved silently without lights or fanfare.

***

Elly and Hank reached the hospital and parked. The car was warm and made them lethargic.

"Hank, I want to put this lovely necklace back in its box. It isn't something I want to wear in the hospital."

"You are right, of course," he agreed as he picked up the box from the back seat and handed it to her.

"I need my scarf too."

When Elly felt ready, they both got out of the car without enthusiasm. "I hope we find that it was a minor problem and I can take him home."

Hank put his arm around her as they walked to the hospital entrance in silence. The bright neon lights made them cower and cover their heads. Inside the hospital it could have been one in the morning or the afternoon it was so full of light, commotion, and activity in the emergency department.

"My son, David DeMartini, was admitted this evening. How do I find him?"

"The admissions desk is down that hall," the clerk said, motioning them in the direction.

At the admissions desk, Elly was required to fill out some forms for financial coverage for her son. She was irritated by the process, but she knew that it was necessary. It seemed an eternity before they let her go.

With circles under their eyes and a general feeling of exhaustion, they took the elevator and were alone again. Hanging together like when they were children, they waited for the elevator doors to open onto a quiet floor. They walked briskly to the nurses' station, and Elly asked, "I am David DeMartini's mother, and I want to know his condition."

"Ms. DeMartini, Dr. Andreesen has been trying to call you all evening. David is not doing well, and he wanted to know if you want us to do everything we can to keep him alive or if you want us to only do comfort care?"

Elly put her hand over her mouth to choke back any cries while she thought for a moment, and then she spoke in a shaky voice, "Just comfort care."

"Thank you, ma'am. I'll take you to his room. Your other son is there too."

Hank felt awkward and hung behind them as they went into the boy's room. He felt like a fifth wheel and decided to stay in the hallway. As Elly entered the room, she realized how dimly it was lit. On the bed the small shape of a child lay with an oxygen mask on his face. He seemed quiet and comfortable, so Elly sat down next to Ted.

"Where did Hank go?" Elly asked, concerned for him when she realized he was no longer there. Then focusing on Ted, she asked, "Tell me what happened, and then you should go home. You look like you have been through a disaster."

"I have, Mom. I needed you so much."

"Hush. I am here now."

"He got sicker around six, right after his meal. He hadn't eaten much, but he choked a bit on it. Then he got really short of breath. I called that number you gave me, but I only could leave a message. And the only other number was the doctor's number, so I called him."

"You were perfect, and you did the precise job excellently. I'm really proud of you."

Many possible problems were running wildly through her head. She thought of aspiration and pneumonia as the most likely culprits. "Okay, Ted, you need to go home and sleep. I will ask the hospital for a cot for me, and I will stay here until morning. Then I want to take Davie home."

Ted looked at her in appreciation. "Love you, Mom," he said as he got up to offer his chair for Hank, who had just come in. Then he turned to his mother and said, "I just thought of something I need to ask you about. There was a visitor here tonight. The nurses called me away and were very secretive about the man who came to visit. They sent me down to the cafeteria for a cup of coffee, but it was closed. They must have known the cafeteria would be closed. I felt they were hiding something."

"How do you know there was a visitor?"

"Because Davie said his lover came to visit him."

"Oh, my God, and you didn't see him?"

"No."

Hank could keep quiet no longer. "This man gave Davie AIDS? And he is a grown man, not some kid that Davie was fooling around with?" he whispered hoarsely.

"Shush. Davie will hear you. I know what you are thinking. Yes, this is a case of statutory rape."

"I'll be right back. I'm going out to talk to those nurses," Hank said with some urgency.

Hank stormed out of the room and then calmed himself down before he approached the nurse's desk. The nurses were working on charting and softly talking among themselves. When Hank came up to the desk, they tried to avoid his gaze.

"I want to talk to the nurse taking care of David DeMartini."

"That's me. I am Janet. What can I do for you?"

"I am the family's lawyer, and I understand that you allowed a man to visit David and sent David's brother on a false errand to hide this man's identity. Do you realize that you may be an accessory to covering the identity of a felon?"

"I don't know what you are talking about," the nurse responded with a blush.

"We know this man visited because the patient said so."

"Maybe the patient is delusional, sir."

Hank glared at the nurse and felt frustrated because he didn't have any proof. He turned on his heels and walked back to Davie's room.

"They are denying that anyone visited. Elly, they are claiming that Davie is delusional and that there was no visitor."

A few minutes later, the CNA, Doris, arrived with the cot for Elly to sleep on. When she was safely in the room and the door was shut, she whispered, "There was a visitor here tonight. The nurses are not telling the truth."

"How do you know?"

"When the boy's brother left, I came in to straighten up a bit and take vital signs. While I was doing that, this man came in to visit the patient."

"What did he look like?"

"He was tall, about your height, sir. He has gray and black hair like he dyes it, and he was dressed in a black suit with a white shirt and no tie. He is fifty years old or more."

"Thank you. You are a peach. What did you say your name is?"

"My name is Doris Perez. I won't get in trouble, will I? I need this job."

"We will protect you, Doris. You are being an excellent citizen."

"I am sorry. I am taking too much time. I have to hurry, or they will get suspicious," she said as she started to take the cot apart so that Elly could sleep on it.

"I can manage the cot. You go and get your other chores done. Don't worry about this cot," Elly assured her.

When they were once again alone, Elly got busy with the cot. She wanted it to look like the CNA had made it up for her.

"I should be going. I am sorry to leave you," Hank said quietly.

Ted was interested in Hank's leaving. "I have classes tomorrow, and I have to go too. Could I bum a ride from you, Hank?"

"Certainly. Do you need to go to the east bay or your mom's apartment?"

"Just to the apartment, then I can take BART in the morning to the university."

"Ted, please take care of Fred. He needs food and water. And ask the attendant to walk him."

"I set it up by phone when I found out I had to stay here with Davie, so don't worry about Fred. Everyone loves him."

***

The Next Morning

The San Francisco streets were wet with a recent rain as Reggie walked briskly to Arnold's office on Montgomery St. He liked the stately building. It was full of substance with the marble walls, and it oozed wealth. This was all he wanted, a place to grow and dole out revenge. It was a nice address for an up-and-coming attorney, and the city offered more interesting cases than Palo Alto. All of this hinged on his talk with Arnold Smith this morning, and he was well prepared. Riding up in the elevator, he thought of how he was going to sell himself to Arnold. After all, they had a common enemy, Elly. It would be easy to convince Arnold of his worth.

When the elevator doors opened, Reggie stepped out on the plush carpet and walked through the sliding doors to the receptionist desk.

"I have an appointment with Arnold this morning. I am Reginald Sloan."

She smiled back at him. "Please be seated a moment while I locate him."

A few minutes later, Arnold came out of the offices. "Reggie, how nice to see you. Come back to my office, and we will have a nice talk."

They discussed pleasantries and shared a joint. "I haven't seen you in years. I understand that you are looking for a position in this office. You would be a handsome young asset to this organization with all your experience."

Reggie observed that Arnold was not a well man. He had lost weight, and his gray skin was pocked with large wine-red lesions. He saw opportunity in Arnold's demise.

"What sort of a position are you offering me?"

"You are coming from a partnership with Henry Dreassler. Have you formally gotten out of that partnership?"

"Not yet. I didn't want to burn my bridges until I had looked at all of my options. There is also another subject I want to talk to you about."

"Yes, and what is that?"

"I have heard from selective sources that you know of a *doer*. I want to put a contract out to kill Elinor Longacre."

"Oh, I didn't know you had a problem with her."

"That scheming bitch took my lover from me. I want to get back at her in the worst way."

"I appreciate your problem. She isn't one I would miss. What is the time frame you need to work with?"

"She needs to die before she can marry Henry Dreassler. The two of them will be a catastrophe for both of us if they are wed."

Arnold stared in shock at Reggie for a moment, "My *doer* is on the run from the law at the moment, but I will do my best to find him."

***

At the federal offices in Salt Lake City, an FBI man contemplated a recent phone call. The call was from the sheriff of Washakie County, Wyoming. A black rancher was complaining that a group of wild men burned a large cross in his front yard, and he wanted them arrested for trespassing.

"Evidently, he followed them to their compound. He did this in the middle of the night. I didn't know we had KKK in Wyoming," said one agent to another.

"They are probably a white supremacist group. We have lots of them in Wyoming, Idaho, and eastern Washington. They are like the KKK, but they don't have the same community backing that the KKK did in the South at one time. These folks tend to isolate themselves in walled-off compounds. Their walls are wood or barbed wire and sometimes both."

"What do you want to do about the complaint? Did the sheriff feel he didn't have the manpower to handle the situation?"

"Yes, he wants help. He said he has a skeleton crew and he wasn't interested in taking on these radicals without more men."

"This might be off the subject, but didn't we get a memo about a wanted killer called Jason Roberts a while back? The last they heard about him was that he was heading to the Middle West and that he might have joined a white supremacist group. Could he be part of this bunch?"

"I remember that tip was from my buddy Joe Sanchez. Yeah, I went to school with him. Let me call him and see. If he thinks this is a lead, we should follow up."

The agent flipped through his Rolodex. "Yes, here is his number. I'll call him."

Then he phoned the agent and said, "Joe, how is the wife and family?"

"Fine and dandy, what's up, buddy?"

"We have a complaint about a white-supremacist group in Wyoming. I was wondering if you have any suspects who might be mixed up with a group like that."

"It is interesting. I just got news that we are looking for George Collingers. He is wanted for the murder of a police officer in San Francisco. You might turn up Jason Roberts too. He is a hired killer. Both men are on the run, and they may be partners. This is an Aryan Nation type? Many times criminals like to run with these characters because they feel safe. I will fax you some pictures and information."

"Much obliged. Looking forward to your fax."

***

Back in Davie's room in the hospital, his mother pitched and twisted fitfully on the cot. Every bone and muscle ached. The room was just lit by a large nightlight on the baseboard near the bed. Elly could hear the soft rhythm of Davie's breathing. He sounded clearer, and his breathing wasn't as rapid as it had been earlier. This was reassuring. Mechanically, she checked her watch. It was almost 7:30. The nurses would be getting ready for the shift change. Maybe this was a good time to freshen up and go to the cafeteria for breakfast. In the room's facilities, Elly found the water cold, and as she splashed her face, she heard someone come at the door. Quickly, she dried her face and opened the door.

"Oh, Dr. Andreesen, you are just the man I want to talk to."

"Hello, Elly, you must have slept here last night. I am sorry the accommodations are not four-star, but we make due."

"That isn't what I want to talk about. We had a visitor last night, and I want to know why the nurses would not give us his name. They even denied he was here. They sent my older son on a wild goose chase down to the cafeteria even though they knew it was closed so that this man could sneak in and visit Davie. Don't you think that's a bit irregular?"

"I'm sorry you are upset. You can leave a note on the chart that Davie only can have family members visit. Would that help?"

"Are you saying that you don't know about this man who visited? If he is the man who gave my son AIDS, then he is guilty of statutory rape. Is he Arnold Smith by any chance?"

Defeated, Dr. Andreesen turned crimson and moved to the other side of the bed. "I am sorry, but you are right. Now please, Ms. DeMartini, we need to talk about your son's care."

Elly stood with her mouth open. A million thoughts were rushing through her head. Then she swallowed hard and said, "Yes, what do you want to ask?"

"I want to discuss with you ways to nutritionally support David. If we put a nasogastric tube in, he can go home and be more comfortable. However, if he has malabsorption problems and develops diarrhea, then our only choice is parenteral nutrition."

For a long moment, Elly considered the options. "I like the parenteral nutrition best to start with. I can manage it at home because I am a nurse and I have loads of experience with this type of therapy. Also, we can avoid the other problems like diarrhea. I have read that those lesions on his body may also be internal, causing malabsorption."

"That is a good plan. I will put in the line today, and maybe he will be ready to go home this evening."

"Thank you, Dr. Andreesen. I know it was hard for you to tell me about Arnold. I don't know yet what I want to do with that information."

"He is dying too, you know. He isn't quite as sick as David, but he is getting fragile. I know you must have a lot of anger about what he did to your son. I want you to understand that Davie was vulnerable because of his sexual needs, and if it wasn't Arnold, it would have been another man or boy. HIV is the thief that is stealing your son's life."

Elly sighed. "I will think about what I will do with this information. I want justice, not just for my son but for other people's sons. Davie is not the only victim."

After the doctor left, Elly sat on the cot and thought. When she looked at her beautiful suit, she realized it was now a wrinkled mess. Her hair was wild, and she needed a shower. She got up and went to her son's side and kissed him on his forehead.

"I have to go, Davie. The doctor is going to put in a special tube in your shoulder so we can make you stronger and I can take you home. Mommy has to go and clean up. I love you, sweetie. I will see you later."

Just as she was leaving, the nursing aids came in to clean Davie up.

***

The rusty sign on the café's door had the uninspiring name T. S. Grill on it. He had walked all night, and was exhausted. He didn't want to look farther. Within moments JR was sitting in the ramshackle eatery, ordering breakfast. Ten Sheep was a small one-street town with rednecks all over the place. He wanted to fit in, and he hoped he looked like one of them with his unshaven face and crumpled clothing. He had stuffed his black attire into a backpack that he had concealed under his clothes last night. As he ate his ham and eggs, he overheard someone talking about the Grigsby Ranch. It seems they had a cross burning in front of their house.

"Hey, Miss Waitress!" JR sang out.

"Yaw? Does you want more java?" she asked.

"I also want to know the best place to hitch a ride on semi headed for an interstate?"

"Go that a way about two miles to the freeway," she said and motioned toward the northeast. "There are usually trucks at the fast-food places under the overpass. They spend the night there."

Another couple of miles did not delight him, but after eating breakfast, he felt stronger and decided to walk in the direction she suggested and try to thumb his way to the highway. He gave her a generous tip and strolled out into the sunshine. He hadn't seen the sun in what seemed like days, and it was welcome. As he walked through the town, he came across a telephone booth and decided to call Barb.

"Hi, any news?" JR said with his voice muffled by a piece of cloth.

"The sickness is still here. The dog is barking. Shall I give him green or red?"

"Red," JR said through the material he held over the receiver.

He left the phone booth feeling in control. Arnold and his friends would have to find someone else to do their evil biding. Even so, it took several hours to get to the highway. Near the freeway ramp going west was the parking area for the semis and some fast-food joints. JR walked into one of the places where he saw the most men. He felt bedraggled and unshaven. Would they reject him for his appearance?

In a corner of the fast-food place, he found the washroom. There he shaved, trimmed his beard neatly, and combed his hair. Nothing could be done about his clothes. They were wrinkled and a mess. He straightened them the best he could and then made his entrance back into the eating area.

JR called out, "Are there any of you who are going to Salt Lake City? If so, I would like to hitch a ride."

***

Elly opened the door and slid into the apartment. Fred met her, wagging his tail to show how much he appreciated her coming home. She crouched down to his level.

"Davie is coming home as soon as he is stable. I know you miss him," she said as she ruffled his ears. "You are better than any man. You are loyal, never grouchy, and always willing to greet me."

She had had breakfast at the hospital, so now she could just go to sleep. She was just slipping into her nightgown when the phone rang. At first, she was going to let the answering machine pick it up, but something changed her mind.

"Hello?" she said weakly.

"Elly? Are you okay?"

"Todd, it is nice to hear your voice."

"You sound really tired. Are you getting enough rest?"

"I have been at the hospital with Davie all night, and I'm beat."

"I just wanted you to know that the DNA report on those bone fragments indicate that they belong to Mike Nikcols and not George Collinger."

"Interesting. I have news for you too. Arnold Smith is ASS. He had the nerve to visit Davie in the hospital. That is a long story I will tell you later, but Dr. Andreesen verified that Arnold is the culprit. What do you need to arrest him?"

"Hmm, I will talk to my DA about what evidence we need to arrest and not have him wheedle his way out of it. I think he is guilty of much more, but we will have to wait for him to make more mistakes. With Mike Nikcols, we don't know what killed him or who killed him. We did find a slug and the gun it came from, but I don't think that answers all the questions."

"Todd, I am really exhausted, and I need to get some sleep."

"I miss you. Could we have lunch sometime?"

"Yes, I will call you when I'm rested."

When she hung up, she stared at the phone. *I would like to see him again just to make sure I am making the right decision. Todd is a good man with lots of integrity. Does Hank have that same veracity too?*

Elly went into the bedroom and slipped into the bed. Fred was close behind. "Freddy, I wish you could talk and give me advice. I know you have my best interests at heart."

Several hours later the phone rang again and woke her out of a deep sleep. "Hello," she said as if she was at the bottom of a deep well.

"Elly? Are you okay?" Hank said, full of concern.

"Yes, I didn't sleep well on that cot at the hospital, so I fell asleep here when I got home. By the way, that mysterious visitor last night was Arnold just as you said."

"That dirty old man should be shot. I called to tell you I love you and miss you so much."

"You are sweet. How are you and Reggie getting along?"

"He came roaring in this morning to tell me he is moving to the city. In addition, he is ending our partnership and giving his talents to another firm."

"Oh, dear, is that going to hurt your office? Do you need to find a new partner?"

"No, I don't think this office will suffer. I asked him which firm he was working with and why. His answers were very vague, and he was more closed about the whole change than I have ever seen him. I think we really upset him and he is running blind."

"Is that worrisome if he is grieving and acting irrationally?"

"Elly, my relationship with Reggie has been in decline for some time. The AIDS crisis really has made me rethink my lifestyle and my love interests. I didn't like his wild parties and loose sexual morals. I thought all that unprotected contact was inviting a epidemic. It reminded me of Edgar Allen Poe's story of the party in the mansion for all those who wanted to avoid the plague, but by the end of the story, they are all dead. For me, Reggie's parties were like that, and I would slip out and go home."

"Oh, Hank, that sounds like so much has been altered because of this terrible disease. You tried but couldn't get Reggie to change his ways. Surely, you both must have lost fiends because of AIDS. I have lost friends and acquaintances like doctors, nurses, actors, and my son. It really makes you feel much less free with your relationships."

"What I really called about was the fact that our day yesterday was interrupted. I would like to make up for that loss. I thought I could drive into the city and have dinner with you."

"Let's wait for this weekend. Davie is coming home today sometime. In fact, when the phone rang, I thought it was the hospital. When he gets here, he will be a handful. His care has become much more technical and labor intensive. In addition, his care is no longer something a CNA can handle alone. What I am trying to say is I am needed here twenty-four hours a day, so going out to dinner will be on hold for a while."

"How about, I bring my favorite nurse a nice dinner, or are you not eating at all?"

"That would be very kind of you. I would like your company. However, tonight I want to focus on my son. He doesn't have many days with me, and I need to be totally engaged in his welfare. I'm also going to try to get Davie's father to come here. I plan to offer the spare room to him. If his son has only a few more days or hours of life, I want him here so he doesn't blame me for leaving him out."

At about four o'clock, the front desk called to say that there was a man downstairs with a large gas tank he wanted to deliver. Elly decided to go down to meet the man. In the lobby she found the man with the oxygen cylinder. With that huge green tank, he was hard to miss. She signed the papers, and he gave her the regulator for the tank.

"Don't take the tank out of the carrier. It is like a bomb, and they have been known to go through cement walls," the delivery man said seriously.

"I'll take good care of it. When I need more, I call this number on the paperwork? And I need a wrench for the regulator, don't I?"

"That's right. Maybe I should help you get it up to your apartment and attach the regulator."

"Thank you. That sounds most helpful."

Elly led him to the elevator. They were silent as the elevator car rose to the eight floor. Elly felt like the tank was another person in the elevator because of its size.

"Do you deliver this sized tank often?"

"Yeah, the AIDS epidemic is good for our business."

"I didn't know it was an epidemic. That *is* very sad."

After he set up the tank, the man explained how to get the proper liter flow and instructed her on turning it on and off. Elly appreciated the information. Now she wouldn't worry about the bomb in their midst.

Elly was relieved when the man left. Fred was growling the whole time he was there.

It was nearly six by the time she got a call from the front desk that an ambulance had brought her son. Grace had arrived at earlier, and Elly took Grace with her when she went down to meet Davie.

The paramedics brought their precious cargo up to the apartment and transferred the oxygen from the small tank to the large one at the same liter flow. They gave the doctor's orders to Elly and the bag of nutritional supplements for his IV.

"These need to be refrigerated. They said it is enough there for a week," the paramedic announced.

"Thank you for taking such wonderful care of him," Elly said as she showed them out.

Elly was happy to see her baby. "Davie, you're home now ... with Mommy."

He weakly opened his eyes and nodded his head with a crooked, trembling smile.

***

The FBI raid came in the middle of the night. They got into the compound of the white- supremacist group by cutting through the wire fence and driving through it with their heavy trucks. They lined up all the men they could find by entering the bunkhouses and dragging them out of bed and handcuffing them. The women were on one side, and the men were on the other side of the compound. The floodlights of the officers blinded their suspects and kept them quiet.

With a megaphone, Rick, the lead officer, announced, "You are being questioned about a raid that you did on the Grigsby place. You were observed lighting a flaming cross on this man's property, and he followed you here when you left.

In a cabin in the back, the wizard was startled out of his sleep.

"Damn it. Who is making that sound!" he roared. The woman he was bedded down with ran in a frantic panic into the closet to hide.

In the dark he pulled on his overalls and his warmest jacket, where he hid his rifle. Through the window Wiz saw the men lined up and shuttered. The coppers had come. Well, he was going fix them. His men all knew that he would shoot anyone who gave information to the coppers. Losing no time at all, he rushed to join his men.

"I don't know what you are talking about copper. We are law-abiding citizens," the wizard announced from the back of the crowd. "Nobody can identify us."

Rick replied, "There are two men who are wanted, and we suspect they are here. If you hand over those men to us without any problem, then we will let the rest of you off with only a fine. I am setting up an office in your bunkhouse, and you will file in one at a time to be questioned. So line up here, and I will see you each, one at a time."

The Feds had frisked the men in the beginning, but they didn't get the wizard's rifle. He had slipped up late in the dark after everyone else had lost their guns. He wasn't handcuffed either.

George was sweating bullets as he stood in line for the interrogation. He knew they had his fingerprints and his picture. *Maybe I could get leniency by testifying about JR. There are several men ahead of me. That will give me time to figure out what to say.*

When it was George's turn, he stumbled his way into the bunkhouse. Immediately, Rick was aware that this might be one of his targets. "State your legal name."

"George Collinger, sir. I know there is a charge for murder on my head. I would like to have leniency because I can tell you about JR."

"When you give us the evidence, we will evaluate the leniency factors."

Without warning, a shot shattered everyone's nerves. Carefully but with a swift movement, Wiz had entered the bunkhouse door. Then he instantly aimed the mussel of his rifle at George's head and squeezed the trigger. The noise rocked the building, vibrated the windows, and made them momentarily deaf. George's head lurched to the side, and then he went limp. His body fell to the floor with a thump. His eyes stared blankly out of his shattered skull as the pool of dark red blood covered the floor. Blood and brain tissue was spattered on the wall, the officers, and the beds. Wiz stood there in the doorway with his rifle in his hands, grimacing sardonically at the officers.

"I don't tolerate squealing pigs, so I shoot them!" Wiz said with a loud, authoritarian voice.

The officers scrambled to gain control. Two grabbed the wizard and handcuffed him.

Rick was fuming with anger. "Who the hell are you that you can walk in here and blast away my witness. Do you know how much time we have spent looking for this man and his partner? George here is a cop killer, and he was ready to spill the information about this other man. You and your damn arrogance have blasted away our chances of bringing both these men to justice."

Wiz hung his head, and in a barely audible voice, he said, "Someone mentioned JR, and I thought it was me or my son."

"Oh, God, I have heard of stupid reasons in my career, but I haven't heard that one. So what is your name?"

"Jacob Reily, and my son is John Reily. I do not stand for squealing from anybody," Wiz announced with pride.

"Well, Mr. Jacob Reily, I am arresting you for murder of an important witness. In addition, I want you to know that I happen to value people who want to tell me the truth."

Chapter 25

A Time for Mourning

Elly's head was hanging over her son, cooing at him to comfort him. Grace stood beside her. Ted was stretched out on the couch, snoring softly. The other sound in the room was the oxygen mask. The flow of lifesaving gas sounded like water running from a faucet. The sound was numbing. They had been at Davie's side all night, tending their fragile patient.

In another part of the apartment, Jerry was rising. Confused by his hangover, he couldn't remember where he was. It took several minutes before he could recall the night before. Then he remembered his little son was in distress. In the distance he heard a woman calling his name.

"Jerry, Ted, come quick I think Davie is going!"

"Dad, come to Davie's side. He is struggling to breathe," Ted, who was now up, bellowed to his father.

"Just hang on. I'll be there," Jerry yelled back as he fumbled for his shoes.

Davie was fighting for every wisp of air. His chest heaved up and down. There was a gurgling sound with every inhalation and exhalation.

"There, there, sonny boy, take a deep breath," Jerry urged, and his voice cracked.

"He has been working this hard to breath for many minutes. It has been so painful to watch," Elly sobbed. "Please, Davie, keep breathing!"

Suddenly, the gurgling stopped. The chest failed to rise. "Oh, God, bless him. My baby, my sweet Davie has gone to his maker," Elly murmured as she fumbled for a pulse.

When she could not find a pulse, she burst into tears. "That awful man killed our son, Jerry. What are we going to do about it?"

"What man?"

Elly looked at him in grief and raised her voice, "Arnold Smith! He raped our son and gave him AIDS! I am going to destroy that man! Are you going to be sober enough to help me?"

"Mom, you are not talking rationally. With Davie gone, there is no one to testify against that man," Ted advised. "Let's sit down and discuss this like adults."

Jerry looked at his former wife with enlightened adoration. *It was a revelation why I had been attracted to this woman in the first place so many years before. Tentatively, I had better sit down in that overstuffed chair and survey my oldest and only remaining son, who dares to give me an order. I can't believe that I only have one son now. It is so strange that I have out lived my youngest child. How can I manage this terrible loss?*

As the morning hours staggered by, he was vaguely aware of the coming and going of people, the doctor, and the little brown girl who helped Elly. It was like a bad dream as he watched Elly wash his son with her tears. Then those men in black came, tucked the body in a bag, and took his baby son away.

The silence of death hung over them like a black cloud.

"It's over. I called the oxygen people, the bed rental people, and the people I rented the wheelchair from. They all promised me to come today. I just can't stand to have that stuff in my house one minute more. It all reminds me of Davie's last terrible moments."

The phone shattered their contemplation. Ted answered it.

"I don't want to talk to anyone." Heartbroken and despondent, Elly was isolating herself.

"It's Todd, Mom," Ted said.

"No one!" she cried out as she ran to her bedroom and slammed the door.

"Mom is too upset at the moment, Todd. Davie just died. Try later or tomorrow," Ted offered.

When he hung up the phone, Ted announced, "He sent his condolences, and he said that you had been such a comfort for him when Gina died that he wanted to do the same for you, Mom."

Elly was so distraught that she just lay on her bed, crying. It took several minutes to get control over her grief. She stood up and looked in the mirror. "Why did I deny Todd the right to share our sorrow with us? Was it just a family affair? Todd loved Davie. Doesn't that make him family? Who do you really love here, missy?"

Does my hate for Arnold cloud my judgment and make me drive others away? Todd was just calling with his concern for Davie, and now he wants to comfort me. I feel all prickly like a cactus. Or am I wallowing in a pity party?

She wilted without grace back on the bed and stared up at the ceiling. *Is this what Davie would want me to do? He liked Todd. He preferred him to his father. With Jerry here, it is a little awkward to have my lover ... or maybe a former lover come here.*

There was a knock at the door. Elly said, "Come in. I'm just sulking."

"Mom, let's get out of here. We are all exhausted. Let's go where we can have some lunch in a neutral place. You must be starving. We didn't have breakfast, and you have said yourself that going without sleep and food makes people more emotional."

"You are right, dear son, and why don't you call Todd and have him meet us at the restaurant in the hotel down the block?"

Ted gave her a winning smile. "Yes, will do. I will also call for a reservation."

***

"I would like to talk to Arnold Smith please. This is Dr. Andreesen speaking."

"Yes, sir, I will connect your call."

"Hi, Larry, what is up? Got a cure for AIDS yet?"

"No, Arnold. I am calling to tell you that David DeMartini died this morning at 6:47. His mother said he went fairly peacefully."

Arnold felt the earth shake under his feet. "That poor boy, I loved him, you know. Such a sweet, innocent boy, and I will miss him."

"You don't feel guilty for giving him HIV?"

"Don't try to make me feel remorseful because I am gay and so was Davie. At that time, I didn't know I was carrying the virus. How do you know? Maybe he gave it to me."

"I just wanted you to know of his passing. Good-bye!"

***

The huge semi with a trailer pulled into a diner on the outskirts of Salt Lake City. The driver reached over to his passenger and shook him awake. "Hey, bub, wake up. Are ya' using drugs that you can't stay awake?"

"I'm sorry. I haven't had much sleep lately, but I am not taking drugs."

"Wal, ya missed breakfast, and we are just outside of Salt Lake. Do you have the change for lunch or a late breakfast?"

"Yeah, I have the money and an appetite. I'll buy you lunch if you would like that. I so appreciate you giving me a ride."

"Wal, I like hitchers so I have someone to talk to, but you snored the whole way. And for that reason, I think you do owe me some grub," he said with a chaw of tobacco in his cheek.

"I am looking for a ride to Sacramento or San Francisco. Do you think one of these other trucks is going that way?"

"Yaw, someone must be going that way. But if not, I'll give you a ride to Reno, and you can find a truck there better than here. Most of these rigs are servicing this valley and not going out of the state."

"Thanks. I think this calls for us celebrating with juicy steaks and baked potatoes with lots of butter and sour cream oozing like a whore's pussy. Are you game?"

***

The Following Day

Elly pondered, *If Davie wanted the same life as his parents, he wouldn't have gone and hung out on 6ᵗʰ Street, begging for a sexual experience that he had always wished for. He would have gone to school, suppressed his sexuality, and hunkered down to study, not knowing the joys of life. On the other hand, Davie was from a different era than his parents. It is a time when men and women have many choices, and they are freer than at any other time to pursue those choices and succeed or die. Davie loved and lost. That is the simple story. This was not a simple chess game. It was a battle of the soul against the body. He wanted both to win, but if you play with fire, you will get burned.*

Then there is Annette, my half- sister, who suffered from a loss of her spouse's love, and it destroyed her. As humans, we find it difficult to live with or without love. I seem to be running in circles. There must be an answer to life's method of doling out the emotional pain. Maybe Davie knew his life was short, and perhaps he wanted to experience it to its fullest. Davie also died from the adoration of love. Is that what love is? A tangle of pain and ecstasy, or is it a maze of twists and turns with an ending that is self-satisfying?

All this thinking was making her hungry. Today she was going to have an appointment with Arnold, and she wanted to be at her very best. *In my heart of hearts, I want answers, and the only way to get them is to go to the source of this angst and ask direct questions. I want to confront him about Davie, Jacob, and all the rest. He knows so much. I am sure of that.*

Over breakfast she worked out questions and tried to imagine the answers so she could comfortably and intelligently respond to them. *He is an ill man, and I don't want to feel guilty that I am not being compassionate; however, I must be assertive with him.*

The taxi arrived around ten. Elly was ready. She had called Todd and told him of her plans in case there were difficulties. In addition, she was taking Fred with her. He was always a good conversation point, and he often put people at ease.

The traffic was light and within a few minutes they arrived at Arnold's address on Montgomery Street. Elly stepped out of the taxi gracefully, turning many heads. Once again, she was in this marble palace devoted to business. She didn't feel as naïve or as helpless this time. She felt inspired, and that would carry her to the goal line. When the elevator landed on Arnold's floor, Fred pulled her out. For some reason, the elevator annoyed him, or he wanted to get on with the business.

Sara, the receptionist that day, was ready for her. "Mr. Smith has some papers for you to sign. Would you like to read them before your meeting?"

"Papers? Yes, I want to read them."

Elly took the papers to one of the chairs and sat down to read. The papers had to do with various properties that she owned. There were many pages, and she felt intimidated by the legal jargon. Now she regretted not having Hank with her for this appointment. She decided that it was best to wait to sign the papers at another time when she could have friendly legal counsel with her.

The receptionist called to Elly and said that she could take her to Arnold's office now.

"Just make yourself comfortable, and he will be right with you." As she left, she closed the door behind her.

"Well, Fred, where shall we sit? Let's take Arnold's chair just to throw him off."

When she sat in Arnold's large leather chair, she felt powerful and in charge. Fred sat under the massive mahogany desk. There was plenty of room, and he could lie down to have a nap. But something kept him on guard. Then she waited and waited. After at least twenty minutes went by, she was going to call the receptionist when the door opened. Now alert, Fred stood at attention.

In walked Reggie, full of self-importance, but when he saw her sitting in his new partner's chair, he swung into action. His voice was hard and filled with hate. "What gives you the right to sit at

Arnold's desk? If you don't mind, please remove yourself, and let me sit there!"

"No, I'm not moving until Arnold walks into this room so I can confront him. You must know that my appointment is with Arnold Smith and not with you, Reggie."

"Arnold is too ill and can't make the appointment. I am his new partner, and I am here to answer your questions."

"I have nothing I want to discuss with you, and I am not moving until Arnold answers my personal questions."

Reggie gritted his teeth and put both hands on the desk. His neck up to his cheeks turned red hot as he growled at her with fury. "Okay, give me your petty questions," he demanded.

His aggressive stance made Fred alert, and he softly snarled.

"My questions are strictly for Arnold. You are too upset to talk sensibly. Maybe I will come back at a different time. There are papers to sign. I understand, and I do not want to involve you."

"You must sign those papers now because they are transferring your accounts to me. Because of Arnold's illness, he feels it would be better if I managed them so we have a seamless transition when..."

"Transition? You? I'm not going to stand for that. This is crazy. I think you should leave this office right now."

"I am not leaving until I have some answers to my questions," Reggie blurted out, and his whole face burned redder with the fire of his anger.

"Okay, ask your questions. I have all day to listen."

Reggie stood up to his full height and asked, "What are your intentions with Hank?"

"That is none of your business. I'm sorry you have lost your lover, but that was more your doing than mine."

"Would you share him with me, or are you going to manipulate him into not wanting me?"

"Reggie, you must listen to reason. Hank no longer wants a gay relationship. He wants a real woman at his side." Fred was audibly growling at her side.

"You bitch! You seduced him with your money, and I despise you. I am fighting back." As he said this, he brought out a revolver from his jacket pocket and pointed it at Elly.

"If you shoot, you will regret it," she screamed as she released Fred.

As the gun fired, Fred leaped over the desk, snarling. The force of his attack deflected Reggie's aim. Elly dropped and dived to the right, but she wasn't fast enough to avoid a bullet in her left arm.

Fred pinned Reggie to the floor with a crashing thud. The gun flew out of his hand and skittled across the room. He felt the hot canine breath in his face, nauseating him. He cringed as the fangs exposed by the growling dog came closer and closer to his face. All eighty-five pounds of Fred were bearing down on him, so he couldn't move.

The noise attracted office people who called 911 and opened the office door. They found Reggie on the floor with a large German shepherd standing on his chest, growling at his victim's face. A handgun lay a few feet away from Reggie's outstretched arm, and they could see feet sticking out from behind the desk.

"Miss Longacre, this is Gregg. Can you talk to me?"

"Call Todd Markam. He's with the police department. Tell him I've been shot," she mumbled with some effort.

To Elly, it seemed like hours went by before she saw Todd's face.

"The ambulance is here to take you. Where is your wound? There is blood everywhere," he said, full of worry.

"I need a tourniquet on my upper arm. I think he hit an artery. I have tried to put pressure on it, but I'm getting weak," she said, slurring her words.

Todd tore off the sleeve of her blouse and made it into a tourniquet above the wound to stop the flow of blood. As he was getting up, the paramedics were gently moving him aside so that they could work on Elly.

Todd came with them to the hospital. As he sat beside her in the ambulance, Elly reached out, grasping for his sleeve for reassurance until his hand was in hers. Fred sat at her side with her good arm around him. Todd ruffled his ears. "Good boy. You saved her life."

***

When all had quieted down in the legal firm, the receptionist called Arnold Smith as she had been instructed. "Mr. Smith, Reggie did not do well today. He shot a gun at Miss Longacre and wounded her. Reggie was arrested and charged with intent to kill. The papers did not get signed as you wanted. I'm sorry to report all this. Miss Longacre brought her dog with her, and he attacked Reggie. So now we only have Gregg in the office. Do you want me to send him home?"

"Oh, dear, I was afraid that he was too hotheaded to handle Miss Longacre. Send Gregg home along with the rest of the staff, and you close up the offices. If the police want to inspect the offices, and files they will need a warrant. So lock everything tight. Are you okay with all that?"

"Yes, Mr. Smith, I will take care of everything."

***

In the evening Todd, Ted and Fred sat by Elly's bed. Her arm was now in a sling, and she was just waking up after surgery.

"The doctor told me you're going to be okay. For a while, we were worried that they may have to amputate your arm," Ted softly whispered in her ear.

"Sweet Ted, you don't have to whisper. I am not dying. That would've been scary. But the surgeon was one of the best, and he pieced it together with a pin here and there. That was what he told me when he explained it to me. Now I want to talk about Arnold and Reggie."

She then turned to Todd and said, "When you question Reggie, please ask him if Arnold put him up to it. I am really worried that they were working together."

"I will do that. Now I want you to rest. Someone from my office or Ted will watch over you constantly to keep you safe. I don't want any unwelcome strangers wandering in and doing harm. We also have that search warrant we need to open Arnold's files."

"If Hank calls or wants to visit, I want to see him. Where is Fred? I want him by my side."

"Yes, he is right here. I will take him to your apartment and feed him, and then I will bring him back," Todd explained and then added, "Yes, I will put Hank on the very short list."

Chapter 26

Pyrotechnics

The truck JR was traveling in arrived in Richmond before dawn. The chap that was driving had been very talkative. He had heard on the news about a raid on some white-supremacist group in Wyoming, and some guy had died in a shooting there. JR was interested in the news, but he acted bored by it so as not to arouse suspicion. Now that they were off the highway, he was hoping he could see a newspaper or something to get more information.

In the local café, he read about the raid in the paper and asked about the BART system of trains and how to get to Berkeley. By ten in the morning, he was in Berkeley, looking for a flop house to stay in on San Pablo Blvd. He found one that was reasonably priced and quiet. There he waited for sundown by sleeping and eating sparingly. Like a cat, the nighttime would bring him opportunities.

On a tree-lined street in another part of Berkeley, a broken man sat morosely at his kitchen table. He couldn't eat, sleep, or pee effectively, and he didn't even want his bottle of whiskey. The emptiness his son Davie had left filled him with hate for the man who had killed his youngest child, his baby. The villain's house was only about ten blocks away. He could almost smell it from here. It had a sickening, deadly odor. Jerry itched to torch it and turn it into a cremation pyre, but he didn't have the mind to plan such an act. Something else had to be done. Maybe the nighttime with its shadows would give him more strength. He went to search for that old shotgun he had inherited. Granddaddy DeMartini had used this gun to hunt wild pigs. Why not use it on another type of hog, a big nasty boar of a man?

***

"Baby, I have heard you have had such a terrible time since I last saw you," Hank said with sympathy.

"Oh, yes," she said with a sigh.

"Are you in any pain? I am worried sick about your welfare."

"Your mother was very right in her condemnation of Reggie."

"That turkey called me from jail and asked me to bail him out. Arnold and the other attorney in his office refused to help him as well. The judge set his bail at a half a million."

"Will he be disbarred?"

"Possibly, especially if he is found guilty, and I think that conviction is easy. He was caught red-handed, and you, the victim, are the perfect witness. I shudder to think what he might have done if Fred hadn't been there. Fred made the front page. Did you know that?"

"Yes, Fred was the hero. By the way, you did hear that Davie died?"

"I'm sorry. I was just so worried about you. Ted was nice enough to call me, but then this thing happened to you the next day. I tried to call you, but I just got the answering machine."

"I need to have you run an audit on my estate. I think Arnold and friends have been stealing money from the estate for a long time. I also need legal advice as to what to do about his negligence and the statutory rape of my son."

"I am so glad you brought this subject up. I was going to offer my services, but it is better if it comes from you, babe."

"I'm sorry, but the nurse and the doctor are here to clean my wound. I will talk to you later," she said and hung up the phone.

"Mom, there isn't anyone here but me. Are you having second thoughts about Hank?"

"I don't know where my head is, but I just didn't want to talk to him any more right now. Besides, I know nothing about my needs legally, and I feel insecure just turning everything over to Hank. But who else do I have with the legal knowledge?"

"Mom, I think you have to trust him. If you find evidence that he hasn't kept your interests in mind, then you can throw the book at him and find another attorney."

"Okay, you are probably right. I am really paranoid right now. Thank you for your clear head."

***

JR watched the sun set as he loaded his freshly stolen car with gear. When all was ready, he drove the car to a nice neighborhood in Albany where the cops would not come looking for it. Then he walked to Solano Avenue for a satisfying dinner. To kill time, he took in a movie at a local cinema. At midnight he exited the theater on a side street so that he was less noticeable, and he walked slowly to his car, keeping out of the streetlights.

He drove up Marin Boulevard to Cedar Street, and then he found a parking spot. Intimately knowledgeable of this neighborhood, he had spent his childhood living there. Houses change, and passageways are altered; however, this time the path he needed was still in place, which was lucky for him. Months ago before the Longacre problem when he and Arnold were just getting acquainted, he had checked out Arnold's house. It had an enclosed sun porch in the back that was quite substantial. The bedrooms were just above this porch, and they formed the ceiling of the outdoor sitting area. The house was black, but as he stood there and surveyed the house, he heard a disturbance at the front. JR realized he had better hurry up his project to take advantage of the noise out front. The ruckus would distract from his activities in the back.

The night was still without wind, so it was good time for a bonfire. The large gas can he had been carrying was full. He had also brought a large piece of cloth and matches. First, he splashed the gasoline over the walls, the wood floor, and the furniture in the sunroom. He left about a quart of the gas in the can and placed it in the center of the room. Backing out, he searched the ground for a rock about two to three inches diameter. Then he took the gas-saturated rag and tied the rock at one end. He struck a match, and the rag burst into flames. Then he tossed the flaming rag into the middle of the sun porch. The flames ran up the walls and licked the upper story. As he backed away from the heat, he said, "Bye-bye, Arnold." Then he climbed through the foliage to his car. . .Now, only Sally was on his mind.

Around at the front of the house, Jerry was yelling obscenities at the same house that JR was torching. "You dirty fag killed my son!" he screamed. As Jerry's voice got tired and scratchy, he raised the shotgun to one of the windows and shot. There was a burst of deafening noise and then a tinkle of glass. He continued to shoot out the windows, daring Arnold to come out.

At the back of the house, the flames, hot from the burning furniture, found more wood to burn in the walls and became a roaring blaze. The flames climbed up to the second story and the widows of the bedrooms. Then the gas can exploded. Jerry continued to shoot out the windows with his shotgun. Soon there was a siren in the distance, adding to the noise. The sleepy neighbors came out to spray their own houses with water to prevent the fire from moving to their property.

When Jerry heard the sirens getting close, he packed up his shotgun and ran to his car. He hid in the shadows and hoped no one saw him. Many people were out of their houses by this time. They were afraid that the fire would attack their homes too. Quickly, he drove back to his house and stuffed the shotgun in a closet.

Chapter 27

A Few Days Later

The halls of the hospital seemed friendlier this morning. Elly was walking to the burn unit to visit Arnold. She pushed the door open with her one good hand and was greeted by a nurse in scrubs.

"Elly!" the nurse said in surprise. "I didn't know you were the Ms. Longacre."

"That is my maiden name. It is so nice to see you, JoAnn. I haven't seen you since nursing school. I came to visit Mr. Smith."

"Yes, he is waiting for you in 311. The doctor said he had to see you, whatever that means. By the way, there is a Margot Carter who wants to talk to you too. She is in the waiting room off the hall where you just came from."

"Thank you. I promise I won't upset anyone any more than I must," Elly said as she walked to the cubicle and slid the door open."

Arnold was sitting in a chair with gauze bandages on his head, hands, legs, even his feet. He had a weak smile on his face.

"Hello, Ms. Longacre."

Elly took the other chair and sat down, setting her cast on the chair's armrest. It was heavy in the sling, and she needed to rest it before it started throbbing.

Taking a deep breath, she announced, "I guess you know we had an audit done on the estate, and we found you have been paying yourself exceptionally well to the tune of several million a year. In exchange for this loss to the estate, we are taking over your law practice, offices, and several of your other investments. Why did you need to embezzle that large amount of money?"

"I was paying scientists to find a cure for AIDS and eradicate the HIV virus."

"That was a noble cause. Why didn't you discuss this with me instead of going behind my back? That's corruption with larceny. I might have agreed with you, and I may have known some helpful scientists. On another subject, it is kind of you not to charge my former husband for shooting up your house and possibly starting the fire. However, what pains me most about all this is the death of my sweet son."

"I'm too ashamed for words. I am grieved that he died. I am probably also responsible for Mike Nikcols, that female officer, Maria, and Jacob's deaths. They were the innocents who got in the way."

"Got in the way? Of what? Your greed? I must inform you that I am wearing a tape recorder that is recording everything we say."

"I thought so. But Elly, I am dying, and I want to make amends for my soul. I don't want to go to hell."

And so Arnold told her the whole story of his desperation to keep her out of the business. An hour later Elly walked out of the room, feeling numb. And wearily, she thought, *I now* must deal with Margot.

The waiting room was close by. When Elly opened the door, Margot stood up. "Elly, I am devastated that you got shot. I told Arnold that I didn't want you harmed. I'm unhappy things didn't go that way."

Elly walked slowly in and took a comfortable chair to rest her aching arm on. "I have to warn you that I am wearing a tape recorder,

Margot. I want to ask you to tell me about the funds you embezzled from this estate."

"It was simple. There was no control after Annette died. I wanted to grow my business, and I needed surgery."

"Surgery? Tell me about it."

"It is really personal, and I would rather it wasn't recorded."

"I can turn off the tape to protect you if that makes you more comfortable."

"I was born a boy, and when I was four, I started to dress like a girl. It was a long battle to become a woman. Several years ago I found a wonderful doctor down the peninsula, who had a program for people like me. All this therapy and surgery was not covered by insurance, so I needed extra money ... and a lot of it. Now I have real breasts, a vagina and all the trimmings. I think I feel like a real woman, but I must take hormones to feel like that million-dollar babe," she said with a smile.

"How fascinating, I would never have guessed that you were a transsexual, and your secret will be mine. On another note, I like that you used funds to grow our business, Margot. That was a perfect use of the funds while there was no one in charge. Let's say you can pay the surgical expends back by designing a spectacular wardrobe for me."

"Oh, that would be delightful. You are such a generous and kind person. Arnold was such a dope."

"And you are going to like this. I want you to expand your operation to New York, Paris, and maybe even Rome. Are you interested?"

"I am fascinated! Elly, you are an angel and a smart businesswoman. I will make us so much money, and we will both be leaders in fashion. I will design the most gorgeous wardrobe for you for five years, and it will be exclusively for you. May I give you a hug and a kiss, dear Elly?"

***

Later as she was sitting in her hospital room, Elly told Todd and Ted about her day. "It is so exciting. I have added a law firm to the Longacre estate. I am putting Hank in charge of it, and we have an expanding fashion industry. Leland, the other cousin, is going to straighten up my bank. Now that things are really getting under control, I am actually beginning to enjoy being an heiress."

Hank opened the door and asked if he could come in. "Hi, guys, how is my sweetheart?" Striding in with a lopping gait, his warm smile lit up the room. He was dressed elegantly in a dark blue suit, and his personality of taking control was in every move he made. With gentleness, he kissed Elly on her forehead.

"Hi. Elly was just telling us how deftly you took charge of Arnold's old office and used Arnold's office value to cover the debts without moving much money around," Todd said. He was beginning to see how Elly could like this man.

"It is nice to see everyone here, and yes, there have been some big changes. I must say it is all functioning really well. Leland is thrilled with his position at the bank, and he will make big changes happen there. By turning it into an investment bank, it will make more money. He sends his greetings to all of you too."

Todd stood to shake Hank's hand. Then he turned to Elly and said with a smile, "Ted and I have some news for you too. I am leaving the police department, and I am going to law school to become an asset to you Elly. Hank, I would appreciate the opportunity to work with you. Will that be possible?"

"Sure, and while you are in school, I can give you free tutorials and guide you through the process of law school. I think you will make an excellent attorney with your law enforcement experience," Hank said and reached out his hand to shake Todd's hand again.

Todd responded enthusiastically and welcomed Hank's outstretched hand.

Not to be outdone, Ted walked over to his mother's side. "And Mom, I am changing my major to accounting so I can be your CPA," Ted said with pride.

Elly loved seeing her men working together. "Maybe I should study business so we can all study together. Oh, in addition, you make me so happy, all of you. There is no one in the world I trust more than the three of you. Also, you have just shown to me the most profound love I could ever ask for. You are truly my wonderful family."